THE PROMISE

THE PROMISE

HIGHLAND LAIRDS OF THE CREST
BOOK FOUR

KIM SAKWA

Taggart
Press

The Promise is a work of fiction. The names, characters, businesses, places, events, locales, and incidents are either products of my imagination or used in a fictitious manner. Any resemblance to actual persons, living or dead, or actual events are coincidental.

ISBN DIGITAL: 979-8-9872899-2-1

ISBN PAPERBACK: 979-8-9872899-8-3

ISBN JACKET: 979-8-9872899-9-0

Library of Congress Control Number: 2023913604

Published in Clarkston, Michigan

THE PROMISE

PROLOGUE

Eight-year-old Brianna O'Roarke awoke with a start. Though the heat of the sun had started to warm her face, she was still so cold her bones hurt. She whimpered and tried to open her eyes, but they stung so much that she quickly gave up. She was confused for only a moment before she remembered: Papa's boat. Something had happened, something bad.

Slowly, memories trickled in, scary flashes that caused her to flinch as she realized why she was soaked to the skin. She was clinging to the hull of Papa's boat, the biggest piece that was left. Brianna's mouth twisted at the realization, and she swallowed hard, then winced at the raw feeling.

"Mama? Papa?" she croaked. Her throat was so dry and scratchy that she hardly recognized her own voice. She felt around herself blindly, and encountering only the cold metal of the hull, started to panic. She concentrated on opening her eyes, swollen from the spray of salt water and the sun. Then:

"We're here, Breea."

"We won't leave you, sweetheart."

At the reassuring tone in her parents' voices, and the confirmation that they were still with her, Brianna finally calmed, letting her lids fall.

Tuning out the sound of the waves and trying to ignore the clammy feeling of her wet clothes clinging to her, Brianna imagined they were back at home, that her mama had just wrapped her in her favorite pink robe after a hot bath. She sighed, picturing the familiar hallway as she skipped to her bedroom, and the soft fluffy rug squishing between her toes as she climbed onto her bed.

As quickly as she'd conjured it, the image of her bedroom at home faded as Brianna tried to piece together what had happened on the boat, and how she'd gotten to where she was now. She couldn't remember exactly what they were celebrating this time, just that they'd set off on Papa's new boat for a sailing trip. They always seemed to be celebrating something; her parents made even the smallest things feel special, saying that it was all possible because of the 'wee bit of magic'. Brianna had never asked what they meant by that, but it was true that her life felt special—whether that was because of her parents' efforts or because they'd actually been sprinkled with some kind of fairy dust didn't really matter to Brianna. It just was. But that was before this latest trip. Now, trying to ignore the icy feeling in her bones, she wasn't so sure she believed in magic anymore, any bit of it.

Usually, Brianna loved their family sailing trips—she loved any trip they took, really—but this time, something had gone horribly wrong. She'd just settled into her bed, a cozy little nook, with fluffy pillows and a few of her favorite stuffed animals when her mama had cried out sharply. Before Brianna could understand what was happening, she remembered that she'd heard her papa on the radio, his voice stern, repeating "Mayday. Mayday. Mayday. This is Excalibur…" She might be just a kid, but Brianna knew that "mayday" meant "help." She'd been startled, too, at his tone and had wheeled around to face him. Papa had caught her gaze and she remembered how his eyes had warmed and stayed on hers as he continued speaking, repeating a bunch of numbers while he pulled her in close, checking the clips on her lifejacket.

Her mama had appeared then, right behind her, muttering "I've got it," and handing Papa something that looked like a flashlight. Papa had attached it to the hook on Brianna's vest, twisting it until it glowed. Brianna remembered it being so bright she'd had to close her eyes. Then lightning had flashed right above them, followed by the loudest clap of thunder Brianna had ever heard.

"Arthur!" her mama had screamed, and the next thing Brianna knew, her papa was pushing Brianna toward her mama, shouting, "Get her out, Mere! The life raft! *Go, go, go!*"

Mama had picked Brianna up and started to run, but she'd taken only a few steps when a huge wave hit the boat and they were thrown. Brianna remembered feeling a rush of heat and icy cold water all at the same time, her arms and legs tangling as she tumbled over and over again in the waves until she didn't know which way was up. Just when she felt like her lungs were about to burst, Brianna had felt Papa's strong arms pulling her up, his gentle voice reminding her that she could float on her back. At some point, he and Mama had found the piece of the hull and helped her climb up onto it.

That had been a day and night ago, maybe more. Brianna wasn't exactly sure how long they'd been in the water, but last night before falling asleep, she'd thought she'd heard her parents whispering.

"They have to be close," Mama had said.

Papa agreed. "I'm sure they are, but they're not going find her tonight," he'd whispered.

Brianna had wanted to know who they were talking about, but she'd been too sleepy to say anything. "It's taking on water again," Mama had whispered, just as Brianna had noticed water pooling under her on the hull.

"I know, love."

Brianna knew deep down that something was wrong, that they weren't supposed to still be out on the water, but she also knew her parents would keep her safe. They always kept her safe, no matter what. The last thing Brianna remembered as she'd fallen asleep the night before was the sound of their voices as they sang her a lullaby.

And now it was morning. Mama and Papa were speaking quietly to one another again, and Brianna let herself be soothed by their voices as she returned to imagining her nighttime routine at home. After climbing onto her bed, she would line up the books she wanted her parents to read to her. She'd just picked one up in her mind, when she heard a noise, a whirring, roaring sound that grew louder and louder until she heard her Mama's voice: "They found her, Arthur. They found her!"

"Breea, wave your arms, baby." That was Papa. Wanting to please him, Brianna waved her arms and kept waving them, smiling when she heard his voice say, "Good girl."

Mama and Papa kept encouraging her, their voices loud and clear even through the sounds of the helicopter that was now hovering right above them. Brianna cracked her eyes open just enough to see it but had to squeeze them shut against the wind twisting her hair around and the water spraying her face. She heard another voice calling her name, a man, but not Papa. "Brianna. Brianna O'Roarke." Then, suddenly, she was being wrapped in a blanket. It felt so good to be warm again, she groaned.

"I've got you," the same man said loudly over the noise. "Are you hurt?" His hands were gentle but firm as he checked her head and then her body. "You're going to be alright. You're safe now," he said, securing her to his gear with big hooks and clips while holding her tight. Before Brianna could register what was happening, he was lifting her from the small piece of hull, talking to her the whole way through. "You're going to be okay," he was saying. "You did it. You're so brave. Your grandfather's waiting for you. Let's get you home."

CHAPTER 1

Present Day

ALWAYS THE PICTURE of calm composure, it wasn't Brianna O'Roarke's quiet, reserved front that was unusual. As she stood looking at the grand hall of her family's ancestral home, Dunhill Manor, no one who walked past her would ever suspect she was feeling anything other than vague interest in her surroundings. Brianna had perfected the stance back in grade school, and it had served her well in the years since, much to her grandfather's dismay.

Ever worried for her welfare, as well as responsible for it, her grandfather had taken great pains to ensure Brianna's emotional well-being. Over the years, this included accompanying Brianna to various means of bereavement counseling. Some of the professionals she'd seen had called her mastery of control a product of conditioning, while others referred to it as an achievement. It didn't really matter which side they fell on, negative or positive, liability or asset, the consensus was always the same: the trauma Brianna endured as a child had taught her to be a few degrees beyond cautious. In the two years since her grandfather had passed, for Brianna, even a 'trust but verify' approach had become no longer an option. She verified first, always, and there were very few who made it into the column of those she trusted.

Today, however, Brianna's deportment wasn't a mask carefully employed to evaluate her current circumstances while she considered her options. No, today was different. Today, Brianna was simply stunned beyond words.

She'd just arrived back at Dunhill, hoping to find some papers that her grandfather might have stored in the family archives before his passing. An appraisal perhaps, or an insurance rider, maybe even an over-looked entry in one of the O'Roarke family bibles, really *anything* of record at this point would do. She needed something that proved ownership of her family's sword in order to approach this Mr. MacTavish with any real confidence. This trip abroad was a last resort. Unplanned, but necessary. Obviously necessary, or she'd never have boarded the plane. Brianna rarely traveled, especially over water, if she could avoid it.

Yet here she was, and within seconds of stepping through the front doors of her family's ancestral home in Scotland, Brianna took her first deep breath in what seemed like years. The shock of familiarity and the sense of being home floored her. Not that she'd ever actually *lived* at Dunhill, but every visit throughout her life had felt as warm and welcoming as if she had. Any remaining tension left her body as she hugged her aunt and uncle, hello, literally sagging against them. She'd forgotten what it felt like to be embraced by family, to be really and truly hugged by people who loved you. The loss of her grandfather just over two years ago had hit her so hard that after the funeral, she'd thrown herself into work and isolated herself from her family and friends. Now she feared that staying away had been a mistake. She loved her life in the States, but this heartening and welcoming *coming-home* sensation was hitting her bone-deep.

It was on the cusp of acknowledging the error of her ways and admitting that maybe she *did* need what family she had left that she glanced across the foyer to the fireplace. At the sight of the barren mantel above it, a new kind of shock shuddered through her body. In a complete one-eighty, warm and fuzzy went to hell froze over in a blink, and Brianna stepped back abruptly.

"What happened to the letterboxes?" she asked, hard gaze turning from the now-bare mantel to her aunt and uncle.

She watched as they exchanged a discomfited look, and then her uncle shrugged, flashing a childlike smirk. Whatever could be funny about the loss of the last of their family's most precious heirlooms, Brianna didn't know.

"We had a visitor, Brianna. Shortly after your grandfather passed. You had already returned to the States. Our family lore unfolded right before our eyes," Uncle Christopher said gleefully, his eyes bright and twinkling as his fingers tapped together in merriment. "Why don't we tell you the story over dinner later?"

Misreading Brianna's stunned silence for exhaustion, Uncle Christopher and Aunt Michelle excused themselves, her uncle reaching for her suitcase as her aunt prattled on about her room being ready.

Feeling numb, Brianna stepped into the great room, where the empty wall that had once been the resting place for her family's prized Wolf sword loomed. A priceless heirloom dating back to the turn of the fifteenth century. A priceless heirloom that her grandfather had sold for mere pennies without telling *her*, the *actual* historian and antiquities cataloguer of the family. Which he darned well knew, since she'd trained at his side since as far back as she could remember! As she returned her gaze to the mantel, horrified could only describe the feeling of seeing it void of the two letterboxes that had miraculously graced that space for centuries. Centuries!

And now, they were gone. The last of her family treasures were recklessly cast away.

Grateful for some time alone to process this latest news, Brianna found her way to her room, a beautiful suite originally occupied by Cateline De la Cour back in the fifteenth century, sister and lifelong companion of Isabeau O'Roarke, the first lady of Dunhill. As family history went, Dunhill was built by Fergus O'Roarke, a castle on a hill fit for a queen. His queen. It was a gift for his bride, the love of his life. Their marriage was a love match. All O'Roarke marriages were, despite that not necessarily being the norm centuries ago. Fate might not have blessed all members of their lineage with longevity—case in point, her parents—but when an O'Roarke *did* marry, whether it lasted years or mere months, it was true and enduring.

Since the loss of her parents, Brianna's faith, if you could even call it that, had shifted. Objects, the only things that truly endured *and* that she could count on, became her primary focus. Counting on people to stick around no matter how much they loved you was futile. So, she surrounded herself with artifacts, the older, the better. They were reliable, always where she'd last left them and in exactly the same state. People, not so much, and in her line of work, avoiding people was easy. Isolating was easy.

The only consolation Brianna allowed herself (a hypothetical and terribly small consolation) was that if she ever *did* find someone she trusted enough to let in that close, she knew that she would follow tradition. She would know true and enduring love. The only question was, for how long? Realizing just how exhausted she was after the long flight, Brianna pushed thoughts of love, trust, and history aside and turned to matters at hand.

After unpacking, she drew a bath, eager to luxuriate in the clawfoot tub some O'Roarke or another had installed during the last century. Arranging her hair in a clip, she grabbed one of the plush, monogrammed fingertip towels from the vanity, then placed it on the rim of the tub. She sank into the hot water, leaning back, her neck on the towel, humming to clear her mind.

It wasn't often that she found herself at Dunhill anymore, but whenever she did, something about the energy in its walls, and especially in this suite, uplifted her in some way. Unexplainable, but no less the truth. Even the shock of the missing letterboxes had started to dull.

When she'd finished with her bath, Brianna wrapped herself in a fluffy robe and padded back out to the bedroom, where she found a tray of refreshments placed on the table by the window. Angry as she was at her aunt and uncle, she couldn't help but smile. A selection of her favorite cheeses and crudités filled the small table, along with a pot of lemon tea. Christopher and Michelle supped on the late side, so it was well into the evening when she was summoned to dinner. As she made her way downstairs, her eyes drank in every detail of the estate, all of it, rich in history. Her fingers trailed along the stone wall of the hallway—touching it made her feel more connected. As much as it pained her to be here without her parents or grandfather, this was her ancestral home, and these walls still brought her as much comfort as they always had.

Upon entering the small informal dining room (first utilized by Fergus and Isabeau's only son

Callum, family lore said), Brianna felt much calmer, grounded even. She loved her aunt and uncle, and their warm and welcoming smiles as she joined them made her feel a bit guilty for her earlier outburst. They always meant well. As dinner was served, she tried to explain how she felt, and why.

"Brianna, just let us explain," her uncle said, cutting her off gently. "We didn't betray our family legacy. In fact, quite the opposite. It was family lore, come to life. *The* lore." He exchanged an excited grin with Michelle while Brianna suppressed a sigh.

Right. The story passed down for generations of the lass who would come to claim the historic letter-boxes. Legend had it that not only would she have the key that would open them, but that her initials would match those inscribed on the boxes. Who knew how many people had heard and repeated some version of that tale back to them? The O'Roarkes had enter-tained a few con artists over the years who claimed to be "the one," certain the boxes were filled with some kind of treasure or priceless artifact, but none of them had been able to produce a working key. Still, her aunt and uncle were easy prey, ripe to be taken. They'd fallen for it each time, hook, line, and sinker.

"I know what you're thinking," Aunt Michelle said, "but this isn't like the others. This one—this woman— was *real*. Initials and everything. A true wee bit of magic, right before our eyes."

"A wee bit of magic," Brianna sighed, unsure how she felt after hearing the details of their story about the woman with the matching initials and key, the woman who found the letters inside and seemed affected by their contents. It was difficult to be angry with them when they clearly thought they were carrying out their family's legacy. Maybe Brianna *was* holding on too tight. Still, a wave of sadness hit her over the loss. How this latest claimant had come up with a key was a mystery, but regardless, the outcome was the same: the boxes were gone. As she stared at the white china plate in front of her, admiring the spray of tiny pink roses dotting its rim, Brianna wondered how they all actually believed that someone would come, that the lore could be true. But they had. Every single one of them.

Every O'Roarke throughout all of history at one point or another was a believer in this 'wee bit of magic'. At one time in her life, Brianna believed in it too, how could she not, her childhood had been truly idyllic. But any belief she'd once had in magic had tragically died with her parents years ago.

"After all that, you still don't believe?" her uncle said.

Brianna paused, choosing her words carefully. "I understand that someone who matched every description in the age-old tale came here, and I can see how happy you are that *you* were the one who fulfilled the lore," she said slowly. "And I believe you, her key fit in the lock." *Or, at least, that the boxes opened.* She didn't voice her emerging suspicion that the locks might just have been old enough that the next key, no matter what it was, would break them. "But magic? How can that be?"

Brianna had never voiced the reason she remained adamantly skeptical even though it was on the tip of her tongue. It always was. One day she'd like to yell at the top of her lungs, "It's not real! *Magic* isn't real! Show me where it was when my parents died!"

"Breea," he started.

"Uncle Christopher, please, for whatever reason, a *wee bit of magic* clearly skipped my part of the family," she said.

"Oh, but no!" he gasped. "If anything, Breea, it's even *stronger* in your part of the family."

Brianna gave a harsh laugh. "How so? A storm appeared out of *nowhere* and destroyed our boat. I've checked the weather reports over and over for that day, and nothing. We were stranded in the open sea for *days*, and my parents who kept my spirits up and never gave up hope *the entire time*, drowned before they could be rescued. Not very magical, I can assure you."

"Oh, Breea." They each reached for the hand closest to them. "I still can't imagine what you must have gone through. A mere babe. It's a miracle you survived."

"So everyone says," she said, more to herself than anyone else, but still, Christopher and Michelle winced. She could understand why, they had always been a very close family, even with an ocean between them. Her parents' deaths had been an enormous loss for them, too. "I'm sorry," she said quickly. "I only wish they'd survived longer, *that* would have been the true miracle."

Brianna glanced up at her aunt and uncle who were exchanging an odd look between them.

"What? What is it?" she asked.

"Oh, Breea," her aunt said, squeezing her hand before casting another glance at her uncle across the table.

Uncle Christopher shook his head. "Don't, Michelle."

"Christopher, it's well past time. She needs to know the truth. If you don't tell her, I will."

Brianna's heart started to thump in her chest. "Please, whatever it is, just tell me."

It was a long moment before her uncle finally nodded and broke away from Michelle's gaze, turning to her. "Breea...your..." he choked on his words, eyes tearing, then swallowed hard and cleared his throat. "Breea... There wasn't any storm, love. The skies were clear that whole week, just as the weather report predicted."

Brianna felt like she'd been slapped "What are you talking about?" she said, not comprehending a word he said. It was as if he were suddenly speaking another language. "I was there when Papa called for help. We were in *real* danger." It had been years since she'd purposely revisited that day in her memory, but thinking on it now, it came back to her, clear as a bell. A shiver ran down her spine, recalling her father's harsh tone, and her mother's frantic look. "I saw the lightning; I heard the thunder. It was a storm, Uncle Christopher." She'd bet every artifact in her collection on it.

"No," Christopher said softly. "It was a fire, Breea. An awful electrical fire, followed by an explosion."

Her uncle took her hands in his and leaned in close. The desperation in his eyes almost scared her.

"What? My God, *what?* Is there more?"

"You were the only one who made it off the boat. *Only* you, Breea."

"*No.*" She shook her head, her face in a determined glare. "No, no, they were with me. They kept me safe until help arrived."

"I have no doubt they did, sweetheart. But I swear on all that is holy and with every shred of O'Roarke integrity passed down through the generations, my dear brother Arthur and his lovely wife Meredith were killed in the explosion that threw you from the vessel."

CHAPTER 2

Scotland 1433

JUDITH FITZGERALD WOULD MAKE a fine bride, of that Aidan Sinclair was sure. The question he kept asking himself, however, was whether she would make a fine bride for *him*. Her brothers had approached him with the prospect upon his latest return from Abersoch, and while he hadn't outright disagreed with the match, he'd told them he'd consider it. But that was months ago, and now they were growing impatient for an answer.

Until recently, Aidan had had little interaction with the Fitzgerald brothers, though he'd enjoyed a friendly rapport with their father, Robert when he was alive. Aidan and the elder Fitzgerald had shared a mutual respect borne out of circumstance when he and his brethren—Gavin, Lachlan, and Dar—first set to secure the Montgomery holdings. Discovering that their travels would be most expedient with the use of Fitzgerald land, Lachlan and Robert Fitzgerald had agreed to terms. Sadly, Robert had passed the previous winter, and within a near breath of his burial, his two sons sought a new arrangement.

Their motivation was obvious. The Fitzgerald brothers hoped to exploit Aidan's newfound influence, power he now wielded having stepped into Lachlan's shoes. Not to mention that which he gained while attending to matters at Abersoch, an endeavor he was honored to be a part of. An esteemed reputation that served him well among the locals and along the border both, the latter ofttimes rife with skirmishes. While their travels for the most part were by land, on occasion, Aidan and his brethren made use of one of Greylen's ships, a journey rife with its own set of complications. His efforts were fixed on the completion of the Montgomery stronghold, well ahead of schedule, Aidan didn't want to jeopardize what now felt like a tenuous alliance with the zealous pair. Nor did he like the idea of creating further far-reaching problems with the misguided men who aligned with them. It was the only reason he hadn't flat-out refused.

He read the brothers' latest correspondence again, a lengthy (and altogether unnecessary) lecture filled with presumption and censure. Concluding a lesson in restraint would serve them both well, Aidan tossed it aside with a grunt.

"Sir."

Aidan peered across the antechamber that had

become his study of sorts, where Henry stood sentinel by the doorway.

"'Tis fine, Henry," he said, and Henry, who was one of the three men who had become his shadow upon Lachlan's departure to the future, nodded and awaited further instruction.

There was still much to do, at present another journey to Abersoch, so thoughts of entertaining a marriage to appease the Fitzgerald brothers would have to wait. Aidan clapped his man's shoulder as he passed, knowing Henry would fall in step exactly two paces behind.

As Aidan made his way through the grand hall, he couldn't help but notice how quiet it was for early afternoon. Not that Pembrooke was ever teeming with inhabitants (at least not like Seagrave or Dunhill Proper), but the absolute lack of *anyone* walking the halls now was cause for notice. While the estate was modest in size, it was nicely appointed and well cared for. As such, a handful of capable staff—a cook and chambermaid who had worked for Lachlan, and Aidan's steward, to name a few—were always scuttling about, quick with warm smiles and friendly chatter. It was something Aidan always enjoyed when in residence with Lachlan throughout the years, the calm and quiet, and the warmth within these walls. Truth be told, Aidan had oft found himself in wonder at just how well these walls suited him, even before they'd been bequeathed to him. Not only the manor itself, but the land it rested upon, and the loch which surrounded much of it. Today, however, that quiet was a distraction. That, and the extra scrutiny he was sure Henry was giving him as they continued through the hall.

"Henry?"

"Aye," his man said, serene as ever.

"What are you keeping from me? I realize I'm often absent but even a half-wit would notice something's amiss in the halls."

Henry paused, which itself was unusual. He was nothing if not alacritous and to the point. "They're worried," he said, then paused again, putting Aidan on alert. "Fairly, Judith Fitzgerald might make a fine future mistress of Pembrooke, but her brothers..." Henry paused again, then gave a small grunt before continuing. "The Fitzgerald brothers have recently incurred a questionable reputation for themselves."

Before receiving the letter from the Fitzgeralds, Aidan hadn't been aware of any reputation of the brothers, good or bad, but their tone in their latest correspondence had made it clear they were very keen to levy this new taste of power bestowed upon them with their father's passing.

Aidan turned to look his man in the eye. "*I* wasn't aware of their true characters until now, so where did this worry come from?"

"The missive you reread only moments ago has been seen by all, sir."

"Ah."

The Fitzgeralds' new standing as untested men of influence was no secret, mayhap not common knowledge, but still. And now, Aidan vividly recalled leaving their missive right atop his desk, obviously in clear view. Mindful of its contents, he made his way to the kitchen where he found his staff, heads all bent together in nervous chatter near the exterior doors. Aidan, adept at moving quietly and always with precision, had to clear his throat to make his presence known. The staff whirled around as one, and upon seeing their fretful expressions, Aidan did his best to reassure them.

"Pembrooke is sacred to me," he said, hand in the air to wave away any concern. "And when I say Pembrooke, I mean all that it encompasses, which includes each and every one of you. As such, rest assured, your future mistress, *whomever* she is, will be a worthy addition."

He looked at the assembled pointedly as he said this, stressing the "whomever" to make his point. Their bright eyes and quick smiles were instantaneous and thus satisfied, Aidan made way for the courtyard, his original destination.

What he'd told his staff was the truth. Aidan *had* always considered Pembrooke sacred. Much of that had to do with Lachlan, whom he held in high esteem. Two years had passed since Aidan had last seen him, but he could still recall the moment he realized that he wasn't merely losing Dar, one of his closest friends, but his lifelong mentor, too.

Dar's plan had always been to return to the future with Celeste, and Aidan had never been so foolish to consider otherwise. But Celeste's unexpected departure (taking with her the sword which they'd assumed at the time was the only key between their centuries) had been difficult to bear. It wasn't until later, when clearer heads prevailed, that they realized there was still a way for Dar to get to his wife, but neither portal on the property at Abersoch held much appeal. One required a jump from high up on the rock wall, and the other lay somewhere within the tunnels, its precise location still unknown. Surprisingly, it was Gwen, Greylen's wife, who told them of yet another portal, one that was much less dangerous and didn't include a literal leap of faith (a leap she feared Lachlan wouldn't survive), but instead a dip into the tide pools.

Privy to this new and welcome information, plans were made, and quickly—so quickly that Aidan hadn't time to fully understand what their success meant. In the short time they'd had left together, Lachlan had implored him to make Pembrooke his own, not only to care for and protect those under his charge, but to safeguard the portal, lest someone accidentally find it, or worse, destroy it. It was an honor that Aidan didn't take lightly. It wasn't until that last day, though, after Dar and Lachlan vanished before his eyes, that a sense of finality pervaded. When Aidan had first joined the men on their quest to secure the Abersoch property, he'd been an eager and dedicated participant, never once imagining he would ultimately assume control.

It had taken Aidan what remained of that summer to fully grasp what this transfer of power truly meant. He'd returned home to speak with his elder brother, Rhys, and to inform him of his plans. While Rhys hadn't been thrilled at Aidan's decision to all but abdicate his familial duties, he understood the gravity of Aidan's new position and the authority he'd assumed. Rhys also had immense respect for Lachlan and accepted that *this* was his brother's destiny. "The mantle suits," he'd said grasping Aidan's shoulder. With his blessing, Aidan felt a great weight lift and his focus shifted in earnest. Nearly two years had passed since then, and with the core structure of the castle at last complete, Gavin and Isabelle could soon make Abersoch their home, thus ensuring their own descendants' future.

As Aidan stepped through the front doors now, his hand brushed the Celtic knot that one of Lachlan's men had carved deeply into the stone years before, casting Lachlan as watchman and protector, and Pembrooke sanctuary of such. A circular knot had been added around it since, as a symbolic gesture to mark the literal title that had been transferred to Aidan those two summers ago when Dar and Lachlan…left.

Aidan stopped atop the steps, flanked by the other two of Lachlan's men, Alan and Richard, as a rider approached bearing Montgomery colors. After Henry retrieved the missive from the courier Aidan cracked the seal, reading Gavin's message. "Our plans have changed," Aidan said, staring out over the horizon. "We head west, to Seagrave."

CHAPTER 3

When Brianna had calculated the route from Dunhill to Abersoch, the Welsh estate where Darach MacTavish had mentioned he was staying, she'd made sure to include a stop at a lovely bed and breakfast along the way. A much-needed and *very* necessary solo retreat on the heels of her aunt and uncle's table-side revelation. In learning the truth about the death of her parents, the news of the missing letterboxes, and even the loss of the sword, took second place. How could it not when the story she'd told herself for nearly her entire life, the premise she'd built her entire emotional value system upon had been irreparably cracked? And although she hadn't realized it at dinner, later, when she was alone in her room, it'd become clear that everything she'd once believed had suddenly changed.

With her head spinning as Christopher told her what he'd learned about the explosion, gathered from reports filed by the coastguard, she'd sat in silence staring at the sconces on the wall behind his head. By the time he had finished, and her aunt and uncle were looking at her imploringly with eyes full of pity, Brianna had already decided her next step. The usual one. Flee.

It wasn't the most mature reaction, but at that moment, it was all she could come up with. The thought of digging through the family archives had lost its appeal. And sadly, that welcoming and warm embrace she'd felt upon arriving, from her relatives as well as Dunhill itself, suddenly felt tainted. Settling on an out, she announced abruptly that she had a meeting with Darach MacTavish in Wales. Of course, Brianna didn't *actually* have a meeting with Mr. MacTavish, but by that point what did it matter? She was in the UK, and so was he. She'd expected some pushback, for Christopher and Michelle to beg her to stay, but at the mention of Mr. MacTavish's name, they exchanged a quick glance before turning to face her, slow smiles spreading across their faces. Oddly, her aunt and uncle seemed almost pleased with the prospect of her departure, but with so many conflicting thoughts swirling through Brianna's head, it hadn't occurred to her to ask why.

In fact, until that moment, Brianna hadn't even considered crashing Mr. MacTavish's vacation, or his business trip, or whatever it was that he was doing there. She'd been satisfied that he'd responded to her call with an invitation to meet with her when he returned to the States. It had been his response that was the motivation she'd finally needed to restart her search through her grandfather's papers.

When she'd come up empty-handed again after her careful plunder of their entire home in the States, she booked her trip to Scotland. She was sad to be leaving Dunhill after only two nights, but it wasn't as if the estate was going anywhere. She told herself she would visit again one day, with the express purpose of exploring its hidden depths at length as an adult. For now, though, she needed a goal, a quest, so to speak, so she'd Googled the best route to the Montgomery estate (and one that included a stop in a lovely little town along the way), then repacked her bags, already feeling a little more clear-headed at the prospect of a project.

She'd still been a bit raw that morning when she said her goodbyes, but optimistic, too. This would be good, and the reset she'd desperately needed. Her aunt and uncle had followed her to her car, then waited while she synced her phone with the car's display, showing the route to the B&B she'd chosen. It was a little more than a six-hour drive, and Brianna was looking forward to a bit of exploration before her dinner reservation.

As she drove, her mind filled with images from those idyllic years of her life, the Camelot of her existence. Now, she wondered if she'd embellished or invented some of those memories. It was only a brief thought—she knew that she hadn't of course. Her early childhood with her parents truly was perfect. What she was really struggling with was unearthing the old family belief in the wee bit of magic. She'd closed the door on such things long ago, but what her uncle suggested was that her memories of her parents surviving those few days floating in the sea with her wasn't a trauma response, but *proof* in magic. Proof that her parents, although very dead, had somehow managed to stay with her until help arrived. It was almost too perfect—leave it to her parents to be the proof—Brianna had to smile. Not that she had decided to accept this hypothesis as true, of course, but it was nice to think that the wee bit of magic she dismissed that day happened right before her eyes.

Preoccupied with her thoughts, the time passed quickly and before she knew it, Brianna was pulling into the car park of the lodging she'd booked. It was still a couple of hours before check-in, so she left her bags with the front desk and walked the short distance into the village. It was a lovely town, and Brianna meandered in and out of a few shops, feeling the first spot of calm she'd had since dinner the night before. On her way back, she happened upon an arts and crafts fair, her favorite kind of thing to explore when she visited anywhere. Thrilled at the run-in, the new Brianna—the one who was supposed to start believing in a wee bit of magic considered that maybe it was destined.

Lost in a plethora of local treasures, she made her way up and down the rows of booths, stopping in her tracks when she spotted a gorgeous, no, *stunning* replica of a fifteenth-century Venetian gown on display. The dress had been cleverly styled with a large leather satchel, worn cross-body. Noble medieval chic never looked so good. Instantly drawn to the ensemble, Brianna stepped inside the tented area to get a better look, then nearly stumbled over her own feet when she saw the woman standing beside it. If Brianna had ever had a picture of a quintessential fairy queen in her head, this woman would be it. Ethereal with long hair and perfect features, wearing a stunning handcrafted gown that appeared to float around her body.

The woman smiled warmly but something about the twinkle in her eye snagged Brianna's thoughts as she murmured hello and fixed her attention back to the display. Still a bit flustered and embarrassed, she took her time admiring the piece before moving on to the table beside it, filled with a selection of gowns, kirtles, and chemises.

"These are beautiful," Brianna whispered to herself, as her hand brushed along the heaping piles of soft linen, wool, and silk. Examining the cuts and colors, Brianna realized the pieces all replicated styles worn throughout Europe during the late Middle Ages. The fabrics though, all spoke wealth.

The woman running the booth sidled up next to her and began rummaging through the messy, but organized piles. "These," she said of the outfits she'd put together from undergarments to gowns. Brianna eyed the woman, her curiosity piqued—the clothing she'd picked suited her perfectly. At least it would have, were she a noblewoman circa mid-fifteenth century England. "And these," said the woman, tossing some hose and a pair of fur-lined ankle boots atop the growing stack.

It really was fine work, almost indistinguishable from the antique designs she'd come across in her career. "These are incredible replicas," Brianna murmured.

The woman smirked, and without breaking eye contact, plucked a few more items from the end of the table. "You'll want these, too."

Brianna looked down and grinned, reaching for the bags the woman had added. Never one to resist a great purse, Brianna couldn't help but be impressed. The woman's selections continued to be spot on. As she examined the silk and leather bags, Brianna gasped when she found a compact mirror inside a matching pouch. Even if they weren't authentic, Brianna was smitten.

"Deal," she said, grinning. "I'll take them."

"Of course, you will," the decidedly odd—yet intriguing—woman said, taking Brianna's credit card and running it. The receipt was printed, but before she handed it to Brianna, the woman gave a small smile, almost to herself, then made her way to the entrance of the booth, where she began defrocking the mannequin of the display gown that brought Brianna in to begin with, gently cradling both the dress and leather satchel that had hung there.

"Oh," Brianna said, raising a hand to stop her. "I'm not sure either of those are in my budget."

"No, they're probably not," the woman said. "But they're perfect. So, it's a gift."

"Oh, no," Brianna said, waving her hand now with purpose. "I couldn't."

"You can," the woman insisted.

It was such a generous gift—and from a veritable stranger at that—that Brianna, never one to feel beholden to someone, decided she'd drop some cash on the table before she left. It wouldn't be anywhere near enough to pay for the dress, but it'd be something. She watched mutely as the woman packed everything in the leather satchel, and when Brianna took the bag from her, she clutched the bundle in her arms, feeling torn. She wasn't sure if she should give it back—it was a very expensive piece. Simple in design, but the leather was supple and worn, without looking used. Not sure what got into her, but certain that the bag felt right in her hands, Brianna decided right then that she was keeping it. The strap went over her head, and she adjusted it cross-body like it belonged there. When she reached for her wallet again, the woman stayed her hand.

"It's a gift, Brianna," the woman said, and for a moment, Brianna froze. How did she know her name? Brianna looked down at her wallet and her shoulders relaxed slightly. Of course, her credit card, which the woman had just run, had "Brianna O'Roarke" printed right on it.

"You'll make good use of them, and that will be payment enough," the woman said.

Brianna held the woman's gaze for a long moment. The sincerity in her voice was unmistakable, and any guile Brianna had felt previously was now gone. This was a gift, and Brianna decided she would accept it as a good omen. After a moment, she nodded and thanked the woman, before sort of floating off down the road, wondering at her new belongings, and the odd and ethereal woman who'd given them to her.

By the time she returned to the bed and breakfast, her room was ready, and her bags had been placed inside. Since she was only staying the night, there wasn't much to unpack besides pajamas and a change of clothes for the morning. As she spread a hand towel on the marble counter to lay out her toiletries, she realized whatever tension she'd felt from her visit to Dunhill felt far away now. Relishing in her little unexpected excursion, she took her time freshening up before dinner, a lovely meal served tableside with a view of a stunning sunset through the picture windows. She capped off her night with a hot shower, and when she slipped into bed, Brianna sighed happily, sinking into a plush featherbed and fine linens.

When she awoke the next morning, Brianna felt surprisingly well-rested. Usually one to toss and turn, especially when away from home, she made a mental note to inquire about the bedding before leaving. While repacking was a bit more challenging considering yesterday's purchases (and gifts), she didn't regret a thing, not even the odd encounter. After a delicious breakfast, eggs Benedict served with the most divine hollandaise she'd ever tasted, Brianna decided to order a boxed lunch to take with her. One less thing to worry about, and given what she'd sampled so far, it was sure to be another win.

Refueled, she and the car, Brianna set off again, intent to hit the gates of the Montgomery property by mid-afternoon. Paying close attention to her unfamiliar surroundings, as Brianna turned down the road that led to the estate, she ran through the words she was planning to say to Mr. MacTavish. If the man even let her in. Her earlier calm started to give way to jittery nerves.

She suddenly felt apprehensive, worried that she would fail in recovering her family's heirloom. She'd been tracking the sword for nearly two years now and finally had an opportunity to negotiate its safe return to the O'Roarke family coffers. She hadn't even known her grandfather had sold it until after he'd died and Brianna had taken on the task of going through his papers and various collections. The shock at seeing the sword's case empty was with her still. And now, here she was, uncertain whether she'd be able to get it back. Losing the sword itself had been one thing, but to learn that the MacTavishes were claiming *that they* were the rightful owners just didn't sit well with her.

Brianna considered all of this as she parked her car and made her way up to the front door. No easy feat since the pictures she'd found of the estate online did *not* do it justice. Brianna had done a bit of research on the property—which was well within her purview as a historian and art collector, not that she had to justify it, but still. She'd dug into everything she could find. And call her crazy (no, don't) but in yet another odd turn of events, she discovered that the estate's owners, the notable Montgomery family had their own mysterious history, loose ends that, from what Brianna could tell, had never been fully tied.

Finding herself on the front steps, she paused before the doors, a stunning mahogany set, inset with leaded beveled glass, and took a deep, fortifying breath. *You can do this Brianna. Time to reclaim your family's history.* Before she could talk herself out of it, Brianna rang the bell, then stepped back, hands clasped before her. The door swung open a moment later, and much to her surprise, it was Darach MacTavish himself who opened it. Naturally, she'd Googled him as well, curious about him and his wife, as well as their connection to the Montgomery family. Still, seeing him in person, this large dark-haired man with a terribly serious look, nearly an arm's length away, was intimidating, to say the least.

"Mr. MacTavish," she said, hating how meek she sounded. She was here to reclaim what was rightfully hers, for goodness' sake! Get a grip, Bree!

"Miss O'Roarke," he said, and for a moment she startled. How could he know her? But of course, the man must have done his own research. That realization made her relax slightly as Mr. MacTavish spoke again. "I wasn't expecting you."

It wasn't a flat-out reprimand, but Brianna flushed all the same, hoping he'd allow her inside. If nothing else, after her long drive, the use of the restroom was necessary.

"I'm sorry to intrude," she said, putting some strength behind her voice this time. "I know when we last spoke you said you would be in Wales at the Montgomery estate for a time."

"And you followed me?"

She shook her head. "No, no, no," she said, waving her hand. "I found myself at Dunhill only two nights ago. Unplanned."

"Dar?" A soft feminine voice called. That was unexpected. Brianna hadn't realized it was a family trip.

Mr. MacTavish stepped back and gestured Brianna inside, his attention now on the very pregnant woman who'd called his name. Brianna recognized her as his wife, Celeste, and saw how his eyes warmed, his entire expression and body language a beacon of true love. Without a word, he pulled her close to his side, then bent down and whispered something to her. It took Brianna's ear a moment to adjust once she realized he was speaking French. "It's Brianna O'Roarke. Christopher and Michelle's niece."

Celeste glanced over at Brianna, so briefly that she almost missed it. "As in…" Celeste whispered back, also in French.

Brianna, suddenly even more uncomfortable at the idea that even Celeste knew who she was, looked away just as she caught Dar nodding.

"Why is she just standing in the doorway? Have you invited her inside?"

Dar glanced back at Brianna and was about to

answer when Celeste sighed. "As in *all the way inside?*" she said.

"She has questions about the sword," Dar told her. "We were supposed to meet at the end of the month."

At this, Brianna glanced back at the pair, and when she did, she caught Celeste's eye for a millisecond. The other woman was looking at her differently now, with a bit more wariness.

"Then why is she *here?*" Celeste asked her husband. "In Wales?"

Brianna could hear them perfectly, even from across the room, but she did her best to remain aloof and pretend she didn't understand. Might as well learn as much as she could, since it appeared the MacTavishes *were* being secretive. He must have sensed she was all ears because Darach glanced at her then and started speaking in a different language again. Scots Gaelic. She knew that one too, but stopped short of rolling her eyes. They'd have to do better than that if they hoped to keep her in the dark. All O'Roarkes spoke enough English, French, and Gaelic to get by, and some spoke even more. Credit all the way back to the De La Cour sisters—according to all records, Cateline had taught her nephew's second wife, Margret, the language back in the Middle Ages, and then Margret had taught her children, and their children taught their children, and so on. And thus began the family tradition, which had since been passed down through the generations. Margret was responsible for another tradition as well. According to some letters that Brianna had come across,

Margret had been the one to ensure that all O'Roarke females were proficient in some sort of weaponry, primarily used for self-defense, though at the beginning, protecting her husband Callum had been her motivation.

Brianna waited patiently, admiring the staircase to her right and an enormous ballroom that overlooked the grounds. While the MacTavishes discussed the merits of inviting her to stay, a man who by his looks had to be Darach's father, appeared from another part of the house. He smiled warmly at her, before interrupting the couple, still deep in debate. When he spoke, he did so firmly, pointedly, *and* in English, obviously for her benefit.

"She's an O'Roarke. She stays."

CHAPTER 4

When Aidan and his men crossed onto MacGreggor land, dusk was fast approaching, and was long gone by the time they'd reached the outer gates of Seagrave Castle. A celebratory flair rent the night air as they entered the bailey where large bonfires illuminated the courtyard, crackling and hissing as embers danced in the air before turning to naught. It was a sight not altogether unusual as Grey and Gwen set the firepits ablaze whenever they received guests, and as their numbers increased throughout the years—his brethren and those in their closest circles—with each successive marriage and bairns that followed, so too did their zeal for merrymaking and revelry. It was fast becoming a familiar sight and one that oft caused Aidan to ponder his future and that of his destiny and subsequent lineage.

Loath to interrupt the children, who despite the late hour were caught up in a game as they ran to and fro, Aidan stayed his horse, content to observe from the perimeter. He breathed in the welcome scent of firewood, taking note of the changes since his last visit. He sent a nod to Grey on the keep's steps, who returned the acknowledgment, his wife Gwen tucked protectively in front of him. After the loss of a babe born without life and the difficult year that followed, it was good to see that Gwen was clearly expecting again. Gavin (Grey's best friend and former first in command) and his wife, Isabelle (Grey's sister) had returned to Seagrave months ago. At first, to offer their support to Gwen and Grey and later, with their impending move to Abersoch not so far away, they'd decided to stay. Aidan knew that Lady Madelyn, Grey and Isabelle's mother, was thankful to have them all under one roof again, and although still in very good health, Aidan also knew from experience, that traveling back and forth was never what he would call easy on a body.

Turning his attention back to the young ones who were making another pass from one end of the courtyard to the other, Aidan smiled when Tristan, Gwen and Grey's eldest boy, gasped and stopped in his tracks as he noticed Aidan atop his steed in shadows. Aidan had a soft spot for the boy, who often sought his favor and followed him about the castle. So when Tristan jumped atop a boulder and pointedly caught his eye, Aidan knew what was coming. The boy lifted the hood of his cloak, concealing his face in shadow— a fine emulation, indeed, as Aidan was wont to observe— and spread his arms dramatically, declaring, "Keeper of the realm, the mighty bear has arrived." Aidan chuckled, as did the other adults. As the children went back to their games, Aidan and his men saw to their horses before leaving them in the capable hands of James, Seagrave's stablemaster.

When Aidan finally made it through the courtyard toward the keep, the children were gone and off to bed. Inside, he spotted Grey on his way upstairs and Gwen on her way down.

"Speak in the morning?" Grey asked as he turned, toddler in his arms.

"Aye," Aidan nodded, nothing was so pressing that it couldn't wait until the morrow.

"You're in Callum's room," Gwen said. "But head to the kitchens first, Cook knew you were coming and made you supper. I'll have Anna see to a hot bath in the meantime."

He stopped her as she made to pass and fixed her with a concerned look. "You're well?" He asked.

She nodded, a crooked smile tugging at her lips as her eyes suddenly filled with tears.

His heart nearly twisted clear around, "Och, Gwen," was all he could manage.

"Don't make me cry," she said swatting his chest, before waving him off. "Eat. I need to find Anna." She paused a few steps down the hallway, "And tell your men," she said, all trace of tears gone as she pointed to Alan, Henry, and Richard, as always close behind him, "I win."

He grinned at her recitation of the MacGreggor creed. "As always, my lady," he conceded, with a nod.

Gwen smiled, satisfied, then continued down the

hall. Watching her go, Aidan made eye contact with Grey, who'd been observing from the landing atop the stairs, grinning too at his wife's rejoinder. While the castle might now be quiet, it was common knowledge that Gwendolyn MacGreggor was carefully guarded. And while Grey's men might not stand the mere pace behind her as they once had, she had eyes on her at all times. Plenty more than his three.

With a salute to Grey, Aidan and his men made their way to the kitchens, toward the large corner spot where they often took informal meals. Cook beamed when she saw him—she had a soft spot for them all, but with Dar gone and Callum prospering once again at Dunhill, he knew she enjoyed his visits all the more. He wasted no time in going to her, fishing out the pouch he'd brought stuffed with herbs plucked with care from Pembrooke's small but bountiful gardens. She eyed the contents with delight then shooed him to the table. She needn't ask twice.

He joined his men, not surprised to find one of his favorite meals waiting beneath the covered platters, a dish Gwen had dubbed *pot roast* cooked with root vegetables and served with bread still warm from the oven. A divine repast indeed. He sent thanks Cook's way and heartily dug in. When they finished, they cleared the table to the good-natured grumbles of servants still busy in preparation for whatever meals would be served on the morrow. Then Aidan left his men by the doors before turning to go upstairs.

The room, once occupied by Callum after his first wife Fiona passed, had later become Aidan's when in residence. He thought back to the various stages he and his brethren had gone through over the years, all seeming at one time or another to come full circle. Having been fostered together as young boys—he, Greylen, Callum, Darach, and Ronan—their bond was as unbreakable now as it had ever been.

It mattered naught if they saw each other but once a year, which had been the case for nigh on a decade. It was a solemn observance that called them together every year, a commemoration to Allister and Fergus, Grey and Callum's fathers, who'd each been instrumental in their development. While Lachlan had played an essential role in their training, and in all their lives, it wasn't until later that they'd learned he was the true force behind their brotherhood. It was no wonder they all revered the man so.

Shaking off the twinge of melancholy he sometimes felt when thinking of Lachlan and Dar, Aidan unpacked his satchel, looking forward to a hot soak. Steam was still rising from the large tub which had been placed before the fire, a sure sign Anna had her hands in its timing. Aidan thought again how good it felt to be back at Seagrave, the castle bursting with life and love and joy—and sorrow, too, which had its own beauty. What these walls had seen over the years. What grand stories and displays of honor and valor. After his bath, memories of the past stayed with him as he sank beneath the linens and closed his eyes.

Aidan slept soundly, always a boon when at Seagrave, which had not only the comforts but the true sense of home. He'd just finished shaving and was running the back of his hand across his jawline when a soft rap sounded upon his door.

"Enter," he bid with a grin, knowing it was Tristan.

Not a moment later, the boy dashed over, eyes gleaming, hand out. "May I hold your medallion?" he asked.

Aidan smiled and shook his head. "If but I had it."

Tristan's eyes grew wide. "What happened to it? Did you forget it? Did you lose it? Did...did someone *steal* it?"

The boy was so expressive, Aidan chuckled. "Nothing so wicked," he assured him, "Save a blow to my pride."

"Nay!" the lad gasped.

Aidan ruffled his hair. "Aye, it happens to the best of us."

At this, Tristan seemed skeptical, which wasn't at all surprising considering his parents.

"Truth be told," Aidan continued, "I was felled by a wee kitten."

"You were not!"

"I see you've inherited your mother's spunk, along with her jargon," Aidan said with a laugh.

"Don't remind me," Grey said as he walked in, his bluster belied by literally *everything* when it came to his wife. "Breakfast?" he asked reaching for Tristan's hand.

"Papa, Aidan lost his medallion."

Grey said naught to the boy but did raise a curious brow in Aidan's direction as he held the door open.

Aidan shrugged it off, grabbing his cloak before

following behind. In a stark, but pleasant contrast to the calm of Pembrooke, the hallway was nearly bursting, filled with squeals and chatter as everyone made their way downstairs to the great hall. A round of musical chairs later, mostly precipitated by a cherub face with serious intent, platters hit the table and another round of chaos ensued as plates and bowls were filled. Aidan enjoyed the ruckus, helping when he could by snagging a fast-passing dish as little arms reached out in vain.

A few moments later, the children finally settled to eat, and a bit of calm reigned for all of a breath until Tristan made the proclamation yet again, that of Aidan's medallion and its missing nature. Hoping the mention would pass without fanfare amidst the crowded table, Aidan took a deep sip of Cook's morning brew, relishing the pleasantly strong flavor as he put on a deliberate air of nonchalance. He was intent on remaining silent on the matter and was almost sure it *had* gone unnoticed until a head snapped in his direction and a set of eyes zeroed in on his.

"Wait," said the culprit. It was Gwen, of course, who of all present would pick at it. He glared at her from across the table, which made her burst out in laughter. "You'll have to do better than that, I'm married to *him*," she said with a head motion to her right where Grey sat. "Was it truly lost?" she asked.

Aidan shook his head. "Nay. I know precisely where it lies."

"Oh. I thought maybe…"

"Maybe, what?" he asked as Gwen trailed off. He hadn't considered anything of the incident, at least not until this very moment.

"Well," Gwen started, and Aidan braced himself, suddenly knowing all too well where this was going. "It's no secret that your medallions carry some significance. Like—"

"Not in this case," Aidan said quickly, hoping to staunch whatever nonsense she might weave. While Margret may have been wearing Callum's lost medallion, and Gwen had found solace in Grey's before they wed, there was no said significance in the case of Dar and Celeste. To further squash any forthcoming argument to her point, he added, "Let's move on from the matter to something real. I've been approached to marry Judith Fitzgerald."

At this, Grey and Gavin regarded him with utmost seriousness while the women gasped, looking horrified.

Aidan shrugged, outwardly projecting indifference, yet suddenly he felt anything but. "I haven't yet agreed," he said, hating the uncertainty that crept into his voice. "Though if I refuse, her brothers will not let it go lightly."

"If not for her brothers and the men that they are, one could do worse than Judith Fitzgerald," Grey said slowly. Nigel and Gil Fitzgerald's reputation as brutes and bullies, at the least, was known widely, as everyone—even the women nodded at Grey's statement. "However," Grey continued, "to speak it bluntly —Judith is wholly of our time, is she not?" It was a question of much import, considering. "If there is anything to be gleaned from our combined experience, your match is likely to be with a lass brought here from a future century."

Gwen nodded slowly. "You know, I'm not one to readily agree with my husband, but in this instance, I believe he's right."

"He's right would've sufficed," Grey suggested with a grunt.

While the two bickered about Gwen's choice of words, Aidan silently sorted through the events that had led to the loss of his medallion. It had been a day of celebration some months ago, to mark that the construction of the Abersoch estate was for the most part complete. Struck with a bit of melancholy at the realization that this also marked nearly two years since the departure of his friend and mentor, Aidan had sought a bit of solitude and headed toward the nearby shore in the early evening hours.

He distinctly recalled the moment he nearly squashed the kitten when it darted in front of him, made all the more surprising as he'd never seen one about the property before. At the sight of it, he'd stumbled, and as he righted himself from an almost embarrassing spill, a flash of metal caught his eye, whirling through the air before bouncing upon the ground with a clack, and landing just out of sight in its final resting place. At the time, he'd chuckled at the comical display, glancing down to confirm it was his medallion that had flown through the air.

The medallions themselves, that he and his

brethren each had, those carved for them when they were still young boys, had never held so much significance to Aidan—it was the real presence of his brethren he cherished. But *this* medallion held much significance. Lachlan had forged it himself, etching the symbol that was unique only to him (the same symbol that was now carved at the entrance of Pembrooke) on one side, and a bear on the other mere days before he left.

Eyes out in case there was another kitten of the same litter roaming about, Aidan went to retrieve it, feeling a bit emotional as he recalled the moment Lachlan had given the medal to him. When Aidan finally spied *where* it had fallen, he couldn't help but chuckle again, this time at the irony of it all. He'd been just about to fetch it when Duncan, in need of assistance, chose that very moment to call out to him. Though he planned to return later that night, Aidan had yet to make it back. Seeing the stricken faces around the table now, he wondered if he'd been wrong. Was the medallion in fact, more consequential than he'd thought?

To Grey's question about Judith, he must admit that he, too, had considered the very same when he was first approached. After all, Maggie had been at the abbey for well over a year before meeting Callum. It had been a fleeting thought, however, as was any thought of a future bride at that moment. The information that Judith was a Fitzgerald, a fifteenth-century Fitzgerald, same as her brothers (though, Aidan assumed, not *just* the same as her brothers, as they were an exceptional breed), precipitated another round of questions and caution, not only from Grey and Gwen, but Gavin, Isabelle, and Lady Madelyn chimed in, too. Even Anna sent him a worrisome look as she reached for a babe already in need of a morning nap.

When it became clear that Aidan had no more to say on the matter, chatter picked up around him, and Aidan was grateful when Henry interrupted their meal, a hand on his shoulder as he bent to quietly inform him of a problem with the ship's inventory. With a brief goodbye and a nod of thanks to Cook, Aidan left the table, never happier to be flanked by his men. From the enlivened chatter he left behind him, it was obvious his presence was hardly necessary.

If only they knew the truth of it.

It wasn't until they reached the steps that would take them out of the great room, that Gwen called out from the table. Aidan had just lifted his hood, one foot atop the stone floor of the foyer, a breadth away from freedom, and paused at the sound of his name.

"Aidan," Gwen said a second time. "Where is your medallion? You never said."

A smile tugged at his lips, at the irony of it all. For now, he was fully aware of the implications of that day. He turned, delivering the news with the air of intrigue it deserved. "It lies at Abersoch, Gwendolyn. At the bottom of a tide pool, to be precise."

CHAPTER 5

With Lachlan's declaration of Brianna's O'Roarke-ness, it seemed that everything was put to rights. Like Brianna was accepted as family or near-to. Whatever that meant, the effect was instant. The tension, worry even, that Dar and Celeste had been exhibiting vanished in a blink.

In a flurry of apologies, warm welcomes, and formal introductions, Brianna's bags were collected from her car, and she was escorted upstairs. It all happened so quickly, and although she insisted (more than a few times) that she'd be quite fine with the room she'd booked at the B&B, a solid thirty minutes from the estate, it would never, *ever* compare to the feelings she experienced being under the care of this family. As Brianna followed them down the hallway, she slowed behind Dar, who stopped as a quiet but excited voice called out, "Papa".

Making a quick detour inside, they fawned over the adorable toddler (who Brianna learned was named Griffin) bouncing on tiptoes, arms stretched, eager to be picked up out of his crib. After a quick diaper change, still a bit sleepy and rightfully shy at seeing a stranger, the boy clung to Dar, staring at Brianna over his father's shoulder as they continued to the next set of doors which opened into a lovely suite. Instantly drawn to the spectacular ocean view, Brianna made for the large bank of windows, framed with panels of beautiful neutral fabrics. She turned back to her hosts to excuse herself to unpack, and everyone started speaking at once. Dar and his father explained they had business to attend to, probably whatever it was that brought them to the estate in the first place, and Celeste had to fix Griffin a snack.

Brianna waved them off with a grin, then turned to find her toiletry bag. Her suitcase was already set atop a luggage rack, nestled between an opened armoire and closet door, so she figured that while she'd been taking in the coastal scenery, one of the men must have placed the smaller bag inside the gorgeous bathroom she spied through the French doors on the other side of a cozy sitting area.

Taking her time, she freshened up, delighting in how the day had taken a turn she'd never expected. At first, she reached for just a few necessary items to leave by the sink, but then caught in a whim, she emptied the entire bag. She did the same with her suitcase. Not that there was so much to unpack in the first place, but oddly, she felt just as at home here as she did at Dunhill. It felt right to fully settle in. She stacked some items on the shelves and in the drawers of the armoire then started hanging up a few blouses and cardigans. When her hands brushed over the soft leather satchel at the bottom of her suitcase, Brianna decided to empty that too—no sense in the gowns getting wrinkled, plus, she was excited to admire them again. She just finished rolling the last pair of hose and was trying to decide whether to place the leather bag on the shelf or hang it from a hook when she was interrupted by a knock on the door. Intrigued, she tossed the bag in her empty suitcase and hurried to answer it.

Opening the door, Brianna was greeted by Celeste, Griffin in her arms.

"It's incredible how you can still hold a toddler while being this pregnant," Celeste said with a soft laugh, motioning to the boy somehow plastered to her side as Brianna waved them in, laughing.

Celeste laughed, too, and gave a *what can you do* shrug. "I thought you might be hungry, so refreshments are on the way. It's easy to overdo it, though—the chef here is amazing."

Celeste went on to explain that getting ready for dinner this far along *and* with a toddler in tow, wasn't anywhere near as easy or quick as it used to be. Growing up an only child, Brianna didn't have a lot of experience with children, but she didn't hesitate to offer to watch Griffin.

Celeste smiled and waved her off. "That's so sweet, but I was on my way to hand him off to Dar. Is there anything else you need?"

"I'm good. Really." Brianna returned Celeste's

smile, feeling her sincerity. And since it had been hours since she'd eaten her lunch at the Inn, she was looking forward to whatever was on the way up to her room.

"Alright then, dinner's at seven, nice casual," Celeste said as she turned to leave. Brianna was about to shut the door behind her when Celeste stopped short at something that caught her eye. "May I?" she asked, pointing toward the closet.

Wondering what it could be, Brianna nodded and was surprised when Celeste stopped in front of the luggage rack.

"I haven't seen a bag like this in …" Her words trailed off as her hand touched the leather.

"In?" Brianna prompted, still curious, when Celeste didn't finish.

Celeste turned to her, a wistful look on her face. "In a very long time. You're lucky to have such wonderful family treasures. It's a wonder…a miracle really, how they've stood the test of time."

At that, Brianna felt a momentary flash of anger. First at the reminder that Celeste's family had possession of her true family prize, and then how that made her think of the others that had been lost, the letter-boxes most recently.

"Oh! Oh no, Brianna." Celeste said with a shake of her head, reading her look. "I'm so sorry, that must have sounded so insensitive." She was suddenly falling all over herself. "Dar told me earlier that you're here about the sword. I honestly didn't know you were looking for it. That *anyone* was looking for it."

Brianna felt her shoulders relax—Celeste was being upfront with her, she wasn't pretending Brianna didn't have a claim to the sword.

"May I?" Celeste asked again, motioning to the bag.

Brianna nodded and handed the bag over. Celeste opened the satchel, then stared at it a long moment, peering inside and inspecting the lining. When she looked back up at Brianna, it almost seemed like Celeste was tearing up. It struck Brianna as a little odd—but then again, she'd been rendered near speechless by the whole experience at the woman's clothing stall herself, so who was she to judge?

Giving Brianna a somewhat watery smile, Celeste reached out and squeezed her hand affectionately. "We're family, Brianna," she said. "Maybe not a direct blood relation, but the connection between your family and mine runs deeper than you know."

Something about the way she said it, the look in her eyes, the warmth of her grasp, touched Brianna in a way that few had in her lifetime. It sounded silly even to her, but Brianna *could* feel the connection between them, even before Celeste embraced her with Griffin still in her arms. She'd heard it when Lachlan had said it earlier, but in that moment, Brianna truly realized that to this family (the MacTavishes), being an O'Roarke carried weight.

Just as Brianna was about to pull out of the hug, she felt Celeste tense and heard her whisper, "Oh my God." With her back to the closet, Brianna wasn't sure what caused the reaction, but the impromptu hug ended, and she saw that Celeste looked oddly spooked. Mutely, and with her gaze fixed over Brianna's shoulder, Celeste handed Griffin to her so quickly, that neither had time to react, leaving Brianna bouncing the toddler on her hip as they both watched his mom frantically examining the dresses Brianna had just hung up.

"Where did you get these?" Celeste asked after what must have been a full minute, clutching the material of the gown that Brianna had been gifted.

Unsure what had come over her, Brianna covered Celeste's hands, doing her best to gently pry them away before Celeste did any damage to the expensive piece. Brianna was a little irked by Celeste's display—the dress deserved some care, and she was suddenly feeling very possessive of it. "I found them at a local art fair yesterday, on my way down here," she said, relaxing when Celeste let her hands drop down by her sides.

Celeste stared at the two garments for a long moment, then spied the ankle boots beneath them, and went bug-eyed again. "You found these too?" she said, snatching them and holding them up.

Not wanting Celeste to tear her whole closet apart, Brianna settled Griffin on the floor and gave him some of the tissue paper that the dresses had been wrapped in to play with. The boy immediately started happily crunching and crinkling the paper, and Brianna turned back to Celeste, who was now looking inside each boot, scrutinizing every inch.

"Well, technically I didn't find them," Brianna said,

reaching for the shoes. "The woman who ran the booth picked them out."

Celeste got very quiet again, and then she said, "Ah. What else did this woman pick out?"

"Are you okay?" Brianna asked, beginning to wonder if she should be worried, maybe Celeste was having some kind of pregnancy hormone-induced breakdown, if that was even a thing.

Celeste leveled her with a very clear 'I'm not crazy' look. "Humor me, please."

Brianna took the hint and shrugged. "Everything, I guess," she said, gathering all the items and placing them on the shelf. She even grabbed the bag from her suitcase. "So these, and…" she reached out, tapping the hangers that held the other chemises and gowns she'd purchased.

Celeste was quiet as she took it all in, and then her mouth gaped as she looked back at the shelf. "Wait, the bag too? It wasn't yours to begin with?"

Feeling increasingly uneasy, Brianna nodded. "No, she used it to pack everything."

A look crossed Celeste's face then, one that Brianna knew all too well. It made her feel guilty for questioning Celeste's sanity moments ago. Celeste was clearly processing Brianna's words, and so Brianna gave her the space to do so, waiting patiently, hoping to be clued in. When it seemed like she'd made a decision, Celeste took the bag from the shelf, and opened it, waving Brianna closer.

"Look," she said, pointing out the small letters embossed into the leather underneath the Celtic design, most of which was hidden beneath Celeste's fingers. But that didn't matter, because at the sight of the monogram, Brianna's heart skipped. She recognized it instantly. It was the insignia inside every O'Roarke bag. Inside her carry-on, her cosmetic bag, the tote she used for work, her grandfather's wallet, still in the valet atop his desk where she'd placed it shortly after he'd passed, and on the coin purse she'd inherited from her mom and always carried with her.

"I don't understand," Brianna whispered. She'd thought the satchel was a recreated general design—beautiful, but a replica—but it seemed like it not only was real vintage but had also belonged to some long ago O'Roarke. Taking it from Celeste's hands, Brianna looked at the bag differently now, with all the reverence of a family treasure—which it seemed like it was, as Celeste had said only moments ago. Brushing her fingers over the insignia, her eyes landed on the Celtic knot etched above it, and she startled, bringing the bag closer.

"Did you see this?" Brianna couldn't believe her eyes. She hadn't taken much note of the design before, but now it was all she could focus on.

Celeste peered inside and shrugged. "It's the design on all the bags, isn't it?"

"Not like this." This was what she had always thought of as *hers*, the Celtic knot made with six braided lines that had captured her heart when she'd seen it for the first and only time when she was a little girl. It had made such an impact on her that she'd sketched it and doodled it almost absentmindedly for years. It had stayed with her so fully that on her eighteenth birthday, she'd had it tattooed behind her ear exactly as she remembered it: a Celtic knot made of those six intricately–braided lines, surrounded by a circular knot. It had been no easy feat, on a tattoo so small.

Unsure of what it meant to be seeing this singular design again after so many years, Brianna kept the details to herself as Celeste took a closer look.

"Oh, you're right, Brianna," she said, though there was an odd hitch to her voice. "This is different."

Celeste shot Brianna an odd look, one that made her skeptical all of a sudden—did Celeste know something that *she* wasn't sharing? Not that Brianna could talk, she supposed. Her skepticism was usurped by another thought and her eyes shot to the gowns. She touched the material again, seeing these, too, in an entirely new light. She turned to Celeste, who was watching her intently. "You know…I said to her, the woman, that these were incredible replicas, that I couldn't believe they weren't real—the material, the craftsmanship…" Brianna murmured, remembering the exchange so clearly now. "And she smirked."

"Okay," Celeste said, leveling Brianna with a very intense stare. "This woman. What did she look like?"

Brianna told her about the woman, how she seemed almost ethereal, a dead ringer for her very own fairy godmother.

Celeste lay her head in her hands. "Oh, Brianna, this isn't good."

"Why? What do you mean?" Brianna's already quickened heart rate started to race.

"I have to get Dar and Lachlan," Celeste said, scooping up Griffin and darting out into the hall. Before Brianna had any time to process what had just happened, they were all in her closet, looking through the garments and paying particular attention to the satchel, and the design inside. Brianna knew the moment they saw it that it meant something to them, too. Whatever it was, they were troubled by it.

After several minutes of this wordless gaping and looking around at one another, Brianna was about to break the silence and ask *what* was going on when Dar spoke up.

"We can't be sure it was Esmeralda," he said, looking at Celeste and Lachlan, who didn't seem to agree.

"Who?" Brianna asked, all but fed up with the whole thing. "What is going on?"

Dar, who had been holding the satchel and examining the marking on its inside turned to Brianna. "The woman who we believe may have given you these things."

This didn't really clear anything up. "You know her?" Brianna asked. They all nodded but based on the energy in the room she wasn't too sure it was a good thing. "So, this means something then…?" Obviously, it did, but dragging it out of the MacTavishes was taking forever.

Celeste nodded. "Yeah, it does. Probably that you'll be taking a trip."

Could these people be any more cryptic? *Hello?!* What did that have to do with anything? "Despite what it might look like, I am not a frequent traveler," Brianna said, hoping this would be followed up by further explanation from Celeste—or Dar, or Lachlan, for that matter. But her comment was met only with non-committal grunts, aside from Griffin who thought it funny.

Griffin's laughter seemed to be the distraction everyone needed because her hosts immediately shifted gears, made a fuss over the time, and left her to get ready for dinner.

Brianna decided to put the weirdness of the whole thing aside for the moment and bring it up again at dinner. There obviously was more to the story—to this Esmerelda person, and the fact that the replica (or so she'd thought) bag she'd given her had the O'Roarke insignia *and* the singularly unique Celtic knot imprinted on the inside—but there would be time to ask questions later, after the MacTavishes had recovered from whatever their initial shock was.

After taking a shower Brianna grabbed a tea sandwich from the tray Celeste had sent up, nibbling her way through a delicious cucumber and dill triangle as she stood in her closet, deciding what to wear and mulling over everything that had just happened. She reached out to finger the dresses that had caused so much uproar, wondering for the millionth time what was going on. Eventually settling on slacks and a silk blouse, Brianna made her way downstairs where she found Celeste, Dar, and Lachlan, sitting in the formal living room, looking at ease and not at all like they'd had a collective panic less than an hour earlier. Watching them as they spoke among themselves, it was obvious they were close and enjoyed being together. Lachlan saw her first and called out to her.

"Ah, Breagha," he said, and Brianna was startled—she hadn't realized how much she missed hearing her name spoken like that—in a thick brogue—since her grandfather passed. "Come."

Lachlan waved her forward as he and Dar stood to greet her. They were all smiles—clearly also having decided to leave the earlier odd encounter forgotten. They all exchanged a few pleasantries as Dar poured her a drink before they walked over to the dinner table together, taking their seats and settling in for what Lachlan said was one of his son's favorite meals.

Brianna was so charmed by the man, and Dar and Celeste, too, that she couldn't stop smiling from ear to ear. They hadn't even spoken of the sword yet, not really, but she realized she couldn't muster up a reason to care, at least not for the moment.

When Lachlan asked about her parents, Brianna launched into a story she'd never spoken aloud. It was only when Lachlan reached out and squeezed her hand and said, "Breagha, tell us from your *heart*, lass," that she realized she'd been telling the story of her parents—of her life—as if she was at work giving cataloguing dictation, rattling off lists and facts of genealogy and geography. Never quick to tears, Brianna felt a rush of emotion as Lachlan looked deeply into her eyes. "Aye, from there," he said gently.

The effect was startling. In all of her life, at least since her parents died, she'd never felt so unencumbered in the company of ...anyone. Even with her family—her grandfather, her aunt, and her uncle—it was different, they suffered from the same loss she had. Of course, she felt safe and comfortable with them, but everything was tinged with the underlying blight of sorrow. But here, now, with the MacTavishes, Brianna felt something transformative. It was in the air, it was all around them, and she could hardly believe the words coming to her, but it was all just a—and because she was turning over a new leaf, she had to admit it—a wee bit magical. There was no denying that long-forgotten sensation, and when Lachlan squeezed her hand again, she grinned, which caused a tear or two to fall, but she didn't care. Instead, she chuckled for a second from the freedom she suddenly felt.

"I have the most incredible memories of my parents," she said, and that was that. Like a wave, that rush she felt carried her through several stories—of her life with her parents, of what she knew of their childhoods, how they'd met and courted one another—anything she could think of. And unlike the polite listening Lachlan, Dar, and Celeste had exhibited earlier, now they all leaned in, hanging on her every word.

Brianna talked through the entire first course, a chilled array of lobster, ahi tuna, and oysters, each served with a generous dollop of accompanying sauce. Catching a much-needed breath as their plates were cleared, she was grateful to see their second course was *anything but* simple mixed greens salad tossed in a vinaigrette. Brianna laughed softly when a selection of hot breads and whipped butters hit the table. "There's a workout schedule posted somewhere, right?"

"Most definitely," Celeste said, then began telling her about a friend of hers, Gwen, who not only insisted on a daily routine but had their schedule pronounced with all the seriousness of banns. Lachlan and Dar chimed in, too, and before Brianna knew it, she was caught up in an animated regalia of stories about their closest friends and family. She heard about the MacGreggors, Greylen and Gwen (the aforementioned workout queen); and the Montgomerys, not Alex or Amanda, but their relatives—Dar was vague on just how they were related—Gavin and Isabelle. Then there was a mention of their dear friend, Aidan Sinclair, who had apparently worked with them on the castle. Curious about what part they'd last remodeled, Brianna was about to ask when Dar jumped in with a story about another of his childhood friends, Ronan. Her question was forgotten when Lachlan started to speak about the O'Roarkes he knew. Brianna wasn't sure she'd ever met or even heard about that part of the family, and she *would* have remembered since they shared the names of her favorite ancestors, Callum and Margret. It was a wonderful, intimate glimpse into the lives of the MacTavishes as they laughed, shed a tear or two, and toasted to cherished memories.

Feeling the warmth around the table, Brianna envied the connection this family clearly had with their fold. She could feel how much these people meant to them—even though their friends and other family weren't there physically, their love and affection filled the room. It was a sensation that, for Brianna, had lain dormant for years, and feeling that re-emerging magical glow was a bit overwhelming.

There was another welcome pause when Dar rose to fetch a new bottle of wine from the kitchen. Once he returned and began refilling everyone's glasses, Brianna took a deep breath, feeling like the time was finally right to turn the conversation toward the sword, the reason she was even there.

"I'm not sure how to broach the subject," she said, feeling her cheeks warm. "But can we talk about the sword?" Suddenly overcome with emotion again, Brianna felt her eyes well up, a few tears spilling over. "I'm sorry," she whispered, as she wiped away her tears, embarrassed. Lachlan and Celeste, who were sitting closest to her, each reached out to offer a comforting touch. "It's just that everything I've ever held dear, all my cherished family legacies—it all keeps disappearing. And the sword...that sword, means everything to me. It's the oldest piece of our history. Name what you want in exchange. You can have the dresses, and the bag, too if you want! I'm prepared to pay whatever price yo—"

Brianna stopped short for a moment at the gasps, wide eyes, and frantic hands waving her off around the table. Still, she had to say her piece—she'd practiced it so many times on the drive up that the well-rehearsed words fell from her lips anyway. "I'm prepared to pay whatever price you wish to see it returned to our family."

She looked up and was met with three stunned faces, mouths agape, all looking like they were waiting for the floor to swallow them whole. In the silence, the staff reappeared with dinner and the room remained eerily quiet, aside from murmurs of thanks as their entrees were served—steak frites, but a play on the frites, made from a variety of root vegetables instead of traditional French fries. All the while, Brianna was trying to gather the courage to ask what was wrong.

"Sorry, Brianna," Celeste said first, having shared another look with the men. "For a moment, I think we were all concerned that...well, we thought..." her words suddenly failed her.

"What my wife is trying to say, is..." Dar cut in but seemed equally flummoxed. "Well, you see, we've all been in some rather … encountered some …".

"Och, the both of you," Lachlan spat, "If there's anything to be gleaned from our experience, and what we know, it's this, Breagha—that sword is not your legacy, lass. No, let me finish," Lachlan said, no doubt reacting to the confusion and offense that had surely crossed Brianna's face at those words. "The sword *itself* is not your legacy, though it is part of it. *Magic* is your legacy, Breagha, my dear."

"Da!" Celeste and Dar cried at once.

"*What?* She's an O'Roarke, and as close to the tree

as they come. Magic *must* run through the very heart of her. It would be unthinkable for her to not have known even a wee bit of it."

They all turned to look at her expectantly, and even though she was open to it, and truly she *was*, open to it, after years of pushing even *the idea* of the family magic away, her doubt must have shown.

"*Breagha!—Girl!*" Lachlan exclaimed after seeing the doubt on her face. "ALL O'Roarkes believe!"

Brianna shrugged, wishing she could force true belief. Dar and Celeste told Lachlan to ease up a bit, clearly worried his tone may have offended her. It was really kind of them, but honestly, Brianna read Lachlan's words as filled only with affection. It was clear he was passionate about the subject.

"It's okay," she said, "It's just... well, after my parents died, any of that wee bit of magic seemed to go with them."

Lachlan nodded, then closed his eyes for a moment. When he opened them again, he was looking at her intently. "Do you know the history of your family's sword?" he asked.

Brianna shook her head slowly. "Beyond what we know from carbon dating, it's the one piece that's shrouded in mystery." Buoyed by the gleam in Lachlan's eyes, and the grin spreading slowly across his face, Brianna's heartbeat ticked up a notch as she leaned forward and reached for his hand. "You know it, don't you?" she asked, tears suddenly pricking at her eyes as that hopeful feeling danced through her again.

"Oh aye, lass. There's good reason it's shrouded in mystery."

The air nearly crackled in the room with his statement, and as he paused, whether for dramatics or not, Brianna was grateful for the breather, as suddenly her brain was nearly bursting from this new information pinging in her head. While she tried to absorb what Lachlan was implying, Dar and Celeste were doing their best to caution him from saying more—which of course only made Brianna want to know even more. Luckily, Lachlan wasn't dissuaded.

"She has every right to know—especially if it *was* Esmerelda who bestowed those gifts upon her on the heels of visiting Abersoch, no less!" His hand hit the table. "And it's our duty to tell her." He fixed his son and daughter-in-law with a stare so intense Brianna almost started to second-guess whether she *did* want to know. That hesitation lasted only a millisecond though, because there was that name again, Esmeralda, and somehow, she was connected to the sword and to the O'Roarkes. It was all too perfect to be a coincidence, and based on the look that Dar and his wife were sharing, Brianna knew the stakes were high.

"We're in agreement, then?" Lachlan asked when neither Dar nor Celeste said anything. The two paused a moment longer, then seemed to come to a silent consensus. With one more look at Brianna, they turned back to Lachlan and nodded, then Lachlan turned to Brianna and patted her hand. "Sit back, love. We're in for a long night."

Brianna accepted the fresh glass of wine that Dar was handing her and, God help her, she sat there for hours, eating up every single word.

As Lachlan told her about the O'Roarkes of centuries ago, Fergus and Isabeau, Callum and Margret, she listened, rapt. After a little while, it became harder and harder to ignore that Lachlan wasn't talking about these people as historical figures, but as contemporaries, and when Celeste stepped in to explain how the sword had come into their possession—how her sister-in-law, a woman named Maggie had found it after *her* brother Derek, who had gotten it from Brianna's grandfather, passed away—well, Brianna needed to top off her wine to take it all in. If what these people were saying was true, there was more than just a wee bit of magic imbued in her family's artifact, *nay*, her family's entire history—and apparently, it was all magic.

So too, the land of Castle Abersoch that they now sat upon.

CHAPTER 6

"I'll be back in a month's time," Aidan said to Tristan as the boy helped him gather his belongings and place them atop the bed to be packed away.

After three days at Seagrave, they were nearly ready to set sail. When Aidan opened his satchel, Tris went to the wardrobe, dragging his feet a bit to collect the few items Aidan had unpacked, as well as what he'd worn on his journey to Seagrave, which had been freshly laundered. Normally, the boy would swoop his hands across the shelf, happily returning with an overstuffed armload, but today he was dawdling, his mood wholly different.

"I should come with you," Tristan said, handing Aidan a single shirt. "Papa says learning to sail our ships is vital."

Aidan chuckled, then sobered seeing how crestfallen Tristan was, shifting his sights to the floor. He laid a hand on the boy's head, gently tilting it back so he could look him in the eye.

"I was laughing at your father, not you," he said. "And you've got a very valid point. Learning to command the MacGreggor ships is a must, but—and this is a very important but—I believe right now your mama needs you here, especially with your aunt, uncle, and cousins leaving, too." Aidan knew that this last thing was the root of Tristan's melancholy. "Ensuring the safety of one's family is of the utmost importance," he said, leveling Tristan with a serious look.

At this, Tristan stood up straighter, as having a noble cause was wont to make one do. "You're right. My duty is here."

"Aye. For now."

"Do you think they'll learn before I do?"

Ah, another worry now revealed, that his younger cousins might outpace him. Aidan was careful not to laugh again. "I don't believe this is the trip on which your aunt and uncle will apprentice your cousins on nautical arts."

The boy didn't seem so sure, and frankly, neither was Aidan. Sailing ran in the blood of MacGreggors and Montgomerys alike. In this, only time would tell.

"Swords or arrows?" Aidan asked, thinking to give the boy a distraction as they still had some time.

"Both," said the little mercenary, and this time Aidan did chuckle.

After an hour or so in the courtyard with Tristan, Aidan made his way back inside the keep. He was besieged the moment he stepped upon the stone floor. First, it was Anna, inquiring about the household items on their inventory catalogue. Next, Lady Madelyn, imploring him to safeguard a carefully packed trunk, freshly stocked with potions and such. And on the heels of her departure, came Isabelle, with a flurry of questions (all which her husband could have answered for her) regarding their quarters on the ship, followed by a request to stop in Ayr, conditions permitting, and to look at their proposed course of travel. Aidan remained patient through each question and request, most of which had been previously addressed. He understood that while this move was in truth a happy occasion, in the end, the family was separating.

Grateful for a lull in the commotion once Isabelle stepped outside, Aidan lifted his hood. He heard Gwen snicker, "That helps" and turned to see her watching the whole ordeal, with Greylen at her side. Aidan gave her a sheepish smile and pushed his hood back. Gwen laughed again in response and made her exit as Greylen motioned Aidan toward his study. Certain that Grey had been subject to his own form of besiegement, Aidan gladly followed him down the hall, and hopefully to a prolonged moment or two of quiet.

As they entered Grey's study, Gavin, who was waiting inside, seated at Grey's desk, rose, ceding the chair. Old habits that were reminiscent of a time when Gavin was Greylen's first in command. Aidan sat in one of the two chairs facing Grey's desk, shifting his legs as Gavin made his way to the other. Aidan accepted a stack of papers from Gavin, a sheaf of shipping logs, details on the crew and course, and results from the most recent inspection.

Two ships were set to sail for Abersoch, one purposed for supplies, as well as the last of the luxuries Isabelle and Gavin were taking with them; the other would carry their most precious cargo, their four children. With the local authority at each port handsomely compensated, the plan was set: the ship carrying Isabelle and the children would lay anchor in the cove at Abersoch, with the cargo ship docking in a neighboring port. As they neared their destinations, it was decided that Gavin would transfer to the cargo ship to make his permanent presence known at the public dock. From there, he would oversee the transfer of their goods by land, which was much more convenient than doing so by long boat. Everything in the logs looked in order until Aidan reached the page that showed that Gavin had stationed him on the cargo ship.

"Nay." Aidan shook his head, taking a quill from Grey's desk to make the change. Until now, their journeys by sea had required the use of only one ship. "We've two ships. Isabelle and your children. I sail with you. Alan and Richard can sail on the other ship."

Technically Aidan wasn't pulling rank, though he could, being that he had been charged with installing the Montgomerys in their new seat. However, since it was Gavin who was behind the commission, it was a little hazy. His decision, however, was met with nods from both Gavin and Grey.

With their final plans settled, Aidan tossed the

revised passenger list on Grey's desk, and sat back, eyes closed, to enjoy that moment of quiet he'd sought before. At the distinct sound of heavy, purposeful footsteps heading their way, he cracked an eye open and exchanged a knowing look with Grey and Gavin. They all mouthed the name *Alex* at the same time. With a commanding presence that only Grey could come close to matching, Alex had worked his way quickly through the ranks, earning a coveted place among the inner circle some years ago. Alex had come to them from the MacPhersons to the south, distant kin of Dar's mother Ella. Eager to serve, he had soon proved his worth—he was an accomplished swordsman, to say the least. Though he'd once been a man with a ready smile and well-timed wit, after Gwen's abduction, any trace of lighthearted ease vanished, and his sole pursuit became the protection of Seagrave, the MacGreggors, and most especially, Gwen.

Aidan realized he hadn't seen Alex that morn, and taking in his appearance now as he charged through the study, it was clear he'd been out riding patrol.

"The Fitzgeralds crossed MacGreggor land at dawn," he said in lieu of greeting. "They'll be cresting the hill momentarily."

Aidan shook his head when Grey glanced his way. "They're not here by my invitation," he said. Aidan had had every intention to speak with the brothers on his way to Abersoch, but that was before Gavin had sent word to Pembrooke about their change in plans and before the conversation over breakfast two days past. With a sigh, he rose now to deal with their unexpected arrival. The other men followed, and they'd barely taken two steps down the hall when Gwen and Isabelle came rushing toward them.

"What's going on?" Isabelle said, only slightly out of breath. "Your men just joined Kevin and Ian on the steps and they're not exchanging pleasantries. They're in war mode."

Aidan wasn't surprised. If Henry, Alan, and Richard stood ready for battle, despite that it was altogether unnecessary, Grey's men would comply, reason or not. "It seems the Fitzgerald brothers have come for my answer," Aidan told the women, and was unsurprisingly met by expressions of alarm.

"You're not still thinking about it—about Judith— are you?" Gwen asked.

Aidan gave her his best glare, which she rightly interpreted, quickly rearranging her face and smiling brightly as Alex quickly looked his way, apparently waiting to be clued in. Surprised it wasn't common knowledge by now, he told Alex of the latest conditions the Fitzgeralds had added to the agreement Aidan had held with their father, the whole unpleasant tale, as they headed outside, joining what appeared to be half of Seagrave's inhabitants. Apparently, *some* sort of news had traveled after all, and they were eager for sport.

Aidan took his place atop the steps, flanked by Grey and Gavin, their men an impenetrable wall behind them. Quite obviously thinking they should be allowed a prime view of the action, Gwen and Isabelle squeezed up next to their husbands, Gwen struggling to position herself best, rounded belly and all, a few swear words escaping her lips as she did so. Aidan wasn't the only one trying to keep a straight face, knowing that even affectionate laughter would draw her ire. Luckily, for them, the riding party was escorted into the courtyard just then, and the men gently pushed the women behind them again.

Still as stone, Aidan waited, wondering at this latest ill-conceived approach from the Fitzgerald brothers. They truly suffered discipline and direction in the wake of Robert's loss, and mayhap never had it to begin with. Why the urgency of getting his answer?

The brothers dismounted, sauntering forward with exaggerated swagger, and clearly no idea of their precarious circumstances. If he hadn't witnessed it himself, Aidan would never have believed such gall, such blatant disrespect. He felt a moment of sorrow for Judith, who was at least nothing like her brothers. The pang gave Aidan pause—because along with it came the consideration that he *did* have the power and opportunity to take her away from them. Odd, but it was the first time he'd felt anything at all regarding the match, temporary though it was.

Gil, the younger Fitzgerald brother, spoke first. "We've come for your answer."

Obviously. Aidan had planned to decline their proposal, yet suddenly all he could think of was their sister, and any harm that might befall her because of his rejection. They would surely take it as an insult, and he had a feeling they would blame Judith. Not that he was suddenly entertaining the thought of marrying her, but he also didn't want any harm to come to her. Faced with the brothers so blatantly now, however, Aidan *did* realize that for months, he'd been utterly and wholly indifferent to the proposition. He should have put it together, for that in and of itself was significant.

"Retreat, while you're still able," he said. "I'll add 'respectfully,' in deference to your sister." With ships to sail, a family to install into their new seat, and many moving parts to make any of it happen, Aidan didn't have time for this.

Gil looked over toward Nigel, his elder by just two years. Nigel glowered but nodded slowly.

"Aye. We will go. You're clearly too…preoccupied to see your error in judgment," Gil said. "But we'll be back. You owe us, Sinclair."

Aidan kept a stoic expression, but inside was marveling at their impudence. These boys would be their own downfall. "I owe no one," he said. "And let me be clear, I knew your father well enough to know, *this*," Aidan said, motioning with his chin toward the brothers, "shames his memory." The last was an insult, and they knew it.

They stepped forward as if to challenge him, showing yet another level of stupidity. Luckily for them, the men they traveled with, held them back.

Still, Gil spouted, "Until we have your answer, you'll stay off our land. Our agreement is over."

A round of sirs was called from the line of soldiers behind them. Aidan answered since the insult was directed at him.

"Don't kill them," he said, and with that, Aidan dismissed the Fitzgeralds entirely.

CHAPTER 7

Brianna's head was still spinning, long after dinner. She just couldn't get Lachlan's final words—the hardest to believe in a series of hard-to-believe words —out of her head. "Fate will take you where you're meant to go, Breagha, I'm certain of it—whether you're ready for it or not." He'd said it so seriously, too. She'd searched for any kind of twinkle in his eye, a smile tugging at the corner of his mouth, but came up empty. So, either he was crazy—along with Dar *and* Celeste, which frankly was hard to believe—or time travel was real, they knew how it worked, and they were convinced that she was next.

She tossed and turned most of the night, kept awake by all the possibilities of *what-ifs*. Mainly, *what if* they were right? It would certainly explain how Lachlan, Dar, and Celeste had all sat at that table, delivering clear, watertight stories that felt natural— not memorized or fabricated—making it nearly impossible to deny their credibility, *or* at least that

what they'd told her was something that *they* believed.
Unless all three were suffering under the same
unlikely delusion, they had her almost convinced.
What if they were right? Yet every time Brianna
teetered on the side of believing them, her more
sensible side—the side that an accredited historian
who dealt in facts—said it was impossible. But,
what if?

What if every choice she'd made in her life had led
her *here*, to this very place to embrace her destiny—
which according to the MacTavishes was hundreds of
years in the past, her own family's *gloriously-magical*
(their words) past? No wonder her aunt and uncle had
been only too happy to let her go call on the
MacTavishes. Celeste had shared with her that it was
she who had been the rightful claimant of the letterboxes—that the letters inside had been written to her
by Dar centuries ago. Maybe Uncle Christopher and
Aunt Michelle hadn't been duped after all.

The new-leaf side of Brianna let herself imagine.
She could visit her family, and see the letterboxes *and*
Dunhill Manor in all their splendid and original glory.
Good Lord, she could meet Cateline De la Cour
herself, her favorite ancestor and true trendsetter of
her time! For a moment, Brianna let herself get
excited about the possibility of exploring in real life
what she'd spent over a decade discovering in old
dusty sections of libraries. Maybe it *was* part of her
journey, her soul's journey. Maybe that part of her,
the terribly wounded part that she'd locked away,
would finally get a chance to heal. Based on what

Lachlan, Dar, and Celeste had shared, if this *was* her destiny, as it had been for them and several of their friends, then there wasn't anything that could stop it. Unable to wrap her head around the implications of what that would mean for her entire perception of reality, Brianna settled on one thing: she would speak with her hosts in the clear light of day, and try to get some sleep tonight.

When she finally tossed the covers aside the next morning, she wasn't sure what to expect when she went downstairs. Would her hosts be sitting around the table laughing, ready to explain that it had all been an elaborate joke? Or would they double down and continue to insist it was all true? Oddly, Brianna was beginning to feel that it seemed more likely that the time travel story was real.

When she entered the kitchen where the MacTavishes were setting up for breakfast, Brianna noticed that something felt different. An urgency, something in the air.

"What is it?" she asked, feeling suddenly apprehensive.

Dar glanced at Celeste before he reached for an envelope that Brianna hadn't noticed, propped up against a fruit bowl. "When you arrived yesterday, I sent a courier to retrieve this."

Brianna took the envelope and gasped as her eyes caught the familiar, flourishing script on its front. "I don't understand?" she whispered, as her fingers brushed over the letters of her name. "This is from my grandfather. But... how do you have it?"

"I believe it was given to Derek along with the sword." Dar looked at Celeste, who was staring at him now, crestfallen.

"You never told me," Celeste said.

"I meant to. I'm sorry, love. It was hidden in our safe. I may not have found it or thought to look more closely if we hadn't sold the house. I just wanted to be sure nothing was left behind."

"Wait," Brianna shook her head, "You've had this… for how long?"

"Not very. But as it only said 'Brianna' on it, with no surname, it wasn't until your call that I realized who it belonged to."

Brianna barely waited for him to finish speaking before she had the envelope open and was unfolding the single sheet of paper waiting for her inside. She began to read:

My dearest Brianna,

If you're reading this, then I suppose I've departed this earthly world, and you've discovered that the sword is gone. It's imperative that you know that I was of sound mind when I sold it to Mr. Lowell, and while you may scoff at the dollars and cents of it all, I hope you will trust my judgment enough to know that it was the right decision. Rest assured that I believe this transaction was not only necessary but required to ensure our legacy and an outcome that even I (a full believer) never imagined. That's all I'm able to say for now, but one day, you'll know why I've done this. I think you'll find that some part of you knew all along.

My eternal love,
Dougal O'Roarke

While vague, her grandfather's cryptic words gave credence to Lachlan's. Somehow, in some way, Brianna shared something deeper than family ties with this group of people. It was a lot to take in. All of it. Overloaded and overwhelmed, the newly minted *fly-by-the-seat-of-her-pants* Brianna went back into hiding. A necessity, in order to process this whirlwind. At the very least, she would take a pause, using her standard cloak of 'when in doubt, do nothing' mode.

Thankfully, when she excused herself with a mutter of "I need some time to think," she was met with understanding and warmth.

Lachlan gave her a fatherly smile. "Take all the time you need, lass."

Grateful, Brianna slipped the envelope into her pocket and padded back upstairs, the cup of coffee Dar had insisted she take with her in hand. Once in her room, she did what she did best, and what had allowed her to excel in her particular line of work. Narrowing her focus, leaving the stories, the connections, the coincidence, and all the odd occurrences by the wayside, Brianna immersed herself in her surroundings, paying particular attention to the *things* around her. Her safe place. After a long shower, dressed in her favorite soft linen chinos and a simple top, she reached for her walking shoes but paused when she caught sight of the ankle boots from the fair. Selecting those instead, she tried them on and was surprised they were so comfortable—not only were they a perfect fit, but they were supportive, too. She took a moment to admire how they pulled her outfit together before grabbing a lightweight jacket and heading downstairs. On her way to the gardens, she passed through the kitchen, stopping short when she saw Celeste and Dar there, enjoying a bit of alone time sans Griffin.

"Oh no," Brianna whispered, then blushed and covered her eyes.

Celeste and Dar laughed a little and waved her on. When Brianna was nearly out the door, Celeste called after her.

"Hey," she said. "If you explore the tunnels, just be careful around the cliffs."

"And stay out of the water," Dar added.

They really were serious. Brianna raised her hand and assured them she would avoid the water, which really wouldn't have been a problem anyway. Funny how vast open spaces scared the bejesus out of her, but mention of a dark, claustrophobic cavern piqued her interest.

Ditching her original plan of exploring gardens, she passed through them and instead found her way to the tunnels on the far side of the property. Although the area was graced with a pretty sitting area, the entrance itself was hidden behind a beautifully manicured hedge. It was meant as a deterrent, but Brianna reminded herself that she had permission (as long as she didn't jump) and squeezed through the dense vegetation.

Once inside, she brushed off her jacket and waited for her eyes to adjust, wishing she'd grabbed a flashlight. She smiled a moment later as soft lighting flickered to her left, and realized she must have triggered a sensor. The lanterns brightened the tunnel ahead as if calling her name, and she tread forward, excited to see what she might find.

Oddly, other than a few sitting areas nestled in the occasional alcove she passed, she didn't come across much. Still, there was something compelling and inviting about the space, an energy that spurred her on, and Brianna lost track of time, winding her way through the cavern. When she heard water sloshing, she was confused and wondered if she'd somehow descended to the shoreline. It seemed impossible given how high up she'd been at the start, but as she followed the sound, bright light spilled into the passageway just ahead, and when she turned, she had to shield her eyes from the glare as she stepped into the large opening.

When her eyes adjusted, Brianna just stood there, absolutely *stunned* by the most beautiful, picturesque, and *yes*, God help her, magical setting she'd ever seen in her life. It was a hidden grotto, rival to none, with burbling tide pools cloistered beneath a natural rock ceiling. Worthy of any mythical court, yet far enough from the shore and open sea that it still felt safe,

Brianna was giddy at her find. She was no expert when it came to geology, but she was a sucker for a pretty stone, and in an area as rich in minerals as this one, Brianna wondered if she might even get lucky and find a crystal.

Excited by the prospect, Brianna walked the rocky shelf between the gravel beach and hidden cove, crouching now and again in her search for treasure, always being careful with her footing. After making her way around the pools that were still full, and without spotting anything interesting in them, she worked her way back toward the rock wall where the pools were mostly empty in the wake of the receding tide.

A bit disappointed she hadn't found anything, not even a polished stone, Brianna scanned the area one last time. Her gaze landed on a cluster of flat-topped rocks bathed in sunlight. *Perfect,* she thought. If she wasn't going to be returning with her pockets full of pretty stones, then she could at least rest for a bit, and take in this beautiful setting. Making her way over to the rocks, she sat down gently, enjoying its warmth, and lifted her face to the sun. After the whirlwind of the last few days, it felt so nice to take in a deep, cleansing breath, and just relax—like, truly relax. She was having such a lovely time, all her questions and uncertainties temporarily forgotten—until a shout from afar nearly gave her a coronary.

Brianna looked up and saw that the shout had come from Dar, who was heading her way briskly, with Celeste and Lachlan in tow. Not sure what had them all so alarmed, she waved so they'd know she'd heard him, then stood to join them. When she looked back up, they were all running toward her, and Brianna saw that Celeste was carrying a large bag...a satchel she would swear even from this distance was hers. Actually—*was* that her satchel? They were shouting something, but the wind had picked up enough that Brianna couldn't make out what they were saying. As they moved closer, the gusts intensified, echoing so loudly, she had to cover her ears. Feeling their urgency, Brianna started to hurry, moving at a steady clip, and trying *not* to imagine what kind of bad news they were running to deliver to her.

Closing the distance between herself and the others, Brianna passed another tide pool, and a bright glimmer caught her eye. She hadn't meant to stop, but the collector in her got the better of her—as did the fact that she was almost certain she'd inspected that pool thoroughly already. Blocking out the calls from the MacTavishes, barely audible over the sound of the now howling wind, Brianna looked toward the spot where she'd seen the glint. Her breath caught when she saw it, a large golden coin of some sort, lodged in amongst the rocks. Like a moth to a flame, she was drawn to it, and reversed course, making her way to a shallow slope she'd noticed on the other side.

Operating in work mode now, Brianna's focus narrowed as she ignored all other sounds and senses. Not her best move as it turned out. Nearly there, she slipped on a mossy stone and cried out as she stumbled. She flailed her arms, doing her best to avoid a haphazard fall, but gravity had already taken over. Using her forward momentum, she pushed herself up at the very last second, and without thinking, leapt straight toward the center of the pool. In those few seconds between her slip and when she landed, everything became eerily quiet, and a flash of what she could only describe as *energy* surrounded her—it happened so fast that she didn't have time to be scared. Bracing herself, she landed hard, stumbling to her knees, her hands scraping the gritty sediment on the bottom of the tide pool. Dizzy, her heart racing from the adrenalin rush, Brianna stared at the rocky basin, blinking slowly until everything came into focus. She checked her hands as she caught her breath, picking out a few pebbles stuck in her palm, then once she ascertained there'd been no real damage, she turned her attention back to securing her treasure. As luck would have it, she'd landed inches from the coin and carefully dislodged it from its resting place. Holding it in both hands, she grinned broadly—it was a prize more than worthy of her embarrassing spill. What she'd first mistaken for a small coin, was actually a large hand-forged medallion. Although she couldn't determine what exactly it was made from, it was in such good condition, that it appeared to be almost new. Brianna held it up to catch the light, admiring the beautiful circular infinity knot carved around the edge, floored that she'd found such a gorgeous artifact. When she turned her attention to the design on the face, her breath caught at the image of a beautiful and formidable bear, set in relief. Bears had always been an omen of good luck for Brianna—her father's name, Arthur, came from the Celtic word for bear. She smiled, brushing her fingers over the raised contour, before turning it over to look at the back. Brianna nearly dropped it when she saw the etching on the back. It was the same knot, *the* knot, the circular symbol that until yesterday had eluded her for most of her life. With a bear on one side, and that unique Celtic design on the other, she knew the medallion meant something. This couldn't be a coincidence.

Excited to show the MacTavishes what she'd found, and hopefully get some answers, Brianna stood, waving it in the air and grinning like an idiot. But as she stared down the shore, not only was the path that they'd been on empty, it—and the rest of the scenery—was altogether different. The wide gravely expanse between the rock wall and open sea was gone, and the rock wall itself, from the cliffs and grotto where she'd first emerged from the tunnels to the shore far down the property line, was lush with vegetation that she was certain hadn't been there before.

As she struggled to comprehend what had happened, she felt that odd energy-like sensation again. Like a buzzing in the air around her. When her bag appeared next to her, with a *plop,* Brianna froze and an ominous feeling crept over her—that some-how, she'd done exactly what she wasn't supposed to do. Hoping she was wrong and doing her best not to panic, Brianna placed the medallion in her pocket, then bent to pick up her satchel. But as she riffled through it and saw that Celeste had packed everything Esmeralda picked out for her, her heart rate started to ramp up again—exponentially. Trying to control her shallow breaths and ward off a full-on panic attack, Brianna looked down the empty path again, hoping desperately that she would see Celeste making her way toward her. *Oh no. No, no, no.* She'd just wanted some time to explore her surroundings and *not* think about the MacTavishes' extraordinary proposal and all that went with it.

Had she really...*time-traveled?*

Staring at the empty expanse, Brianna wondered how she'd gone wrong. She was certain she'd heeded Dar and Celeste's warnings. Hadn't she? She'd avoided the water, and as for the cliffs, well, she hadn't even gotten close to an opening, so she surely hadn't jumped. But then the memory of how she'd pushed off the rock—an instinctual, almost uncontrollable action—flickered into her mind, and she recalled how she'd leapt into the air before landing in the center of the tide pool. Wait. *Did that count?* As she looked back down at her bag, Brianna had a feeling that it did. No wonder they'd been running toward her—they knew, and she'd been oblivious. A strange yet vaguely familiar feeling came over her then, as she pulled herself up and out of the shallow tide pool. Fear. Real and total fear and uncertainty. She hadn't felt it, not like this, not in decades—not since the night her parents died.

Shaking, and wondering what she was supposed to do next, Brianna's ears pricked at the sound of a faint, wispy cry. Grateful for something, *anything really* to focus on, she turned toward the sound where a tiny little kitten stood only a few feet away.

"*Oh*…hi, baby." Thinking it was an odd spot for a kitten to be wandering around, Brianna gave a cursory sweep of the area, but couldn't see any signs of its mama or litter mates. "Where's your mama? Did you get lost? Or fall?" Brianna asked, looking up at the craggy rock wall.

The kitten just stared at her, then emitted another wispy yowl. Worried the little creature might run away if she reached for it, Brianna took a moment to brush the sand from her hands and her pants, smiling when it started walking toward her with an unsteady gait. Looping the strap of her satchel over her shoulder, Brianna adjusted it on her hip, then reached for the kitten, now at her feet. The sweet baby started purring as soon as Brianna cradled her against her chest.

She stood that way for a moment, giving and taking comfort too, until the distinct sound of horses in the distance put her on high alert. Brianna turned and nearly dropped the kitten when she saw a sizable contingent of men galloping down the long narrow stretch of shoreline. They road three abreast, filling the whole beach from the shallows to the rock wall, a sight both beautiful in its symmetry and terrifying for its testimony. Brianna blinked, wondering if it was merely a figment of her imagination (or, had she somehow hit her head after becoming airborne and not noticed?) or was this more evidence that what she'd been told was true—time travel was indeed possible, and she'd just done it. After a few seconds, there was no denying—a figment, it was not.

As they rode closer, Brianna suddenly realized what she was wearing—*pants*, for starters—and reached into her bag, shifting the kitten to one arm so she could dig for fabric. Grabbing the crimson dress, she put it over her head, tugging the material over her modern outfit. With seconds to spare, she clutched the kitten and considered running, but the men stopped not ten feet from her. When one dismounted and began to approach her, she stood her ground, not that she had a choice, and decided to give it her best.

"Are ye lost, lass?" he asked, his Scots Gaelic more proof of what happened.

Apparently, Brianna's best was silence at the moment. She hoped he thought she was shaking from being cold.

"Are ye hurt?" He asked, concern replacing curiosity. "Can ye tell me your name, lass?"

God help her, she hoped she was making the right choice. "Brianna," she told him. "Brianna O'Roarke."

CHAPTER 8

Blessed with clear skies, a brisk wind, and friendly waters Aidan spent the first two days of the journey to Abersoch just as he'd suspected—working alongside Gavin and Isabelle to instruct the twins and their younger brother about sailing. It was a boon, reminiscent of his younger days when Allister and Fergus had done the same for him and his brethren. Even Captain John, the MacGreggors' eldest and most seasoned commander, recounted a few tales to the boys, including the times Isabelle snuck aboard.

So absorbed in their duties, the time passed quickly, and on the third morning of their journey, they made port in Ayr—their one and only planned stop. With a short list of supplies to gather, it was originally slated as a brief excursion, but they hadn't taken into account that they'd be visiting at the same time as the annual fair, so they'd extended their stay through the afternoon. While Aidan and Gavin followed along behind Isabelle and the children, providing occasional counsel to the twins as they bartered for goods, Isabelle took the opportunity to collect what amounted to a trove of fabrics. With her arms filled with silks as well as the baby, she exited the booth she'd been in for quite some time.

"I seem to have run out of coin," she said, handing a pile of fabric to Gavin.

Aidan chuckled, smitten as he watched their clear love for one another. When Isabelle turned to him and thrust something his way, Aidan was quick to respond, surprised to find baby Emmalyn suddenly in his arms.

"I need two hands," Isabelle said with a shrug and smile, before returning to gather her purchases.

While Gavin helped the twins, Aidan settled Emmalyn against his chest—the youngest of four, the baby was used to being passed about—and waved Isabelle off to finish her purchase. Looking through the crowd as he waited, he nodded to his men, as always mere paces behind, and saw many of their crew enjoying their extended respite on land. Aidan smiled when Emmalyn cooed and snuggled deeper against him. He was patting her back when something odd caught his attention—just up ahead, the throngs of fairgoers seamlessly parted and a familiar, though unexpected figure appeared. "Esmerelda," he breathed as if Emmalyn could understand.

Although he was focused on the mysterious woman who'd played a part in all their lives, he was still able to catch Isabelle with his free hand, who, gasping as she exited the booth, had stumbled, and nearly fell headfirst to the ground at the sight of Esmerelda.

Sensing a change in the air, all vestiges of ease vanished, and Aidan stood straighter. He transferred the baby to Isabelle, then moved to stand in front of her, signaling to Gavin across the path with the boys, to stay put as he did so. Reading his silent command, their men surrounded them, much to Gavin's displeasure.

For all their posturing, Esmeralda didn't slow, showing absolutely no emotion as she strode right up to him and stopped a hair's breadth away. Wishing to get whatever this was behind him, Aidan waited rather uncomfortably as her head tilted back and her iridescent, swirling blue eyes locked on his. Give him any other task, *any*, and he was steps ahead, but in *this*, magic, there were no guarantees. All he was sure of was that a promised fate always bore a cost.

After a moment, Esmerelda spoke. "You've accomplished much, and more than proved your mettle, Aidan Sinclair, but your task is far from over. Tread with caution, the path ahead is not a smooth one."

Aidan knew better than to ask any questions, he just held her gaze and gave the nod that he knew she was waiting for.

Satisfied, Esmerelda turned to leave and Aidan felt his muscles slack but a second until Isabelle managed to step around him and called after the departing woman.

"Wait!" she said, raising one arm, the other still on Emmalyn.

Esmeralda stopped and turned. "Isabelle."

Isabelle froze, and Aidan put a protective hand on her shoulder. "You know my name?" she asked.

"Of course. I know all of you, as well as your parents."

"Why did you lie to Maggie and Callum?" Isabelle asked quickly, as if she knew she'd soon lose her nerve.

Aidan quickly pulled Isabelle behind him again, worried the enchantress would take insult, but Esmeralda bristled more at the gesture than Isabelle's words and wasted no time in taking him to task.

"I wasn't insulted by her question, Aidan Sinclair," she said, getting ever closer to him. "Your lack of faith in my character, however, gives me great pause. Now, move."

The last thing Aidan had intended to do was anger Esmeralda, yet he'd done just that. A sorry accomplishment of which he believed within their circle he was the first. Glancing at Gavin, Aidan waited for his nod before he moved slightly to the side. When Esmeralda stepped into the space he just vacated, he felt a change in her.

"Fiona was with child—a girl—and died. So, I told Callum he would welcome a boy so he wouldn't be reminded of Fiona and the girl she carried."

Esmerelda's blunt words were a complete departure from her usual veiled musings. It was obvious she cared, and deeply. Aidan watched as Isabelle bowed her head, all trace of bravado gone.

A moment later, Esmerelda turned to him. "You

waste a precious commodity, Aidan Sinclair. The wheels of fate are already in motion."

And with that, she turned to leave.

Aidan gladly watched her go, more than ready to put the entire exchange behind him. He vaguely felt Gavin give him a solid push to get to his wife, and stumbled to the side in response, his eyes locked on Esmeralda until she disappeared into the throng of festivalgoers.

"Round the crew," he told them, knowing without a doubt, their time here was done.

What he didn't mention was the sudden urgency he felt to heed the mystic's warning and be on his way.

CHAPTER 9

Brianna was escorted from the shore on horseback. Although she was an accomplished rider thanks to the years of lessons her grandfather had urged her to take, she was grateful to merely be a passenger this time, seated with the guard who seemed to be in charge. As they made the arduous trek to the bluff above, Brianna realized that if not for her exploration of the tunnels, she never would have found herself by the tide pools. Consumed with thoughts, not so much on *how* she came to be here but *why* she'd felt pulled toward it each step of the way, she was thankful for the silence as the men navigated the steep path—and for Kitty, too, who still purred against her chest.

When they reached terra firma, Brianna's breath caught as the castle came into view. So, this was Abersoch in its original form. Like a true beacon on a hill, the castle seemed to glow in beautiful glory. Its style reminded her at once of Pembrooke, the estate not so far from Dunhill that she'd developed a deep attachment to as a child, and where she'd first seen that specific knot that seemed to be everywhere now. She sat straighter in the saddle, hit with a rush of memories, and her eyes teared up. Brianna could still recall the day her grandfather had taken her there, and how seeing that design for the first time, carved deeply into the stone, had affected her.

She was still in somewhat of a stupor as she was helped down from the horse but nevertheless made sure to pat the animal affectionately before ascending the steps that led to the front doors. Suddenly shaking and chilled to the bone, Brianna stood in the massive entryway where she was turned over to the care of a man who seemed to be in charge. While he exchanged a few terse words with the guard who'd brought her inside, Brianna took in her surroundings, clinging to Kitty and feigning an air of detachment, all the while hoping she wouldn't be turned back out.

"I'll check on ye in the morn, lass," the guard said, and his words—clearly indicating that she would still be here in the morning—pulled her from her stupor.

Brianna wasn't sure why he'd taken such an interest in her welfare but appreciated it all the same, and nodded, murmuring a thank you before he turned to leave. His boots sounded loudly as he made for the door, casting a serious pall on her predicament as she turned to face the man she'd been left with, who by now she assumed was the chamberlain of the estate. The man wasted no time in exerting his authority and showing his displeasure, pointing at Kitty, and shaking his head.

"Please, sir," Brianna breathed desperately, clinging to Kitty like a lifeline. "She's free of fleas," she said, though that was a total guess, "she'll cause no harm."

Luckily, the guard who'd taken her from the shore was still in earshot and called from the doorway, "She's an O'Roarke, William."

"Very well," said the man, still looking skeptically at the fur ball, but when he next caught Brianna's eye, she saw that his expression had softened.

Once again, the O'Roarke name had proved to mean something, and Brianna let out the breath she'd been holding, grateful her ancestors made such a favorable impression.

As the man—William—gave a final nod to the guard, he signaled to a young girl who Brianna hadn't noticed, standing by the stairway. She quickly came forward and William, addressing her as Lilly, instructed her to take, "Miss O'Roarke to the north guest chamber."

Relieved to have been accepted, Brianna followed the girl up the stairs, her hand skimming the stone wall as she admired the excellent masonry. Led to the very same guest room she'd slept in last night, Brianna stood just inside the doorway, taking it all in. While it was devoid of modern luxuries, the room was still somehow oozing warmth and charm, and, she noted, appointed with a few pieces that seemed to be ahead of their time.

Sage green and ivory linens adorned a large four-poster bed with ribbons of matching fabric curling about the posts. A vanity and two wardrobes flanked a large, framed mirror, resting upon the floor. Deep sills ran along the north wall, which faced the sea, each housing clear leaded glass windows, a luxury Brianna knew was usually saved for royalty or the church. She caught her breath as Lilly released a series of metal hooks, pulling the window open and securing it thusly to the wall. The fresh air smelled wonderful but quickly chilled her, and Brianna shivered, cuddling Kitty.

Lilly noticed as soon as she turned around, looking horrified to have distressed her. "Just the one," she said by way of apology, explaining that although the guestchamber had been fully prepared, they weren't expecting it to be occupied when the Montgomerys arrived. "A wee bit of airing and I'll close it up tight," she said, making her way to the fireplace and lighting the kindling, already piled high.

While Brianna warmed herself by the fire, a large wooden tub was moved from behind two privacy screens and placed in front of the hearth, followed by a steady stream of household staff, all carrying buckets of steaming water. Brianna surmised the buckets must be kept ready and lying in wait somewhere, a detail she couldn't remember ever reading about but was grateful to discover, even if it was only in practice here. Once the tub was full, a long, polished board was affixed to the rim, and promptly filled with toiletries. While Brianna looked around the room for a suitable and safe place for Kitty, she noticed yet another quaint sitting area boasting a simple table and beautiful chairs. As Lilly busied herself lighting the candles set in lanterns throughout the room, she saw Brianna's gaze fall on a door in the corner and explained that it was a private latrine.

"Do you need help with your bath?" Lilly asked, and as she started to unpack Brianna's satchel, her eyes wide as she pulled out the Venetian gown, darted to Brianna and back to the fabric.

While Brianna let the girl reconcile her disheveled appearance with the luxurious garments, she suddenly realized whether appropriate or not, Lilly's staying meant that she would see the decidedly modern clothing under her dress. Thinking best how to avoid this, Brianna watched the poor girl become increasingly alarmed as each and every garment she removed from the satchel and gently shook out was, at best, damp.

"It's okay, Lilly, we can lay them on the hearth, I'm sure they'll be dry in no time."

By the look on her face, Lilly did *not* agree and instead gently gathered all of Brianna's belongings in one fell swoop before hurrying out the door. While happy for the privacy, and more than ready to give the wooden tub a try, Brianna wondered if there was a way to lock or bar her door. All too soon, Lilly flew back in, Brianna's clothing nowhere to be seen and carrying what looked like a robe of some sort.

"Did you need me?" she asked. "For your bath?"

Brianna smiled. "Nay, I'll be fine."

Lilly left, though not before laying some linens over the rim of the tub. Brianna barred the door behind her, then placed Kitty in a basket she'd spotted across the room and undressed, hiding her modern clothing and the medallion in the back of one of the wardrobes. While she soaked in a large wooden tub, the fireplace crackling and heating the room, Brianna learned she wasn't a bath snob after all—hot water, a splash of heather-scented oil, and a pretty bar of floral soap could be appreciated, even centuries in the past.

After donning the robe that had been left for her, Brianna unbarred the door and sat on the hearth to dry her hair in front of the fire. She had just started brushing the strands between her fingers when Lilly came back, carrying a tray filled with ribbons and a pretty comb for her hair, as well as a basket of fresh straw for Kitty. It went beyond good training, this quiet, young girl, considered everything!

Lilly made three more trips that night: first, a tray for dinner which thoughtfully included something for Kitty too. At the sight of food, Brianna suddenly realized that it had been hours since she'd last eaten, and wondered what she might be in for. Luckily, the cook was set on perfecting a few recipes ahead of the Montgomerys' arrival, and it smelled divine. She had to admit she was a bit obsessed with the pretty dish it was served in, too. When Brianna lifted the lid, she grinned at the unexpectedly familiar sight of pot roast and quickly dug in, enjoying tender pieces of meat and root vegetables roasted to perfection.

It was sometime later, as Brianna stared at the fire petting Kitty that Lilly brought in a chemise for her to sleep in. As Brianna slipped it over her head, the material fell about her body perfectly, and she marveled again at how lovely everything was. This castle clearly employed a deft-handed seamstress and had no shortage of luxurious fabrics. After Lilly turned down the bed and extinguished the lanterns around the room, she quietly let herself out. Exhausted, Brianna sunk into the mattress, surprised it was so soft, and promptly fell asleep.

BRIANNA SPENT the next three days under the watchful eyes of the congenial, but *very* tight-lipped household staff. Teetering somewhere between sheer panic and utter bewilderment that she'd well and truly *time-traveled* hundreds of years into the past, it took nearly all that time to trust she wasn't going to be thrown in a dungeon (not that she'd seen one), or hear cries of 'off with her head' (which, if memory served, was still some years before this era), or watch as a woodpile or gallows went up on the grounds somewhere. Once she realized she truly wasn't in danger, of any sort, Brianna felt her walls slowly come down, letting in the pure exhilaration of actually *living in history.* It had her in a constant state of sensory overload.

Still, she kept much to herself, well aware that her unexpected appearance had not only caused a stir but added to the staff's responsibilities. Brianna had gathered—through Lilly—that they were readying the castle in preparation of receiving Gavin Montgomery, his wife Isabelle, and their four children. Their excitement was evident, and after a few days, Brianna decided she was excited to meet them, too. These were people the MacTavishes had spoken of so fondly, their closest friends in the fifteenth century— the *ascendants* of the very famous twenty-first century Montgomerys, Alexander and Amanda. Brianna wasn't ashamed to admit, she felt a little starstruck at the prospect.

Based on her recent experience with the MacTavishes, it was clear that the Montgomerys were of similar ilk. It showed in the feelings amongst the staff and even the castle's guard. The pervading joy was at first surprising, in a redundant *everything* was surprising sort of way.

She'd learned that Duncan, the man who'd found her by the tide pools, had been until recently, second in command to Greylen MacGreggor, and now oversaw the castle's security, a position he took with the utmost seriousness. Duncan checked on her daily and continued to assure her that once his commander arrived, they would safely see her home, to Dunhill Proper. Since Brianna had never said *where* home was, not once, and neither had she been specifically asked, she just nodded and demurred. Once the Montgomerys arrived, she'd decide what, if anything, she should tell them. Hopefully with their help, she would figure out the mystery of Pembrooke, the medallion, the Celtic knot, *and* how they were all connected. Despite all of this, she'd almost broached the subject with Duncan several times, especially once she realized he was familiar with the people she'd heard the MacTavishes talk about, but stopped herself each time. Initially, she'd attributed Duncan's honorable behavior, and that of the men under his authority, to her clothing, which she knew suggested noble or highborn status. As the days progressed, however, Brianna learned firsthand that the men who were installed to guard the Montgomery stronghold were in a word, chivalrous.

The interior personnel, who frankly *all* appeared to be of the same family (at least three generations of them), were managed by William. From chambermaids to laundresses, and even the well-appointed kitchen staff, their dimples and good nature were obviously hereditary, and their competence, too. Watching their daily routine was fascinating, exciting even. Brianna was witnessing what she'd learned in history books and scholarly texts displayed in real time, right before her eyes.

With very little to do throughout the following days except wait for Mr. Montgomery, who would assign someone to escort her, God willing, to Dunhill, she walked throughout the castle and explored the grounds. From what she could gather so far, the castle was complete, at least for the time being. Not a bad starting point, if she said so herself. Brianna had of course examined structures like this before, but seeing it newly built instead of in varying degrees of restoration after hundreds of years, she could appreciate its beauty, both aesthetically and structurally. It thrilled her to know some of the men who'd had a hand in its construction—Dar and Lachlan would no doubt be proud of what their original vision had amounted to.

From her conversations with the staff, which usually turned into her peppering them with questions, eager as she was to learn if what she'd read in books was truly accurate, Brianna discovered that the Montgomerys planned to settle into their household, first, and see to any modifications the following spring. She couldn't imagine what, if anything, would need to change. Dar and Lachlan had done a remarkable job—not to mention their friend, Mr. Sinclair, if she remembered correctly, who not only began the project with them but took over when they'd left. In less than three years a sound and fortified structure stood complete with a trustworthy staff, and formidable men installed to guard the Montgomery stronghold. Brianna supposed their mass fortification had to do with safeguarding the portal as well.

On her fourth morning at Abersoch, Brianna awoke from an incredibly sound sleep. She stretched contentedly before pushing the bed linens aside, smiling as her fingers brushed against the material. Everything was so much more sumptuous than she'd expected, despite all her reading and historical knowledge. Not only were the bedclothes surprisingly soft, but the mattress and the pillows were, too. She'd expected coarse or even crude appointments, honestly in just about everything, but it was far from the case, or at least in the case of the Montgomerys and their station.

Using the cushioned footstool beside her bed, a

lovely fifteenth-century original, replete with an embroidered cover, Brianna stepped down before reaching for Kitty who had taken to sleeping at her feet. Just as she started straightening her bed, a knock sounded on her door.

"Come in," Brianna called, as she continued her one-handed chore, knowing it was Lilly, who'd become a welcome sight over the last several days.

"Ah, good morn Miss O'Roarke," Lilly said brightly, setting down the tray and basket before rushing to the other side of the bed to help her. "I brought fresh food for your companion," she said of Kitty, taking the time to, as she always did, fluff the mattress from beneath before smoothing every wrinkle from the bed cover once they finished.

While Lilly saw to cleaning and straightening her room, not that it needed it, Brianna grabbed Kitty's bowl of food from her breakfast tray and set her down to enjoy her morning feast. Thank goodness they knew how to feed a house cat—Brianna balked at the idea of setting her out to forage for her meals. The kitchen staff also surprised her with a handful of treats that were surely before their time. Like the ginger-mint tea, she was sipping on now. She wasn't complaining, but at the same time, she wondered how a fifteenth-century estate in Wales stocked a perfectly crunchy granola or was partial to serving fresh fruit instead of the preserved fruit that Brianna knew was the favored option of the time. Either it had some-thing to do with the fact that some other modern women were living amongst these families as Dar and

Celeste had said there were, or her history books had gotten it wrong. Maybe both. She'd made a few casual comments in passing, but they'd gone unnoticed, so rather than risk raising suspicion, she let it go.

Brianna chose clean undergarments and a shift, then grabbed Kitty, who was tangling between her feet. As she made way for the latrine, another surprise, and a very welcome one, Lilly reached for the kitten. They'd fallen into a routine these last few mornings, and Brianna honestly couldn't say that she minded it very much. It seemed that Lilly was happy, too, especially to have an indoor pet. Brianna's first suspicions—that the entire household staff was all part of a family—had proved true, and it was lovely to see, charming even, especially at mealtime. Not that she was allowed to eat with them (as that would be "below her station," per Lilly), but she also refused to let them serve only her at that large table in the great hall—they had enough responsibilities without having to accommodate an unexpected 'noble' guest. She did break protocol on occasion, if one considered an occasion at least twice a day, when she returned her tray to the kitchen, raving about another successful meal, and then lingered to take a cup of tea and chat.

"What dress shall I wear today, Lilly?" Brianna asked, as she skimmed over her growing collection of gowns, which now included the three from Esmeralda and two others that had been added to her wardrobe since her arrival. Lena, Lilly's aunt, and an accomplished seamstress had insisted on fashioning the extras. At first, Brianna had sharply objected, already feeling like she'd been given so much, but when Lena explained it was more time-effective in the long run, Brianna had relented. Besides, the additions were beautiful, and considering that Brianna didn't know how long she would be here, well, a few more outfits would help. She found herself falling into a comfortable pattern and was surprised that she liked having people about. Holding up the dark blue gown with flared sleeves, Lilly nodded, helping her into it.

Brianna had just finished putting her hair up when she heard happy shouts from the grounds below. Curious and cradling Kitty against her chest, Brianna raced across the room to the stone sill, gasping at the sight of a magnificent ship in the distance, watching as it changed course and veered into the bay.

As the ship slowed and drew nearer, she could make out a man standing on the deck, large in stature, his face hidden beneath a hooded cloak. Two other men stood sentinel behind him, a clear show of might, and one Brianna noticed echoed upon the bluff, which was lined with soldiers. She heard some indiscernible shouts called from the deck and watched as the crew scrambled to heed orders, furling the remaining sails and dropping their first anchor and then another to moor the ship. A longboat was lowered into the water, and netting secured to the hull—and throughout it all, not once had the cloaked man nor his guards moved. It wasn't until the women and children were safely aboard the longboat that they broke form. Brianna had to admit it was a formidable display, worthy of the castle's proprietor.

When they reached the dock, Brianna leaned out as far as she could without falling, fascinated as she watched. The cloaked man—Mr. Montgomery, Brianna surmised—stood, his polished boots hitting the dock one at a time. Then, as he surveyed the coast, the rock wall, and the castle itself, he removed his hood, and Brianna gasped, stepping back. She was surprised both by how *handsome* he was and her reaction to the reveal. Brown sun-kissed hair, broad shoulders, and sinewy arms, visible even from here. Shaking off whatever it was that struck her, Brianna reminded herself that he was married and was, in fact, now helping his beautiful wife and their gaggle of children onto the dock.

Brianna continued to watch as a parade of people disembarked the ship, followed by trunks and wrapped packages, until the Montgomerys disappeared from sight, to ascend the steep path. It was some time before they reached the top of the bluff. Then, they rode to the courtyard on horseback, he was carrying a baby, a young child, and two other older children were with soldiers. The whole family was met at once by Duncan. Mr. Montgomery slid off his steed, his large hand lingering to give a string of affectionate pats as he listened intently, before transferring the baby into his wife's arms.

Then his gaze shot to the castle, and the very spot where she stood.

CHAPTER 10

It wasn't at all unusual for Aidan to be met by Duncan upon his arrival. What *was* unusual, however, was the news he brought with him: an O'Roarke, here in residence, and awaiting escort to the O'Roarkes at Dunhill Proper. Aidan tried to reconcile the information, so far from anything he expected—although, what he had expected had involved a portal between realms and the warnings of a powerful enchantress, which was rather unusual too. The boys, already eager to see their new home, shrieked excitedly, running ahead to meet their kin (blood relation or not, according to Gwen and Maggie they were all family just the same), Isabelle close behind.

Aidan listened as Duncan updated him on the men who'd been sent to meet Gavin, confirming they'd arrived at the port on schedule, and that their progress toward Abersoch was already well underway. He would still be an hour or so on the ride, mayhap more with their fares, though far less effort than using the steep path.

Standing in the courtyard, surveying the castle's exterior and the final details, finished in his absence, Aidan was struck with an immense feeling of satisfaction. It was done, well and truly. He knew that the interior was likely to be shining too, the staff, though small in number had been hired for their excellence, as well as their discretion. When Gavin arrived with the rest of the family's belongings, their mission at Abersoch would be complete, and his time here done.

Aidan clapped Duncan on the back, feeling a bit victorious, as they walked through the courtyard and up the steps. He heard gleeful chatter as he opened the doors and stepped inside, smiling as he took in the scene. The three boys gathered excitedly around who Aidan assumed must be their would-be cousin—the mysterious O'Roarke guest. The first thing he noticed was how pretty she was, with a lovely smile, warm eyes, and long, straight hair.

"An O'Roarke, you're sure?" Aidan asked Duncan. All the O'Roarkes he knew—save a small few by marriage, had thick, unruly hair.

The woman in question turned to Isabelle and curtsied then as if she were queen. At this, Aidan suppressed a smile. Aye, an O'Roarke indeed, and no doubt close in relation to Margret.

Duncan chuckled. "What do you think?"

When Isabelle noticed Aidan's presence, she took the woman's hand and brought her forward, clearly having already made her acquaintance. "Come, let me introduce you," she said excitedly.

The O'Roarke woman met his gaze squarely, her head tilting back as she neared, her startling blue eyes framed with thick lashes. Aidan had to admit they were O'Roarke eyes—almost exactly the same as Callum's, save the sharpness of his gaze. Her hair was wrong, but her eyes…her eyes fit.

"I'm pleased to meet you, Mr. Montgomery," she said.

"Oh, oh no, no, no," Isabelle laughed softly, "This isn't my husband, Brianna. This is Mr. Aidan Sinclair."

The woman looked confused at first, but he would swear recognition flashed in her eyes at the mention of his name. While Isabelle explained Gavin's temporary absence, Aidan wracked his memory, trying to recall mention of a Brianna O'Roarke, but came up with naught. Aidan decided he'd have to ask Callum from which part of the family she hailed.

"Forgive me, Mr. Sinclair," the woman—*Brianna*, demurred.

"What brings you to Castle Abersoch?" Aidan asked, wishing to hear her speak again as another thought crossed his mind. And frankly, if not for Duncan informing him that she was an O'Roarke from the onset, it would have been his first, especially on the heels of Esmerelda's warning.

She stared at him for a long moment, which meant that she was either reticent about her answer, or was choosing *what* to answer, either of which might confirm she was exactly what Aidan suspected. Unless he were being foolish, and it was nothing of the sort. Regardless, after so many days in residence, one would expect a ready answer to such a simple question. Finally, she said, "Family."

Puzzled by her hesitation and the possible motivation behind it, Aidan pressed. "Family? Is that so? I know of no O'Roarkes in this vicinity. In fact, you're a long way from Ireland, lass."

Her eyes widened momentarily, perhaps surprised by his scrutiny before she quickly demurred. "Indeed, sir. But my family settled in Northern Scotland some years ago."

Isabelle elbowed his side, pasting a rather mad smile on her face, clearly urging him to change his tone. Right, a guest. Supposed family. Blood kin, no less. Until he could speak with Gavin, and question Duncan, and perhaps the staff, he let it go.

As the children continued to run in circles, the staff gathered what belongings they could, and Aidan and the men (Duncan, Henry, and Richard) took the rest and made their way upstairs. The boys, still taken with their guest, followed, chatting incessantly all the way to their new chambers, where they quickly lost interest in her as children are wont to do. Leaving Isabelle and the boys to settle, Aidan continued down the corridor, walking behind Miss O'Roarke. She turned after a few steps.

"Are you following me?"

He was, but to her, he said only, "My chamber lies beyond yours."

She nodded and remained silent down the hallway

until she reached her door, then turned. "Mr. Sinclair, I only wish for safe passage to Dunhill," she said. He noted a slight desperation in her tone, which once again stirred his suspicions. "When Mr. Montgomery arrives, I'll inquire about a suitable escort."

"Indeed, Miss O'Roarke," he said, inclining his head, leaving off that suitable or not, *he* was her escort.

Aidan did not see her again until dinner. Yet from the time they'd parted until the moment he laid eyes on her again, he thought of little else. Something about Miss Brianna O'Roarke continued to gnaw at him—something not quite right, though he had yet to determine what. He'd questioned Duncan about her arrival and was told that a small vessel had been spotted close to shore the same day she'd arrived but wasn't certain whether Miss O'Roarke had been aboard. She'd seemed skittish, Duncan said, and had given no indication of having arrived by boat—or by any means at all, for that matter. This raised more questions than it answered for Aidan. For one: why would someone want to pose as an O'Roarke? Other than the use of the tide pools, which he was nearly certain no one else beyond the Brotherhood knew about, what reason was there for anyone to infiltrate Abersoch? He thought momentarily of the Fitzgerald brothers, but dismissed the notion just as quickly— they were far from clever enough to contrive anything of the sort. And, while Miss O'Roarke's reticence rightly made him suspicious, it was her odd and perfectly timed arrival that truly set him off.

He considered, too, whether she might be from the twenty-first century, like Maggie and Gwen. She was found upon the shore after all, with no evident means of transportation. But, again, he dismissed the idea— not only had he heard from the staff that she spoke Scots Gaelic flawlessly, but the cadence of her words and her accent placed her *here*, in both time and place, as did her personal belongings, taken (without objection, he'd been told) and laundered upon her arrival. The refined quality of the fabric and the impeccable stitching of the garments, even the delicate lettering of her name, discreetly embroidered on each piece, had been appreciatively noted. He was surprised by his disappointment at the realization that she couldn't be from the future. Suspicions aside, she was beautiful, and clearly had her wits about her. In truth, were Miss O'Roarke—if she was who she said she was—to be his match, it would be no hardship. She seemed immediately more plausible than Judith Fitzgerald, who he hadn't given one moment's thought to in days.

Aidan recalled Esmeralda's warnings again and wondered if perhaps Miss O'Roarke was merely another obstacle to be dealt with, a necessary distraction from the tide pools and the possibility of the woman he was supposed to fall in love with. Some roadblock fate tossed in his way. Or, he considered again—*was* her reason for being here something more perilous? It seemed more and more unlikely that she had arrived under truly nefarious auspices, though still, something tugged at him.

When Aidan entered the great room that evening,

he saw Miss O'Roarke seated by the fireplace with
Gavin and Isabelle, speaking cheerfully. None of them
had noticed him yet, so he took the opportunity to
pause for a moment in the doorway to observe her.
She was lovely, with hair the color of honey, and a fair
complexion, near perfect, save an appealing sprinkle
of freckles across the bridge of her nose. She laughed
softly then, a pleasing sound and for the moment, he
laid aside his doubts.

"Ah, there he is," Gavin said, spotting Aidan and
waving him in, "Come, a well-deserved toast."

As Aidan stepped forward, his smile came easily;
Isabelle looked so happy. Gavin, too. When they all
stood, he couldn't help but notice Miss O'Roarke's
gown, a stunning piece that indeed spoke wealth. She
wore it well, regally even. Surely that counted for
something.

He accepted the drink Gavin offered, and the
heartfelt praise that accompanied it. "'Twas an honor,
my friend. Nothing less," he said, humbled.

Miss O'Roarke had been looking around the room
with a keen eye, then turned to him. "What you've
accomplished in such a short period, Mr. Sinclair is
truly remarkable," she said. Her praise seemed
genuine, her smile, too. "I consider it a privilege to
have explored it first-hand, the attention to detail and
quality of work—it's all well above the standard."

"Are you familiar with architecture, Miss
O'Roarke?" he asked. An odd look, perhaps surprise,
flickered across her face, though why she would be

suddenly surprised by a topic she'd begun herself made no sense. Unless, of course, she was hiding something—again, he wondered if her appearance was as innocent as she claimed.

"Ah, well, yes, I..." She trailed off, her eyes growing wide for a moment before she collected herself. "It's just that growing up with such a grand example of what's possible, perhaps, has given me a bit of an appreciation."

Unconvinced, Aidan raised an eyebrow. He'd known many who had grown up in grand estates who still knew nothing of the craft.

Miss O'Roarke must have noted his skepticism, because she spoke again, this time more quickly.

"Well, Fergus, my great-uncle, did build Dunhill Proper, a castle for his queen, after all. And I must confess, Mr. Sinclair, when I saw Abersoch for the first time, it reminded me of another castle, one that captivated me from the first, in fact, the words 'shining beacon' flashed through my mind at the very sight of it," she said charmingly, her slender fingers dancing through the air.

"Oh, my," Isabelle remarked. "High praise indeed."

"As intended, truly," Miss O'Roarke said, raising her drink.

Aidan joined in with the others in salute, but still, something nettled at him. "You never said, but how did you come to be here, Miss O'Roarke?" he asked.

He watched her closely, how she swirled her brandy for several long seconds before looking up.

"Ah, well, I…I was ferried here," she said, with a decisive nod.

While that confirmed what he'd been told by Duncan, Aidan wondered at her hesitation, as well as the odd manner in which she described her journey. As a guarded look crossed between them, a trill of laughter from Isabelle drew his attention.

"'Tis the funniest story, Aidan." Isabelle laughed and reached for Miss O'Roarke's hand. "When Brianna told the children she was ferried here, they thought she'd said *faerie'd*, as in a fairy magically brought her to us." Isabelle laughed again. "You should have seen the way she indulged them, pulling faces, and telling them a tale about being on a quest for a lost family treasure, then pleading with them to keep her secret. Oh, they *loved* it!"

As Aidan turned back to Miss O'Roarke, the oddest feeling came over him. "A quest for treasure? Faerie'd, Miss O'Roarke?" he said, resisting the urge to alight his digits as she had done.

Her distinctive deep blue eyes held his, and she shrugged, then waved her fingers again, as a smile and blush spread across her face. Plausible indeed.

"'Twas kind of you to play along, Brianna," Gavin said, the slow cadence of realization in his delivery, barely detectable. "You know how silly children can be."

Aidan glanced his way, and when he met his friend's eyes, he noted that Gavin had a curious look about him, too. Looking back to Isabelle, he saw the realization cross her face as well, and it was then that all eyes shot to their guest. The very plausible Miss O'Roarke, quite possibly *faerie'd* here from the future.

Miss O'Roarke shifted in her seat under the weight of their stares.

"Do you believe that's possible, Miss O'Roarke?" Aidan asked, his tone light, yet he was oh so curious at her answer. "Faeries, I mean?"

"I've come to believe that anything is possible, Mr. Sinclair. Even magic. I was recently reminded, and rightly so, that we O'Roarkes must believe, if only a wee bit," she demurred. A vague and clever answer, timely too as dinner was served. "Oh, it smells divine," she said, changing the subject. "If I'm not mistaken, it's the same meal I had my first night here."

"A favorite of mine," Aidan said, which was true. What he was curious about was whether she knew the twenty-first-century approach that Gwen had introduced them all to. "Are you familiar with the dish?"

She narrowed her eyes for a moment, so quickly he might have missed it, then looked at him curiously. "Meat and vegetables? I am, I'm quite partial to both."

"*Pot roast*," Aidan said, watching her closely.

She held his gaze a moment, then looked down at her plate. "What an interesting choice. Clever, too." She smiled, clearly amused, but then quickly turned her attention to Isabelle like the subject had little meaning to her.

Stymied, Aidan continued to observe her throughout dinner. She was a mystery, intriguing and fascinating with a quick wit, and though he was still harboring suspicions, he also found her rather exceptional. She was impeccably well-mannered, and more knowledgeable of both artifacts and commonplace items than anyone he'd ever come across in his life. She marveled over a covered dish as if it rivaled the discovery of fire, then cooed about a silver platter and even served praise to a linen square, that frankly he was never sure served a purpose to begin with. She did this with almost everything at her fingertips and within sight. She grew more and more animated with each detail she pointed out, admired, and described. She even spotted a collection of wooden chests, clear across the room, declaring them *O'Roarkes*, and excitedly telling them all where one would look to find the unique insignia. She was correct, of course—Callum had made those chests for Gavin and Isabelle in celebration of their new home. So, there was something off about her, that was to be sure, but she also seemed so entirely delighted by her surroundings, that Aidan could no longer conclude that she posed a threat or had ill intent of any kind.

As the table was cleared, they decided it was best to retire. After such a long day, not to mention the journey itself, Isabelle was nearly asleep at the table. "Come, Bella. Time for bed, love." Gavin said softly, gently rousing his wife before helping her up.

Aidan turned his attention to Miss O'Roarke, who was watching Gavin and Isabelle with a somewhat wistful expression. Unthinkingly, he shared a candid smile with her, which she returned. He still wasn't altogether sure what to make of their guest, and as the group made its way upstairs in a quiet procession, he began to sort it through. He was acutely aware of her walking beside him, but so deep in thought he hadn't realized they'd arrived at her door until she stopped.

"Good night, Mr. Sinclair," she said.

"Good night, Miss O'Roarke."

CHAPTER 11

Brianna was up and out of bed earlier than usual, excited to embrace the day and looking forward to spending more time with the Montgomerys and Mr. Sinclair. With Kitty still sound asleep, she threw on her robe and washed up. Then she sat at her vanity, twisting her hair, and knotting it on top of her head with a silk ribbon. As she stared at her reflection in the mirror, she imagined her hair in its natural state, unruly at best, which she'd always been told was a dominant O'Roarke trait. She'd been straightening it for so long, that she almost forgot how to manage it with curls, but her latest Keratin treatment would only last a few more weeks, a month at most.

Deciding she would cross that bridge when she came to it, Brianna carried on with her morning routine. She'd just taken off her robe and was about to get dressed when she heard a knock on her door. Figuring it was Lilly, here to help her get ready, Brianna waited for her to enter as she had every other morning. When she didn't, Brianna assumed her hands were full, and hurried to help. She opened the door, only to see Mr. Sinclair in all his stalwart glory taking up the entire space. His eyes, a stormy shade of green this morning, enhanced by the tawny color of his hooded cloak, sent a shiver down her spine that surprised her. One he had to have noticed once he shifted his gaze to her face from the messy knot on top of her head. Suddenly, Brianna realized she was only wearing her chemise, without even a robe to shield her from his penetrating looks. To his credit, Mr. Sinclair regarded her squarely, his eyes never straying downward.

"Mr. Sinclair," she said, glad that her voice came out steady. "May I help you?"

"You said family brought you here to Abersoch, yet you never explained," he said, searching her face with an imploring look.

He was so candid with his question and seemed so genuinely curious about the answer that Brianna stepped back and waved him inside without thinking. After a brief hesitation, he nodded, and made the *lonnnnng* journey from just beyond her doorway, to just within. His cordial restraint wasn't lost on her. If there was anything she'd learned this past week, it was that these people could be trusted, and that continued to be proven over and over. Even Mr. Sinclair who she'd sensed had been wary of her, at least at the start, was here, speaking to her without artifice, and again she found herself leaning as closely toward the truth as she could without broaching it. "I really did come to retrieve a family heirloom," she said.

He seemed to be considering her words at length. "I see. Did you find it?"

She shook her head. "I did not."

"Would you care for my aide in your quest?'

His words harkened brave knights and fair damsels in her mind and when she smiled, he did too. "I believe that our prized Wolf sword is out of reach now."

She was surprised how easily those words came out, not that it wasn't the truth, she *had* gone to Abersoch to retrieve the sword, and it *was* out of reach, hundreds of years out of reach—it was her delivery that shocked her. She'd never been the best flirt, in fact, awkward would be a more appropriate descriptor, but even to her ears, that had sounded a little flirty. She hadn't even meant to try and wondered what had come over her, but she paused when she saw something shift in his eyes. He was still smiling, yet clearly calculating something, too. "I am sorry for your loss then. 'Tis a prize indeed… with or without the stone."

At this, Brianna faltered. Stone? What stone? When she'd mentioned the sword, she forgot that he would know of it. It took her a second to realize what he meant, and she stepped closer, suddenly desperate to hear more, forgetting herself completely. "Wait. You've seen it? The jewel?" she whispered, holding her breath. She thought she remembered Lachlan or Celeste mentioning something about a jewel, maybe, but they'd said so much, she couldn't recall. But hearing Mr. Sinclair speak of the stone, *the* stone, that went in the hollow beneath the family crest was something she wondered about her entire life.

He nodded. "Aye, a priceless beauty."

"What color is it?" she asked, unable to contain her excitement. "My grandfather said sapphire, but we've never been sure." So engrossed in knowing, she thought nothing of his renewed scrutiny.

"Truth be told, lass, I'd say O'Roarke blue. The very shade of your eyes."

While he was doing nothing more than paying homage to lineage and calling her eyes blue, which they were, the way he said it made Brianna grin like an idiot. But her schoolgirlish reaction was fleeting— as she stared up at him, she began to wonder if...if he knew of Pembrooke. If he knew of the sword, if he was close with Callum—Dar, she remembered, had said they were brethren—he would know the area around Dunhill. "Do you know of Pembrooke, Mr. Sinclair?" she asked.

"I do."

Brianna felt her eyes go wide. As much as she'd wanted to reclaim her family's sword, Pembrooke had eluded her even longer, and to be in the company of someone who knew of it was nothing short of a miracle. She realized quickly that she might have come on a little strong, and at the expression of curious fascination on Mr. Sinclair's face, she tried to calm herself down, all the while her brain was pinging out of control. It must have taken her a full moment to breathe and another to find her voice.

"Do...do you think I," she stammered when she was finally able to speak, shaking out her hands in nervous anticipation, "...do you think that whoever escorts me to Dunhill might take me to see it? Pembrooke, I mean?"

Mr. Sinclair nodded. "Without question."

The rush she felt was euphoric.

"Oh, Mr. Sinclair—*Aidan*!" In her excitement, she shrieked and threw her hands in the air, but thankfully stopped herself before she started drumming them against his chest. Mortified at her near faux pas, Brianna pulled a face, which embarrassed her even more. Fanning her cheeks, she started pacing to gather herself, realizing self-consciously how all of this must look. She couldn't remember the last time she'd been so unguarded in front of another person, let alone a stoic, fifteenth-century Highland Laird. Once she'd calmed herself down, she turned back to him, relieved to see that he didn't appear to be offended. He did have an odd look on his face, though definitely more of a smile than a scowl.

"My apologies, Mr. Sinclair," she said, keeping her voice as calm as she could. "You have no idea what this means to me. Truly, this is one of the most remarkable moments in my life." She laughed at her own words and covered her mouth, returning the warm look he gave her. If he only knew how ridiculous that statement was. Of course, it was remarkable to finally see Pembrooke again, but she'd had a string of extraordinarily remarkable days lately.

In need of an outlet for her delight and thinking it wise *not* to take it out on Mr. Sinclair, Brianna all but floated to her bed, and reached for Kitty, holding her close and then rocking her in a little dance. "We're going to Pembrooke, Kitty," she whispered in the cat's ear, slowly swirling her around, and stopping in her tracks when she realized she was making a spectacle of herself. Again.

Thankfully when she glanced his way, Mr. Sinclair —*Aidan*—just looked amused by it all. "Ill-advised," he cautioned, shaking his head and looking pointedly at Kitty.

Brianna couldn't help but roll her eyes. "She's free of fleas," she said, with much more certainty now than when she'd said the same to William on her first day at Abersoch. "And the staff's already quite fond of her." He didn't seem to be swayed and had another thought. "You're not superstitious, are you?" She'd read conflicting historical accounts on the matter, especially when it came to cats.

"Hardly," he scoffed, though she could tell he wasn't offended. In fact, he seemed rather amused.

Brianna realized then that she liked talking with him. She hadn't had the chance to do so before—not like this, at least, not one on one. Coming off of the wonderful dinner last night, this warm and friendly rapport that seemed to be growing between them, felt natural, effortless even. She was still sharing a playful look with him, with an ease that was already well out of character for her, when a boyish grin broke across his face, and she felt her cheeks warm at the sight of it. Good grief this man was handsome. Being around him sure beat the piles of books and dusty artifacts she normally surrounded herself with, any day—she'd never met anyone else who she would ever have said that about.

"The last time I saw a kitten, I was nearly felled by one, and—" he'd started his reply so playfully, but then Brianna noticed something shift, and Aidan strode forward toward Kitty, brows furrowed.

Brianna instinctively stepped backward and kept going until she hit the wall behind her. She couldn't imagine what had him so intent on reaching the cat, but he was mere feet away now, and she finally put out her hand, flattening it against his chest when he reached her.

"Stop," she cried, suddenly afraid for Kitty. "Don't hurt her, please. Please."

At this, a mixture of confusion, consternation, and frustration crossed Aidan's face before he softened, obviously contrite at having frightened her. He heaved a small sigh, then shook his head.

"I mean her no harm, lass. I swear it on my life. I wish only to see her up close."

She hesitated, still uncertain. What could he need to look at Kitty for?

"I swear to you, Brianna," he said, and something about the pleading way he spoke her name softened something in her. "Please, lass."

She relented and removed the hand that was shielding Kitty. At once, something like recognition flared in his eyes.

"Where did you get this cat?" he asked.

"I found her. By the shore," she whispered, confused and wondering what all of this was about.

He stared at Kitty a moment longer, then looked back at her again, gave a short nod, and abruptly left.

She was still standing there, staring at the door when he strode back half a minute later. No knock, no formality, and in fact, she would swear something about him had changed—he seemed altogether more relaxed, almost casual.

"We leave within the hour, lass," he said, as if the previous two minutes had never happened. "Do you need help packing your things?"

Brianna decided not to mention the thing with Kitty, either. "Within the hour? So soon?" she asked. How sudden. How odd. "Today?"

"Have you reason to stay longer?"

"Well, no, but I…I just didn't realize …" Her words trailed off.

He smiled. "Nor did I."

Brianna ignored the oddness of his answer, still confused at the quick change in plans, not that they'd actually discussed when she'd be leaving. She'd thought to broach the subject with Gavin today, but if she had to leave now, at least it appeared that Aidan was the one who would be escorting her. "Do I need anything in particular for our travels?"

"Anything of importance to you—save the cat."

Then he was gone. Again.

It didn't take her long to pack. She started with her medallion, tucking it into a pocket she'd found, cleverly hidden inside her satchel. She was surprised how quickly the satchel filled up—with her new garments, and some personal items, like the combs and ribbons, and soaps that Isabelle insisted she keep, she now needed another bag to fit it all. Isabelle brought her a lovely leather tote. It was an exquisite piece that she insisted she have despite Brianna's protests.

For the first time, saying goodbye was difficult. She'd only just met the Montgomerys, but felt so comfortable with them and welcomed, that she could have easily stayed longer. She was even going to miss William, who'd warmed considerably since her arrival, and Duncan as well, who wouldn't have a soft spot for the guard who acted more like a guardian than a gatekeeper. But when it came to saying goodbye to Lilly, she was hit with a wave of emotion that she frankly hadn't expected. They hadn't shared any deeply personal secrets or anything, but Lilly was the first person she'd bonded with here, a companion of sorts, and Brianna had become so fond of her.

"You are a gem, Lilly. Sweet, smart, and an asset, to this family, and yours." She tried to keep her voice low but knew the others overheard. While they waited for her to gather herself, she stood in the entrance, wondering if she'd ever see Castle Abersoch again. And if she did, whether it would be in this century or hers.

"Time to go, lass."

Brianna whirled around at the sound of Aidan's voice. He'd been readying everything for the journey, and now it seemed like he wanted to get them on their way. Brianna gave the castle one last sweep with her eyes, trying to commit it all to memory, everything in it, as well as her experience here.

"Ready," she said with a sigh, feeling melancholy, but for once, not bothering to hide it. Brianna 2.0 was a bit messier, it turned out. Aidan gave her a much-appreciated sympathetic look, and even Kitty mewed, stirring against her. His eyes shot to the cat snuggled up against her chest.

"You disobeyed me?"

Steeling herself for a confrontation—since she'd purposely misunderstood him about bringing Kitty along, and he'd clearly noticed—Brianna feigned ignorance with a, "Whatever do you mean? I followed your orders."

He pointed to Kitty, who was safely tucked into the sling-like contraption that Lena had fashioned, sort of like a baby carrier so Kitty would be snug and safe while Brianna had both hands on the reins. "I said, '*Save* the cat,' Brianna."

Tilting her head to the side, she fixed him with a blank stare. "And I have."

He gave an exasperated sigh, and if she were in a better mood, Brianna would have almost found the reaction funny on such an otherwise stoic man. "*Save* the cat, Brianna. I said, *save–save*."

She knew what he meant, obviously, but remained silent. She was not giving up Kitty, ever.

Aidan stared at her for a long moment, and Brianna thought she saw a smile pulling at the corner of his mouth. He just gave her a nod, however, and turned away.

The matter settled, Brianna shifted her thoughts to the journey ahead. As she walked to the stables, she imagined it would be nice to ride and see the land—*rustic* maybe, but still nice. She couldn't imagine how long their whole trip would take, but remembering that it had taken well over ten hours in her car, she knew it would be several days, at least, on horseback. Curious about their route, she asked Aidan which towns they would pass through, remembering how much she'd loved her stop in Carlisle, just a week ago (give or take a few centuries), which was the strangest thing to realize.

"Brianna." He said her name so softly it barely interrupted her thoughts.

When his voice registered, she turned, taking in the sight of him standing in the courtyard, holding the reins of two horses, and realized she liked the way he'd said her name and his casual yet all-business demeanor. She also liked the way he looked in the bright sunlight as he stared back at her, his hair ruffling in the breeze and his linen shirt open at the neck. She liked his well-fitting trousers and polished leather boots, too, and that hooded cloak draped behind his back. She just liked *him*, she guessed, shrugging absentmindedly as she mused. Not that she *liked*-liked him, she'd never *liked*-liked any man enough to go on anything more than a first date, but with Aidan...maybe she did. The thought was startling, along with the realization that he was watching her, too, his head tilted to the side, curiously. She'd forgotten how transparent Brianna 2.0 was and quickly looked away. When her eyes landed on the horses themselves, it dawned on her that there weren't any supplies tacked to the saddles. Confused, she saw Aidan's man, Henry, waiting near the path that led to the shore, and she suddenly felt ill, all traces of her Aidan-induced glow fading in an instant. It hadn't occurred to her that their journey would be by ship. She looked out at the bay, where the ship they'd arrived on was still moored. She was familiar with this kind of ship, having previously seen one reconstructed after its remains had been found off the East Coast. It was one thing to admire a grand mid-fifteenth-century ship on exhibit, quite another to be expected to board one and sail upon it. Images of the Excalibur flashed through her mind, and sounds she'd worked so hard to forget rang in her ears. She couldn't get on that ship. She shook her head, backing up.

"I can't," she said, feeling herself go numb.

"Can't what?"

"Travel by sea. Board that ship."

Aidan looked at her curiously. "I assure you she's sturdy, with a capable crew."

"It doesn't matter how sturdy she is," Brianna said, struggling to keep her voice even, "or how capable the captain and crew are. The sea is unforgiving, Aidan. I lived to tell that story once, and I'm not sure I could give it another turn."

At this, he laid the reins over the horse's mane and walked toward her. When he was merely a pace away, he stopped and stared deeply into her eyes.

"Brianna. Do you mean you were in a boating mishap?"

She wasn't sure he even blinked, so intent was his gaze. Honestly, given all she knew about fifteenth-century customs and culture, she was surprised he was even trying to understand.

"I was. As a child. I haven't been aboard a ship since." She realized this contradicted her story about being "ferried" to Abersoch, but after their earlier conversation, she had a feeling he already knew.

Aidan nodded slowly, then turned away for a moment before he spoke. "To be clear, at least between you and I, you did *not* arrive by *ferry*, then?"

She shook her head. "I did not."

There was that look again, one she was coming to associate with him. Free of artifice, yet shrewdly intu-itive at the same time. And what she was reading there now wasn't so much suspicion, which he'd obvi-ously had before, but more like she was a puzzle he was intent on solving (though, obviously, Brianna was holding some key missing pieces back). When he spoke, he betrayed none of that, however, and his tone was straightforward and even. "We have two choices, Brianna. One, you remain here at Abersoch while I attend to an urgent matter. I'll return for you within a fortnight, mayhap sooner, then take you home by land."

As she did the math in her head, she began to wonder if she'd ever see Dunhill or Pembrooke, or for that matter Aidan again. Who's to say what could happen in the interim? It was true no matter what century.

"And two?" she asked, although she was almost certain she already knew.

"We get on that ship. And you trust that I'll keep you safe."

She looked out at the ship he was asking her to sail upon and honestly wondered if she even could. It might be greater in size than her family's boat, but there were no lifejackets or fire extinguishers, no radio to call for help, and no helicopter to rescue them from God only knew what. Just the open sea, cold and unforgiving. When she looked back up, he was waiting patiently, like he had all the time in the world. He didn't even prompt an answer from her. She was surprised to find that she was actually torn between staying behind and watching him go or facing her fear and boarding a ship for the first time in over twenty years. As she looked between the ship and Aidan, wondering what she should do, he stepped closer and filled the space between them. Then he reached for her hands and looked deeply into her eyes.

"I'll come back for you, Brianna," he said, as if to

save her from the torture of trying to decide. She was touched by his concern, which she was coming to realize was just how he operated—by her observation, he'd been nothing but considerate it seemed, to everyone around him.

He stood there, watching her for a long moment, she could feel his hesitation in leaving her. It struck her, and not for the first time that she and Aidan might actually have a connection. It was a new feeling for her, and one she found she liked. Eventually, she felt him start to pull away, and she grasped his hands.

"I'll come," she said, without thinking. He seemed so surprised (and, frankly, so was she), that she said it again, more firmly this time. "I'll come. I want to go with you."

"I'll protect you with my life, Brianna. I swear it."

Strangely, she found she believed him, this veritable stranger who up until a few moments ago, she'd merely considered an honorable man kindly seeing her home. An appreciated gesture, but nothing more than that. But now she wondered. What was it Lachlan had said? *Fate will take you where you're meant to go.* She'd been so skeptical of it all, typical Brianna 1.0, looking at it from a purely intellectual standpoint. But now she had no other recourse but to give over to it, whatever *it* was. Maybe the magic wasn't about time travel or even experiencing history firsthand, maybe it was about something more, something she was just beginning to discover. She'd been so lost in thought as Aidan helped her on the horse, she didn't notice he'd turned the other away until he came up behind her. She closed her eyes as he took the reins and his strong arms surrounded her, finding comfort, too, in the soft sound he made to nudge the horse forward. She couldn't be sure, but she thought she heard him whisper something that sounded like, "From this day forward, Brianna."

CHAPTER 12

The wind had picked up significantly by the time Aidan had situated Brianna on the longboat. They were sitting across from one another and quarters were tight, so her legs were perched between his. Her tension at being aboard a boat was clear—she was all but clutching Kitty as she looked out to sea. She shivered, and without thinking, he removed his cloak and then wrapped it around her. When he lifted the hood, he was grateful to see a spark of appreciation in her eyes—the first hint of life since they left the bluff. Whereas before, she'd been so unguarded and carefree—so full of pure delight at everything around her —since they'd left the courtyard, she'd been mute and expressionless. It was a sorrowful change, and he was surprised at how deeply it affected him. He couldn't imagine what she was feeling, but as he held her gaze, he hoped that one day he would earn the honor of her confidence.

It was true, he'd been wary of Brianna at the start,

but that had quickly shifted. With each ensuing inter-action, the riddle of her untangled just a little bit more, and though he had yet to receive a blunt confession from her about where she was from, *truly* from, Aidan was utterly convinced Brianna O'Roarke was his intended match. While the list of her attrib-utes was fast growing as he learned about her, there was something *more* and beyond the obvious of her physical appeal, and even that of her wit. He could not pinpoint exactly *what* it was, truly, it was immaterial and a sensation wholly new to him, but in Brianna's presence, he felt...rightness. Yesterday he'd consid-ered her merely more plausible than Judith—today, plausible did not come close to the degree of his conviction, and God help anyone who dared say differently.

Now, as he held her gaze, that little bit of appreci-ation she'd graced him with faded and her bearing grew so serious, her eyes big and haunting as she stared up at him, that he began to question his ratio-nale in taking her. He was on the cusp of signaling the crewmen to turn back and return to the dock when Brianna reached for his arm. She shook her head, and he knew somehow, she had guessed his intention, surprising him yet again. Some strands of her hair had loosened from the neat pile on top of her head, and he reached out to tuck them back inside. Just as he did so, she whispered something that he couldn't hear over the wind. When he pulled back and asked her to repeat herself, she said, "Do you believe in magic?" He couldn't be sure if she was picking up their conversation from the night before, or if her question was singular in nature.

To grant himself more time to formulate a reply, he tucked one last strand behind her ear, then draped the hood of the cloak back over her head, just so, to frame her face. When he met her stare, he found so much earnestness there, he answered in kind.

"I believe there are things I do not understand and cannot fully fathom or explain. But I have seen first-hand, situations that are seemingly impossible, yet they are very real and exist."

She did not blink as he spoke, but searched his eyes, clinging to each and every word. Considering the gravity of the matter—a bridge she'd crossed between centuries—he understood her reticence, well aware she was testing his measure and worthiness. Her decision to trust him, needed to be hers and hers alone, and while he was certain he had it—her trust—at least in part (ergo their tight proximity on a boat in the water), he remained captive under her penetrating gaze, unwilling to move or even blink, lest he lose it. He was relieved to see life spark in her eyes again but pitied anyone subjected to such scrutiny.

When she finally leaned closer, he did so too, and she said, "Do you believe in destiny?"

"More than most," he said without hesitation.

It seemed he'd passed whatever test she'd set out for him because Aidan could swear he felt her relief as her shoulders dropped. When she laid a hand on his leg and inched even closer, so close he could see the varying flecks of blue in her eyes, he nearly forgot to breathe.

"If I told you something... something that seems impossible but—" Brianna's eyes widened as the boat rocked, and Aidan braced her as she lurched forward, carefully tucking her head beneath his chin. He, too, was stunned to realize they'd reached the ship. He couldn't recall ever being so immersed that he'd forgotten his surroundings. Ever. As he stood, he lifted her with him, her pet happily purring between them. In that moment, he was glad for the small boat's unsteadiness. He helped her find her balance, then gently released her. It was not acknowledged, but in those brief moments that he'd held her, Brianna had wrapped her arms around his waist and held him just as firmly.

After Henry gathered Brianna's things (everything else had already been taken on the ship) and made his way aboard, Aidan helped Brianna from the longboat. There was no evidence of everything that had just transpired between them, and though she had yet to look at him since pulling from their embrace, he could clearly see how focused she was on the task before her, and how the reality of the upcoming journey was sinking in.

When she reached for the ladder, he covered her hands as they gripped the rungs. "Like this," he said, repositioning them for the best stability. She nodded and then looked up to where Henry now awaited her. "You'll be there in no time. I'll be right behind you," he said.

She looked at him then, again so seriously, his
heart clenched, and he wondered if this was what his
brethren felt each and every day—if so, he wasn't sure
how long he might survive.

"Brianna?"

"What if fate is bringing me full circle?"

Aidan shook his head. "If I thought for one second,
that boarding this ship would cause you harm, I
would not let you do so."

Brianna gave a small nod, then focused on the
rungs again. As she began climbing, she whispered
something to herself, and though he couldn't be sure
he'd heard her correctly, Aidan would have sworn
she'd said, "Fate will take you where you're meant to
go." He watched her go up, rung by rung, unable to
believe it possible that Brianna had steeled herself for
the climb by whispering the very words Lachlan oft
said to Dar, especially in the days leading up to their
departure. By the time he'd shaken off his stupor,
convinced he must have misheard, he had to scramble
up the ladder to meet Brianna, where she was waiting
on the deck beside Henry. Aidan gave her a close look
as she adjusted the carrier Kitty was in, and smoothed
the material of her dress, but her face betrayed
nothing of the words she'd just whispered, and so he
decided he'd move on from it too, at least for now.

After giving her a few moments to gather herself,
Aidan showed her about the ship. Much like their
walk from dinner last eve, he was again acutely aware
of her beside him, and again favorably so. He waited
patiently each time she stopped to examine some

aspect of the ship or another, paying particular attention to each of the masts, mechanisms and all. The crew, all familiar to him, save one, nodded politely and busily went about their duties.

"Ah, I see we have another sailor aboard," said the captain, chuckling as he approached, no doubt having noticed Brianna's keen attention to the ship. "Sailor-*ess*, that is."

Though Brianna smiled at Captain John, who Aidan had always considered friendly if a little forward, she nervously laughed off his words. "Oh, no, sir, just interested in the ship. Do not rely on me to sail!"

As Aidan made formal introductions, he explained to Brianna that Captain John had been instrumental in teaching them all to sail when they were young, lasses included.

This brought a true smile to her face, and she said, "My father taught me as well. I was told it was an O'Roarke tradition started by Fergus himself."

Captain John was looking at Brianna curiously and scratching his chin. "An O'Roarke, you say?" he asked, shaking his head. "I've yet to meet one who doesn't have a wild mane of hair.

"Unless it's from your mother's side, I suppose, but even then, every O'Roarke bairn I've ever met has inherited the hair." The man, more familiar with the family and its branches than Aidan was, continued to look at Brianna, who had visibly reddened and was absentmindedly running her fingers through her hair.

Right. "Always a first, Captain," he snapped, bristling at the Captain's impudence.

Aidan grasped Brianna's hand and led her away as Captain John shouted, "Not an insult, just an observation, Sinclair!" to their backs. "Welcome, aboard lassie!"

It did not matter to Aidan that he'd had the very same thought about Brianna's *very* un-O'Roarke locks, what mattered was that he hadn't come out and said it to her, lest it hurt her tender feelings. Grumbling to himself as they crossed the deck, Aidan stopped only when Brianna whacked his arm. Whirling around, wondering what on earth had gotten into her, he saw Henry giving him an odd look as well. He reined in his impatience at the sight of Brianna attempting to catch her breath.

"Sorry," she said, shrugging, a small smile growing across her face. "I did *try* to get your attention. It was hard to keep your pace, you were practically dragging me down the deck."

Right. So much for being level-headed. He grunted something he hoped might pass as an apology and was about to start off again when she placed a hand on his arm.

"What he said was true. It *is* an O'Roarke trait to have wild curls, and I guess sometimes I'm a little sad that my hair isn't the proud marker of our heritage that it could be."

He wasn't sure what to make of that except that she was trying to make him feel better.

"Would you like to see your quarters?" he asked, choosing to change the subject entirely.

"I wouldn't like to do anything aboard this ship, but since we're here, getting settled would be nice."

As he led her below deck to the well-appointed cabin that had been set aside for her, he was careful to point out markers along the way so she could easily find her way in the event neither he nor Henry were with her. Inside the room, fresh linens had been laid on the bed, and Aidan was pleased to see that a bouquet of flowers had been set on a table. The staff at Abersoch had been sure to tell him that they had liked having Brianna as their first official guest, and it showed. As he started to point out the cabin's features, she leveled him with a look. *Right.* He was acting like a dolt.

"Ah well, yes," he said, recovering himself. "My quarters are just beyond this one, should you need me. You remember how we got here?" She nodded as she placed Kitty on the bed, beside her bags, which Henry had brought down. "If I don't see you on deck once we're underway, I'll come check on you. Either Henry or I will always be close at hand."

Once he was sure Brianna would be alright, Aidan headed above board to speak with Captain John again, seeing as their first conversation had ended so abruptly. The man laughed when he saw him, then held up his hand as he finished calling out orders to his crew. Once they'd left the cove, he grinned and said, "She suits, Sinclair."

Obviously. Aidan knew John wasn't expecting a

reply, merely relishing the fact that he'd lost his head. An affliction that was new to him. So, other than fixing him with a glare, Aidan ignored the man's words, and instead asked about provisions. Although Aidan hadn't planned a long stay at Abersoch to begin with, now that they were leaving a day or two ahead of schedule, he wondered what, if anything, might still be unaccounted for.

"All set, aside from a few men, down after drinking some tainted ale," Captain John said, then explained that they'd made a few substitutions, which would account for the unfamiliar face Aidan had seen as they'd boarded. The captain assured him that the sailors were qualified, but as they were true unknowns, they were of course being closely monitored. The other ship, now empty of supplies, would be a day behind, and the current plan was to make port in Ayr again and stay overnight. While not optimal, under the circumstances, it was sound.

Aidan was eager to formally end whatever hopes of an alliance the Fitzgeralds thought they might still have regarding their land, as well as their misguided plan that he would wed Judith. Though he'd been able to put them off somewhat easily up until now, he'd realized that it had been a mistake to entertain their proposal in the first place, and not cut ties at Seagrave when he'd had the chance. Now, Aidan hoped a demonstration of respect (not that they deserved it) in speaking with them directly might well ensure that Judith would not be cast in an unfavorable light— both to future suitors or her brothers.

Aidan had yet to inform Greylen and Callum of his plans to meet with the Fitzgeralds. He'd planned to do so in person, but now with this extra day, there was a very real possibility that word might reach them first. He passed Henry, who was keeping watch on Brianna's door, as he headed to his quarters to pen the missives to his brethren. Though vague in detail, lest the letters fall into the wrong hands, the task still took some time, and when he finished, Aidan was eager to check on Brianna and see how she was faring. He hoped some fresh air and maybe some refreshments would sound appealing.

Leaving his cabin, he was surprised to find the hallway empty. If Henry was gone, that surely meant Brianna had gone above board, but still, he knocked just in case, chuckling as he did. He was feeling a bit lighter now, clearer, and looking forward to speaking with her, and hoping she'd be open to a few, well-posed questions.

As soon as his boots hit the deck, he heard a commotion across the bridge. Before he could make a guess at what could be causing such a stir, one of the crew, a man he knew well from over the years, came running his way. Seeing the urgency in the man's eyes, a sense of foreboding settled upon Aidan. All he could think of was how Brianna had worried she might be fated to go down with the ship, and he went running in the same direction. Aidan pushed his way through the crowd, bracing himself for what he might find, wholly unprepared for what he saw when he broke through. Another of the crew—one of the substitutes by the unfamiliar look of him—had somehow gotten a hold of Kitty and had her by the scruff. It seemed he was threatening to throw her overboard, while the rest of the crew tried to reason with him, warning the sailor that he was making a terrible mistake.

Terrible did not even come close, Aidan was furious.

The horror on Brianna's face, as she watched this man dangle her precious pet over the railing, was painful to take in. Henry was holding her back, most likely from trying to charge the man herself. Had this interloper a shred of common sense, the look on Henry's face alone would have ended the situation. Catching Henry's eye, Aidan signaled he would take the man down—gladly. On Henry's nod, he stepped up behind the sailor and swiftly rendered the man unconscious with a quick and firm application of pressure to his neck. Before the man went down, Henry was there, glowering, as he plucked Kitty from the man's arms, eager to return the cat to Brianna. Aidan watched the tearful reunion with relief, then looked down at the man stirring by his feet.

"Confine him below," he said to the crewmen who had assembled. He thought nothing of his tone until he saw the look on Brianna's face.

If she only knew the true breadth of his anger. He was beginning to calm, but rage at what had been done to her was still simmering when he approached her. When she looked up at him, he did not hide the ire that was still surely evident on his face—her wide-eyed disbelief confirmed it. When he spoke, however, he made an effort to keep his voice even.

"I would ask that you do not let the behavior of one man, unknown to us save for today, jade your opinion of the rest of the men aboard this ship, nor anyone you encounter under my employ," he said. "I cannot speak on the character of those I do not know, but I promise you, Brianna, while I still breathe, I will protect, honor, and serve you at the expense of all else."

He wasn't sure if she understood the implications, nor did it matter. He looked deeply into her eyes, offering a silent prayer that the trials they had endured today might have satisfied Esmeralda's warning.

In his bones, however, he somehow knew they had not.

CHAPTER 13

Brianna stayed in her quarters for the rest of the afternoon, recovering from and processing the incident on deck. Although the encounter itself had been short-lived, and the man who'd endangered Kitty was no longer a threat, Brianna found herself having a hard time getting over the trauma of it. She knew she and Kitty were safe, but as she'd been learning lately, knowing something, and feeling it, were two entirely different concepts.

After Henry had escorted her below deck and made sure that she and Kitty were settled comfortably, he'd pointed to an area just beyond her door where he said she'd be able to find him whenever she needed. He'd been about to leave when Brianna had called out to him to wait, wanting to thank him. When he turned and looked at her, however, a fresh rush of tears prickled at her eyes, and she could only mouth the words as her throat clogged with emotion.

His nod was curt, but his eyes were brimming with warmth and understanding.

It was almost ironic. When she'd asked Henry to escort her above deck earlier, it had been an act of bravery on her part, eager as she'd been to prove to herself that there was nothing to be afraid of on this ship. And, she'd been curious to see what it would feel like, to be sailing as an adult, looking out at the open sea. Brianna remembered how it had inspired awe in her as a child, but honestly, she'd never thought she'd revisit it again. Ever. Nervous, timid even, she'd kept her focus on the ship itself, trying to admire the detailed woodwork while gathering the courage to stand at the railing. Henry was behind her, but clearly not close enough, because as she'd been watching one of the sailors coil a rope, she was caught off balance by a blow to her chest. She'd been so stunned by it, that it took a second to realize that Kitty had been ripped from her carrier. Frantically, Brianna had looked around until she saw Kitty, squirming and writhing in the arms of a man with a crazed look in his eyes—and who was clearly afraid or maybe superstitious of cats. As terrified as she'd been, Brianna felt an overwhelming rage take hold, and Henry had had to hold her back, with repeated assurances to her that Kitty would be returned. In between his efforts to keep her calm, Henry had also warned the sailor who'd snatched Kitty that he was making a horrible mistake. His words had been so carefully metered, but when it became clear that the man wouldn't listen to reason, Henry's tone changed. In a voice that would have scared her hair straight if she hadn't already had a Keratin treatment, he told the sailor that Kitty was a beloved companion to *Sinclair—and the House of Pembrooke* as if Aidan had descended from the most powerful dynasty on earth, and was now keeper of the realm.

Brianna had been so floored by the whole thing— it was like she'd suddenly been thrust onto a movie set just as the gauntlet had been thrown down, and the battle of good vs. evil was about to commence. Good grief, she'd almost looked up to see if the dragons had been released! When Henry whispered to her again, however, it was to say, with utmost confidence, that the man would be punished (or was it 'killed'? She really couldn't recall, nor would she, if pressed), Brianna sobered instantly, realizing that as crazy as this new reality was, and it *was* borderline insane—it was hers, and it was crucial that she stay focused.

It was then that she spotted Aidan, quickly making his way around the crowd that had gathered. When he reached them, Brianna saw him share a brief look with Henry as he moved steadily, determinedly, *furiously* toward the man holding Kitty. Henry had bent down to Brianna to tell her he had to step away for a moment so he could retrieve her pet, lest she be harmed or dropped when Aidan felled the man. At first, Brianna thought he was exaggerating, but no, that's really what happened. It was all over so quickly, that she'd barely had time to blink (let alone *think* about what she'd heard less than a minute before), and then Henry was back, and Kitty was tucked safely into her arms. At that point, all of her attention was on her dear kitten, and Brianna looked her over carefully, grateful she seemed okay. She was shaken, yes, but hopefully, she'd forget about the incident with her next bout of purrs.

It wasn't until Henry closed the door after her silent thanks that a wave of exhaustion hit her. Brianna rubbed her chest, wincing a little at the tenderness she found there. All she wanted to do was lie down and cuddle Kitty, but she wasn't sure she'd actually be able to relax. So, she compromised and sat down on the edge of the bed, Kitty in her lap, and listened with an open ear, hoping to hear Aidan's heavy steps headed her way.

Hours later, she was still waiting, with supper already come and gone. A tray had been delivered to her room, and she'd eaten as much of her meal (far better than she expected considering they were on a ship) as she'd been able to. Still rattled from the afternoon, and worried that she hadn't seen Aidan since, she wasn't very hungry, and pushed most of it around on her plate, feeding bits to Kitty. Brianna looked at the door again, wishing for the hundredth time Aidan was standing on the other side. She knew this unusual (for her) attachment she was feeling was premature, maybe even irrational, but that didn't mean it wasn't real, or she could pretend it didn't exist. Whatever it was, she couldn't help but feel like he was avoiding her, though she couldn't figure out why.

Finally, Brianna decided she'd had enough. She'd spent most of her life keeping people at bay, doing her best *not* to feel, or at least not let it show when she did, but with Aidan—a man she'd known for all of (or barely) a day and a half—she was beginning to wonder if there was an off switch. It seemed impossible even to her, but what wasn't at this point? She and Aidan had a connection—that couldn't be denied, though whether it was just basic human attraction or on a level more supernatural, she had no idea, and didn't think it mattered. But because of it, Brianna was somehow tuned into his frequency, and she just had this *feeling* he was struggling with something—something bigger than rescuing her cat or making sure she made it to Dunhill safely. She wasn't trying to claim that she was suddenly so evolved and emotionally mature that she knew *what* he was struggling with, but she was pretty certain that whatever it was, Aidan was having his own 2.0 experience. And though she was recently getting the hang of this relating-to-other-people thing, *that* was something she knew about. If he felt only a fraction of the emotional roller-coaster that she'd been feeling, well, this fifteenth-century Highland Laird was in for the ride of his life.

After making sure Kitty was safe and secure in the little area where she'd sectioned off a pen of sorts, Brianna got up and strode to the door. On the other side, Henry greeted her and smiled warmly, as if he hadn't been standing there for long hours, with, by the looks of it, nothing to do.

"I'd like to go up to the deck again," she said,

steadying herself with a breath. "I'd like to find him. Aidan, I mean."

He seemed pleased by her statement, and if he noticed her faltering, didn't say anything about it, just helped her up the step-like ladder. He stayed close behind her until it was clear that she had not only found her balance but wasn't showing signs of having a trauma response to being back on deck, then gave her some breadth and backed up two whole steps.

Once up top, she carefully scanned the area and was relieved that the sympathetic gestures that had been cast her way earlier were now replaced with sure nods and smiles. Another benefit to spending most of your time with books and artifacts: they don't fix you with pitying stares after you embarrass yourself in front of them. The deck was full, but there was no sign of Aidan. After looking past the captain again, on tiptoe this time, and still coming up empty, Brianna turned her sights to the prow of the ship. The relief she felt when she saw him, standing there, at the bow staring out at sea, was a bit staggering.

The sun had just dipped over the horizon as she came up beside him, standing close enough to feel the rustle of his cloak against her dress. That in itself was a thrill she hadn't been expecting, or one she'd ever experienced before. She said nothing but felt him shift half an inch closer to her as she placed her hands on the railing and stared ahead, too. It really was a gorgeous sight. They stayed that way, quiet for a few minutes until he finally spoke.

"Seeing you fret over Kitty earlier," he began

slowly, measuring his words, "realizing we had allowed someone of such ill character within our ranks…we do not subscribe to such."

Brianna understood what he meant, fifteenth-century speak wasn't all that difficult to follow, even if you didn't already know the language as well as she did, but she was becoming increasingly aware of how the words carried a different weight. Regardless of this unexpected learning curve, the one thing that Brianna was sure of was that Aidan Sinclair was a man of integrity, and didn't mince his words. He said what he meant, so it was clear that this blight had truly taken its toll on him. She wasn't sure if her visceral reaction was to what he'd said, or simply to him, but she found that all the other noise in her head was gone, quieted once she saw him. She'd planned to ask if that was why he'd been avoiding her all day— guilt over bringing the man aboard—but when she turned and found him already waiting, eager even, to look into her eyes, his earlier anger gone, she wanted only to reassure him.

"In the short time that I've known you, Aidan Sinclair, *that* has become blazingly clear."

Aidan nodded. "I'm humbled by your ready defense, still, I wish you did not have to endure what that man put you through today."

That she really and truly felt for him, when she'd barely before felt for herself, softened her reply from its typically dry delivery. "That makes two of us."

His grunt was subtle, as well as the slight move-ment of his chin bobbing, but he said nothing. After a moment, he reached out, as if to brush hair from her face, though she was sure there were no errant strands to speak of. Still, she closed her eyes and covered his hand, letting the comfort of its weight flow through her. Brianna 2.0 was bolder, seemingly more mature. At least with Aidan. They shared a cautious smile, and she let her hand fall away. He did too, but only after he placed the imaginary strand behind her ear.

"When I realized you'd ventured above board of your own accord, I felt…" he let his words trail off, then shrugged. "Mayhap this will sound untimely or surprising, but 'twas pride, I felt. No easy feat, considering your experience, Brianna."

Brianna returned his shrug, glad that their easy, friendly energy of earlier seemed like it might return. "Well, I did have Henry lumbering close behind," she said and smiled.

"Aye, he does that." His smile reached his eyes this time.

"I only came up to see how it would feel to look out at the vast, open sea, but I never even had the chance to do that. My eyes went straight to Kitty, and I never saw beyond her."

Sweeping his arm out toward the ocean, Aidan gestured that she do so now. She hesitated, and he encouraged her with a look and a nod. Taking a deep breath, Brianna turned and placed her hands on the railing, fixing her gaze on the water. As she did so, she felt him step closer still.

"And now?" he asked.

"I see a sunset so beautiful and so peaceful it hardly seems real. Even the water appears tranquil." She just stood there staring, and breathing.

"Aye…" He trailed off again, and Brianna heard a small sigh escape him. If he wasn't such a formidable presence, she would have thought he was nervous. After a moment, she caught Aidan turning to her in her periphery, waiting until she looked up at him. His expression was one of concern, and when he spoke again, his tone was so sincere. "I would not ask, save for your very own words just moments ago, so, now I wonder, how it *feels*."

She was surprised he'd paid such close attention to what she'd said, and, that he'd picked up on the fact that she hadn't answered his question. A question, she realized now, that he'd truly asked in earnest. It was a big ask, even for this 2.0 version of herself.

At her hesitation, he nodded, and made a small barely perceptible sound, then looked back to the sea as if to show her. "When I look out, I feel measured and unencumbered, even with a world of pressing matters."

Her heart broke a little at his words, sentiments that reminded her of her father, always so happy to leave everything behind, so he could focus on his family. She took a deep breath, gathering a bit more courage, maybe, she considered, even pulling some from Aidan, and when she looked back out at the vast waters this time, she allowed a rush of emotion to hit her, and she shook her head. It took her a moment before she was able to speak. "I feel sad…when I look out, I remember them, and I can *feel* how good it was." She swiped away a tear, she didn't want to cry and wasn't trying to draw Aidan's attention. "And it reminds me that once they were gone, I never felt it again."

"Brianna—"

"No, it's okay." She turned to him. "Who am I to think I should've had more? I'm lucky for the time we were together." She shook her head, suddenly filled with remorse. "Until a few days ago, I never even let myself think of them, not really, not to remember…or feel that essence of our family…*here*." Her hand covered her heart and she felt like it was all suddenly unraveling, that the carefully protected shell she'd encased her deepest wound inside was cracking. Or maybe *she* was the one unraveling, feeling safe and protected in Aidan's presence, at least enough to be vulnerable.

She took a deep breath and continued, "I'm not sure I would've ever faced this," she said, waving her hand at her surroundings, "boarding a ship, sailing the open sea. I'm not sure my courage would have ever been put to the test like it has today…like it has this entire week." She searched his eyes then, wondering how or if to broach what she'd almost blurted out on the longboat. She'd been so desperate then, feeling as if her life was coming to an end, but now she wasn't so sure anymore.

"I would welcome your thoughts, whatever they might be," he said, seeming to sense her hesitation. "I realize I have failed you already, but you will never find a more loyal subject."

She had never met anyone who spoke with such depth, let alone spoke to *her* like that. And, although she'd never before allowed anyone close enough, Brianna was certain, it would have changed nothing—because she hadn't been ready to receive it. If not for the sequence of events that had led her to Dunhill Manor last week, and all of those that followed, she could not have opened herself up before this, and certainly, not like *this*. Yet, as she stood on the prow of what was surely one of the grandest vessels of its time, sailing across the open waters of the Irish Sea, Brianna was suddenly absolutely certain that fate had indeed taken her where she was meant to go. Toward this man, who regarded her with such reverence, and who moved her so deeply.

She placed her hand on his chest, leaning in ever so slightly. "You did not fail me, Aidan," she said, speaking firmly, and not allowing herself to falter. "I believe that you, and this place, are my destiny."

At this, she saw his eyes widen for a split second before he knelt in front of her and bowed his head. "And I would seal our fate." His words were spoken like a solemn oath, and although she had no idea what their future might hold, she knew from that moment on, they would somehow be tied together forever.

CHAPTER 14

Aidan was speaking with the captain the next morning when he spotted Brianna across the deck. Pleased as he was to see her, he was surprised she was up and about so early. He'd hoped she might find her way to a deep slumber and stay abed at least past dawn, especially after everything that had transpired the day before. She'd not had a moment's calm from morning til night, it surely had taken a toll on her. That she'd faced each incident bravely and with grace, yet still had the temerity to search him out and confess her suspicions to him, had humbled him perhaps as never before. It was a moment that he suspected would be etched in his memory forevermore, the image of the last rays of the sun, set alight between them, while he bound himself to her before God. He could still feel the touch of her slender hands upon his head as he swore his allegiance to her on bended knee. It was an oath and promise he would take to his grave. He thought of how her fingers had brushed through his hair as he looked up at her, her hands cupping his face. He could barely breathe for the depth in her eyes and deliberation in her touch. They barely knew one another, he had not even pressed his lips to hers, and yet Aidan knew in his bones that Brianna was his forever. It was fate, to be sure, but there was something about her, something more that had clung to him since the first moment he'd seen her, too.

"What does this mean, Aidan?" she'd whispered the night before, her eyes searching his.

If she only knew how quickly their circumstances had shifted with her confession of destiny. She'd asked him with such candor, he knew that he had gained her trust, and he would not spare her the truth.

"It means I have promised myself to you, Brianna. My words are consent to consider us wed—" At this, her eyes flashed in alarm. "*However,*" he'd continued. "'Tis still only my consent. I do not intend to force your hand, though I have hope that in good time, when you are ready, you will give yours."

She'd remained quiet, her expression still so serious, but had nodded, her eyes filled with understanding. Their easy patter abated then, simply due to her sheer exhaustion. She'd been through enough for one night, mayhap a week, and when he asked if she would like to go back to her quarters, she appeared grateful and allowed him to tuck her arm into his. Entwined together, he walked beside her, even more aware of her energy than usual, how it blent with his. When she turned to say goodnight, he saw the faint shadows beneath her eyes and gently swept them with his thumbs just before bending so his lips touched her brow. She'd given him a soft smile before closing her door slowly, their eyes never breaking contact until the last sliver was gone.

Aidan watched her now as she scanned the deck, her search, it seemed, over when their eyes met. He inclined his head, considering himself more than fortunate, as a modest smile tugged about her lips, and she made her way over to him. He felt a warmth, a flutter perhaps, in his chest, which he was beginning to associate with Brianna, as it happened each time he caught sight of her. He'd been noticing it ever since their first dinner at Abersoch—was that really only two days ago?—when she'd first danced her fingers in the air. Before now, he'd never given thought (or perhaps not enough of it), to what being matched or being in love would feel like. It was one thing to consider the *idea* of the woman he was supposed to fall in love with, but he'd never been *in* love before. Nor was he quite certain he was now, at least not yet, but he'd never felt this kind of protectiveness, possessiveness even, for anyone. It was new territory he tread, to say the least.

As she continued across the deck, Henry lumbering faithfully behind her, that physical sensation he attributed to her happened again, this catch or swell, and he was certain now that it wasn't *merely* attraction. Aye, he was attracted to her, madly so. Once he let himself accept she was the woman he'd been waiting for, it had only intensified. Her appearance and demeanor mattered not. She could be gowned in finery and regal in bearing, fashioned for the day in her highborn attire, determined to face her fate, or clad in merely a shift, her hair arranged in disarray atop her head, barefoot and filled with innocent glee, an image now seared in his mind. But he'd known many a fetching lass in his lifetime and not once had any sort of physical attraction been accompanied by this, this sensation.

When she caught his eye again, they shared a smile, a genuine one this time, and he froze. Had he been in battle, he'd be dead. Felled on the spot. He supposed being aboard the ship allowed him some breadth, but he knew he'd better get a hold of himself before this premature besottedness caused a problem.

"Good morning," she said softly when she reached him.

"Aye." That it was. "Good morn, Brianna."

"What's that?" she asked, her head tilted to the side as she pointed down to the thin leather braids in his hand. He'd nearly forgotten them himself.

"I made a yoke of sorts for Kitty."

"You did?"

God help him, when she beamed, he felt a bit lightheaded. Then he realized she did not have Kitty with her. "You didn't want to bring her up with you?" he asked. At her look, he assured her, "He will be gone on the morrow. We'll make port early."

"Oh." She was clearly surprised by this. "We're stopping? I assumed we would sail straight to Dunhill."

"Nay, we'll dock at Seagrave first. 'Tis a short ride from there."

Her eyes narrowed, then she said, "There's more?" Of course, there was, but he only just realized it himself. She nodded, perhaps sensing his hesitation, "Aye, there is."

"Perhaps, *short* isn't the most accurate description," he said, considering how best to tell her they'd oft time made use of the cottage between Seagrave to Dunhill to break up the journey.

"I don't mind riding, Aidan. In fact, I enjoy it."

"I'm pleased to hear so. The journey, while possible to complete in a day, can be lengthy. So that you do not need to ride for so long, how do you feel about an overnight stay in—"

He stopped short when her mouth fell open, and she clutched his sleeves. "The family cottage! We're going to the O'Roarke family cottage!" She was beside herself like she'd been when he told her she could see Pembrooke. "What's wrong with that? I'd love to see it with my own eyes!" In her excitement, she drummed her hands upon his chest, then pulled a silly face and stepped back, blushing. "Sorry."

He chuckled, "No need. And I'm not sure there's anything wrong about making use of it," he said shaking his head.

"Oh." A flush swept her fair skin from just above the cut of her dress to her cheeks. "You were implying—"

He shook his head, his heart racing with what she'd thought he'd meant, what he realized she might be open to. "Nay. In truth, I imply naught." He paused, wondering if he should inquire further, but decided to leave it aside for now, as time and circumstance would provide. Instead, he held up the braids he'd fashioned the night before. "Come," he said, reaching for her hand. "I'll show you."

Her excitement—in the change of subject, or the yoke itself—was evident, and she placed her slender hand in his. How easily the gesture came to her, the first time she'd held his hand since all that had transpired the night before, it gladdened him.

It was a day Aidan enjoyed as never before. While wholly chaste, there was a shared intimacy in how they spent time in each of their chambers as they ventured back and forth with Kitty, and up on the deck too. Aidan could almost feel their closeness and familiarity with each other growing. It pleased him how Brianna took great interest in his belongings and travel bags, large and small, examining them and exclaiming over their small details. When they happened to be in her quarters shortly afterward, she went immediately to her satchel, and it almost seemed like she was about to share something with him, but then appeared to change her mind. The look on her face made him think it was more than just the elegant craftsmanship of the bag, and he had to admit, he was slightly disappointed when she put it down, but even more curious. No matter, he was a patient man, for now, it was enough she considered it.

Later she'd made a simple loop, knotted from a thin strip of leather he had left over from Kitty's harness, and she taught him a game of cats and bairn beds something or other. That had inspired him to show her a few silly games, too, ones he hadn't played since he was young—though playing them with Brianna, clasping and unclasping their hands was quite different from playing them with the kin he'd grown up with. There was one she'd excitedly declared *a thumb war*, which he countered with another he learned as a young boy. Brianna had built upon that one, adding a few silly ditties, though he'd stopped her whence her songs had started to describe some peculiar characters and circumstances, especially one Miss Lucy.

At the end of the night, after watching another sunset together, they'd returned to his quarters and she'd fallen asleep next to him whilst he read through the list of supplies he'd need to gather from Ayr. He smiled down at her, pleased to have made her feel so secure and so safe. Then, he laid his head back against the wall, Brianna nestled into his side, and Kitty curled between them.

Aye, the Fates had shone down on him indeed.

THERE WAS a marked chill in the air early the next morning as the ship passed through the Northern Channel and entered the Firth of Clyde on their approach to Ayr. The sun had yet to crest the horizon, and still, Aidan couldn't pry Brianna away from the prow, her eyes drinking in the sights cast only in the pre-dawn light. He watched as she leaned into the railing as if she'd never before had a care of being aboard a ship or the sea itself. When he came up beside her, she tilted her head toward him and smiled. He wasn't so foolish to think that her happiness was only for him, but surely, he was partly responsible for eliciting it. Aidan was learning, and quickly, that when it came to Brianna, he seemed to feel first and reason last. As afflictions go, it was something he could live with, even if it was something to get used to. He returned her smile and, at the sight of her shivering, draped his cloak over her shoulders. When she stepped back into him, seeking his warmth, he gave it to her gladly, wrapping her in his arms.

They hadn't spoken of their exchange the other night, the vows he'd made, nor did it seem to matter. The facts as they were had been acknowledged, and time would take care of the rest, as it already seemed to be doing. Mayhap by the time they arrived at Seagrave, or perhaps Dunhill, what was fast growing between them—companionship and friendship, to be sure, but also attraction, affection, and the hint of more along that line—would be enough to build the foundation of a solid relationship. He was certain now that she was his by fate, and so it seemed more than prudent to take her to see Dunhill, where she wished to go. Afterward, however, Brianna would live with him, as his wife, at Pembrooke. He couldn't say for sure if she was aware of this, but considering how she was always so assured in her desires (something they had in common), he was not eager to bear such news to her yet. But all of that was secondary because in all his wonderings about who was to be his fated true love, never had he imagined *this*. If he felt only *this*, to its exact degree, and no more for the rest of his life, he would die a happy man.

Reining in his erstwhile thoughts, Aidan forced himself to refocus on what was in front of him at that moment. Remembering what he'd come up here for in the first place, he shared what he knew would be a pleasant surprise. "I sent Henry for a warm beverage," he said.

She shuddered against him, but he knew it was not from a chill, he had enough heat for them both. "Not to sound ungrateful, but the last warm drink I was served on this ship was disgusting," she said. "Let's just say the cook aboard this ship doesn't quite have the skills of the cook at Abersoch."

Based on his newly refined and *'modern'* tastes, thanks to Gwen and the many new spices and ingredients she'd added to their fare, he could only imagine and chuckled. "You'll be pleased with this one."

At this, she turned, there, in that small footprint of space. Facing him now, with eyes sparkling and her hand shielding the side of her face against the sun that was finally beginning to rise, she said, "A warm morning beverage, I'll enjoy? Do tell, Sinclair?"

Her sweet playfulness momentarily stunned him. In the second it took for his words to come forth, a blush had swept across her cheeks and she looked away for a moment to cover her embarrassment.

Finally, Aidan managed, "I found some tea, in my bag. A blend with bits of citrus rind. A far cry from the warm ale you were probably served yesterday, I'd say."

At this, her eyes widened and he knew she was pleased. "I don't know how to thank you," she said, growing serious. "You've been so thoughtful and considerate." Then she rubbed her arms and wrinkled her nose. "And I really like your cloak."

He chuckled, well aware that it was more than the cloak that was the true cause of her smile, but then sobered. "You owe me no thanks, Brianna. I meant it when I said I'll always see to your welfare."

Her eyes shuttered a moment. "I know that shouldn't make me feel so nervous, but…" she let her words trail off.

"But?"

Her cheeks reddened again. "Well, suddenly I have, or almost have, a husband and what goes with that," she said, and he was stunned for a moment at how forthright she was being about the prospect of their coupling.

Aidan felt his body responding to what she was suggesting and took a breath to quell the sensation. Aye, he wished to bind their union physically, but he did not sense that Brianna was anywhere near ready yet. She mayhap felt the growing attraction between them, and by all evidence, she trusted him now, but Aidan was confident that if they took this time to know each other better, their bond could only be stronger for it. While it did not matter to him, he was certain that to Brianna it would. Patience had never been a problem for him, and Brianna's continued trust was worth the wait.

He shook his head. "In due course, Brianna, we're in no hurry for such. *I* am in no hurry," he corrected, knowing prudence was key.

Her relief was evident, but in the next breath, her brows furrowed. "But...not because, because you don't want to...with...me?" Her voice became increasingly lower with each word until he was forced to shift his focus from her eyes to her lips to make out what she was saying.

He hoped his astonishment, that she could even entertain the thought, was clearly written on his face. "I assure you, that is not the case," he said.

She gave him a doubtful look (that he quickly countered), before supplying an explanation of sorts. "It's just that every O'Roarke marriage throughout history..." she paused when he raised a brow at her words *throughout history* (it was hard to let it pass unnoticed), then she hurried on. "Well, it's just that they're all..." she hesitated again, her eyes darting anywhere but his.

"Brianna, what are you trying to say?"

"They're all love matches, Aidan. When an O'Roarke marries whether it lasts years or months, it's true and enduring. It's always been this way."

"And that's a problem?

"I was just worried for a moment when you said... *that*," she jerked her head to the side, "about sleeping together."

Aidan considered himself a patient man, at least he

had just moments ago, but he had no idea what Brianna was getting at.

She sighed when he didn't reply, clearly frustrated. "When you said you didn't feel the need—

"I will stop you there." Aidan put a hand up, realizing Brianna had misinterpreted his intention. He'd merely wished to put her at ease, not to make her question his attraction to her. "If I had known those words would cause you a moment of uncertainty, rather than the calm that I intended, I would not have uttered them. To be clear: I want you, Brianna. I have since the moment I suspected that you were the woman I'd been waiting for, and each one that has followed. The moment you give your verbal consent —*if* you give it," he added, wishing immediately that he had not, "we'll be all but wed. From there, I will *eagerly* await our physical joining. And though we are still new to each other, there is no doubt that our union will fulfill the standards of your lineage." Aidan paused, a little out of breath, emotion coursing through him. How could she not see? He wanted to ask if he'd dispelled her worries, but over her shoulder, he spied a castle atop a wild bluff, and he knew she'd want to see it. "You'd best turn, lass," he said, motioning with his hand and nodding in the estate's direction.

She did a quick pivot, clearly grateful to be given a moment's distraction, and nearly swooned in delight at the sight of it. She gasped then said, "Oh, Aidan. Thank you."

While he hadn't slayed a dragon, he knew she took

great interest in things and her surroundings. With her hands clutching the railing again, her attention now elsewhere, he turned to leave her to her enjoyment, but she reached out.

"Don't go," she said, keeping her eyes on the intricate architecture for another moment before facing him. "I'm sorry, this is all so…I don't even have the words right now."

"You've no need to apologize. I cannot mend what I don't know is broken. Though to be clear, naught is broken." At her look, he chuckled, then motioned for her to carry on, happy to simply stand next to her. A few minutes later Henry appeared bearing the aforementioned tea, he took it and then placed the warm cup in her hands. He knew she liked the drink because he'd asked the staff, eager to make her journey as easeful as possible, but this tea was from his collection. Even her hum of delight as she inhaled the aroma was beguiling. She took a long sip, then turned, granting him a smile, and pressed the cup back into his hands.

"You have to try this," she said. "I think it's my favorite so far."

Aye, his, too, but he took a drink as if it were new to him. All in all, it was another transformative morning, one he was all too pleased to tack onto the one before. Perhaps, like the braids that wound around his unique crest, another thread had been added to it, one they were weaving together.

He remained by her side as they sailed into the harbor, pointing out landmarks and answering her questions about the town of Ayr. He watched her as she took in the crew mooring the ship at port, not surprised when the thought crossed his mind that Brianna O'Roarke may well have regained her sea legs. He left her for a short time, to see to the man who'd threatened Kitty brought up from where he'd been secured below. After tossing a pouch of coin his way, Aidan warned him to steer clear of them, now and in the future, and waited until he was taken ashore.

Glad to have that behind him, he went in search of Brianna and found her watching as a group of fishermen set off from the harbor. After deciding it was best to leave Kitty in the safety of her quarters, he helped Brianna to the longboat. She was surer this time, an altogether different experience than the last. Her legs were between his again, her hands touching him almost casually as she cast her sights here and there.

She spied him marveling at her turnabout. "What?"

"You—flourishing," he shook his head. "'Tis the true sight to behold," he said.

By her small smile, he could tell she appreciated his praise. After a moment, she shrugged. "How do we grow if not by facing our fears, right?"

"Aye, you are correct."

"I would have preferred to ease into it. Maybe you could have asked me to spend a day on the beach first, like a normal date, but," she shrugged, doing that dance with her hands he was so fond of, "c'est la vie."

He looked at her curiously. Not over her suggestion of modern courting, in which he was all too happy to indulge; he was stirred by her use of French, her words, spoken as an expression. He'd heard many unfamiliar expressions from Gwen and Maggie, *especially* Gwen, but not this. It was true, he supposed, that many could quip a phrase in a foreign tongue, but he wondered suddenly if Brianna spoke the language. Curious, he said, "Tes yeux sont la plus belle nuance de bleu que j'ai jamais vue de ma vie." *Your eyes are the prettiest shade of blue I have ever seen in my life.* Oh, aye, she knew it, God help him, her smile ignited his, and his chest nearly swelled to bursting as a flush swept her cheeks.

"Je suis flatté. Merci," *I'm flattered. Thank you,* she said, her hand squeezing his leg as they rocked.

He was still lost in her eyes when she reached out to brace against him as they came along the dock. Forsooth! She'd done it to him again. He laughed it off, but knew he'd better get control over *this... her,* if he were to regain any sense of the order and control he prided himself on.

Once ashore, with Brianna safely at his side, he led her through the town of Ayr, nodding to those he knew, and others acknowledging his presence as they passed. Even with the fair still on, it was an orderly place. But it suddenly occurred to him that Brianna was quiet, unusually so. When he turned, he wasn't sure what to make of her expression, "Brianna?" he prodded.

She just shook her head, eyes wide, and continued to look around. He mirrored her expression in hopes of prompting a response. Her eyes darted nervously, and when she realized he wasn't moving, she finally whispered. "I'm a bit overwhelmed."

Right. He was traipsing her through a thriving port town when her exposure thus far had been significantly more contained. "How can I help you?" he asked stepping closer.

"Do I look okay?"

This set him back. "Pardon?"

Her eyes darted around again as she nervously smoothed her dress. "Brianna, you look just as you should, like you belong here, and lovely to boot," he added appreciatively. He wondered if he should take her back to the ship, then thought of Isabelle and how happy and distracted she was a few days ago, and wondered if maybe the fair would do the same for Brianna. He stepped closer to her and took her hands, smiling softly and looking deeply into her eyes. "We have two choices." He felt her relax at once, whether from his familiar words or merely shifting her focus from everything around her, did not matter.

"One?" she asked, softly but eagerly.

Right. He chuckled. "One, I can take you back to the ship, where we can spend the day. You can sing your silly ditties all afternoon while I imagine up new games that allow me to hold your hands. I'll send Henry to fetch supper for us, and tomorrow we'll be on our way."

"And two?"

"I have it on good authority, that the annual fair is brimming with wares."

Her eyes widened. "A fair? With crafts? And decent snacks?"

He grinned. "Aye, just yonder."

She turned her head, peering around again. "You're sure I look alright? My dress? My hair? People were staring."

Ah, now he understood. "I've been to Ayr many times. Even before traveling to Abersoch, these last few years. 'Tis only common courtesy. And you're passing better than alright."

She nodded and graced him with a small smile, but still seemed lost in thought. He was happy to give her a bit more time, but then her face fell, and a small sound escaped her lips, her eyebrows still knit in consternation. He wanted to offer some words of comfort, but he did not know what had caused her such trouble so suddenly. After a moment, she seemed to right herself, and a look of relief crossed her face when he tucked her arm in his and began walking again.

CHAPTER 15

Brianna wandered in and out of stalls for most of the afternoon, she had a pouch filled with coins that Aidan had pressed into her hand hours ago but had yet to buy anything. It wasn't that she hadn't admired some lovely items, she had—fabrics and jewelry, painted tiles and tapestries, wooden bowls and iron pots, and even some things that might be useful, too, like soaps, sachets filled with dried flower petals, kerchiefs, even little covered tins that she could use to keep her things in—but she couldn't enjoy the experience like she might have if she didn't feel so...out of sorts.

She probably wouldn't have felt *quite* so terribly self-conscious if she hadn't noticed a man looking at her so oddly, almost with scorn, but it happened so quickly she couldn't be sure. Besides, after Aidan had assured her that there was nothing wrong with her appearance, she'd felt silly for being self-conscious, something she'd never worried about before.

Realistically, she knew that she was dressed appropriately for the time, (more than, considering the quality of her clothing), but she'd picked up on some lingering stares as she and Aidan had started their walk through town. It was obvious that he was well-known and respected, and she supposed that he *had* been keeping her rather close, so maybe it was that they'd never seen him with a woman before. Or that they were used to seeing him with a different woman...other women. It was when she'd had that thought that she'd winced earlier, and, okay, maybe made a sound of disgust. Aidan had been concerned, as nothing ever seemed to get past him. Since there was no way she was going to tell him she was jealous of a possibly non-existent, imaginary woman, or maybe a string of women, it took a few minutes to convince him that she was fine.

Once they'd started walking again, he'd pointed out the local market streets, and just beyond it, the fair, easily large enough to rival any back home. Livestock and horses, tents, and rows of stalls, open tables, and food and drinks galore. It was something that should have been enjoyable, an experience of a lifetime especially for her, but after her day with Aidan yesterday—so simple and on the surface innocuous, but brimming with meaning and connection underneath. She'd never imagined having anything like that with anyone, let alone a man with such a presence and immense power. But Aidan was also thoughtful, measured, and deliberate, and so she found his words and deeds all the more meaningful and romantic coming from him. He hadn't pressed her about her past, or how she came to be here, even though she knew he had to suspect. She almost showed him her medallion but changed her mind. Later she thought she'd show him the insignia inside her satchel, but again hesitated. She couldn't imagine it would be long before he spotted her tattoo and would recognize the symbol. "Pfff," a breath escaped her as she realized that she'd unwittingly branded herself as property of Pembrooke. *Huh*. She paused. Maybe that made *her* of the house of Pembrooke too.

When she felt a set of hands on her shoulders, she prayed they belonged to Aidan, then realized they must, considering how close he'd stayed to her. He and Henry had been following along behind her, watching her from a respectable distance, if three feet was the current standard for a respectable distance. Though they did afford her a bit more space if she stepped inside a stall *after* they'd deemed it safe for her to enter. It was sweet if not a little overkill.

When she turned, Aidan was gazing down at her with concern, and she counted her blessing again. Fate and destiny aside, if this truly was her home now, her life, spending it with Aidan Sinclair was the best outcome she could've imagined. Aidan Sinclair, *and* the House of Pembrooke. She brushed her tattoo, as she covered his hand, wondering again what all of this meant. When she'd asked him before if he knew of Pembrooke, she'd never imagined that he would know it so well because it was his home— or, she considered now, was that the reason why she'd been so fascinated with it ever since she was young? Another connection leading to their ultimate fate?

"What is it?" Aidan asked, his eyes searching hers.

"What is what?" she asked, liking the weight of his hands on her shoulders, pouting a bit when he moved them.

"Well." He sighed, holding her head in his hands. "You've been looking for hours and have naught to show for it."

"I'm sorry." She shrugged. It was all she could offer.

"Brianna, you seem forlorn, yet you should be beside yourself. I brought you to a mecca of the very things I've seen you delight over time and time again."

She smiled. That was sweet, and true, but she had so much on her mind. She was so confused.

"I'd love some more of that tea you found," she said, realizing that she'd be happy going back to the ship. Wow, that was powerful—choosing an afternoon talking and playing games over a day spent examining historical objects. She almost laughed remembering how Aidan had gone on about Tiny Tim trying to eat the bathtub for some time. It was a good thing she hadn't told him it wasn't wood—porcelain might have sent him over the edge.

"I've plenty more tea. But I'll do better than that. We'll sup at the Inn tonight. The food there is almost as good as what you'll find at Abersoch. But first, you *must* find something for yourself in the stalls."

"But—

Aidan shook his head. "Humor me, one item, no matter."

Brianna smiled, suddenly feeling a bit lighter. Maybe she'd just needed some direction, or maybe Aidan suggesting dinner with her in town had something to do with it. There was a pretty comb she'd seen, and those tins she was kind of obsessing about now. She was trying to remember exactly where she'd seen the tins when she spotted a man behind the stall nearly dragging a gaunt and bedraggled mare along beside him. Brianna was horrified at the sight. That poor thing, she'd clearly been mistreated, and looked so hopeless.

"Does my item have to be in a stall, Aidan?" she asked, laser-focused on the mare.

"Where you find it matters naught."

Her decision was made then and there. "Aidan," she whispered, clutching his cloak and nodding toward the mare. "I want her."

Aidan stepped back at her tone and turned to see what had caused her sudden reaction. He wasn't pleased either. "We can try," he said, shaking his head, "but I beg you, don't get your hopes up. And if you show too much interest, he might refuse just to see *you* suffer, aye."

"Like you wouldn't believe."

He grunted, so she was pretty sure he understood what she meant.

When the man was close enough, she called out, "Sir," surprising herself with her boldness. He ignored her and kept moving. "*Sir.*" Brianna hurried through the back of the stall and came up behind him, trying not to look at the mare, lest she start crying and show her hand. Still, the man paid her no mind when she called after him again. Steeling herself, she ran ahead of him, and stopped, out of breath, but placed her hand out, and said loudly, "*SIR!*"

Not happy that she'd interrupted him, he snarled, "Out of my way, lass."

Brianna planted herself in front of him. "Sir, I only need a moment. I would like to purchase your mare."

He looked at her oddly. "Why? She's not for sale."

"I'll give you my entire purse." She had no idea how much the money in the small bag was worth, but when Aidan pressed it into her hands, she was surprised by its weight. He'd only shrugged and winked, so she was pretty sure he'd passed her the medieval equivalent of a Black Card. Some of the booths Aidan had guided her toward were filled with very expensive wares, so she wagered it was quite a lot.

The man looked at her for a long moment, then at the horse, seeming to consider her offer. Brianna knew she (and the mare) probably only had this one chance. If she didn't get her now, the man might later be angered by the exchange and abuse her even more. Brianna said a litany of silent prayers, and when he pointed at the bag in the palm of her hand, she made an effort to remain expressionless.

"How do I know it's not filled with sand or worthless pennies."

He had a point, but she acted as though he couldn't

be more wrong. "I assure you, it's not," she said, leaning into her air of authority, then spilled the contents into the palm of her hand for him to see. Oh, good Lord, these weren't even coins. Aidan gave her a bag filled with what looked like pure minted silver. The man went bug-eyed, he clearly liked what he saw.

"You mean to offer all that, for her," he said, elbowing the mare (probably to get whatever last jabs in that he could, Brianna thought). The mare didn't make a sound, though Brianna caught a slight movement in her nostrils.

It wasn't easy, but Brianna continued to feign indifference while funneling the coins back into the bag. "The choice is yours. It's just that I'm in need of a horse, the reason is unimportant." Then she cast what she hoped was a conspiratorial look, evil liked company.

He sneered back, a little gleeful. Sick man. He gave her a curt nod, then held out his hand.

"The reins, sir."

They made an awkward but even exchange, passing reins, and the bag filled with coins at the same moment. Once Brianna had possession of the horse, she continued with her stoic charade, though she did gently motion the mare to safety. Then, she stood in front of her, waiting for the man to leave, and if justice served, he'd fall into a ditch and never get out. Just when she thought the whole unfortunate episode was over, her breath caught as none other than the rough sailor who'd grabbed Kitty walked up to the man.

"That's her, Da," said the sailor from the ship. "she was with the man who threatened me," he said, jabbing his finger in her direction.

Brianna steeled herself for another confrontation, but this time the stakes couldn't have been higher. Somehow, she knew she could do it, because in those few seconds that had followed this new and impending threat, she'd fully dug her heels in, not just to her immediate situation, but to fate, destiny, and the fifteenth century itself. This was her new reality, and she liked who she was in it. These men would not bring down the house of Pembrooke—*her* house—not on her watch.

Summoning all the bravado she could, Brianna stood tall and proud, then took a step forward. "I can assure you, *Sir*, he did no such thing," she said, disdain lacing her words. She knew she was laying it on thick, but with her adamant denial of Henry's threat, such an insult couldn't be allowed. If God was going to strike her dead for lying, at least she'd saved the mare and Henry's reputation. A small price to pay for belonging to Sinclair and the House of Pembrooke. She puffed up a little more at the thought, surprised again by the extra bolt of confidence it brought.

"Is that so?" The man was looking between her and his son, skeptical.

Brianna knew this wasn't over, but hoped if she hit the right tone and chose the right words, it might be. "I said it was. Do you think I would lie? Do you know who I am?" She kept her tone even, trying for regal. Her delivery must have hit correctly because she detected a bit of fear in the man's eyes, and she wasn't ashamed to say that she felt completely emboldened by it. "I am Brianna O'Roarke. I can trace my family lineage for nearly a millennium. Furthermore, I am promised to Sinclair and the House of Pembrooke." She threw that one in for good measure, recalling how it had sounded so theatrical when Henry had said it the other day. She wanted to add, 'Be grateful, I don't release my dragons!' but knew that would be too much, and possibly more confusing than anything else, so she settled on just thinking about it, which was just as empowering. Then she made a show of straightening her skirts, quite proud of herself, before turning with as much regal flair as possible.

She nearly tripped at the sight of Aidan and Henry, who had somehow managed to come up behind her while she was busy ensuring the survival of their dynasty. Their show of solidarity—arms crossed and glowers icy enough to freeze a man dead —warmed her heart, and she beamed.

Take that, you miserable knaves.

She walked past the men with her mare, and when she brushed up against Aidan, he squeezed her arm, and she knew he was pleased with the show she'd put on. She had no idea where she was going, but it wasn't long before Aidan was beside her. He took her free hand and walked them around the tents and then pulled her and the mare off to the side. While he looked over the horse, Brianna stroked her snout and whispered sweetly into her ear. "It's okay," she crooned "One day you'll live with us."

At this, Aidan's head whipped around, but she dismissed him with a shrug, not sure why he was so surprised. If he was just waiting for her 'verbal consent' or whatever, wasn't living together at some point pretty much a foregone conclusion? The mare nudged her hand, and she resumed petting her behind the ears. Wordlessly, Aidan came up beside her and started giving the horse some affection too. He shook his head, smiling as he reached out to her. "What you did today is commendable, Brianna. It's one thing to see an injustice, another to take action to correct it."

Brianna stepped into his arms and fell into his embrace, only realizing then how scary that whole encounter had been. She felt his chin dip down to graze her face. She liked that and leaned into his touch.

"Do you think she'll be alright?" she asked, pulling away and looking up at him.

"Aye. We'll take her to Glenn, he has stables nearby and cares for many horses. I'm not sure she'd make any journey right now, be it by sea or land. But I think he'll take care to see that she thrives. If she has the will."

"She does."

"Aye, if she's anything like her new mistress, I've no doubt."

Brianna warmed at that. "Thank you," she said. "For standing by me. For supporting me and believing in my cause."

His fingers brushed down the side of her face. "Brianna, you make me proud, lass." He gave her another squeeze and gestured to take the reins from her. She stroked the mare again, and whispered, "He's good people, don't worry."

Something had shifted between them, Brianna could feel it. Whatever it was, it had occurred in the time since she'd first seen the mare to now, and as they began walking again, she leaned against him, and he wrapped his arm around her shoulders as if it was the most natural thing in the world. After a moment, he pulled her closer to graze her with his chin again, a gesture she was growing quite fond of.

Aidan spoke then. "If I told you I knew where we could enjoy a feast of whole grilled fish, roasted vegetables, and mayhap a spot of fine wine, would you be interested?"

She stopped and looked up at him. "Don't tease me, Aidan Sinclair, or I may have to release my dragons."

When he smiled down at her, he wore a look she hadn't seen before, though if she had to guess, it was the look of a man who was about to kiss her, or at the very least was thinking about it. Never in a million years (or seven hundred give or take a decade or two) would Brianna ever have imagined that the spark she'd been missing for so long would be ignited on a worn dirt road in medieval Scotland with a fifteenth-century Highland Laird. Something about it was so bittersweet.

Aidan's expression changed to one of concern, and he cupped her face, looking deeply into her eyes, "Brianna? Are you alright, lass?"

She didn't realize she'd been looking at him so intently, but she smiled and nodded, "Yes. I think I found the magic, Aidan."

"Aye, I believe we both did."

BRIANNA WAS HAVING the most wonderful dream about the visit she and her grandfather had made to Scotland when she was still a little girl. It had been a couple of years after the accident that took her parents. In her dream, they were inside his office at Dunhill, which was strewn with opened files and piled-up objects. Papers were tacked to the wall, alongside all kinds of maps, ancient-looking ones hung beside more modern ones, seemingly with no rhyme or reason.

Then, her eyes shot open, and for a moment, Brianna couldn't tell if she was dreaming or awake. She'd forgotten about those years and her grandfather's obsession with some family mystery or another. Still half-asleep, she closed her eyes again, hoping to go back there, and must have dozed off because she saw herself again as a girl, and her grandfather was running down the hallway toward where she was playing in front of the fireplace. Brianna looked up when she heard him hooting and hollering, startled when he scooped her up and spun her around, laughing as her jacks scattered all over the place. This was the day her grandfather had first discovered Pembrooke. Brianna remembered how it had looked to her when she first saw it—the most beautiful fairy-tale castle she'd ever seen—and how she'd gone off to play while her grandfather studied the stonework.

Now, Brianna woke again with a start, the images still so present in her mind. She hadn't thought about that day in years. She was surprised she'd dreamt about it, just as it had happened, and desperate to go back again, she quickly laid down and closed her eyes. As if she was meant to see it, her dream returned, and there was the little garden she'd found at Pembrooke, and the rock that had those initials carved into it, she'd forgotten all about them...as she knelt, brushing her hand over the deep etchings to sweep away the dirt, she heard someone call her name. But...it wasn't her grandfather's voice, and that confused her because he'd called her just after she'd found the rock and discovered—

"Breea. Wake up, sweetheart."

Startled, Brianna froze. Mama? Was that Mama calling her? Mama wasn't at Pembrooke.

"Breea, come, love, you must wake up now."

Papa? She felt a rush sweep through her from her head to her toes. They were here! She could feel them! Mama, Papa! She tried turning around but, couldn't move.

"Breea, you need to get up."

She wanted to tell them she was trying but she couldn't. "Mama? Papa? Where are you?"

"BREEA!"

Brianna bolted upright with a gasp, hearing Aidan as he bellowed her name and pounded on her door. "Brianna!" he hollered again just before her door splintered open and he rushed inside. He started grabbing things and throwing them in her bag, then reached for Kitty and secured her into her sling, which he flung around Brianna's shoulders. All this while she sat there dazed, confused, and wondering what on earth was happening.

"Aidan, what—"

Then she smelled it. Her face fell and her stomach dropped as she looked at him in horror. "Fi..." *fire*. She couldn't get the word out. It didn't matter that they were close enough to land to swim to shore, they had to survive the fire and get off the ship first. *Oh, God, no! Nonono...*

"We must go," Aidan said, grabbing her and pulling her from where she was frozen and scared in the bed. He pushed her behind him as they entered the hall-way, which was crowded as everyone scrambled for safety. When they reached the ladder, he pushed her up from behind, stopping her before she started up the next.

"Nay, there!" he said, pointing to a set of stairs she hadn't noticed before. They led to a less crowded part of the main deck, but after Aidan hoisted her into Henry's outstretched arms and he set her upright, Brianna stumbled as images from her childhood flashed before her eyes—the eerie darkness, the odd glow of firelight, and the unforgettable sound of crackling wood as the vessel that was supposed to keep them safe was now compromised. For a moment she felt terror's grip, watching the men jumping into the water below but then Aidan's strong arms wrapped around her, carrying her away from the frenzy and setting her down to help Henry, who was taking an ax to part of the railing. Aidan began ripping it away with his bare hands, then turned back to her.

"When I say jump, jump," he said, eyes blazing. Brianna stared at him. She'd never seen him so intent. "Do you understand? Brianna—do you understand?"

She felt Kitty curled up against her and panicked. "Take her," she said.

He shook his head. "My weight—"

She felt her eyes widen, as she realized they would sink beneath the surface first, then would have to swim back upward. He grasped her arms. "Brianna! Out, not down. As far as you can." She felt herself nodding but saw his face set grimly. She hadn't realized she'd backed up, until he lunged for her, sweeping his arm around her back and using the momentum to propel them both forward and off the ship with enough force to clear the anchor lines. He let go of her just before they hit the water.

It was cold, but it wasn't the icy chill that stunned her, it was being surrounded by saltwater as she sank beneath the surface. A sensation she'd never wanted to feel again. Brianna fought back her fear, pushed through her memories, and kicked until she broke the surface, gasping and calling for Aidan.

"Aidan!" She spun around, waiting for him to resurface. "*Aidan!*"

She started to panic but saw him then, swimming toward her. "It's okay," he said, reaching for Kitty the second he was next to her. "We're okay. On your back, you know how to float, aye?"

She nodded and grabbed his face. "You're okay, right?"

He nodded back, then smiled and leaned in and kissed her, so quickly that she knew it was just to reassure her. Still, the feeling of his lips on hers and the look in his eyes righted something in her and she felt herself calm ever so slightly.

"We're unharmed," Aidan said. "I swear it. Look."

He was right, the harbor was filled with small boats already helping sailors from the water. Some had even made it to the pier and were already being lifted to safety. They weren't out in open waters, after all. Aidan let Brianna make her own assessment and he must have felt her relax, because he turned her around and swam toward one of the boats that had come to help, pulling Brianna along with him. Suddenly remembering Henry, Brianna whipped around but saw that he was swimming with steady, sure strokes right behind them.

After Aidan had settled her in a safe spot, wrapping her in a blanket that someone had pressed his way, he left to help the men trying to douse the fire. She wasn't sure how long she sat there watching, but it was sad to see Captain John finally give up and jump from the deck. It didn't appear that anyone was hurt, but she hoped the ship wasn't a total loss. When Aidan came back, he nodded to someone behind her, and she turned, not realizing that he'd stationed a few men to watch over her.

"Come," he said. "I've secured lodgings for the night."

She didn't ask about the accommodations, but she'd already decided that she wasn't going to be sleeping alone. She hadn't quite figured out what that looked like yet, although the reality was setting in, in the immediate future (like, soon), but after tonight, she was grabbing the O'Roarke lore by the horns—starting now. Soon, they arrived at a quaint cottage just beyond the outskirts of town. Aidan introduced her to the owners, Adam and his wife Charlotte, who greeted them outside. Brianna thought that Adam had the unmistakable look of a warrior himself, and it suddenly occurred to her that Aidan wouldn't choose just anywhere for them to stay. He'd selected this inn not just for its solitude but because he knew she'd be safe there.

Once inside, Charlotte fussed after her while Adam and their teenage son helped Aidan and Henry gather supplies to take back to the harbor. When Charlotte started leading her upstairs, Brianna looked over at Aidan, wondering if this was goodnight.

His eyes were already on her. "I'll be up before I leave to go see to the ship, but not for some time," he said. When she entered the room, Brianna found it was already warm, with a nice-size bed, a small table for private meals, and a dressing area. She smiled in anticipation of a hot bath, seeing a few large pails of steaming water and a stack of linens set beside a substantial tub.

After settling Kitty in a spot by the bed, Brianna

reached for her bag, still waterlogged even hours after it had been pulled from the harbor. As she was inspecting the seams, looking for any damage, her fingers met a hard disc, and she breathed a sigh of relief. Her medallion was still secure inside, right where she'd tucked it into the secret pocket the morning they'd left Abersoch. She'd almost shown it to Aidan that day they'd spent together on the ship, but something had stopped her. The medallion was so meaningful to her, with what she thought of as her symbol on one side, and the image of the bear on the other. Even the infinity knot, etched into the rim moved her so. But that day on the ship had been filled with its own meaning, and although, according to Aidan, they were nearly married after he'd pledged himself to her, she wasn't quite ready to share the medallion with him, not yet. That all seemed so long ago now, but in reality, it had only been three days, days which felt like an entire lifetime. How else could she explain such a transformation in herself? How else was it that this medallion—a medallion that fate had almost literally handed to her, that she was sure was truly meant to be hers—had already slipped her mind? As she looked at it now, she marveled at how her focus had shifted so completely from her shiny (and very significant) object to Aidan, Kitty, and those around her. She placed it beneath the linens for now and then dumped the rest of the contents of her bag on the floor. Aidan had managed to grab a few of her things from the ship, but they were all wet. She did find a comb though, and Kitty's harness that she put by the hearth to dry. Charlotte said that she'd left some things for her to wear and took her clothing to launder. When Brianna hesitated, the woman patted her hand.

"We've known Aidan a long time, I promise to take great care of your things."

Brianna nearly teared up at her kindness and warmth. "They're only things. It's okay, I'm just a little turned around."

"Och sweet, you've surely been watched out for, he's good to the bone."

Brianna nodded, even more emotional now. "Thank you." The woman hugged her as if she could sense she could use it.

Since Aidan said he'd be a while, Brianna took her time bathing. The hot water felt so good, she soaked for what felt like ages and still had time to wash her hair before Aidan came up. The shift that had been laid out for her was plain but it was soft and fit her well. She'd just worked the comb through her hair and was knotting and pinning it up onto her head when Aidan rapped on the door and called her name.

"Come in," she said, her words muffled slightly as she spoke around the hairpins she held between her lips. She couldn't remember if she'd locked the door or not, and kept working at her hair as she made her way over. Aidan had just stepped inside as she was reaching for another pin, and when he spotted her, he stopped in his tracks. Brianna froze too, but she wasn't really sure why, other than a reaction to Aidan doing it first.

"Are you okay?" she said, finishing up with her hair.

"Breea...I...you..." She wasn't sure if he'd meant to call her Breea, or if it had happened inadvertently since he was clearly at a loss for words, emotional even, but she liked it. And seeing Aidan this way was certainly something. Not that Aidan was a cold man, far from it, really. Brianna knew that he felt deeply, but he was always so measured, always in control, even when he was furious. Something had shaken him, and she rushed over, truly concerned.

"Tell me," she said, placing her hand on his chest while reaching for his face.

He covered both of her hands with his own, staring down at her, a look of disbelief on his face. She waited for him to speak, but he just shook his head. He seemed so torn, like he was struggling with something, but then he wrapped her in his arms, and for a moment she forgot everything and just held him back.

"I have to go back," he finally said, rubbing his chin on her head before pulling away.

"I don't need more time," she blurted out, suddenly scared that if she didn't say it now, she might not have another chance. That there might not *be* another time. She'd already awoken to another fire and found herself in yet another churning sea...life was too precarious, too short to risk losing what fate and destiny had gone to great lengths (nearly unimaginable lengths) to provide for her.

"More time?" he said almost absentmindedly as he rubbed her arms.

She knew then he had to be overwhelmed with everything else, otherwise he wouldn't have had to ask. Brianna placed her hands on his chest and looked up at him. "Aidan...I want to be yours," she began, noticing how his focus sharpened as she stared into his eyes. "Until my last breath." They weren't the exact words he'd said to her that night on the ship, but she could tell he knew what she meant. His eyes closed and he bowed his head, and when he looked at her again, with such emotion, she knew that this was where she was meant to be. He drank in her entire face as his hands moved up her arms and over her shoulders, up until he grasped her head in his hands. Then he bent to brush his lips over hers. It felt so good, that first *real* touch, and she nudged him back, her hum vibrating between them. He pulled away, staring at her, shaking his head for a second, before he looked down at her lips, and swept his thumb across them. His grip tightened, tilting her head just so as he bent down and pressed his lips to hers again, so fully, so passionately, so desperately, that she was stunned by it. And then he was gone. She stood where he'd left her, staring at the closed door, her hand covering her lips as the feeling of his kiss lingered. She still didn't know what had happened, or what was bothering him, but she knew that Aidan was right, their marriage *would* fulfill the O'Roarke lore, she could feel it already.

CHAPTER 16

The sun was just beginning to rise when Aidan and Henry, made their way back to the harbor laden with supplies to appraise the damage. The smell of burned tinder wafted through the air, and when they reached the water, Aidan took in the remnants of the ship, somehow an even sadder display now after the fire was completely out than when he'd pulled Brianna from the deck only hours ago. Pushing those particular thoughts to the side for now, he focused on the task at hand, monumental as it was. It might take days before a full assessment could be made, but now, in the clear light of day, it appeared the ship might be a total loss. He'd decided he would give the news to Grey himself, which meant he and Brianna would be finishing their journey on horseback.

Aidan spent the remainder of the day with John, making arrangements to haul the ship to the dockyard for a full inspection. It was the captain's first major loss, and unsurprisingly, he was taking it hard, bearing the full responsibility of such a large number of men, and the exorbitant material cost. It gave Aidan no pleasure to see him like this, and so he was quick to remind him that other than a few minor injuries, no one had perished, and the ship, even favored as she was, was merely a vessel and could be rebuilt.

Still, something gnawed at the back of Aidan's sleep-deprived mind. It wasn't lost on him that they'd gained the ire of at least two men—the sailor and his father. He considered that the fire might have been set purposely. As he and the captain compiled a detailed account for Grey, they inspected what they could of the hull and decks and catalogued an inventory, paying particular attention to signs of foul play. It was a boon their other ship, which had initially been set to arrive later that day, had sailed into the harbor ahead of schedule. They'd be able to make good use of it housing their displaced sailors and considering how labor-intensive the coming days would no doubt prove, having the additional crew would be necessary. Alan and Richard, he'd heard, were none too happy when they spied the ship's condition. As Lachlan's men first, they'd seen him safely through his years, and after being charged with a 'whelp' as they called Aidan, times such as these might challenge their sound reputation. Their relief was noticeable when they spotted both he and Henry, hale and hearty. They took over questioning the remaining crew who might have seen something the night before that was significant only in hindsight.

By the time they'd had things sorted and the men disbursed to sup and sleep, it was dusk. They'd all only been abed for a few hours before being awoken in the wee hours to the fire, and that added to the long day that followed, meant that exhaustion would soon set in. Aidan could feel it himself already, but with the meager belongings he'd been able to recover from the ship, much of it still wet, salvaged from the debris, he also needed to make a few stops in town. They were in desperate need of supplies, too, even more so after the fire. Thankfully, his last planned stop was the bathhouse, as Aidan was eager to wash off the last remnants of soot and salt water. As he made his way back to his lodgings, he finally paid heed to his thoughts of Brianna. First and foremost, that he'd (unwittingly or not) somehow placed her in harm's way at nearly every turn—taking her aboard the ship, the sailor, the fire—it was a blow the likes of which he'd never before experienced. That *he* hadn't directly harmed her mattered little, for he still bore responsibility. It was not lost on him, either, that Esmeralda's warning seemed now *wholly* insufficient in light of the occurrences that transpired these past four—God help him—just *four* days!

He hoped that these four days had pacified the Fates and that he and Brianna could know some semblance of peace for the foreseeable future. Not that what was whirling around his mind, nor what he'd felt physically when he'd seen her the night before was exactly peaceful. That he'd secured only one room for them both hadn't been presumptuous, aye, they'd achieved a level of comfort with each other, but he'd selected these lodgings because he knew the owners personally. Adam had been a fierce warrior in his day, and in the years Aidan had been coming to Ayr, he'd become a good friend, too. He knew Brianna would be safe there. They only had one room, which they let out discriminately. In the chaos of the evening before, he hadn't thought to tell Brianna to consider the chambers hers alone, so when she'd bid him enter and greeted him as she had—with such easy familiarity, in her bedclothes, smiling around a mouthful of hairpins, her eyes dancing— he'd been so overcome by the sight of her, he'd nearly fallen to his knees. He couldn't even attribute it all to lust, though his attraction to her was undeniable. No, what struck him then was not passion-driven, but something more pure, something so overwhelming that he couldn't yet name.

When he arrived back at the small cottage, Adam and the men he'd enlisted for the day to watch over Brianna were outside, not so subtly engaged in a game of swordplay. Henry, Richard, and Alan gladly joined them. Once Aidan made his way inside, Charlotte greeted him with a smile.

"Ye were right, Aidan," she said, beaming as her boy reached for his bag, which held the garments he'd purchased for the morrow, and a few other strange items—trews made of some odd material and a knit shirt—he'd found tangled within Brianna's dresses and had plucked out just before they'd fallen into the laundress's hands. He smiled, and had he been less tired and a wee bit less apprehensive about the prospect of how Brianna might feel after a day to herself, mayhap spent brooding (not wrongly) about being in harm's way again, he might have chuckled.

Charlotte gave him a knowing look just as Brianna's head popped up from where she was sitting on the floor across the room, her smile wide, her eyes bright.

"Aidan!" she called, clearly well-rested. "I didn't even hear you come in." She jumped up and hurried over to him, reaching for his hands, nearly beside herself over whatever she was about to say. "Did you know Charlotte has the most beautiful collection of painted tiles from all over the world?"

Aye, he did, but Aidan mirrored her delight as if he hadn't a clue, pushing through his weariness, grateful she'd passed her day so happily. With her hands still gripping his, a grin still on her face, he felt the tension leave his body. Something must have shown on his face, however, because she furrowed her brow then, and looked at him closely.

"Are you alright?" she asked.

"Merely tired," he said, which was the truth. He was more weary than he could ever remember being.

Still, concern marred her features, and she motioned toward the stairs. "Why don't you get some sleep, I can stay down here."

He was shaking his head, thinking nay, he'd rather stay awake for hours than be without her, but the words wouldn't come forth. Still, she seemed to understand and told Charlotte that she'd come down for their dinner later. Then she took his hand, guiding him upstairs and into their room.

"Come, just rest," she said, telling him she'd managed to get a few hours of sleep already.

Aidan followed her to the bed, and when she climbed onto it and gestured him over to her, he couldn't get there fast enough. He laid his head in that spot just atop her chest and beneath her chin as their arms wound around each other, and he sank into her embrace, speaking softly as she asked him about the ship, Captain John, and the crew, all the while stroking her fingers through his hair. He fell asleep within moments, feeling her heartbeat, and inhaling her scent.

Sometime later, he awoke with a start, bolting upright, and scanning the empty room. He was in Ayr, at the lodge. Brianna. Where was she? Kitty was curled at the end of the bed. He'd slept deeply—judging from what he could see outside, the night would soon be upon them. He was about to go in search of Brianna when the door opened, and her silhouette appeared.

She smiled softly when she stepped into the room and saw he was up.

"It was getting late, and I didn't want to keep Charlotte up," she explained, lifting the tray she held, and motioning to Charlotte's son behind her who held another. "So, we brought up dinner."

Aye, he could see that. He watched as she showed the boy where to leave the trays, then pressed a coin into his hand, winking at Aidan as she did so. Aye, she was getting her land legs as well. While she fussed about the table, Aidan saw the boy out, then turned to Brianna again—*his wife*. The words rang in his head as if it just dawned on him.

She looked at him curiously. "Are you okay?"

"I'm suddenly reminded of the vows we made to one another—our marriage consent, church or no," he said.

He almost laughed at the look on her face. "Suddenly?" she said. "*You forgot?*"

It was the first true bright spot in a long, wearisome stretch and he felt his grin as he held her gaze, shaking his head. "Nay, Breea. I will never forget. Not the vows we made, nor one single moment we've shared since the very first. And if that," he said pointing at the table she'd set so beautifully for their supper, "tastes as delicious as it smells, it seems tonight's boons are indeed plentiful." Her eyes narrowed a fraction, and he laughed as he walked over to her. "'Tis no ploy. I did not forget."

"If you say so." She rolled her eyes.

He cupped her face, touching his lips to hers, nuzzling, just a wee bit before pulling back to look into her eyes. He'd woo her over supper and looked forward to each second, but for now…as he looked at her upturned face, her pretty blue eyes and those freckles spattered just so across the bridge of her nose, and her lips still slightly parted, he repeated, "I did not forget." Then he kissed her again, a slow drawing upon her lips, listening for her hums of pleasure and learning what she liked. Aye, he liked that too, and when he brushed across them again, he tugged with deliberation before changing direction, tilting her head back while deepening their kiss. When she made that sound again, a deep reverberation from her mouth to the base of her neck, it went right through him. His eyes shot open and he took a step back.

Brianna stared at him wide-eyed, with a breathless look he imagined mirrored his own.

"What happened?" she asked.

Such a simple question, yet he wasn't sure how to answer, rendered mute at how he'd reacted to her, and what really amounted to nothing more than mild (mayhap a tad more) kissing. Her look prompted an answer. However, his true reply, which would have been something such as *Your lips and the sound you just made...that vibration along the column of your neck, set me afire,* was a sentiment he was surely not sharing with her, especially the afire portion. What he said was, "I thought to have a small taste of you, Miss Brianna O'Roarke, and then sit to enjoy your company over this supper that truthfully, smells *utterly* divine."

"It is," she said dryly. Her flat affected tone belied the smile that tugged at the corner of her mouth. "I helped make it for you, Mr. Sinclair," she added, raising a brow.

Aidan struggled to keep his expression placid, too. In any other circumstance, he would have countered her retort and carried on what he sensed would fast become a verbal joust. However, this was no game. He wanted her. Not it. Still, he was curious. "What is it?" he asked.

"Coq au vin," she said, jutting out her chin.

She had him so engaged in this seemingly innocuous exchange that truly was anything but. "*Coca-what*," he said, his ever-increasing desire for her warring with his desire to match wits.

At his look, she said. "Chicken stew."

"Ah," he said. "Coq au vin sounds better. Will it keep?" he asked.

She smiled, breaking the ruse. "Aye."

At this, Aidan could hold back no longer. "I would have you now, Brianna O'Roarke."

"Then why are you still talking?" she said, taking a step toward him. "It *is* destiny, and we *are* married, are we not?"

He chuckled at her frustrated tone, but when he considered her comportment up to now, he was nearly convinced that his wife was as pure as the first snowfall. "This has been truly enjoyable, highly provocative even," he could tell she liked his praise. "But I find myself wondering about your experience."

"You...you want to hear about my *experience*..." she sputtered, clearly taken aback. She paused an overly long time before saying, "With..." her hand flung out, "doing..."

She couldn't even say the words, confirming he'd been correct. He chuckled, then shook his head at her look of embarrassment. "Nay." He pointed at her, and she froze in place, which was fascinating in itself, though he did not want her to feel ridiculed. "Tis not directed at you. You merely surprise me..." his words trailed off at her quick smile. "...at almost at every turn."

"Almost?" she said stepping even closer, her fingers lightly gliding across his arms.

Oh, to be sure, my Breea. Her controlled composure was fully back in place now, but he was not fooled. It was an air, and as he traced the side of her face, looking deeply into her eyes, he cared not. He knew that she would trust him in everything that was about to follow, and would look to him as her guide, so he would show her.

"You, Brianna O'Roarke are a riddle I'm unsure I'll ever completely solve, nor do I think I wish to," he said. "But I would swear to you again, I will honor and protect you until my last breath."

Whatever she'd found in his candor, his words pierced that shell of hers and he felt the change, he saw it in her eyes, now open and vulnerable, he felt it in her touch when her trembling hand covered his.

Gone was all trace of artifice, even in her tone when she whispered to him, "Show me."

"*Aye.*" He nodded, unsure if the word escaped his lips as he reached out to pull her into his arms, for the first time, feeling her entire body pressed to his from head to toe in anticipation. The sensation was so stimulating, that his own hands shook as he tilted her head back, and covered her lips with his, feasting on her mouth, for long minutes, yet he never felt sated. He could not touch her enough, could not hold her to the degree he needed, and when he finally pulled back to look at her, he knew that she felt it too.

His hands skimmed down her body to remove her outer dress but became lost as he gently caressed her through the garment, her soft hums of enjoyment sounding throughout, from the swell of her breasts to the backs of her thighs, and every dip, and curve, and slope, and crevice between. It was long minutes later that she'd lifted her arms for him so he could finally remove it while leaving her shift in place, and when she reached for his shirt, he was quick to oblige and threw it to the floor. He'd intended a night of slow, leisurely pleasure, awakening Brianna gradually to shared passion, but he had a feeling it would be anything but. He'd never been so desperate for a woman before. Needing a diversion from their bed, at least for a few minutes, his eyes bored into her, and her pulse beat wildly at the base of her neck in response, her breaths coming in quick bursts, which surely did not help.

His hand flattened against her chest, and he strode forward moving her with him, until her back was pressed to the wall. And when he gathered the hem of her shift, bunching it in his hands, as his fingers brushed passed her knees and then her thighs, stopping at her hips, she nearly swooned, or mayhap it was him that nearly swooned. He avoided touching her intimately just yet twisting the material from her shift around his hand, before bringing his fist up against the wall and pinning her securely in place. His eyes flared as she gasped, and when she started to pant, merely in anticipation, he nearly lost himself then and there. *Slow. Down. Aidan.*

He nudged her face with his, and when she tilted her head back and opened her mouth for him, begging for her need to somehow be satisfied, he did not hold back and kissed her deeply and wantonly, pressing his body to hers while pulling and suckling on her lips. She matched him move for move with her mouth, all the while scoring him with her nails, clutching him anywhere she could. He cupped her breast, pressing and fondling her as he kissed and nipped his way across her collarbone and the column of her neck, then lifted his head so he could gauge her reaction to his touch. The need and desperation on her face and in her eyes shook him in a way he'd never experienced before, and he wondered if he appeared just as desperate as she. He surely felt it, and took mercy on them both, gliding his hand down to cover her mound, groaning deeply as she pressed herself against him. Then she reached for his breeches and unfastened the ties to free him, his head fell back as she wrapped him in her hands. He grunted, taken aback by the sudden escalation, and especially Brianna's eager curiosity.

"Breea…" He barely heard his own voice. "Brianna."

She looked up then, her eyes wild from their fore-play, and for a moment he considered taking her now, here, but he could not take her against the wall. At least, not tonight. She was still staring at him when he told her to unhand his member, his trousers, or both so he could take them to bed.

She shook her head, her eyes growing even wider at his suggestion, and tightened her grip. "I can't let go," she whispered. Then she moaned as her head fell back against the wall.

Right, he hadn't let go either. His hand was fastened to her, clutching her possessively. When he chuckled, she did too, and they each drew in a much-needed breath. He took advantage of the moment and swept her off her feet before she knew what he was about and had them atop the bed in seconds. Stopping again only to discard the rest of their garments, he pulled her beside him and began touching her again, this time from head to toe, keeping watch for sensitive areas. His fingers spread her nether lips, gliding his hand from the entrance of her sex to her hooded bud, she moaned, pressed against him, and he nearly came undone. So close he feared he would not regain his control, he spread her wider even more, then teased his fingertips about her entrance to coat her exposed pleasure point with moisture, gliding over her, begging her release. He watched her reach the pinnacle, her breaths quickening, her hands grasping his arms, as she moaned.

"Breea," he breathed with her, adding more pressure to push her over the edge.

He was wound so taut he nearly exploded when she gasped his name but continued to caress her. Then she was reaching for him, motioning him to her, and he settled himself between her thighs, leaning his forehead to hers. "The last thing I want is to hurt you," he said, knowing that for a brief moment, he would. "Forgive me." Then he grasped her hips and thrust himself deeply inside.

She cried out, her hands digging into his shoulders, as she tried to push herself away.

"Be still, Breea," he begged, his firm grip keeping her in place. "I promise, this will quickly pass."

When she opened her eyes, she whispered, "It's already gone." Surprise was in her voice as the tension left her body.

He pressed his forehead to hers, kissing her as he braced his arms behind her. He watched her eyes widen in surprise as he slowly began to move inside of her, enjoying how she moaned from the pleasure of it. His expression mirrored hers as he quickened the pace, sinking deeper, and knew he was done. He forgot to breathe as he gave in to the intense pleasure of being surrounded by her, and thrust forward one last time, overcome in rapture as he released.

CHAPTER 17

Brianna awoke with a smile, humming quietly at the feeling of Aidan behind her, the weight of his hand covering her thigh possessively, even in his sleep. If she hadn't already, after last night, she considered herself lucky on all fronts that fate had chosen Aidan for her. She had a new appreciation for his all-business demeanor, too, especially now that she knew how his focus could be directed toward *that*. He'd been just as thoughtful and deliberate afterward, too, when he'd gone downstairs and returned with large pales of hot water and bathed her, which didn't bother her at all, considering how deep in each other's business they'd just been. Then they'd sat before the fireplace, eating Coq au vin, not caring that it was nearly cold, while Aidan sang her praises. And not just for the food. When he took her back to bed, he'd tucked her in his arms, and she fell asleep as he ran his fingers through her hair.

It had all been such an incredible experience, one

she never imagined, and, she shouldn't have to say, especially in the fifteenth century, but it was still difficult not to. It was true that she'd been taken with Aidan, fascinated even. He was strong and powerful, clearly intelligent and attuned to his environment, all of which were attractive qualities, even before you took his good looks into account. But last night, what she'd felt between them had been different. It was electric, the only word she could think of. Their chemistry seemed about to combust, and she'd found it impossible not to respond to him.

When she thought about all the moments that had led up to last night, most of which (or all) were significant in hindsight, not to mention intense, was it really any wonder? Brianna smiled, thinking about how even despite his initial doubts about her, she and Aidan had shared an easy rapport and camaraderie from the start. She remembered how their energy had been so surprising and refreshing, synergistic even, though now, looking back, she considered that maybe what was between them at the core *was* more innate. If they *were* fated, maybe that's just how it worked, naturally (or was it *un*naturally?). How else could she explain that in less than a week, she was waking in his arms, as his wife?

Brianna felt her cheeks heat just thinking about the way he'd touched and looked at her, but what surprised her most was that while it was happening, not once had she felt awkward or inexperienced even though she was, and he knew it. She'd only felt intense desire and intensely *desired*. She'd been so caught up in the moment, especially once she could feel his erection pressed against her, thick and throbbing, and filled with so much heat, she'd become desperate, frenzied even, reaching for him, touching him, holding him in her hands, which was crazily more thrilling, and more exciting than any artifact she'd held in her entire life.

Smiling at the thought, she stretched a bit, noticing how tender she felt in ways she certainly never had before. She'd been fully sated and well-loved, to be sure. At that thought, she paused, suddenly uncertain. She'd been well-loved but maybe not *loved*-loved. Aidan had certainly *tended* to her, and she knew he cared for her…or had he cared *after* her? She knew she mattered to him, so did it really matter whether or not what he actually felt for her was *love*? It only took a second to poke around with that thought to realize that, yes, it did. Brianna sat upright, not liking how she suddenly felt. Insecure. She may have only recently begun to re-embrace the idea of the O'Roarke wee bit of magic, but she'd always held dear the fact that all O'Roarke marriages were the products of true and enduring love. She looked over, and of course, Aidan was staring at her with the oddest look on his face.

"Breea, what is it?"

Well, she didn't want to say now.

"Did you have a bad dream? Did I hurt you?" He sat up and reached out so gently as if she suddenly might break.

She wasn't sure why she was filled with doubts all

of a sudden, but it was true that they'd never really spoken about their *feelings* or if they had any. Yes, he'd said they'd fulfill the lore, and yes, he treated her like she was special and showered her with praise. He even vowed to honor and protect her and see to her welfare, and she knew he meant it, but being destined or fated or whatever it was and then vowing to be together because of it, wasn't the same as realizing you liked someone, and pursuing the natural course of things from there. Not that she had ANY experience in any of that, destiny and fate aside, but still, beyond agreeing with her that he felt the magic too, which might have (for him) been about the physical, Aidan had never once said he liked her or cared for her, or verbally expressed having feelings for her. Just that she was pretty, or passing fair, which was basically the same difference, and supported the physical part, not the other.

She took a deep breath and turned to him. "I know this is going to sound silly, but...you're happy, right? Passably at least? I mean, I know we...I know it's because of *fate*," she did a little one-handed air quote thing, "but...happy is a good start, isn't it?"

While he gave her his full attention, he wore the look of someone trying to decipher another language. After a moment, he cocked his head to the side, still staring at her curiously. "What precisely do you wish to ask me? Please, be very clear."

Brianna took a breath. "Do you like me?" she asked, cringing inwardly, but she desperately needed to know.

His eyes narrowed, then he shot upright and pulled her close. "Brianna. You ask me this, in earnest?"

Brianna felt herself redden. Well, when he said it like *that,* it was kind of hard to believe. Still, she shrugged and nodded. Feelings aside, her reasoning was valid.

"Breea." He shook his head. "Have I given you cause to believe that I don't?"

"No. But that's my point. Here we are..." she trailed off and gestured to the tangled bedclothes, their intertwined limbs. "But are we here because we know that's what's expected of us? By fate or whatever? Would we be where we are now otherwise?"

Aidan shook his head. "Does that matter? In truth? These are not ordinary circumstances—as you know, better even than I."

Brianna nodded—he had a point. Though they'd never said it out loud, that she'd somehow landed here from the future was an unspoken constant between them. Still, she felt uncertain.

"And regardless," Aidan continued, "what we shared last night was true passion. We are rife with feelings, you and I...feelings that are new to both of us, just as we are new to each other..." He'd been tangling his fingers in her hair, but gently grasped her neck, bringing her a fraction closer to him. "Let us explore them, enjoy those feelings, let them happen, and grow as if we *hadn't* been drawn together by a prewritten plan. Aye?"

She felt his words move through her, scattering

her fears, and proving them to be unfounded. She
realized that Aidan had never given her a reason to
doubt anything, that fate had chosen so well for her.
At this thought, she smiled softly, and he did too.
Feeling happy and secure, she leaned forward and
brushed her lips to his. "Thank you," she whispered.
She was so grateful as she settled against him, that he
always knew just what to say to help her through
something or see it differently.

They lay that way for a few minutes in easy
silence, Aidan running his fingers through her hair
while Brianna closed her eyes, enjoying the sensation.
Then she felt him stiffen, his fingers suddenly frozen
in place. Confused, she looked up toward him just as
the oddest look crossed his face.

"Breea." The breath literally escaped him, and he
sat fully upright, taking her with him. His eyes fixed
on hers, staring so deeply, but she couldn't be sure
what had happened, what had struck him so suddenly,
until he tilted her head to the side ever so gently, and
pushed her hair over her shoulder as if to get a better
look at her neck. Then, it was Brianna who froze in
sudden realization as Aidan's fingers brushed over her
tattoo, and he whispered something, clearly to himself
since she was right there, and she couldn't make
it out.

"How do you have this marking?" he asked her, his
eyes darting quickly to hers, fingers now pressed into
the tattoo.

Instinctively, Brianna moved to cover the knot

with her hand, but her reach met Aidan's hand instead, and she rested hers on top of it.

"I saw it once," she said vaguely, suddenly feeling protective of it.

"*This* knot," he said, moving her hand to look again. She shivered as he brushed over her skin with his fingers. "You saw *this* specific knot—*this* circular symbol?"

She nodded, unsure where this intense surprise had come from. She'd thought at first that he was just shocked that she had a tattoo at all, but it didn't seem like he cared about the ink itself.

"Nay," Aidan said. "This knot is uniquely mine."

At this, Brianna's breath caught. She kept still, but her eyes darted to meet his. She'd always felt that this specific knot was *hers*. "What do you mean?" she whispered, unsure if she felt so weird because he was claiming it, a symbol that she'd never previously seen anywhere else in her entire life, or if because deep down, something was telling her that the knot being personal to them both was more significant than a simple appreciation for Celtic art.

"When Pembrooke was passed on to me, this symbol was created," Aidan said. "A braided thread was added around the knot that my brethren and I have shared for years as our symbol of loyalty to one another, making it mine, while still tied to them."

"That's where I saw it, Aidan. When my grandfather took me as a little girl." She could still remember tracing her fingers over the symbol, cut deeply into the stone.

KIM SAKWA

Brianna's heart started to beat wildly with all that this implied. "So…I didn't just permanently connect myself to Pembrooke, but to *you*? I did this years ago, the second I was old enough to get a tattoo—well before I knew you ever existed." Thinking back, she suddenly remembered the medallion. "Aidan…" She gasped and shook her head, then scooched from their bed, wrapping a blanket around her as she rushed over to her satchel.

"Brianna?"

She heard him call her name but was so singly focused on finding the medallion that she didn't reply. She reached inside her bag, then into the pocket hidden on the side. Finding it empty, she had a moment of panic before remembering that she'd taken it out of the wet bag the night they arrived. Looking around the room, she saw the stack of linens by the tub and rushed over, breathing a sigh of relief when she found the medallion hiding beneath it. She picked it up and held it to her chest, rubbing her fingers over the cool metal, feeling the etchings on its two sides under her fingers. It was in that moment that she had the sudden realization that it was the *medallion* (which she truly believed was always meant to be hers) that had brought her here and to Aidan. She would have never stepped (or, okay, fallen) into the tidepool otherwise. Anxious to finally show him what brought them together, she turned back toward the bed …and ran right into Aidan, who had come up close behind her. Seeing him in the clear light of day, bare-chested, with just a linen wrapped around his waist, looking so handsome and so formidable was a bit shocking if not distracting.

"What is it?" he asked, his eyes searching hers.

"I found something," she said, then slowly lowered her hands.

When she opened them, revealing the medallion, he went quiet as he stared at it, his fingers brushing over the symbol on one side, then turned it around and studied the bear on the other. When he looked at her, his eyes were filled with emotion.

"You found this?" he asked, his voice catching ever so slightly.

She nodded. "Yes." She hesitated, but then added, "At Abersoch. Look, it has the symbol, *your* symbol Aidan." She laughed and brushed her tattoo. "*My* symbol. And Aidan, it even has a bear on the other side." At this, she teared up. "My father's name was Arthur."

Aidan didn't need any further explanation. With even more emotion showing in his eyes, his head shook slightly as he traced the side of her face with his hand. "Arthur. Bear."

Brianna nodded, smiling through her tears. "Yes." She hesitated then, something tugged at her, something she should know, but in her excitement, she couldn't quite grasp what it was. Figuring it would come to her eventually, she showed him the rest of the medallion's details. "And, look, this knot around the rim..." She traced it with her finger. "It's an infinity knot, the endless knot. It's all connected, the things that have become our symbols."

He shared her awe, and grasped her head in his hands, kissing her forehead, before pulling back to look at her.

"Breea," he said, looking at her intently, "this...this medallion is mine."

"Yours?" She breathed. So many things were swirling in her head, and she suddenly remembered the thing she hadn't been able to a moment before. "Aidan...Aidan means bear, too."

He nodded. "Aye, my brethren and I each have a crest. This one, however, was forged by my mentor. I never thought to see it again—I dropped it weeks ago..."

They stared at each other, eyes widening at the same time, and not missing a beat, said together, "In the tide pool."

Something lit in his eyes then, and he dragged her in for a firm kiss. "Brianna," he said, once he'd pulled back, "you worry that what we...that —*this*," he said, motioning between them, "what we share is naught but an illusion because fate pushed us together, aye?"

She shrugged. "Maybe?" However, her feelings said differently. Feelings she couldn't deny having that were amazing and terrifying at the same time.

"What if it's nothing of the sort?" he said, his breathing ragged. "What if fate brought us together *because* we should be together? What if we would always have found one another..." He paused, then stated out loud what had never been said between them, "Had it not been for the centuries between us? What if you were supposed to be born here, in this time, to fulfill your destiny? I say fate did not bring us together now to fulfill its natural order, but to correct its mistake."

"And maybe that's why I was so drawn to Pembrooke, and to this specific symbol?" Brianna wanted to believe him so badly, it was the most incredible, romantic notion she could ever imagine, but...she felt herself hesitate, drifting off into a series of rationalizations that still failed to explain how she was here, in the fifteenth century, with a man she was sure she could love, and maybe did already. The weight of what finding herself in love would mean started to settle on her. If these were only the beginning hints of what she might feel for him, she wasn't sure there was enough magic anywhere that she could endure losing him, losing someone else.

Aidan gripped her by the shoulders—firmly, but not roughly. "Do not go behind your wall, please. I will not hurt you. I will not leave you. Ever."

She swallowed hard, feeling tears prickle, but held them back. While she knew her reasoning had been valid from the start, Aidan had hit on something far more profound. He pulled her into his arms, his lips pressed to her forehead.

"You are not alone anymore," he said. "You are Brianna O'Roarke, of the House of Pembrooke, by right and by marriage."

She fell in love with him a little bit then, or, if she was being honest with herself, a little more. He hadn't actually come out and said that he loved her, and come to think of it, he hadn't even said he liked her, but neither mattered anymore, especially since his actions spoke loud and clear. Aidan Sinclair got her in a way no one else ever had, and surely that counted for even more.

She pressed her hand to his chest, and stared deeply into his eyes, repeating his words, as if saying them aloud would seal her fate. "I am Brianna O'Roarke, of the House of Pembrooke, by right and by marriage."

"Aye," he breathed, so moved, he grasped her head and covered her lips with his.

She clung to him, kissing him back, wanting to believe it with everything in her being. She hummed, and when he answered with his own, she felt it rumble deep in his chest.

His hands slid down, and when he lifted her, she wrapped her legs around his waist and continued to kiss him as he carried her back to bed. She almost asked him to make love to her, but stopped herself, wondering what she should say, or how.

When he drew back and looked at her, he must have read something there. "I beg of you, lay your worries aside."

Since he'd already gone so far to allay them all, at least for now, technically she wasn't worried, but she still felt herself blush as she nudged his lips with hers, and whispered against them, "I was wondering how to ask you to make love to me without naming it so."

If his grunt was an indication, she guessed he knew what she meant, and a moment later, it became clear that he did, when he covered her mouth and kissed her, deftly settling her beneath him. Then he pulled back and stared down at her for a moment.

"When I look at you, Brianna, and when I hold you..." his next words were whisper soft, "like this..." he pulled her closer before continuing, "or when I'm granted a mere touch in passing, I have never once, felt *this* sensation that I feel with you, not once. I've yet to name it, for I've never known it ... but there is no doubt in my mind that *love* is precisely what we have between us, and what we are making here."

At this, her heart turned over, and her hands framed his face, this beautiful man who had never once failed to show her in word and deed his reverence for her. Her words were whisper soft too. "So, it would be alright to ask you to make love to me directly, then?"

"'Tis required."

Brianna felt the last of her defenses give way. Whether fate had brought her where she was supposed to be, or to where she should have been all along, it almost didn't matter. She just knew that there was nothing for her to fear anymore. "Will you make love to me, Aidan?"

"With everything that I have, Brianna...and with all that I am".

CHAPTER 18

There was little in Aidan's life that had ever made him feel truly encumbered, not family responsibilities, not stepping into Lachlan's shoes (and thus ceding his birthright to his brother Rhys), nor even the magnitude of finishing the construction of Abersoch. Truthfully, he'd been content with his life up to that point and had felt quite in control. And, despite all that had befallen him these past days (including the very real possibility that his foes, whomever they might be, could strike again at any minute), neither did he feel encumbered now. He found that rather curious and wondered how that was even possible. He'd gained a wife, a companion who was and had been from the start, a constant in his mind and for the most part at his side, and yet, if pressed, he'd say he was content, and without a doubt, in control. To be sure, Brianna required some extra care and concern, but surely the vast changes she'd endured were deserving of such. Giving Brianna the attention she currently required, was a privilege, and there truly was no place he would rather be.

If not for the underlying sense of urgency to return to Seagrave, so he could deal with the Fitzgeralds once and for all, now compounded by the fire and delivering the news to Grey, Aidan would have gladly stayed abed with Brianna all day. He'd have been happy, too, just walking about town, sitting beside her by the sea, or any number of things she wanted, just as long as it was with her. Though he'd begun to sense it on the ship, the feelings he had for Brianna had grown and continued to do so with each passing moment. He wondered if they might level off at some point, stop compounding one day, and felt a flash of alarm when he considered the magnitudes of despair his brethren had been subjected to. It was necessary to remain aware of such possibilities, but he need not give sway to such worries. He was well-prepared to see to Brianna's safety and taking measures to fortify their means still more before leaving.

Though he was loath to end their time in Ayr, making haste was of the essence. After they'd packed up what was left of their belongings, he'd watched Brianna say goodbye to their hosts, extending her gratitude for their care, then staring wistfully at the cottage as if committing it to memory, just as she'd done at Abersoch. "We'll visit again," he'd told her, squeezing her hand, and not letting go.

He kept her close as they walked to town. She was quiet beside him, and seemed content, petting Kitty and looking about. When she craned her neck for the third time, he turned to follow her line of sight, wondering if she sensed something he had not.

"Is everything alright?" she asked. "Are you looking for something?"

That she asked this as if her own behavior hadn't caused his hackles to rise was rather brash, Aidan thought. "I'm wondering what has *your* attention," he said, "and frankly, if it should have mine as well." Vigilant as he'd been—and even more so after the fire that he and his men had concluded was most likely no accident—her watchfulness gave him pause.

She smiled and tilted her head to the side, shielding her eyes from the sun. "Sorry. It's just that I haven't seen Henry. Or Alan or Richard?"

Ah. Now he understood. For a moment he thought he'd lost his edge and there had been a true threat he'd not noticed. "They're close by, just giving us a bit of breadth."

He watched her turn, scanning the area. "Are you sure? I don't see them anywhere."

He chuckled. "Never more, trust me." They'd bedded down just outside the cottage, keeping in clear view lest anyone think to cause mayhem. He whistled then, and they showed themselves, obviously close enough that they'd heard Brianna's concern since it was she they all looked to.

She beamed at them, as she rubbed his arm, and said, "I do trust you, really. I was just a bit stumped since they've been so present up to now."

He'd just made eye contact with the men himself

when Brianna's words sank in. She'd said them so easily, so casually, but the significance was profound. He stood a bit taller even, his chest expanded too, for he had truly earned the honor of her trust. Smiling like a sotted fool, he took her hand, "Come," he said leading her to the tanner's.

The tanner, whose services Aidan had availed of several times in the past, waved when he saw him approaching, then held up one finger before disappearing into his shop. A moment later, he reappeared, and Aidan held back a chuckle at Brianna's gasp when she saw his arms laden with the rest of their bags—the ones he knew she had given up as lost in the harbor for good.

"Oh, Aidan, how...?" she said before dashing over to the tanner, and running her hands first over the leather case Isabelle had given her. Aidan was glad to see that all of their bags had been mended, the leather returned to its previous luster, not that he'd had any real doubt in the tanner's skill. He'd also purchased two more bags needed for their journey and a few other surprise items he had yet to pick up.

The man dropped the iron stamp bearing Pembrooke's seal in Aidan's hand, then showed them the mark he'd branded inside all the bags, including the new ones. When Brianna saw that it was their symbol, she gasped again, and glanced at him, her eyes dancing in delight. When Aidan pointed to her bag, thinking they should mark that one as well, she shook her head and opened it showing him that it was already there.

He reached out, brushing her hair from her neck, then leaned down to whisper into her ear, "Because you belong here."

While Aidan paid the man, Brianna started to gather their purchases while praising the man's work and thanking him.

Aidan deftly took the packages from Brianna, tucked them beneath his arm, and led her away to their next stop. She was so busy talking as they walked to the tailors that she didn't realize where they were until they'd stepped inside. Once she looked around, her eyes lit up.

"Oooh," she said, and Aidan chuckled not at all surprised by her delight. While the fair had an abundance of nice wares and expensive fabrics, none rivaled this particular establishment. Brianna gasped again when he pressed more than a few pieces of silver in the owner's hand. Then her mouth nearly hit the floor when the tailor nodded and set the wrapped packages before them.

"What did you get?" she asked excitedly.

In lieu of a response, Aidan winked, then set the new bags from the tanner on the table, ready to be filled.

While the tailor opened the first wrapped package, Brianna gasped again.

"For me?" she breathed, as she reached out, examining the garments he'd had made for her. "How did you… I still have a few things, but you lost nearly everything."

"We're both in need."

Then she saw her gown, the only other garment he'd been able to salvage, and which the tailor had used to gather her measurements. She was admiring her new shifts, and dresses, and his new garments as well. "These are lovely," she said, first to the tailor who beamed, and then to him. She turned just as Aidan was donning his new cloak, and her eyes went wide again. "Oooh," she exclaimed, then reached up to smooth the material over his shoulders.

He gave her a quick kiss, then reached for the last package and handed it to her.

"What's this?" she asked, looking at him curiously.

"Mayhap you should open it."

She looked between him and the bundle so many times, he wasn't sure what to make of her hesitancy. Finally, she unwrapped the brown cloth to reveal the garment underneath, and her look was priceless. You'd think he'd given her a trunk full of jewels by it.

"Aidan!" she cried before she even unfolded it all the way. "My very own cloak? And it matches yours?"

He nodded, smiling broadly now. "You'll have more for the seasons, but this one should get us home." That their cloaks matched was simply because the color made it easy to blend in, but he enjoyed Brianna's delight in it just the same.

Just now, Henry was picking up the clasp he'd had specially made for her cloak at the blacksmiths, and he couldn't wait to give it to her.

She was so excited and animated, that she didn't notice that when they left the tailor's, he was leading her to the shoemaker. Outside the door, she stopped short.

"What's this for?" she asked.

"You're in need of boots."

"I have boots."

"'Tis riding boots you need, love," the word slipped out and although their eyes met, the significance was clearly at his ease and use of an endearment. Still, in light of their earlier discussion, it was a welcome slip to them both.

After helping her out of her ankle boots and into the new tall riding pair, he waited as she walked a few paces, to and fro. "Aye? 'Tis a good fit?"

"Yes," she said, looking at him curiously. "They're very good. How did you know my size?"

He held up his hand. "Your wee foot fits right here, like so," he said tracing the path with a finger, just as he had done when they were aboard the ship and she'd tucked her feet up beside him that day they'd played games and conversed for so many hours.

She smiled and hugged him, trying to be quick, but he held her there, in no rush, then tilted her head back and kissed her.

"One more stop," he said.

"Good lord, Aidan Sinclair, what now!" she said, shaking her head and laughing.

The apothecary already had their items ready, necessary supplies to replace those that Gwen had carefully selected and were now lost to the sea. At the least, a good needle and thread along with a few herbs for poultices would get them to Seagrave where Gwen would be able to properly equip them again.

"Right," he said, adjusting her cloak about her shoulders, their errands finally complete. "Let's get some horses for the journey, check on your mare, and be on our way."

Glenn was waiting for them when they arrived at the stables. He had a good selection prepared, and brought out a few he thought would suit. After looking them over, Adian nodded to the pair he'd chosen.

"Ye made a sound choice. Yer men too," Glenn told him, pointing to the horses the others had chosen.

"What do you think?" Aidan said, turning to ask Brianna. When he did so, he discovered she was no longer at his side. He worried for a moment before spotting her over by her mare. "Breea." He motioned with his head, *here. Come back.*

Mouth set, she shook her head, hair fluttering. He knew she intended to take the mare along with them, and he wasn't sure how to argue in the face of her determination or honestly if he even wanted to. When he crooked a finger, she shook her head again, darting her finger, arrow-like, toward her mare. He would gladly have her take the mare, save the very real fact that the mare might not make the journey, not in her current condition. He sighed, not looking forward to disappointing her. She must have realized his intent, since her face fell as he approached her, and he took her hands. "I know you want to bring her with us. I fear she won't make it."

"I think she will, Aidan. Please. I won't be riding her," she stressed. "The other you chose for me will suit just fine."

He closed his eyes, knowing he shouldn't even entertain the idea, yet he bent his head to hers, and whispered, "Let me look her over." She nodded, and he could see her struggle to control her emotions. "If not today, I'll send for her after she's had time to regain her strength."

Brianna squeezed his hands, but kept her expression neutral now, trusting he would keep his word and allowed him to inspect the mare more carefully.

He approached the mare slowly and was surprised when she didn't shy away. If he wasn't mistaken, she actually tried to stand tall. Hard not to admire. "Good girl," he said, using sure strokes to comfort her and feel for lame or tender spots. It seemed impossible she didn't have one, yet he could find none. Aidan half wondered if she was somehow holding back, so she could make the trip with them. He waved Glenn over, and after a few minutes, Aidan asked Brianna to join them.

"I believe you're correct in that she can make the journey, but this decision must be yours. If there's trouble, she may not be able to keep pace, and we may not have the luxury of finding shelter for her."

Her face set determinedly as he spoke. "I won't leave her behind. She'll come with us, *and* keep pace, I know it as surely as I know I'm to make this same journey with you. She's had a few setbacks, but she belongs, Aidan, just as much as I do. She has the strength for it."

Aye, based on Brianna's impassioned declaration, he had no doubt, and no desire to contradict her further. So, he just nodded, then framed her face, and bent to press his lips to hers. Then, he fished out a saddle blanket from his bag. "Then we have to get her accustomed to this first."

Brianna nodded, and her shoulders relaxed as the remaining tension left her body. She helped him secure the blanket around the horse before leading the mare out of the stables, to the area where his men were waiting, arming themselves with the weapons they'd gathered from the forgery earlier.

"Are we expecting trouble?" Brianna asked as she watched them.

His men looked to Aidan to answer her as they secured their scabbards and swords.

"While I have sway throughout most parts of Scotland, and some distance beyond our borders," he said, leaving off that it was very possible that they'd encounter a threat his influence wouldn't quell. He continued, choosing his words carefully, "Not drawing attention is always best."

In answer, she raised the hood of her cloak.

"Precisely," he said. "However, now that we're leaving the burgh and traveling such a fair distance across the land, ensuring our safety rests solely in my hands."

While they divvied the quivers and bows, and a

few extra daggers, Henry unrolled a cloth to unveil the last of their weaponry.

"Oh, those are nice," Brianna said, eyeing the set of daggers.

"We're pleased you like them, they're yours," Henry told her.

"Really?" She looked at him then, and he saw realization pass through her gaze. Mayhap this was the first time she understood that something of visual appeal also had a more vital purpose.

"Aye." He attached a scabbard to her belt and another around her calf. She appeared hesitant at first, yet when he asked her to reach for it, the quickness and agility with which she moved made it clear that she had handled a dagger before. How shrewd of her, and how shortsighted of him to mistake her pause for reluctance to wear the weapon, and not see it for what it was—a calculated appraisal that revealed her proficiency. Once he adjusted its placement, she reached for it again, nodding soberly to confirm it was placed correctly.

"Come," he said taking her hand.

"Where are we going?" she whispered.

He grabbed the pouch Henry had picked up from the jewelers as they passed him, stopping just beyond a nearby copse of trees.

"I wanted a bit of privacy, to give you this," he said, placing the pouch in her hand. "And no, 'tis not another weapon. Though you'll have your own in time, crafted just for your proportions, of course."

Her eyes widened briefly as she looked at him,

weighing it with her hand. "What is it?" she asked, curious but again hesitant to open something.

"A gift."

"You got me a gift?"

Aidan shook his head in wonder. He'd never known someone so seemingly unaccustomed to being taken care of. At her continued disbelief, he chuckled and nodded toward the pouch.

"But you've given me so much already," she said, still protesting. "You spent the entire morning, showering me with all kinds of things."

"Necessities."

She shook her head. "Aidan, what you call necessities, to me feels like so much more."

"Have I ever told you that I was a patient man?"

She nodded. "You did...on the ship."

"Ah." He smiled. "'Twas once true, then."

She laughed, her eyes bright again, which had the most magnificent effect on him. She finally untied the ribbon and opened the small parcel. When she saw what was inside, her eyes darted to his. "Aidan." She gasped as he helped her remove the clasp he'd had forged for her. "It's beautiful."

"As are you," he said, taking it from her and attaching it to her cloak. "I had this made to symbolize our union. Our shared symbol united by a braided chain.

She covered his hand. "An endless knot."

He looked at her and nodded. "Aye, we are bound for, and throughout, eternity," he breathed, cupping the back of her head to kiss her. Feeling how delicate she was beneath his hands, he became serious again, and pulled back to look at her, choosing his words carefully. "I don't expect it," he began, "but if there's need, do not hesitate to use your weapons, unlikely a case as it might be."

It was not a complete falsehood—Aidan did not fear a threat was fully imminent, but he would not be a fool in thinking there wasn't some possibility.

She straightened, her next words delivered plainly, with no trace of a boast. "Well, I won more awards in archery, but I can throw a dagger, too. Lessons care of my grandfather."

She had been prepared well, but if she had to fight on this journey, it would not be for sport. "When you're defending yourself, it may feel different."

She nodded gravely. "I hope I don't find out, but you can be sure that I won't hesitate."

They were on their way a short time later, but just before they lost sight of the town, Aidan made a point to stop, allowing Brianna a turn to say her goodbyes. When she'd had her fill, she nodded in his direction, then pulled her mount around and carried on. They stopped twice more that day, once for a brief respite, and another to water the horses. Neither had been prompted by Brianna and though she took advantage of each, dusk was full upon them by the time they stopped for the night.

Brianna's mare, who was attached to Aidan's horse by a lead, appeared to do fine throughout the day, though Aidan knew he'd need to check her thoroughly, as she was certainly quite weak. He was surprised to see that she'd fared so well, especially considering their pace. Brianna, however, was not surprised at all.

Once he'd dismounted, Aidan noticed that Brianna was still atop her horse.

"Do you need help?" he asked. He had to admit that his wife was an excellent rider, but it had been a long day.

The corners of her mouth turned upward. "I think I do. I loved riding today, but I'm not sure I can swing my leg up over the saddle right now." She laughed as he reached for her, and once he'd lifted her clear, she wrapped her arms around his neck. He closed his eyes, surprised by the gesture. Not that they hadn't been openly affectionate, he'd merely been caught unawares by the sudden casual intimacy and took full advantage now to hold her tight for a long moment.

After he was sure she could stand, he helped her remove Kitty from her sling and gathered their bags. "Let me check on your mare, then we can wash up."

"I would love that, too! Except…does that require walking?"

He chuckled, and after turning their horses over to Henry and checking on Brianna's mare once more, he tried to carry her, but she insisted on walking herself. Then, after giving her some privacy, she joined him for a quick wash in the stream.

"I'd give you the brightest smile," she said when he handed her a small tin of scented soap. "But I'm suddenly so tired."

Finally, something that didn't surprise him. She

should be exhausted. "I'll imagine it then," he said, lifting a few strands of her hair that had fallen loose of their knot while she washed her face. "Here," he said, reaching for the soap, when she finished, then motioned for her to turn.

"Bless you," she breathed, humming as he washed her neck and back, gently kneading her muscles. "How are your legs?"

"Sore, but I'm sure by morning...or at least *a* morning in the near future they'll be better," she said, turning back to him.

He chuckled. "I'll make them better shortly." At her deep blush, he added, "I meant I'll rub them for you."

She shook her head, eyes gleaming. "Not better, Aidan Sinclair, but I like the way you're thinking."

He laughed, unsure he'd ever been so completely happy in his life.

CHAPTER 19

When Brianna awoke the next morning, it was still quite dark. She felt around the makeshift bed that Aidan had made by some stroke of genius the night before, set up in a soft grassy spot, adding a bit of cushion beneath them. It was surprisingly comfortable—or had been while he was next to her. Realizing Aidan was already up and gone, Kitty too, Brianna sat up and noticed it wasn't quite as early as she'd thought. A soft predawn glow lit the horizon, and she scanned the area where they'd made camp, stopping when her eyes met his. Her smile was instant, and she could feel the warmth in his eyes even from here. He was standing by the fire, Kitty in the sling, which he'd draped over his shoulder. *God, she loved that man.* Gaping at the realization, of how it had come so naturally, she covered her mouth with her hands. Aidan's head cocked to the side as he looked at her curiously. Yes, her feelings were quickly growing, but the way it hit her today was startling. Good, but startling. Brianna 2.0 had evolved way beyond her expectations, not that she'd really had any to begin with.

She stood, wrapping one of their blankets around her shoulders, and grabbed the dagger Aidan left within her reach, securing the scabbard around her calf. Then she slipped on her fur-lined boots, which he'd thoughtfully placed beside the bed before making her way over to him. He had a steaming beverage in one hand and pulled her in close with the other. He kissed her forehead. "For you," he said and pressed a cup of tea in her hand.

Brianna took the mug gratefully. "You know you're on my short list."

He winked, seeming to understand what she meant. "I'm no fool, Breea, and haven't a care *where* I place in your pecking order. I'm merely glad to have made your *list*."

She was a little undone by his reply. Sure, she enjoyed feeling witty—and, shockingly, *being* witty with him—but he had to know, he *was* the list. She took a sip, humming in pleasure before burrowing against him, loving how the weight of his head felt atop hers. "You sure know how to make a girl happy."

He pulled back, lifting her chin. "'Tis only your happiness that concerns me." When she blushed, thinking of the ways he had surely done that, he chuckled. "I was speaking in general."

She shrugged, then smiled coyly, something she was getting more used to, petting Kitty from her perch.

"How are your legs?" he asked her.

"Aidan," she whispered. "Shhh."

His innocent massage last night had been anything but. Maybe it had started out that way—after he'd gotten her comfortable, he'd sat at her feet and began rubbing her aches away. How he'd found each and every muscle that needed attention was impressive, but at some point, his intentions had shifted to something more amorous. She knew she was partly to blame, and it probably hadn't helped that she'd moaned and squirmed the entire time. Aidan had been gentle but diligent, hitting everything from her toes to her glutes, but then he'd retraced his path, using his lips. He told her how fair her skin was, and she knew he didn't mean she was prone to sunburn (though she was), but that he thought she was beautiful. The way he flattered her so easily, so naturally, was romantic, and she totally had a thing for his fifteenth-century vocabulary. When he began kissing her inner thighs, she'd nearly jumped out of her skin, and then he'd shimmied her shift, the only thing she had on, above her waist, cupping her bottom in his hands. She'd held her breath, wondering what sort of pleasure she might be in store for, and then she wasn't able to wonder anything coherently at all because he had her writhing and whimpering until she'd cried out his name. When she reached for him, desperate to feel him inside of her, she heard his breath catch as he sank in deep and stilled for a long moment. It was the most incredible sensation, and her legs, which by that point were working just fine, had wrapped around his waist, and this time when he began to move, she'd met him thrust for thrust. Her nails had scored his scalp and his shoulders as he rode her, hard and fast. The pleasure was so intense, it nearly overwhelmed her, and when he released just moments later, she found that equally gratifying. Truly, it was an amazing end to an incredible day.

She looked at him now, smiling and shaking his head, obviously aware of what she'd been recalling.

"Breea." When he pointed at her, chastising yes, but teasing her too, all she could do was shrug and bite her bottom lip. "*Breea*, I beg you. Cease." He said, reading her clearly.

She spun around to compose herself for a second or ten, then turned back to him again. "Sorry."

"Don't be," he said with a chuckle. "I look forward to having you again later, truly. We just haven't the luxury now."

"Anyway," she said, pasting on a serious look. "My legs feel fine."

He gripped the back of her head and dragged her in so he could kiss her soundly. "Aye, they do."

So much for her all-business approach, not that she was complaining, not one bit. She'd never realized how much she would enjoy this kind of attentive affection and was happy, maybe even relieved, that Aidan seemed to give it so easily. He took such good care of her, looking after her in every sense. It wasn't lost on her that this was all just the beginning. She thought about it, how or what that might look like in the very near future, to be living together at

Pembrooke. Would he be home all the time? Would he have to travel? Would she go with him? Would they have children? Would it matter to him whether they were boys or girls? When she glanced over at him, her eyes met his—he'd been looking at her curiously again, which wasn't all that surprising since that was usually how he looked at her.

She took another bite of the sandwich he'd given her when he'd sat her down with Kitty. When he'd first offered it to her, she'd been taken aback. Not that anything seemed wrong with it, but it clearly *was* a sandwich, appearing in the fifteenth century well before its time, so she just hadn't expected it. She wasn't sure what was in it, but the bread was a soft grainy roll, and whatever was inside was the perfect combination of sweet and salty with a hint of spice, and just plain delicious.

"Did you make this?" she asked, and her voice cracked slightly, as Brianna was surprised by a swell of emotion.

"Are you unwell?" Aidan asked. He had the oddest look on his face, though, again, that wasn't altogether alarming. "Breea?"

The sandwich was just really so good and had been prepared almost daintily, clearly made with such care. That he'd done this for her when she was certain he'd have been content with a hunk of torn bread and a few course wedges of cheese overwhelmed her. She took another nibble, trying to figure out exactly what was in it. When she finished chewing, she asked again, "*Did* you make this?"

Aidan nodded. "Aye, just before you awoke."

Gaping again, she just looked at him in awe, shaking her head. Aidan reached for the sandwich then, and she pulled it to her chest, swatting his hand away.

"Is it bad?" he asked, clearly having gotten the wrong impression.

"Bad?" she croaked, shaking her head in wonder. It was delicious. The roll wasn't too hard or crusty, and it wasn't too cumbersome to take a bite. She opened the pocket he'd sliced into the small loaf and saw thin slices of apples and cheese evenly layered and…and… "Is this *fig*?" she asked.

"Aye, a spread."

"You brought a *spread*?" she cried.

His brows furrowed. "Nay, only figs."

Well, he certainly hadn't thrown it together, that's for sure.

"Breea?"

Brianna held up her hand and shook her head again, then turned to the side, looking away. She just needed a moment to compose herself, which wasn't so easy to do when he was watching her so closely. After she'd managed a breath, she gave him a lopsided smile, then pressed the roll back together and took another small bite. "It's just *really* good, Aidan."

He seemed to understand then that she just appreciated his attention to detail, and gave her a quick nod, before going back to breaking down their camp.

This was merely the beginning of a pattern that continued for the next several days, with Aidan seeing after her, her mare, *and* Kitty with the utmost care. Even his men were considerate, and still all the while so diligent in their duties, foremost of which she now realized was providing protection for Aidan, and now for her. Brianna tried to make herself useful as much as possible, always asking if and how she might help, but it appeared they had a system of sorts and were simply happy to have her along. Aidan's men had also been giving them a bit more breadth at times, especially once they'd made camp for the night, and after securing the perimeter. The same was true for most mornings until they set off again for the day.

It seemed impossible (though she shouldn't be surprised by what was possible anymore), but so far, every day she'd spent with Aidan was equally exciting and overwhelming—Brianna was sometimes almost frightened by the intensity of these new and budding feelings and emotions. It seemed like a whole new world had opened up for her. Before Aidan, she'd been so singularly focused on the *things* around her. And while she still took time to commit certain sights to memory, the objects, structures, and even the places now ranked far below her concern for Aidan, Kitty, her mare, and even Aidan's men.

She'd been so sheltered, or maybe just so shut off for years, that Brianna was surprised she loved touching and being touched so much. Sexually, sure, that was entirely brand new to her, but really, she just craved Aidan's physical contact. It was incredible that she could just reach out as he passed and feel her fingers brush his shoulder, hold his hand, kiss him, even just press her lips to whatever part of him was in reach, be it his back or his arm, or rub her face against his chest when he held her at night. It seemed that now she'd been awakened to the pleasure of touch, she couldn't get enough. She'd been so tired the last few evenings, that after they'd washed up in a nearby stream, Aidan literally rubbed her to sleep, sensing her exhaustion. She'd been sure to wake up extra early to catch him before he left their bedroll. At first, she worried she'd miss him, but after he'd made love to her, he confessed that he lingered, waiting for her to stir.

"If you feel but a fraction of what I do…leaving our bed without looking into your eyes…without touching you…holding you…without losing myself *in* you…'tis nearly impossible. So, waiting for you to stir is no hardship, Brianna."

Swoonfest!

With so much to focus on once they began riding for the day, it was usually during these predawn hours, still lying in his arms that Brianna wondered about their life at Pembrooke.

"Aidan?" she asked one morning about a week into their journey.

"Aye," he whispered, still quiet, and rubbing her back.

"You want children, yes?"

He grunted, pulling her closer. "I desire a keepful of bairns, with you, Breea. With eyes blue like a starlit sky and hair as smooth as a glassy lake."

She chuckled and was about to confess her days of

smooth and straight hair would soon be abruptly coming to an end, but he rolled her beneath him, eyes shining. "In the quest to carry out our legacy for the house of Pembrooke, we need to be diligent."

"Well, when you put it like that it seems rather necessary," Brianna said, grinning.

He made love to her again, and Brianna was sure that it *was* love, if the depth of emotion in his eyes and the reverence of his touch was any indication.

They quietly made their way back to the stream afterward and washed before breakfast.

"Ready?" he asked, once she'd dressed, making sure that her daggers, which he had insisted she wear daily, were tightly secured.

When she nodded, he said, "You're in for a treat today."

"Aidan Sinclair." Brianna shook her head, enjoying their easy banter. "Don't you know? Every day has been a treat."

He liked that, and made a point of showing her his appreciation with a kiss. When he pulled back, he stared into her eyes, and said, "I can't wait to get you home, lass."

Once he'd spoken the words, Brianna noticed something cross his features, worry perhaps.

"I didn't jinx us, did I," she joked. It was only when she saw something flare in Aidan's eyes that she understood she was making light of something that carried real weight. Despite everything, Brianna realized she'd still been seeing things through the lens of a historian—she still, for the most part, had felt removed from the actual consequences of living in the past. But that look in Aidan's eyes shocked her into her current reality. The observer perspective wouldn't work anymore. While it had to be true that jinxes and spells in the fifteenth century probably had a different connotation than where she came from, in light of her journey to this century, she couldn't downplay it either.

"Nay," he said, then gave her an unconvincing smile.

Brianna cringed inwardly. What if she *had* jinxed them? Or something worse?

"Breea?"

She sighed. "Sorry. I just," she reached for his hands, "You don't think we're..." she looked around. Even though the rest of their party was well out of earshot, she still leaned in close and whispered, "You don't think we're cursed or something, do you?"

Mercifully, Aidan didn't even flinch. "Nay, not at least for you simply saying you've enjoyed our days together. Nor my wish for us to be at Pembrooke and start our lives anew."

While his reply didn't quite assure her that jinxes and curses were impossible, Brianna decided not to press it any further. She could tell Aidan was anxious to keep moving, and not because he believed they could be jinxed or cursed or that the end of this journey meant the end of their troubles. But she couldn't quell the feeling that something was preoccupying him. Whatever it was, she decided, that she'd trust him to tell her if and when he felt it was necessary.

So far, he'd never rushed her on any of their mornings, and even though the few people they'd happened upon along the way all had been familiar to Aidan and his men, she sensed traveling out in the open like this wasn't his first choice. They were armed, sure, but she was certain he'd chosen their path based on the quickest and safest route possible with her, Kitty, and her mare in tow. Still, something about their conversation made her look at things differently, with a bit more caution. This feeling stayed with her as they returned to their camp and joined Aidan's men for a quick breakfast before getting ready to set off for the day.

While Aidan and his men finished breaking down their camp, Brianna checked in on her mare as she did every morning. And, like she did every morning, she marveled at how much the horse had improved.

"You just needed someone to trust, didn't you?" Brianna cooed and stroked her snout. Her mare (Brianna had yet to come up with just the right name) neighed and pressed against her hand. "I know, I'm feeling rather sure of myself, too."

"As you should be."

Brianna startled for a second but relaxed almost instantly as Aidan came up beside her. After looking the mare over, too, he gave a nod and addressed the horse. "My wife was right, Merri. I'm pleased to see how you've fared. You'll flourish at home, sweet, just wait." He turned to Brianna then. "Would you like to lead her today?"

Brianna nodded, surprised at the offer, but knew it was because they'd both won his trust. Then, something else struck her. "Did you call her Merri?"

"Aye." He winked at her. "You've got your kitty, Kitty, and now you have your mare, Merri." He bent to kiss her. "The dragons will have to wait."

"*Dragons*?" she said, a half-smile on her face, trying to figure out what he meant.

"Breea, we're speaking of the House of Pembrooke," he said, looking aghast. "You think a House as powerful as Pembrooke wouldn't have *dragons*?" He leveled her with a serious gaze that he managed to keep for just a few seconds before he chuckled, pulling her close, still laughing against her lips as he kissed her.

It was then Brianna remembered her earlier comment about releasing the dragons and laughed, too, blushing both because Aidan had remembered— and because she'd almost—*almost*—truly wondered if he'd been telling her the truth.

Yeah, Aidan definitely got her.

She was still in a dreamy mood later that morning when Loch Ness came into view and was stunned by its sudden appearance. She'd seen the lake before, of course, but here, and now, it was as if it were brand new. She stayed her horse, soaking it all in, then glanced over to Aidan to see if he was as taken with it as she was. He'd clearly been waiting for her to catch his eye, she couldn't be sure how long he'd been sitting there, but his look was brimming with awe, too. She held his gaze, and was overcome with a rush of emotion at the realization that his look of awe had nothing to do with the lake, and was all because of her. It was an enlightening moment, and she felt a little guilty for the years she'd spent being jaded.

For the next few nights, they made camp on the later side. Aidan and his men were happy to be nearing their destination and had taken to riding a bit longer to further close the distance. Talk in the late evenings had turned to Seagrave and Aidan's friends who resided there, Greylen and his wife Gwen. Brianna recalled Dar and Lachlan speaking of the couple, too and was excited to meet them. It felt like an entire lifetime ago that she'd visited the MacTavishes at Abersoch, but in reality, it had only been a couple of weeks.

The next morning, after another impassioned pre-dawn effort to establish their legacy, thus ensuring the house of Pembrooke's survival, Aidan led Brianna to a nearby stream. She could tell the area was very familiar to him, and although the sun was just beginning to rise, he pointed off in the distance, telling her she'd soon have a hot bath, a soft bed, and fare that was sure to please her. His mood had been somewhat lighter these last few days, and while he still kept up his running commentary on the land, always quick to point out new flora and fauna for her benefit, she noticed this morning that he stopped several times to listen and scan the area before moving on. She was always quick to follow his lead, and so stopped abruptly each time too, wondering if there was something she should be looking for, but then he always moved on in the end. It happened once in the water too, as they bathed, but then something shifted, and in an instant, his face set. He pressed a finger to her lips, then motioned with his head, they needed to leave. He didn't look alarmed, just alert, so she didn't panic, but still, she'd never tried to be so quiet in her life.

They were just starting to get dressed, when Aidan's head shot up, and he turned to look in the opposite direction. Brianna held her breath, by now truly scared, she was about to ask him what was wrong when he covered her mouth with his hand. She froze in place, half-dressed, with her eyes darting to the rest of their clothes, a bow and quiver, his sword, and their daggers. It was all easily within reach, but when she met Aidan's eyes, she knew whatever he'd seen was bad, so she made no attempt to gather their things. A moment later, he was covering her with her cloak and pressing her daggers into her hands, before securing his. When he looped the quiver over her shoulder, her heart dropped a little more. He'd never had her use it before, and it had been years since she'd last shot at a target. She stood a little straighter as he retrieved a single arrow, pressing the shaft against the bow before wrapping her fingers around both. Her eyes darted from side to side, as she tried to figure out where she'd have the best advantage, but Aidan squeezed her hand.

"Not now," he said, his voice low but crystal clear. "When I tell you, make for our camp. Forsake not one second, Breea. Flee, as if the fires of hell are at your back."

She nodded. He didn't want her to look back.

"If you need to defend yourself, do not waver. Be precise, aye?"

She nodded again, understanding that he was telling her to aim to kill.

"If you stand right where we slept last night and look toward the fire pit, Seagrave lies due north," Aidan continued, "by foot, you'll reach its border well before dusk. Trust no one until you cross MacGreggor land. They will not patrol beyond it. No one, Breea."

She felt tears pool in her eyes as she nodded, her heart thumping wildly. Did he think she might have to reach safety alone? Or was he merely preparing her for the worst? He was so grave, his face set in an expression she'd never seen on him before. Aidan stared into her eyes for another second before saying, "Never forget who you are." Brianna trembled slightly, wondering if that was his way of saying goodbye, if these would be the last words she ever heard him speak. It was true that O'Roarkes only married in the case of true love, but there had never been a guarantee of the longevity of those marriages —was her promise of a true love match already coming to an end? Before Brianna could fall into a doom spiral, Aidan turned and suddenly made himself so large, it was like he grew to twice his size. He was obviously shielding and protecting her, but she wasn't sure from what. Still, the movement brought her back to her senses.

Brianna heard a disturbance behind them from their camp, breaking the eerie quiet that had settled over the woods. When she turned toward the sound, Brianna saw their horses flee the area, her mare taking up the rear. Then, just as Aidan reached behind him to squeeze her wrist, she saw what he had seen. The men. There were at least eight of them, creeping out from hiding spots all around the stream where they'd just washed, obviously having lain in wait to catch them. The thought of them watching her for so long without her knowledge sent a shiver down Brianna's spine. When something sounded behind them again, she tightened her grip on Aidan's shirt, but he just squeezed her wrist again, rubbing his thumb on her palm, a calming gesture. As soon as she turned, Brianna saw it was his men approaching, which he must have known. She said a prayer as Aidan scanned the area, one arm keeping her snug up against him. By the time Henry, Alan, and Richard reached them, the other men were only several yards away.

Brianna had no idea what their plan was, if Aidan and his men even *had* a plan, but it was clear that all four of them worked seamlessly together, and could read one another's expressions and intent in an instant. Right now, it seemed like they were all focused on the strange men moving closer to them. Then, Aidan's arm moved from her back, and she knew it was almost time. When Aidan reached for his sword, his men did the same, the movement so fluid Brianna felt like she was watching in slow motion. She saw Aidan's stance shift as he gripped the hilt with both hands, power radiating from his torso and hips as he swung it through the air and bellowed, *"RUN!"* before lunging forward.

HER HEART BEATING WILDLY, and all at once terrified, Brianna turned and ran back toward their camp. Between her breathing and the sound of blood rushing in her head, she couldn't hear anything behind her. She was tempted to turn around, but Aidan was counting on her not to. She kept repeating in her head the words he told her to remember. *I am Brianna O'Roarke of the House of Pembrooke, by right and by marriage.* The brush scratched her face, hands, and legs as she flew through it, but she kept going. She stumbled a few times over some roots or branches but pushed herself back up each time she nearly fell. Her grip was so tight on the bow and arrow, that her fingers were numb, and her knuckles raw from scraping the ground as she tried to keep low. When she finally reached the perimeter of their camp, it was obvious that Alan, Richard, and Henry had scattered their things. They'd probably let the horses go too, so they wouldn't be stolen or hurt or, God forbid, worse. She knew Kitty had to be somewhere, and scanned the camp wondering where they'd hid her. After a moment's frantic searching, Brianna decided she'd have to come back to scour the area later.

Remembering Aidan's instruction, she found the spot where they'd slept and stood there to get her bearings. Thankfully, her grandfather had taught her how to find due north in one of their informal lessons. As she headed off, Brianna whispered to herself, *Oh, please, please, please, don't make me do this alone...*

She heard movement behind her, and she froze. For a few seconds she was overcome with fear, then Aidan's eyes flashed in her mind, and his parting words: "Never forget who you are."

She would not fall apart. *I am Brianna O'Roarke of the House of Pembrooke.* Gathering herself, the words a mantra in her head, she turned to see a man she didn't recognize, fast approaching, but still a safe distance away. Aidan's voice rang in her ears: *Trust no one...* Everything she'd been taught in her youth came back to her now. But this wasn't a competition or target practice with her grandfather. There'd be no awards ceremony or blue ribbons. *Defend yourself...* Planting her feet, she gripped the riser and nocked the arrow, extending her arm as she drew the bowstring, finding her anchor like an old friend, level with her jaw. Aidan's words again: *be precise...* Staring down the arrow shaft, she took aim, dead center, on her mark ...*do not waver...*Completely still, Brianna could almost hear her grandfather's voice in her ear, he and Aidan trading off guidance in her mind: *someday Breagha, you may have only one opportunity and only one arrow...don't be rash.* With a deep breath, her lungs expanded, and the movement stretched the span of her arms, that fraction of an inch further to set the tension...*wait for it, girl*...there!—she opened her hand, her eyes followed the arrow's path as her fingers swept passed her ear and the arrow struck her target. She watched blankly as her would-be attacker fell to the ground where he'd stood and Brianna allowed herself a moment to accept what she had done before she turned.

Seagrave. Due north. Run. *Trust no one.*

CHAPTER 20

Grateful to hear Brianna's footsteps retreat, Aidan shifted his focus to the man in front of him, Gil Fitzgerald, grunting as his sword met metal on its downward strike. Each moment they kept these men engaged was another for Brianna to reach safety. By now, Aidan believed he had accounted for all of their assailants, each one familiar to him—both Fitzgerald brothers and their attending men, who were always looming with covetous eyes during his visits with the Fitzgeralds. It was a pattern that had worn his patience, managing the brothers and their ill-timed summons after Robert's death.

Grunting as he staved off an impressive blow from Gil, Aidan pushed him back with a swift kick, noting with surprise that he'd underestimated Gil's proficiency. His foe was surprisingly agile and quick on his feet. Pivoting quickly, Aidan spotted Alan, Richard, and Henry thick in the fray, all handling themselves extremely well. He noted that at least one of the Fitzgeralds' men seemed to have been felled.

"Took you long enough," Gil sneered, pulling Aidan's attention back to him. "We'd thought that after you survived the fire, you'd have made your way with more haste."

Aidan bristled at Gil's tone but kept his composure. It seemed the Fitzgeralds were more than just a pair of irritating bullies, but men who were capable of much more brutal acts. So, not only had the brothers been responsible for the fire, but they'd presumed, correctly, that he'd travel straight to Seagrave. Aidan was surprised they'd had the patience to wait and wondered just how long they'd been following him and his company. Mayhap he'd underestimated them in this too. He allowed himself a moment's self-doubt. Had he taken no measures? Been oblivious? He knew this was untrue, that he and his men had been as careful as they could have been, and the degree of danger they now found themselves in was grave only for Brianna being left on her own. He could handle the Fitzgeralds, this he knew. He would, in truth, relish the opportunity.

"Imagine our surprise to see you in Ayr— *and* to see what's kept you lingering so long. A woman like that… 'tis understand'able," Gil added, leering perversely at Brianna's retreating back. It was all Aidan could do to hold his ground and not foolishly attack him right then and there. "Fear not, Sinclair, we'll find another for our sister, and as for your *woman*," he said, obviously unable to see what Brianna was to him. "We'll see to her too."

If Aidan could kill him twice for the suggestion, he would, but his fate was already sealed. Terminally so. The brief rise of the brothers Fitzgerald would end today, at the hand of the House of Pembrooke, beginning with Gil.

Gil smirked then, and Aidan found his timeliness almost amusing, until he spoke.

"Nigel should have her by now," Gil said, eyes glinting. "The girl, that is. I can only imagine his delight at being alone with her."

Aidan didn't waste time turning to confirm Nigel's absence, he just held Gil's stare, and ground out, "Right." Then, he tossed his sword in the air, and as Gil's eyes followed the sword's arcing path, Aidan reached for his dagger. When Gil looked back at him, Aidan sneered and lunged forward. "The hell he is," he said, sticking the blade right into Gil's throat.

As Gil sank to the earth, Aidan wrenched his blade free, feeling no remorse. Turning, he looked quickly for Nigel among the felled bodies and those still fighting but didn't see him. Heart pounding, he grabbed the collar of one of the two men who'd surrendered and demanded to know Nigel's whereabouts, trying not to picture his hands on Brianna. He learned that Nigel had never been there at all, but had been lying in wait with at least one other of the Fitzgeralds' party back at their camp. Aidan's pulse quickened even further. *Nay.* He'd sent Brianna, straight into the hands of the enemy. He stumbled as he reached for his sword, which was still lying on the ground beside Gil, then ran. He didn't have to imagine the fires of hell at his back, for they were there, spurring him along.

He followed the path she'd taken through the brush, spotting the places she'd stumbled and fallen. He noted blood marring the edge of a jagged rock and knew that it was hers. When he stood next to the site of their bed, he saw her shallow boot prints in the soft earth. By the looks of it, she'd spun around, then set herself straight and in the direction he'd bade her go. But...Aidan followed the tracks and saw that she'd backtracked a pace after turning, her direction now due south. In this direction, her prints were deeply set —in a shooting stance. Turning to follow her sights, he ran to inspect the area and came upon a man, struck dead in a small clearing. So she'd taken him down, and with a single shot, from the looks of it. *Well done, lass.* But this meant that Nigel was still out there —and so was Breea.

Aidan quickly picked up her trail as she left their camp, heading due north just as he'd told her, thinking only of getting to her in time.

CHAPTER 21

With her eyes fixed on the higher terrain ahead, Brianna ran as fast as her legs would carry her. She'd never been so scared in her life, not even during the days she'd spent at sea after the accident as a child—at least then, she hadn't known she was alone, and had been oblivious to the real dangers that lurked. Today was different. She'd had to face Aidan, the man she loved, for quite possibly the last time and just…go. He'd given her the tools and guidance to ensure she reached safety, but still, she was doing this alone. She wondered if this was history just repeating itself. If maybe she *was* jinxed, or cursed, and her fate was to keep reliving the trauma of losing the people who mattered most, over and over again. *No,* Brianna told herself. She would not end up alone, her marriage of true and enduring love a mere memory to last her the rest of her days. Aidan had shown her how to believe in her power. He'd instilled her with love, with hope, and with confidence, and set her free to live. He'd made sure she had a fighting chance, and there was no way that he wouldn't fight, too. This time had to be different. And he *would* return, he had to.

Looking around, Brianna knew she needed to keep moving. Stuck on a stretch of grassy meadow, not far from their camp, she longed for cover, but the tree line was still in the distance. She thought she heard someone behind her, and nearly jumped out of her skin, but kept going, hand hovering over where her dagger was sheathed. When she turned and scanned the area, however, she saw no one. That was the one small advantage of being out in the open, she decided. If she was vulnerable to being spotted, so was her enemy. She couldn't be sure if there were more of them, or if they would even pursue her if there were. It was only now that she had the chance to wonder if the attack had been a random ambush, or if the men were after Aidan specifically. Looking back one last time before going on, she picked up her pace. The sooner she could put herself at a higher elevation and more cover, the better.

Just as she made it inside the tree line, Brianna thought she heard another sound, like the rustle she'd heard before. Instinctively, she reached for her dagger, but again, when she turned she saw nothing but the meadow stretching behind her. Deciding she was just imagining things, Brianna took a moment— and a much-needed deep breath—trying to shake off the heebie-jeebies. With her frazzled nerves quieting back down, she focused back on her goal: Seagrave. According to Aidan, she had a five, maybe six-hour hike ahead of her. She wasn't going to win any medals for speed, but she could go steady all the way. Nothing like a dose of clarity to keep her motivated. And tucked back into where the brush was growing thicker at the base of the small copse of trees, she was somewhat hidden now, too. Feeling ready to keep going, Brianna turned—right into a man who was standing there, silently looming behind her.

She screamed, then stood frozen as he leered down at her. Taking advantage of her stunned fear, the man grabbed her wrist, jamming it hard against his knee. She cried out again as her dagger fell and pain radiated up her arm. Smiling, he wrenched her shoulder, dragging her in close. She felt her quiver smash up against a tree and knew her arrows had fallen to the ground. The sudden clarity of her defenselessness—one of her daggers and arrows both out of reach—brought her back to the present and she even started kicking and clawing anywhere she could, but by then, the man had gotten the upper hand.

He sneered at her, then said, "Oh, keep fighting, lass, we like that."

Brianna shivered. She knew exactly what he meant, what he wanted, and knew she had to get away *now*. She needed to regain control. *Breagha—think, girl!* Her grandfather's voice rang in her head, and it was all she needed for her lessons to come back to her again. She let her body go completely limp, becoming dead weight, then dropped to the ground. He was still standing right over her, but it gave her the seconds she needed. The man grumbled, and she thought she heard him make a nasty comment before he reached for her. But she was ready this time, having grasped her other dagger from the scabbard around her calf, which the man hadn't seen, hidden in the folds of her cloak.

Her attacker wasn't nearly as large as Aidan, but even so, she doubted a strike, from this angle would be fatal. She had this one chance to incapacitate him and cause as much damage as she could, and when he lifted her, she wrapped both hands around its hilt, then, using all of her strength, she jabbed upward, striking him right in the gut. He yelled out, and with her hands still in a death grip, her face set, teeth grinding, Brianna wrenched it as hard as she could, then pushed him back, trying to pull the dagger free. He gasped, his eyes wide with disbelief, and grabbed at her hands as he fell, taking her with him. She screamed, wrenching herself and the dagger from his grasp then scrambled backward across the brush.

She watched for a moment as he tried to stand, roaring with rage. Realizing that she'd done less damage than she'd hoped, Brianna stood rooted to her spot, terror struck for another second before snapping out of it enough to get her limbs to move, then turned onto her knees, righting herself. As she stood, she reached down to scoop up some of the fallen arrows but dropped the dagger in the process. In her attempt to retrieve it, she stumbled twice before finally leaving it behind to run for higher ground.

It wasn't until she'd made it further up the hill, trying to put as much distance as she could between herself and the man, that she realized her mistake— and just how grave her situation was. The trees here were more spread out, providing less cover. She searched frantically for a better spot, and when she found none, she turned to look behind her for a split second. Heart pounding, she clocked that the man wasn't far behind her now and that he wasn't alone. She whipped back around and kept going. Brianna knew what she had to do, but when she looked down at her hands, she realized she'd only managed to gather one arrow amongst a few large twigs.

Someday, you may only have one.

CHAPTER 22

Aidan had just breached the clearing between hillsides when he heard a scream. *Brianna*. Turning toward the sound, which had come from the woods lining the expanse, he changed course, a brutal combination of fear and anger pushing him forward. Snarling, he ground his teeth together as he tried to ward off thoughts of the sort of danger she was in. He heard another scream, but this time it was not Brianna's, but a man's. Aidan knew he was nearly within reach of her, but the copse of trees was laden with thick brush, hindering his view. Still, he knew he must be close, his line of sight narrowed, and... *there!*

He spied movement, a mere flash of a sleeve, through the branches, and at the very same moment, Brianna screamed again. Aidan roared, charging headlong through the thicket—but when he broke through to the other side, there was no one. She was gone—he'd missed her by precious seconds. Panic rose in his chest as he searched for her trail, drawing back abruptly when he saw something glinting on the ground. Breea's dagger. As he moved closer, he found her quiver and scattered arrows strewn about the brush, and then he saw her *other* dagger…soaked in blood. Good God, she was defenseless, mayhap wounded. Frantically searching the hillside, Aidan's gaze finally landed on someone, but it wasn't Brianna. It was Nigel, making his way up the hill, stumbling as he went, yet moving with dogged purpose. Another growl escaped his lips as he reached for Brianna's daggers, sheathing them both next to his, then headed straight for Nigel, scouring the hillside for Brianna as he did so. Finally, he spotted her, high up on the hill, standing against a tree trunk, hood drawn in hiding. She looked to be uninjured, and his relief was so great he let out a sigh.

But, as he looked closer, it appeared that she wasn't hiding at all. Nay, she'd chosen her position with care, blending into her surroundings. He watched as she began to move, slowly, purposefully, her face set in determination as she drew her bow. Had she not seen him, heard him? Knowing she'd already taken one man's life, he wished to spare her the burden of yet another—and to be fully truthful, Aidan wished to slay Nigel himself. Nearly in reach of his foe, he called out to her sharply. At the sound of his voice, Nigel turned, startling when he saw him, and reading his intent clearly as he reached for a dagger—Brianna's. It would be a fitting end, for the anguish he'd surely inflicted upon her.

"Aye," Aidan said, thrilled at the fear on Nigel's face. "Your brother's waiting for you." Nigel's eyes widened as Aidan lunged forward, striking with precision. Aidan held him as he slumped to the ground. "Since I'm a man of my word, you'll have my answer now. I would have wed your sister, but only to save her from harm, at the hands of you and your brother." With a twist of the dagger, he finished him, then wrenched his blade free, eager to reach Brianna.

As he stepped over Nigel's body, he looked up the hill, anxious to meet her eyes. But the instant he caught sight of her, he realized his mistake. Brianna's aim had never been on Nigel at all, for her bow was still set, and her sights elsewhere—there must still be another. Aidan froze where he stood to give her a clear shot. Be it his last moments on this earth or not, his eyes never wavered from her face, set so beautifully in concentration as she aimed with deadly intent. He remained completely still as she released the arrow, never once allowing his eyes to stray, even as her arrow sailed passed him, so close he felt the air shift just before it met its mark, felling the man who'd come up behind him, near enough that the man's sword clattered at Aidan's feet.

For a mere blink, their eyes locked, then Aidan broke his gaze from Brianna's and turned to collect the fallen man's sword, staying low as he grasped its hilt. Seeing no more of the Fitzgeralds' party skulking up the hill, he stayed his ground a moment longer until he was confident the danger had truly passed. Then he quickly made for Brianna, who'd been watching him just as closely, and only now let down her guard, sliding along the tree's trunk until she rested upon the ground, her bow held steady in front of her.

CHAPTER 23

Heart still racing, Brianna tried to catch her breath as Aidan sprinted up the hill toward her. Even though it appeared they were out of danger, she felt like they were still open targets and kept looking around, terrified someone else would jump out at any second. As soon as Aidan was close enough, she loosened her grip on the bow and reached out with her good arm, desperate to touch him, keeping her sore arm tucked securely in front of her. She hadn't even had the chance to look at it yet but knew it had to be at least badly bruised.

"Breea." Aidan's voice was ragged as he fell to his knees just before her, grasping her shoulders and bringing his face level with hers. Slowly, he pushed her hood down, breathing her name again, and searching her eyes, as he gently brushed the hair from her face. "Are you injured?"

She grasped his hand, marveling at how familiar its shape already felt to her, the comfort she drew from it. "I need my arrows," she said, returning to her present urgency. "They're at the bottom of the hill. My daggers, too."

He seemed startled by her request, then something shifted in his expression, and he stared at her so intently, like he was trying to figure her out. Frustrated at his lack of action, her eyes darted from side to side, keeping watch in case anyone else appeared.

"*Aidan*, please, we're defenseless."

Finally, he moved, shaking his head. "Nay, Breea. We are not."

Before she could protest, he took his firm hands and framed her face, blocking her periphery, making it so she could look only at him as he stared deeply into her eyes.

"I am armed," he said, his voice sure and even. "I've two swords, and six daggers, two of which are yours, and in a moment, I will retrieve your arrows. But you must know, we are not defenseless, and you are no longer on your own." He still hadn't moved, or for that matter, let her move, but Brianna felt her breathing begin to slow, and when her shoulders relaxed, she made a sound close to a sigh. Aidan nodded approvingly. "Aye," he said, then waited another moment before he released her. "Are you injured?" he asked, sliding his hands over her head, pressing gently as he went. She noticed a cut beneath his eye, then, and reached out. "Brianna." Aidan waited until she looked at him again. "Did he hurt you?" he asked, more urgently this time.

Oh. Her eyes widened at the thought, but she quickly shook her head, realizing she must not have answered him before. She could see his relief, and whispered his name, tracing the thin cut along his hairline, and the one beneath his eye. "Breea. I'm whole," he assured her. "A few scrapes, nothing more."

"What about Henry?" she asked. "Is he okay? Alan, Richard?" She tried not to think about Kitty or their horses, otherwise she'd only imagine the worst.

"I'm sure they're close behind," he said, continuing his careful but earnest inspection of her. As his hands skimmed her shoulders, down her arms, she winced, which made him stop at once. "You *are* injured."

She shook her head, confused for a moment, then she remembered, her wrist. The man had grabbed it and slammed her arm so she'd drop her dagger. *Her dagger!* She'd dropped them both.

"My dagger. Aidan," she said, suddenly feeling more exposed. "And my arrows." Brianna gestured toward where they lay. "You said you'd get them."

"I will." He nodded slowly, then leaned in, trying to get a better look at her hand. She wasn't even sure he'd touched her yet, but she cried out in anticipation, and his eyes shot to hers.

"Sorry. It's just tender. I'm jumpy."

He nodded, and pulled his hands back, giving her wrist a good look from where he sat, grimacing before he pulled back her sleeve. He was so gentle, so quiet, even when he sighed, closing his eyes and shaking his head before looking at her again.

"Breea," he said. "You wielded the bow…with this hand?"

Brianna looked down at her right hand, the injured one. Yes, she'd used her bad arm, but what other choice did she have? She wasn't paying attention to her injuries at the time, she'd been running for her life, and cover—and stopping that man from attacking Aidan.

"It's my dominant hand," she said, which should have been excuse enough. "I needed my aim to be true."

If he was unhappy with her answer, he hid it well and said nothing more on the matter, just looped her bow over his shoulder. "I need to wrap this, but let's get down the hill first. Then we'll need to make haste for Seagrave. Brace your arm." He said no more, just carefully lifted her, grimacing when she winced, and carried her down the hill. Once she was settled, she burrowed against him and for a moment, forgot they were more visible now. "I see no one," he said, correctly guessing why she had stirred, then gently pressed her back.

When he reached the area where she'd dropped her arrows, he shifted her slightly but kept her in his arms as he bent to grab them and the quiver, too. "Until your arm heals, you'll trust me to see to your defense," he said, looping her quiver over his shoulder.

There was a hitch in his voice that Brianna caught immediately, and her fear took a backseat for a moment. She tugged on his shirt to get his attention,

276

and when he looked down at her, though he was every bit the implacable warrior ever in control, she knew him well enough now to see the pain and sorrow he tried to hide from her.

"Aidan," she said, her tone deadly serious, "I will *always* trust you. I hope I'll never be in that position again, but...it was *your* strength and courage that guided me through."

Brianna held his gaze for a long moment, watching as his expression softened, and he lifted her just enough to nudge his face to hers, a touch they both needed. She'd just settled against his chest again, feeling his strong, and very sure arms giving her a gentle squeeze, when Aidan suddenly tensed and stopped short. She let out a muffled shriek and whipped her head around to see what had caused his reaction, but a moment later, relaxed her death grip on his arm. At the bottom of the hill, standing in the meadow, was Merri, looking completely unharmed. At the sight of her, Brianna's breath caught. *Her horse.* She was nearly in tears from the relief, and as her heartbeat once again started to slow, Aidan gave her another gentle squeeze. When she turned to face him, she saw that his eyes were glassy, and when he spoke, his voice welled with emotion.

"She came back for you."

Somehow, Brianna wasn't surprised, even amidst all the chaos. Merri's return just confirmed what she already knew, what she felt—they were meant to be together, all of them. "We're a family, Aidan," she said, settling against his chest again, "of course she returned."

His mouth set for a moment, his grip on her still tight. After a second, he grunted, and with a nod, continued forward. When he reached a soft patch of grass near to where Merri stood, waiting, he gently set her on the ground before turning to the horse.

Brianna kept a watchful eye on the hillsides while Aidan gave Merri a quick once over, whispering praise and affection into the mare's ear, loud enough for Brianna to hear. His inspection complete, he gave her another well-deserved pat, then untied one of the bags tacked to her side.

"Merri was carrying our supplies from the apothecary," he said, relief filling his face as he knelt beside her to unpack it. He was so outwardly calm and in control again, at once her fierce warrior and soothing protector.

"You need to drink something," he said, opening a skin of water he'd pulled out of the bag.

She nodded, realizing suddenly that she was beyond parched, which reminded her again of the peril they were just in. Aidan must have noticed the look cross her face.

"Breea." His hands cupped her head as she sipped the cool water. "You're safe now."

She took one last gulp, then met his eyes. She was starting to believe that they were safe, but... "I killed two men, Aidan." She was whispering, but still, she'd needed to say that out loud.

"Who had no regard for your life nor mine," he said not missing a beat.

He was right, obviously, but that didn't mean there wasn't a lot to process. She wasn't sure she was able to talk any more about it at the moment, and Aidan seemed to sense that. When she said no more, he just nodded and helped her take another drink before looking at her arm again. She hadn't seen what he'd purchased from the apothecary back in Ayr, but as she watched him open some of the pouches, she could see that they were filled with different kinds of herbs and powders. He mixed a few powders together first, in a small drinking cup before adding some water, turning it into a milky liquid.

"I can't account for the taste," he said, grimacing, as he knelt in front of her to give her the mixture, "but it will help with the pain, and mayhap calm your nerves."

Brianna nodded and braced herself. She had a moment of panic wondering if she should really trust this fifteenth-century remedy, but then shrugged it off—what other options did she have? And besides, she knew Aidan would never give her anything that he deemed the slightest risk. She downed the concoction, which really didn't taste so bad—like one of the vitamin supplement packets she took mixed with a bottle of water, the kind that didn't dissolve and tasted sort of woodsy—and Aidan nodded, satisfied.

After setting aside the cup, he mixed some herbs with another powder in what served as a mortar and pestle, then opened a small container filled with an ointment of some kind, adding it to the mixture to make a paste.

Brianna looked down at her arm, taking note of the blotchy areas of pink and red already marring her skin, from the top of her hand to her elbow, not to mention the scrapes and cuts she must have gotten from running through the brush. She watched as Aidan gingerly rinsed the raw spots, then applied the salve. She was amazed at how he seemed to be so good at this, too. Once he had finished gently rubbing the salve into her skin, he looked up at her and smiled softly, then stroked her cheek before he took out what looked to be soft spun linen tucked inside another larger pouch.

When he finally wrapped her arm, the pressure immediately alleviated some of the pain, especially in her wrist and hand. Then, he tilted her chin to get a better look at her face, searching for cuts and scrapes, along her hairline. He glanced down after a minute and looked into her eyes with so much care, that Brianna felt it wash over her like a balm. Overcome, she whimpered, bracing his leg. His entire stance shifted in an instant, and he gently wrapped his arms around her, holding her as close as he could without putting pressure on her injured arm, and sinking into their embrace. When he pulled back after a long moment, he brushed his lips to hers, then returned to his careful ministrations, cleaning the scrapes on her face, which Brianna obviously couldn't see, and didn't even remember she had.

"Are there more?" he asked, glancing around her body.

She shook her head. "I don't think so." Though she really couldn't remember. "I don't know, maybe, but just scrapes, I think."

"Will you show me? The last thing I want to worry about is letting something fester."

There were a few raw spots on her knees, and one on the back of her thigh from when she'd fallen to the ground. It felt like there might be a few more bruises on her torso, but nothing too serious. After cleaning and applying salve to those too, he stood and tore off a strip from his cloak.

She was so startled at the sound, she gasped. His eyes locked on hers, and he knelt beside her, calming her with a touch. "I promise you, the danger has passed," he said, waiting a moment before he continued, "We've a few hours ride still. We'll be on MacGreggor land soon enough, but Seagrave lies a distance from the border. 'Tis best to keep your arm secure, in the meantime."

Brianna nodded, she hadn't even considered until that moment that she couldn't ride, at least not alone. "Do you think Merri's ready?" she asked, wondering if carrying the both of them might be too much for her.

"I think she's more than ready, but if she shows any signs of strain, I'll gladly walk and lead her."

Brianna nodded, then something struck her and she gasped again. Aidan's mention of making a sling reminded her that she still had no idea where Kitty was.

"Aidan?" She didn't even have to ask. He must have guessed just by looking at her.

"We'll find her. I would imagine, she's tucked safely away and out of harm's reach."

A few minutes later, Aidan slipped the sling over her head, wrapping the material around her arm so it was cradled. Brianna noticed the difference immediately as her neck and shoulder bore the weight. She gave Aidan a grateful look, but flinched, clutching his leg with her good hand when she heard sounds coming from the edge of the clearing.

"My men," he said, looking at her. She wasn't sure how she knew that, but as if on cue, Aidan's men came into the clearing, their horses led along behind them.

When they got a little closer, Brianna saw that Henry had Kitty's carrier draped over his shoulder, and she appeared very content nestled against him. She clutched Aidan's legs again, so happy she almost cried. She covered her mouth, and when she turned to Aidan, he was already waiting. She was so overcome, feeling like they were really and truly safe, all of them, that she didn't notice much, but what clearly stuck with her was the look in his eyes, and how it filled her heart.

Soon, Henry was beside her, transferring Kitty into her arms. Trying not to lose it and blubber all over Kitty while she cuddled her, Brianna asked the men if they were alright. When they didn't answer, she looked up and saw they were all wearing ghastly expressions. It took her a moment to realize that they might have been insulted that she'd even questioned their welfare—or, more accurately, their ability to handle themselves in a fight. Thankfully, Aidan interjected on her behalf, making sure they knew she was asking in earnest. Before the men could reply, he went on to explain that it was Brianna who felled the man in the field near their camp, and she again felled another within the wood, a short distance behind them.

"Because of Brianna, the Sinclair name and the House of Pembrooke still has a future."

And then, as if she'd been initiated somehow, all three of the men gave Brianna a full accounting of their welfare. They left out the gory details but assured her that they were all indeed hale, hearty, and whole, delivering the news with a notable respect.

While she was proud to have held her own, Brianna would gladly leave the defense to Aidan and the men in the future, and she told them as much.

"Rest assured, I never want to have to do that again," she said, then changed the subject, feeling somewhat abashed at being the center of attention. "Your horses came back, too," she said.

Henry nodded, eyes alight. "Truthfully, 'twas Merri who brought them back," he said. "Right to the very spot where we'd bedded down, then she trotted off, and I can see now where she was headed so quickly."

Brianna felt a rush of tears and looked over at her horse again and then back at all of them. They'd all become so important to her. They didn't even seem to mind that she was a bit all over the place and gave her a few minutes to release some of her pent-up emotions. Aidan knelt behind her though, and held her, while she cried all over Kitty, soothing her with whispers of nothing really, just sounds, as he rocked her until she calmed.

When she'd finally gathered herself, Aidan kissed the top of her head and rubbed behind Kitty's ears, too. Then Henry knelt and motioned for her to transfer Kitty back to him so he could put her in her carrier—there was no way she was going to be able to hold her with her arm in a sling. She nuzzled Kitty a moment longer, then handed her back. Henry stopped short of cuddling the feline to his neck just in time, as all eyes were on him.

Once Kitty was safely ensconced with Henry, Aidan went off to conference briefly with Henry and the rest of his men, who were clustered a few feet away, taking stock of their things.

It was decided that Merri would get her due and carry her and Aidan to Seagrave. Henry would ride alongside them, while Alan and Richard would follow close behind, escorting the men that they must have kept out of her sight but who'd surrendered. By the time Aidan lifted her atop Merri, Brianna could barely feel the pain in her wrist—his concoction was working, or at least the placebo effect was, which was just as good at the moment. When Aidan climbed astride the saddle blanket behind her, she leaned into him, enjoying his solidity. He helped her find the perfect position, unrestrained without a saddle but safe and secure in his arms. She knew he was eager to get her to Seagrave, but she noticed that he still took an extra beat to hold her as she settled against him, a sound of utter contentment escaping his lips. She felt it too, and whispered her thanks.

"Time for that hot bath and soft bed I promised you," he said, rubbing his chin on her head.

It hadn't even occurred to her until he said it again, but she honestly hadn't minded the lack of creature comforts on their journey, or anything about it—at least before this morning. She'd never experienced what it was like to be so close to someone, and if that meant sleeping on the ground every night or bathing in a stream, she'd take both over what she'd had before. A life without real companionship. She knew then that she truly loved him, and that superseded all else. Feeling truly safe in Aidan's arms, it wasn't long before Brianna felt a wave of exhaustion come over her as she slipped into what would surely be a deep and peaceful sleep.

CHAPTER 24

The moment Aidan crossed the border onto MacGreggor land, he and Henry were surrounded by the band of riders patrolling the area. He'd expected no less; these were men who Aidan knew well and trusted, and they sensed his urgency. With no more than a subtle nod to Brianna still slumbering in his arms—a welcome effect of the draught he'd given her —the men tightened their escort to hasten him toward the castle.

If Aidan worried about Merri's endurance, she'd once again proved him wrong. Not only had she thrived throughout the entirety of their journey as one of a herd, but this proud girl was proving herself to be quite the leader as well. He would give her the respect of carrying her mistress all the way to her destination.

It wasn't long before another band of riders appeared in the distance, Alex at the fore. Aidan recognized him at once, his hawkish gaze and acute perception driving him forward with haste, and an urgency that equaled Aidan's. At his approach, the rider next to Aidan fell back, and Alex took his place. "Where are Alan and Richard?" he asked, then pointedly took in Brianna, reposed against his chest.

"Trailing behind. The Fitzgeralds came upon us early this morn. Alan and Richard are guarding the two who survived."

Alex glowered at the news, before charging off to speak to the men he'd been riding with. At his word, half broke in the direction of the castle, the others for the border, no doubt to provide escort for Alan and Richard once they crossed. Alex returned then, taking up Aidan's flank again. Alex was nothing if not steadfast and loyal, so it was fitting that he said no more, and asked no questions. Besides, now was not the time for discussion about Brianna. In truth, Aidan wasn't sure, he even *could* express everything she was to him. Not that the matter was anyone else's concern.

With the final stretch to the castle mercifully silent, save for the steady chorus of hoofbeats, Aidan thought back over his entire history with the Fitzgerald brothers, a span of several years, which had culminated first in their unannounced visit the day he'd left Seagrave nearly a month ago, and finally in their poorly chosen tactic of ambush.

Considering the events of the day, how the brothers and their men had successfully managed to track them and catch them by surprise, caused Aidan to question his judgment. Up until the past few weeks,

Aidan had considered the Fitzgeralds an annoyance at most, one he'd soon be rid of one way or another, leaving any real or imagined alliance (on the part of Gil and Nigel) behind. Had he let his vigilance slip because of it? Lachlan had bestowed upon him a mantle of guardianship, but could he still claim it if his singular attention on Brianna was the cause of their woes? These thoughts plagued him until he crested the hill and the gates of Seagrave were at last in sight. Laying his eyes on the castle should have brought him relief, but instead, the noise in his head became deafening, a brewing tempest, and an omen of the reckoning that surely awaited him.

As they entered the courtyard, Aidan made straight for the steps, eager to get Brianna the proper aid she needed, noting that the riders Alex had sent ahead had done the same, their steeds left in the hands of the castle guards, likely in their haste to seek Gwen. Aidan bent his head, nudging Brianna gently awake before whispering in her ear to tell her they'd arrived. Her eyes fluttered, and he smiled down at her, ignoring his worry and fear as he slid to the ground holding her tight in his arms. Once on the ground, he looked Merri in the eye, offering a brief but necessary thanks to the mare, then hurried up the steps, leaving her in the care of the guard, waiting to take her reins.

He nearly missed a collision with Gwen, who was making her way outside just as he came through the doors. At the sight of him, Gwen stopped short, taking in his ragged and no doubt grisly appearance, before turning to Brianna who still lay half-dozing, half-awake in his arms.

"What happened?" Gwen said hoarsely. She cleared her throat, "Aidan? Tell me."

Realizing what had occurred would remind her of the ambush Grey and Gavin had endured years ago, Aidan hesitated, wishing to spare her unpleasant memories.

"Aidan!" she pressed.

"We were ambushed."

Gwen nodded, then, with her mouth set in a straight line, she scrutinized his face and arms. "Is any of this blood yours?" she asked, pointing to his arms and face.

He shook his head. "Not enough to matter."

She turned her attention to Brianna then, her features softening as Aidan instinctively pulled her closer. Brianna clutched at his shirt in response. She was still groggy, but more alert now as she shifted to stare up at him.

"Oh, hi," Gwen said, unable to keep the smile off her face as she glanced between Brianna and Aidan. "I'm Gwen. You're in good hands. Mine and this guy's." Brianna attempted a weak smile, breathing a barely detectable *thank you*, and Gwen turned back to Aidan. "Let's get her inside," she said, her voice nearly drowned out by a thunder of hooves as another band of riders raced in through the gates.

Aidan turned as he and Gwen hastened forward, and saw Grey riding at the front of the approaching pack.

"He'll find us," they said in unison and continued on their way.

"What happened?" Gwen asked as she led him down the corridor that would take them toward her infirmary.

Aidan shook his head. Brianna hadn't yet told him *how* she was injured. "I can't be sure. We were waylaid." He looked down at her, wondering if she might provide an answer, but when he saw that her eyes had closed again, he just pulled her closer. "I instructed her to run. By the time I found her, I was only certain that her wrist needed attention...I know she has cuts, but...I ..." he stammered, as he laid Brianna down, helping her find a comfortable position when she winced.

Gwen looked at him sympathetically, reaching out to soothe him as she moved closer. Her touch helped, a steady hand to quiet his mounting worries and mitigate the loss of Brianna's weight in his arms.

"You did this? Aye?" she said, pointing to the sling he'd made from his cloak and the clean linen he'd wrapped tightly around Brianna's arm.

Aidan nodded to Gwen, and at the same moment, Grey appeared, clearly having been apprised of the situation. They exchanged a brief look before Aidan turned back to Brianna, who was clutching his wrist, grimacing as she tried to sit up.

"I... don't feel... well," she said in shallow bursts, panting. Aidan quickly helped her up, then stayed close, looking with concern as Gwen removed the sling to get a better look at her arm.

Before Gwen could continue with her examination, however, Brianna started to fan herself with her good hand, and a glistening of sweat started to show on her brow.

"Please, get this off me," she said, struggling to remove her cloak while pushing her hair back at the same time.

Quickly, Aidan pulled it away, then handed it to Gwen so he could sweep Brianna's hair back, twisting it around his hand to keep it off her face and neck. She looked at him with such gratitude, that his heart nearly melted. It was such a simple task, using his hand as her personal hair clasp to keep her nape cool. Still, he was pleased to provide her even a modicum of relief, albeit brief—for no sooner did Brianna's mouth twist sourly, and it was clear she was about to be sick.

In the moment, Aidan wasn't quite sure which was of most importance: holding onto her hair, or finding something for her to retch in. Frozen in indecision, all he could do was cup his hand in front of her as he looked around for something more suitable. Gwen came to his rescue with only seconds to spare, placing a small pot in front of Brianna, which she promptly grasped onto. Aidan offered her the only privacy he could within the small confines of the chamber and turned his head while she emptied the contents of her stomach. Since she'd only ingested some water and the draught he'd given her, it was over quickly—yet long enough for him to catch Gwen and Grey, clearly amused at his reaction to helping Brianna. In another circumstance, he might have laughed at their antics, too—their dramatic stares just before Grey cupped his hands in front of Gwen for her to imitate retching into them—but considering the situation, he couldn't imagine why they'd be so undone at his behavior. He'd no doubt that they'd done the same or more for each other over the years.

Aidan narrowed his eyes at them before turning his attention back to Brianna as she took a ragged breath, and managed to unwind his hand from her hair so he could grab a few linens stacked on the table beside the cot to wipe her mouth. She nodded covering his hand, and took the cloth from him. He reached for another and dipped it into some cool water to blot across her forehead, feeling how clammy she'd become. As he brushed his knuckles down the side of her face, she breathed a little *thank you* and then started to cry very softly.

Aidan felt his heart swell with compassion. "Nay, Breea. Don't cry, love," he said, shaking his head. He held her in his arms as she gathered herself, and once she'd calmed, he asked if she'd like to lay down again. When she nodded, he helped her get situated, pressing his lips to her forehead, and turned, wondering *what* in the blazes was keeping Gwen so long.

He spun around to find both Gwen *and* Grey still as statues, watching him, all traces of humor gone. When a moment later Gwen shook herself out of her stupor and took a step toward him, Aidan could see what had caused her to linger was simply emotion. Pure and sincere emotion, and nothing to jest at.

"I'm sorry. I'm so happy for you," she said softly before turning her attention to Brianna and sitting at her bedside. "I heard Aidan call you, Breea. Is that your name?" she asked, pushing Brianna's hair back.

Brianna tried to speak but still seemed too weak, so Aidan stepped in for her.

"Brianna. Brianna O'Roarke," he said. Then, his tone laden with import, he added. "My wife."

He couldn't see Gwen's face, but her hands flew to her cheeks, and based on the spark in Brianna's eyes, he could only imagine her expression of delight.

It took Gwen another moment to gather herself, though her voice barely concealed her merriment when she asked Brianna, "Do you feel a little better now?"

"I just feel really dizzy," Brianna managed, then started to pant again, struggling to get comfortable.

"Let's give this a few minutes to pass," Gwen said, pressing another cool cloth to her forehead. "Aidan," she said, her eyes still on Brianna's. "Are *you* ill at all? Did you eat the same thing, maybe?"

"Nay, we had nothing," he said, taking a leather strip that Grey had offered to tie Brianna's hair back. "And she, but a draught for the pain and to help her rest more comfortably."

Gwen made a sound, hmming as she looked over Brianna. Aidan, meanwhile, gently gathered Brianna's hair again, positioning it up where she usually wore it atop her head. He was relieved to see a small smile on her face just before she reached for his hand and closed her eyes, seeming to rest comfortably now. After a minute, Gwen looked back at him.

"I don't think any of the powders I gave you would have—"

Aidan shook his head and felt his eyes go wide.

"Wait, *what?*" Gwen said, whirling around so that she was facing him fully.

"My supplies were lost," he said, his heart sinking rapidly. "Before we left Ayr, I acquired new at the apothecary. At least those I could find."

Gwen's easy smile and warm manner dissipated immediately, "I need to see what you gave her, Aidan."

Aidan looked around for a moment, feeling lost, until he felt a hand on his shoulder. Henry. He'd been standing just inside the door this entire time, and now gave Gwen the bag of medicinal items. Although he had a passable knowledge of topical and ingestible curatives thanks to Grey's mother Lady Madelyn, who was a well-practiced healer, Gwen had an advanced expertise that added another vital layer. As such, Aidan knew that as a rule, medicinal compounds were to be avoided, period. Hence the reason he'd purchased single ingredients and combined them himself.

Still, he held his breath, filled with worry again as he looked between Brianna, who blessedly seemed to still be resting comfortably, and Gwen, as she examined the contents of his purchases. Finally, Gwen gave a decisive nod and looked Brianna over once more, taking extra care on account of this new information.

Aidan watched as Gwen spent a considerable amount of time checking her eyes, and her throat, and searching for spots of skin irritation—noting that she managed to do this while keeping Brianna's modesty fully intact. She finished by taking count of Brianna's heartbeats then turned back to him, sighing deeply. "I think she'll be okay."

"You *THINK*?" Aidan said, alarming himself with the ferocity of his words. Her noncommittal answer had jolted him. He wanted certainty, even if that was impossible for Gwen to offer.

At Aidan's outburst, Grey stepped between them, nostrils flaring at the raised tone Aidan had used at his wife, but Gwen clearly cared not. She simply rolled her eyes before turning her attention back to Brianna. Still, over her head, Aidan cast Grey a look of apology, which his friend quickly accepted with a nod.

"What happened to your supplies?" Gwen asked as she started to unwind the linens covering Brianna's arm.

"They were lost in the fire."

At this, Gwen's head shot up and she and Grey spoke together: "*Fire?*"

"You haven't heard?" he asked, calming Brianna with a touch as she stirred from their sudden clamor. He'd been all but certain the news would have preceded him considering the length of their journey.

Grey shook his head. "Nay, I took Tristan to Dunhill, and just now returned."

"Grey." Aidan felt Brianna's grasp on his hand

tighten, and when he glanced down at her, he saw a small smile cross her lips—her touch meant as a bolster. "The ship …the ship was gravely damaged. Mayhap destroyed." He'd hoped to be the one to bear the news to his friend, and in light of the circumstances, as he now knew them, he only wished it wasn't being delivered amidst everything else.

"What happened?" Grey's expression was intent.

"The Fitzgeralds," Aidan said, his mouth set in a hard line. "Gil and Nigel were in Ayr and saw me there with Brianna. I haven't the exact details, but I know for certain they had a hand in it."

"And when they failed…" Grey said, then waved his hand over Aidan's and Brianna's injuries. "*This?*" Grey's expression shifted as he realized the breadth of the Fitzgeralds' wickedness.

Aidan nodded. "Aye."

Brianna was looking at him. Confused. "You knew them? The men who attacked us?"

"Oh boy," Gwen muttered and rolled her eyes. Grey merely stared, clearly choosing to remain silent.

"Aidan?" Brianna squeezed his hand.

"I knew them," he said flatly.

A commotion behind him caused him to whirl around just as Tristan burst into the room, crying out his name. Despite everything, Aidan's heart swelled at the sight of him, and he couldn't help but smile as the boy latched onto him, laying a hand atop his head.

Tristan looked up and stepped back, then gasped when he saw Brianna. "Is this your lady? Did she find your medallion?"

Before Aidan could reply, Kitty meowed from her place in the sling around Henry's shoulder, and his eyes shot to the feline. "You captured the wee kitten, too!" he gasped, and as the young were wont to do, left all his questions aside for the furry little beast Henry held out for him to see.

While Tristan cuddled and toyed with Kitty, Gwen had returned her focus to Brianna's unwrapped arm. She was quiet as she examined it, and Aidan felt the tension in the room rise again. Her eyes darted his way, and she leaned in closer when she saw the unmistakable mark of a hand around Brianna's wrist, looking much worse now, hours later.

Gwen looked up to meet Brianna's eyes. "Are there more?" she asked, quietly.

When Brianna shook her head, Gwen glanced around at Aidan and Grey, and widened her eyes pointedly—it took Aidan a moment to understand that Gwen thought that perhaps there *were* more marks and that Brianna was keeping quiet to spare him. His blood began to boil at the thought that Nigel had…Aidan shook his head to clear it. He'd been certain Nigel hadn't the time to…to cause further harm, but suddenly he wondered. Mayhap there was more to her insistence of gathering her weapons or her mention of being defenseless. His horror must have shown on his face because Gwen cast him a sympathetic but beseeching look.

"Why don't you give us a few minutes," she said.

Aidan swayed, suddenly off balance. Even though Gwen was correct to make sure Brianna received the care she needed, and the privacy she might require, the thought of her leaving his sight—especially knowing that it was exactly *because* he'd sent her off on her own to face abuse at the hands of his enemy— was abhorrent, and too painful to think of.

He could barely account for his behavior or the mania stirring in his head. The thought of her wide-eyed stare when he'd asked if she'd been more harmed than he knew had made him irrational, and knew it wasn't helping matters. Yet he stood there, powerless to move, even as Gwen shared a look with Grey obviously conspiring to see to his departure. Then Grey was beside him, gripping his shoulder to pull him away. Aidan held Brianna's eyes as long as possible, grasping at the doorframe as Grey and Henry finally succeeded in pulling him from the room.

CHAPTER 25

Brianna squeezed Gwen's hand suddenly very aware of what was going on as more of the fog lifted. "Nothing else happened, Gwen," she insisted, as she tried to sit up, knowing she sounded groggier than she felt. Gwen's face was filled with compassion, but watching Aidan suffer like that was awful, they'd been through enough already. "You can't let Aidan worry like that. That man—the one who attacked me—he scared the bejesus out of me, but this," she said, motioning toward her wrist, "was the only physical damage he did."

Gwen reached over to gently help her settle back more comfortably, shifting some pillows behind her and beneath her arm before continuing. "I just wanted to be sure," she said, the worry in her voice unmistakable. "And you're not quite ready to get up yet, even if your brain is saying differently."

Brianna realized Gwen was right. She was feeling more alert now—whatever Aidan had given her for the pain was wearing off, and that, paired with seeing how much Aidan had resisted leaving her side had jarred her back to reality—but her body wasn't responding as quickly.

"It's okay," Gwen said. "It won't last long, just try to relax if you can." She took in a deep, cleansing breath then, encouraging Brianna to do the same. "That's it," Gwen said with a smile. They did this a few times, while Brianna focused on Gwen. She was a beautiful woman, with pretty green eyes and dark blonde hair. She had a wonderful manner about her, too, so warm and caring, exhibited once again as Gwen reached forward and cupped the side of her face.

"I know you don't even know me," Gwen said, shaking her head, "and I can only imagine what you've been through—*and trust me*, my imagination has been stretched beyond its limits," Gwen said this with a knowing look and a slow nod. "But I swear, Brianna, I'm on your side. And Aidan's, too." She paused another moment before going on. "Look. As much as these men—Aidan, Grey, the whole brotherhood—want to shelter us from everything, it doesn't always happen that way."

Brianna reached out and covered Gwen's hand with her own—she had a feeling that Gwen knew this from experience. They shared a deeply meaningful look before Brianna spoke again: "Honestly, Gwen, nothing else happened."

"Alright then…but if you remember something later, I'm here. Keeping things inside can be so destructive, sometimes you don't even realize how damaging it is." Gwen waited for Brianna to nod, then reached for some supplies on a small tray beside her.

While Gwen cleaned and redressed her hand and wrist, she told her about what had happened to her years ago. About her abduction at the hands of Gavin's brother, and how it had nearly broken her. When she reached this part, Gwen turned her head for a moment as if caught up in the memory, then made a small sound and turned back. "Even though I knew it, it was Grey's insistence that I talk about it that let me begin to heal. I can't speak for anyone else, but for me, the difference was remarkable—it really helped. And sometimes I've found that sharing *my* experience can help someone else heal, too." Gwen let her words sink in, then smiled softly, before leaving the topic behind. "I know this isn't your best day, Brianna, but I can't wait to hear all about you. Aidan means so much to us, and to know he's found…that he's found you… Brianna, what is it?" Gwen was looking at her so intently and it took Brianna a moment to realize that she'd started drifting off into her own thoughts.

"I'm sorry." Brianna's head was spinning, the reality of everything that had happened to her over the last several weeks all crashing in on itself, and something Aidan had said echoed in the back of her mind. "I…I think I have so much to tell you, Gwen," she whispered, thinking about the MacTavishes and what they'd told her about the other women their friends had married. "But I need to tell Aidan something." Feeling strong enough, Brianna pushed herself up again.

"Whoa, you might feel ready," Gwen said, easing her back down. "But let's finish wrapping your arm and get a new sling in place before you run off. It's that important?" Gwen asked, sensing her urgency.

Brianna nodded slowly. "I think so. I saw a man in Ayr, the morning we arrived. I didn't say anything to Aidan… because I…I was just feeling so self-conscious that day." She paused for a moment and gave Gwen a deliberate look before adding, "So…out of place."

"Pfft." Gwen nodded. "Been there," she said, her eyes telegraphing her understanding, before adding, "Nice ink by the way." She winked then, and Brianna's heart swelled with excitement, joy, and relief, even at what was all but a clear confirmation that she truly wasn't alone here. Obviously, this wasn't the time for details, but Brianna felt the shift, it put her on more solid footing. Gwen smiled encouragingly as these thoughts whirled in her head. "It's okay, trust me, we'll have plenty of time. Seagrave might have a lot of modern conveniences, but they're not *that* modern. Still, we do excel at a few pastimes beyond the daily grind of fifteenth-century *luxury living*," she said, with air quotes and a little chuckle before ticking off a few. "You know, like close family gatherings, outstanding meals, a few games…even making babies," she added, with an infectious smile, blushing when Brianna chuckled. "Go on, now," Gwen said. "Tell me about this man you saw in Ayr."

Brianna paused a moment to take everything in,

feeling the grin on her face before the reality of the current moment came back to her. She nodded, then took a deep breath before speaking.

"Well, at first, I just thought he was some random guy giving me a dirty look, and made it all about me… God, I even went so far as to imagine he was mad that I was walking with Aidan for some reason." Brianna's mind was a swirl of thoughts that she fought to connect. "Maybe if I'd said something…but I was so worked up at the thought of other women with Aidan before me, or Aidan *with* another woman, that I didn't say anything." She trailed off, upset that she'd been so childish that she hadn't done anything useful about it —at the time, or any of the times afterward.

"Brianna," Gwen squeezed her hand, which got Brianna's attention for at least a moment. "What happened, *whatever* it was that happened, was not your fault. I may be the first person to tell you this, but I assure you, I will be far from the last."

"But what if I could have saved us all from this?"

Gwen shook her head. "Sometimes we can't be saved from *this* or anything else," she said, somehow understanding without knowing any of the details yet.

Feeling a true kindred spirit in Gwen, a shared history, so to speak, Brianna told her what happened, how Aidan had sent her off once it was clear they were in danger.

It still hurt thinking about how in those seconds, she'd thought it might be their last together. "He just wanted to keep me from harm." Brianna felt a new rush of emotion and had a good cry while Gwen soothed her.

When she got ahold of herself, Gwen shook her head and smiled softly. "That's all they ever want, Brianna. Trust me, if you're lucky enough to be connected to one of these men —and I mean that rhetorically since you obviously are—there is no deeper or stronger love. None."

"Gwen." Brianna's voice broke for a second, and she leaned in closer, feeling like she had to say something, but the words wouldn't come.

"Whatever it is, you can tell me. Believe me, it helps."

"I...I killed two men."

"Oh, honey." At her unquestioning compassion and the warmth in her eyes, Brianna broke down again.

"It's a heavy burden to carry," Gwen said, after Brianna told her the whole story. "Whether they had it coming or not."

Brianna looked at Gwen and could see immediately that Gwen was speaking from experience —and yet here she was, seemingly sane and thriving. She was a testament to the truth of her words.

"I just want to ask one more time, and then I'll leave it alone. The man you fought off...you're absolutely *sure* that nothing else happened? That he didn't..."

"I'm sure," Brianna said, shuddering at the thought of what could have been. She clutched Gwen's hand then, "Thank you. For listening and also for sharing your story with me."

"I'm here for you, anytime."

"Can we go now?" Brianna asked. "I really need to see, Aidan."

Gwen nodded, then stood up. "Give me just a second."

Brianna gasped at the sight of her in profile. "Gwen! I didn't realize you were pregnant."

Gwen pulled a face, mouthing 'pastime' with air quotes as she walked over to a set of cupboards lining the wall, pressing a hand to her back as she looked at her supplies before grabbing what she needed. Then Gwen wrapped Brianna's arm and fitted her with a new sling in minutes.

"Alright, let's go," she said holding out her hand to help her.

Brianna leaned back, looking at her skeptically. "I don't want to knock you over."

Gwen chuckled. "I'm stronger than I look. But let's hope we both stay upright, otherwise there'll be hell to pay."

Brianna laughed a little at that, too, and it felt so good to let go for a moment. She pictured the looks on Aidan's and Greylen's faces if they came back to find the two of them sprawled on the floor.

When her thoughts returned to her, she sobered. "Did you know them?" Brianna asked as Gwen pulled her up and she shook off the last of the fog muddling her head. "Those men..." she tried to recall the name Aidan used. "They were brothers, I think?"

"The Fitzgeralds." Gwen nodded. "Until last month, I only knew *of* them, when they showed up, unannounced…" her words trailed off a moment. "But, I think Aidan should be the one to fill you in."

When Gwen opened the door, Henry was waiting on the other side with two other men Brianna didn't recognize standing behind him.

"He's in the study," Henry said at once, looking at her with concern.

Brianna nodded, realizing this was the first time since they'd left Ayr that she and Aidan had been separated. "I'm okay," she assured him. "I need to speak with Aidan, though. Will you take me to him?"

Henry looked at Gwen, maybe to make sure it was okay for her to be walking around. At Gwen's nod, he turned down the hall, gesturing for Brianna to follow, the other men falling into step behind them. Brianna did her best not to lean on Gwen, who had offered her arm. She was so consumed with getting to Aidan, that she paid little attention to her surroundings, though she did note the warmth and cleanliness of the enormous hallway. As they passed through the foyer, it was hard to dismiss the intricate masonry and woodwork, especially on the stunning archway that led into the great hall. Brianna made a mental note to come back and examine it more closely when she was well.

They'd just made it halfway across the entranceway when the boy who'd come running into the room earlier to see Aidan appeared. He looked worried, and when Gwen shook her head in answer to the questioning look in his eyes, his face fell even further. Brianna raised her eyebrows at Gwen, indicating that she could take a moment and talk to him. Gwen smiled, patting her hand appreciatively and they walked over to him.

When they reached the boy, Gwen lifted his chin, smiling warmly down at him. "He's going to be alright, Tristan."

The boy's lip quivered. "Are you sure, Mama?"

"Aye, my sweet boy, I'm absolutely sure."

When he looked up at his mother from beneath his lashes, Brianna saw his eyes were almost the same shade as Gwen's. He looked over to Brianna as if for a second opinion, and she smiled down at him.

"I know we haven't been formally introduced," she said, extending her hand, "but I'm Brianna. Would you like to come with us to find Aidan?"

Based on his expression, it was obvious that Tristan hadn't expected the invite. Her heart went out to the boy, the love he must feel for Aidan.

"Maybe you could help keep me steady, so I don't have to rely on your mama?"

At this, the boy's chest puffed up, his eyes no longer wary. "'Tis my duty to assist you. But, I cannot keep something to myself that may cause trouble." The boy said this to her but kept an eye on the men behind them, too.

Curious, Brianna turned. Taking in everyone's pleased expressions, and Tristan's proud stance, she put two and two together, then gave Tristan a warm smile of her own.

"Not easy keeping a secret around here," Gwen chuckled. "Tristan's been taught exactly what he should share, and what can be kept to himself."

Brianna nodded and faced Tristan. "Well, seeing as I'm determined to speak with Aidan, I think an arm or a shoulder to lean on will do the trick *and* save us from trouble," she assured him.

The boy studied her carefully, his gaze flicking from her to the men, looking for a cue perhaps. It seemed they were letting him make his own decision, however, and Brianna had to say, she was enjoying Tristan's lesson in critical thinking.

After a moment, Tristan gave a deep nod and then offered her his arm, which Brianna made a big show of taking graciously. Then, they carried on down another hallway, stopping when they came to a pair of doors set deeply into the stone wall. Brianna heard muffled voices from behind it, maybe even a shout or two, and suddenly hesitated and backed up.

"What do you think they're doing?" she asked, turning to Gwen.

Gwen thought for a moment, then said, "Well, since the Fitzgerald brothers are dead, I suppose they're either strategizing their next steps or peeling Aidan off the ceiling." She paused. "I think seeing you would go a long way. Would you like me to knock? Or do you want to?"

Brianna took a deep breath. Not only did she need to tell Aidan about the man that she'd seen in Ayr, but she also wanted to let him know she was okay, relatively speaking at least. She was just about to step forward when Tristan squeezed in front of her with a huff and took his fist to the door with more force than Brianna thought possible from a child of his age. His actions were met with grunts of approval from behind them, and Brianna couldn't help but be impressed again by this boy's training, as well as the constant reinforcement from the men around him.

Greylen opened the door a moment later, and Brianna didn't miss how his eyes lovingly swept over Gwen. She hadn't been in any condition to notice it before, but that one brief look just now, was enough for her to know how much he valued his wife. These people just kept going up in her estimation, exponentially so.

There were too many people in the room for Brianna to see more than Aidan's profile as he leaned over a large round table that had been set in front of a wall filled with maps, and something about it struck her, reminding her of her grandfather's study at Dunhill. When one of the men moved, she could see that Aidan was writing a letter. Once he was done, he passed it to one of the guards standing nearby, who nodded and then made his way out of the room. Without looking up, Aidan started writing again, finished another letter, sealed it, and handed it off, too. The second guard gave a respectful nod to Gwen and Brianna as he passed, and it was this that alerted Aidan to their presence.

He immediately dropped everything and hurried toward her in the doorway. He looked…oh, now that she could really *see* him, he looked both beautiful and haggard. That they were both still standing was a miracle, and frankly, something she hadn't even tried to wrap her head around yet. Brianna reached out with her good hand, shaking her head as he got closer. His face was drawn so tight, all she wanted was to assure him that she was okay, that nothing else had happened to her, but he gathered her in his arms so quickly, and as his body and warmth enveloped her, all she managed to do was take in a deep and ragged breath. She felt his body tense and knew he was fighting for control, that he probably thought the worst because of her reaction. She was loath to leave his embrace, but she needed to reassure him.

"It was nothing more," she said, pushing back and looking at him intently, making sure he could see she was fully clear-headed now. "I swear."

His eyes, always a mesmerizing shade of green, shifted now, along with some of his worry. They went so dark they were nearly emerald. He bent, and pressing his forehead to hers, whispered, "You needn't ever swear *anything* to me, Brianna. I merely ... I merely wish to keep you from harm."

She loved that about him, and it was something he'd demonstrated repeatedly, even hours ago in the face of death. Literally. Brianna thought about something Gwen had said, that while awful, considering the consequences, it was probably very true. "Maybe you weren't supposed to," she said.

A low growl sounded from his throat in reply and Brianna frowned. Gwen shot her a look that very much said *Let's keep that understanding between us.*

Yeah, got that. Strong as these men were, their sense of duty was not to be threatened.

Once he'd calmed, Aidan glanced to the sling Gwen fashioned and asked, "Your wrist?" his eyes darting between her and Gwen for confirmation.

Brianna nodded, rubbing his arm with her good hand as Gwen said, "Just a sprain. But that bruising is going to take some time to go away."

Brianna tightened her grip on his arm then, wanting his focus for a moment. "I need to tell you something."

He waited expectantly, worry flashing across his face.

"I think I saw one of those men. Before, I mean."

"Before this morning?"

She nodded. "Yes."

"Do you recall where?"

"When we were walking into town, the morning we arrived. I didn't realize I should have said something, maybe it would have prevented all this from happening."

"Brianna," he breathed, grasping her head in his hands. "You cannot carry this burden, too."

"But," she looked at Greylen. "I'm so sorry about your ship."

"Did you set the fire?"

"No."

"Then you've nothing to be sorry about."

When she started to open her mouth again, both of the men gave a terse shake of the head, making it clear there'd be no more arguments. Knowing that was the end of it, Brianna nodded. "Who were they? Why were they after you?"

Before Aidan could answer, another man came into the room. Brianna didn't think he was one of the guards, but maybe another of their brotherhood, based on his commanding presence, and the way Aidan turned toward him immediately, giving him his full attention.

"I just spoke with Alex," the man said, grasping Aidan's shoulder.

Aidan looked like he was about to reply when the man, who'd nodded acknowledgments to everyone in the room—giving Gwen an especially warm smile— fixed his gaze on Brianna. After a moment, he tilted his head. "Have we met?" he asked, staring deeply into her eyes.

When she looked at him directly, Brianna nearly gasped. She'd never seen anyone with eyes the exact shade as hers, outside of her father and grandfather. Was this one of her relatives? A fifteenth-century O'Roarke? Her thoughts raced, running down the genealogy lists she'd spent years poring over. Then it dawned on her. If she was remembering correctly, this must be—

"Callum," Aidan said, stepping to her side and pulling her closer. "This is my wife, Brianna."

Brianna stood silent as Callum looked between the two of them, studying her with particular curiosity. "From where do you hail?" he asked, laser focused on her eyes.

She was so flustered by his question she wasn't

sure how to answer, but after a moment, just awkwardly waved her hand and said, "From…across the way a bit." She knew her vague answer didn't pass muster, but it was the best she could come up with on the spot.

Callum chewed on that for a moment, literally, and it was all she could do not to shift her weight from foot to foot under his deadpan stare. Finally, he spoke. "I see," he said, in a flat tone, then his eyes returned to Aidan. "And you're wed?" For some reason, he seemed puzzled at this.

"Aye," Aidan said slowly.

Again, Callum looked confused. "You didn't call us together for the occasion?" he asked. "As we've all done to mark affairs of such import?"

"We exchanged vows upon the ship." Aidan's words were terse now, which was confusing since Brianna thought he and Callum were good friends—brethren, actually.

"Vows…on the ship?" Callum repeated. He seemed confused by this. "Did Father Michael accompany you?"

Aidan shook his head.

"What of your sire?" Callum asked, turning to Brianna. "Were your parents in attendance?"

When she shook her head, Callum nodded slowly again, his gaze lingering on her, before he turned back to Aidan. "So, you promised yourselves to one another?" he said almost rhetorically, although scorn edged his tone. "But did not sanctify this marriage in the church, or have the approval from anyone Brianna might call family to act on her behalf?"

Oh, she cringed. Suddenly, what she'd felt was on the up and up, now felt anything but.

"*I* acted on her behalf," Aidan said, pulling her tight to his side, his tone clearly pushing back.

Callum looked at her. "You *are* an O'Roarke, Brianna, aye?" his eyes narrowed at Aidan. "That much is evident—at least to me."

She nodded, getting the clear sense that if her father had lived, he'd have sounded just like Callum in the moment.

"Did you think at *any* point to speak with me?" he said to Aidan, an edge to his voice that hadn't been there a moment ago.

Brianna felt Aidan stiffen beside her. "In regard to *what…?*"

At this, Callum's stance changed, and the air nearly crackled in the room. "Since she's in this land," he said with a sweep of his hand, astutely reading between the lines, "without any family known to her—I'm *referring* to Brianna's hand in marriage," he spat, as the exchange became rather heated.

Aidan took a step forward, so close to Callum, their chests almost touched. "The circumstance bore action. As did yours, with Maggie. Did you seek to do the same when you married a *Sinclair* without speaking with me first?"

"If you'd but take your head out of your—"

At this, Greylen wedged himself between them,

barely breaking the tension as Aidan and Callum continued to glare at one another. Greylen shoved them both back, and then Callum rephrased his question.

"If you'll but think back, you'll recall that *I* in fact did!"

Aidan seemed to consider his words and noted that all eyes were on him. After a moment he nodded. "You're right, you sent word to ask if there was a relation, considering we shared the name, and to ask for my blessing if so."

Callum seemed mollified by his recollection as well as his somewhat chastened tone and gathered himself.

Brianna stood there in shock, slowly piecing together what had happened. She felt awful for both of them, but in the moment, she felt sorrier for Callum. He was quite obviously upset, and all because of family honor. *Her* family honor. She knew from her time with the MacTavishes, and from her years spent studying her family's history, that of all the men of this circle, Callum had a deadly quiet edge, one borne out of horrific loss, an O'Roarke family trait. One she knew all too well.

It was clear they weren't done, however. She could feel it in the air, and she felt torn.

Aidan held her gaze and she knew he could read it in her eyes. "I'm sorry."

She knew he meant it; this day had been tumultuous, rife with it, to borrow a term from her *husband*.

Her husband by consent yes, and even legal according to the times, but now that Callum had mentioned it, Brianna recalled the family bible, in which marriages had been recorded all the way back to Fergus and Isabeau. Some of the pages were smudged and tattered, some even lost, before she and her grandfather had been able to preserve what was left of it, but she realized now that in addition to the names of those close enough to be inscribed within the pages, the clergy who performed the ceremony had always been documented as well. Adding credence to Callum's outburst—they did take sanctified unions seriously. For a heartbreaking moment, Brianna worried that it could even be tied to the lore.

"We need to have a church wedding, and soon," she said reaching for Aidan's hand.

"We will," he said, almost desperately, gently clutching her good hand as he looked down at her. He was trying to give her his full attention, but his eyes were still darting between her and Callum.

There was a long moment in which no one spoke, and the longer it went on, the thicker the tension around the room became. The silence grew deafening and just desperate for it to end, Brianna squeezed Aidan's hand again, hoping he'd keep his eyes on hers.

"You told me you knew those men who attacked us," she said, her voice cutting through the quiet. "Why were they after you?"

Brianna wasn't sure who had truly erred. Her for asking the question again, or Aidan for making her.

But in the end, it was Callum who had the last word, taking his role as her familial guardian with the utmost seriousness.

"Because he was expected to wed their sister."

CHAPTER 26

Whatever reckoning Aidan had imagined, he had not expected it to be rendered at the hands of Callum. Yet, in those few seconds after Callum's proclamation, he remained stunned, watching a series of emotions cross Brianna's face—confusion to disbelief to something that went far beyond hurt the longer he remained silent—the gravity of his mistake suddenly at the fore. He wanted to say something, jump to his own defense, but he found himself unable to speak, for in truth, he had none. What did it matter that the Fitzgeralds had demanded that he wed Judith? Aye, it amounted to no less than extortion, yet he'd kept it from her as if it held some sort of real value. The remorse he felt was so deep, as if someone had reached inside his chest and clutched his heart, squeezing out what so recently flourished and thrived there. It was so painful, this sensation, paired with the look in her eyes as she stumbled over a barely audible yet simple, "Oh...*oh*." It nearly felled him.

And still, words would not come forth. Brianna gave him one last pleading look before she turned to leave the room, Gwen rushing after her. He turned his stare to Callum, who had also not moved, perhaps realizing what he'd just done. In fact, save for the women, everyone within Grey's study remained completely still and silent.

"'Twas not my intention to wound her feelings," Callum said, and the look in his eyes told Aidan that he hadn't intended to wound Aidan, not truly.

Aidan knew this, and frankly, had no one to blame for what had just happened other than himself. He'd never broached the subject with Brianna. Not once. He'd thought—like a fool—that holding his ground, merely focusing on a formal end to the agreement was enough, but the anticipation building in his chest should have told him otherwise. He knew now that he could have—*should* have—found the time to tell Brianna about Judith and her brothers, given her at least some sort of roundabout explanation or another so she wouldn't come by the news...like this. By surprise that is.

Shaking his head at his senselessness, he faced Callum squarely, offering his friend the apology he deserved, tripping over each other's words when they spoke at the same time. Aidan held his hand up and stopped him. "Nay, allow me, please. I owe you an apology, Callum. I can see now why you ...you—"

"Saw fit to kick your arse," one of the men said *almost* under their breath.

Aye, that. It took only a moment for him and

Callum to smirk, and both nodded in agreement as chuckles sounded about the room. They were brothers first—especially in cases such as this—and in the end, all else mattered naught.

"May I offer some advice?" Callum asked once everyone had recovered. When Aidan nodded, Callum pointed toward the door and said earnestly, "Go after her. Now."

Aidan needed no more convincing. With another round of boisterous agreement behind him, Aidan turned and hastened after her. As he rounded the hallway and headed toward the stairs, he found Tristan perched atop the steps of the great hall. Aidan didn't stop but caught his eye and cast a sheepish smile his way, putting a hand to his ear as he started up the steps.

"Never be too proud to admit your mistakes," the lad called out readily, reciting one of the many lessons of their brotherhood creed.

"And?" Aidan said without looking back.

"Even if it pains you...*especially* if it pains you."

Though Aidan had little to cheer about, *that* brought a grin to his face, one that was wiped clean in a blink when he nearly ran into Gwen on her way downstairs, stopping him in his tracks. Not literally, per se, but out of respect, he remained still so she could swat his arm.

"Ooh, what's wrong with you," she said, apparently needing the use of both hands to exert her frustration upon him. Seemingly satisfied with his punishment, she took a deep breath seconds later, then looked at him contritely. "Sorry, I know you already got an earful. I just, I just really like her, and—"

Aidan grasped her by the shoulders, cutting off her speech. "I *love* her, Gwen."

"Oh," she sighed and melted instantly. "I normally wouldn't say this, but it's just so obvious she loves you too." She pulled a face, darting her eyes to the side, and confessed, "Which is why she's waiting for you in your room. Go already."

Aye, he was trying.

He nodded and gave her a smile. Before he continued up the stairs, he pointed to the balustrade when he let go of her. "Have a care."

She rolled her eyes at him, but reached for the railing as he continued to his chamber...*their* chamber. The chamber he was sharing with his wife at Seagrave. He knew he'd much to repair, but for a moment, he was struck at the degree his life had changed since he'd last been here. When he reached the door, he knocked first, unsure what to expect. He was buoyed by her ready call, and quickly stepped inside, momentarily puzzled because she didn't seem to be anywhere within.

"Brianna?" he said, his eyes sweeping the chamber. He was about to call out to her again when he saw her on the floor in the sitting area before the hearth, her legs tucked beneath her, Kitty on the cushion behind her head.

When they locked eyes, she made a face. Her unhappiness with him, the situation, or both, was clear. "If I ever wondered what bringing home someone to meet my parents would be like, I just found out," she snapped.

Right, spitting mad it was, then. He could not really be surprised, given what she'd just learned—and how she'd learned it, but still, he wondered: "Why are you sitting on the floor?"

"I'm filthy," she said sharply. "I'm not going to dirty anything in this chamber until I can bathe and change." She paused for a moment, and he dared not challenge her. "How's Callum?" she asked abruptly, and it wasn't lost on him that her inquiry was meant as a show of familial loyalty.

"Formidable," he said, leveling her with an equal stare. "Much like you right now—*nay*," he continued, holding up his hand as she opened her mouth to protest. "Callum's reaction was appropriate and deserved. I should have expected no less from him, we are as close as true brothers could be."

"I guess that's a good thing, considering, he's my family," she returned, clearly unmoved by any of his words so far.

"And you're *my* family, Brianna. My wife. Aye," he said at her doubtful look, knowing that this too must be addressed. "We've not yet been wed in the church, but we will be."

"It's not even that!" she burst out. "It is, yes…but… you were engaged!…betrothed!"

Aidan made sure his words were clear when he said, "Never, Brianna, truthfully, we were not."

"A technicality, then… Did you have feelings for

each other?" The turn in her tone and look in her eyes sliced through him, she was deeply hurt.

"Brianna, I barely *know* Judith, let alone ever had feelings for her..." his words trailed off at her look, his head tilted, begging her thoughts.

She looked at him a long time, and when she spoke again her tone had lost its edge. "Maybe there's more and you just don't want to say?"

"Do I strike you as a man who doesn't say what's on his mind?"

She made a face and raised her good hand in the air. "I mean...really, Aidan?"

Right. Since he'd no argument, he tried to remain silent and let her continue, though he did grumble which he obviously should not have.

"Oh, *now* you have something to share?" She accepted his contrite look, but after a moment, worry crossed her features again. "Did you though? Have feelings for her?"

Aidan suppressed a sigh. He could not be frustrated that she felt the need to ask him again, considering he'd been less than forthright about the whole subject. "I did not."

"Did *she* have feelings for you?"

He wasn't sure how that would even be possible, but his surprise at her query must have shown. "We were barely in each other's presence. Mayhap twice, three times—ever." He quickly explained how the suggestion of wedding Judith had come about, and its true nature, but she still seemed skeptical.

"Okay…I guess," she added with a shrug. "But…if I hadn't arrived, would you have gone through with it?"

"*Nay.*" His answer was immediate, though he realized he wasn't certain what he would have done. A look must have crossed his face when he realized that in the end, he had considered it. Her alarm was clear. "Nay, Breea."

"You had to think about that."

"I felt sorry for her situation." That was the truth.

Her face fell.

"For the love of God, Brianna. I love you—YOU. I never once had to *consider* promising myself to you. I just did. Period. 'Twas an act in the moment that I knew was right. Providence. Our fate. Our destiny. There was no consideration involved when it came to you—the woman I know is my heart, and has my heart."

When she looked at him, her gaze was still filled with love, but she was wounded by what she'd just learned, not to mention the trauma she'd endured only hours ago.

"I know, in here," she took her fist and thumped her chest, "that you're right, we are meant for one another. But," her voice cracked. "Aidan," she covered her eyes with her hand and wept.

"Breea." He dropped to his knees and gathered her in his arms. He was equally grateful that she welcomed his touch as he was heartbroken by her sorrow. He held her for some time, uttering soothing sounds and rocking her gently as she sobbed in earnest. He felt no hurry, no need to rush her. She needed this cleansing release, this letting go of everything that had been building since they awoke this morning, and that he could provide her this safe haven, despite their confrontation just now, was all that mattered to him. After a few minutes, her breathing slowed, and as she started to calm down, she pushed away just enough to look at him. He wouldn't have thought anything of such a small gesture before this morning, but now, just her being in his arms, looking at him this way, brought a rush of gratitude, love, and warmth. He brushed his lips across her forehead, to the corners of her eyes, and then, unable to stop himself, rubbed his entire face to hers. She seemed to understand that he was undone by it all too and sighed while nodding her approval.

He wasn't sure how long they remained there quietly taking comfort from each other, but when she looked at him again, two things were so very clear: first, his poor Breea had been through hell, and second, to have her safely within the walls of Seagrave was a true blessing.

"I am so sorry for all that you faced today."

Her fingers gently covered his lips. "No," she said so softly he barely heard it. "I'm beginning to think..." Her mouth twisted and her eyes narrowed, but she wore a faraway look, lost in thought for a long moment before returning her focus to him. "What if it was always meant to happen? Some manifestation of what occurred today, I mean?"

That had his attention. "What are you saying?" he

asked, sitting up straighter. This was no restorative musing on the day's events as he'd thought.

"What if our coming together was never about us being together in the long run?" She cupped the side of his face as he slowly shook his head, still unsure precisely what she was getting at, but not liking what he was hearing. "What if this is all we have, Aidan? What if our union isn't eternally viable?"

Her words stunned him. "*Wait* …wha…why?"

"I need to work through this," she said, shifting in his lap to straddle him. He could nearly see the thoughts churning in her head, and though he waited, she said nothing further.

After a minute of this, he could bear it no longer. "Why would you question the soundness of our union?" He asked, adjusting her slightly, but keeping her firmly in his grip.

She appeared startled by the question but then nodded slowly. "Well, I remembered something. With all this talk about family and lineage, and seeing Callum—and knowing I'd read his name before—I remembered this bible we have in my family that's been passed down through the generations."

He believed he knew exactly the book she was speaking of. If so, he'd seen it many times. He'd even watched Callum carefully record his and Margret's name into it.

"It's inscribed with all the names of those who've been married throughout the ages, and…our names are not in it."

"Wait," Aidan said, putting his hands on her shoul-

ders. "Slow down. Your concern is that our names are not written within the pages of a tome that would be nearly a millennium in age by the time you had your hands on it? Were all the pages even intact when you saw them?"

"It's not a concern," she said, somewhat affronted. "It's a hypothesis, a theory routed in—"

"Breea, I wasn't making light of your premise."

"I'm sorry, my thoughts are racing." She shook her head. "They aren't intact, not all of them, but hear me out. What if...if there's something more to why things have unfolded for us the way they have?"

He could tell already, he would not like what she was about to say but gave her the breadth to express herself. In truth, he was happy just to be touching her.

"What if our names aren't in it, aren't included in the sacred family bible because...we don't ... because fate *wasn't* fixing its mistake but was instead following a deliberate plan?"

He grunted. It was worse than he thought. "Brianna—"

"No, please just hear me out."

Although he did not like what she was saying, he smiled and nodded, tightening his grip as he said, "I will always hear you out." Only a fool would dismiss her input, but despite her worries, he was beyond certain they would prevail in the end, regardless of her ruminations and where they might lead.

She told him then of everything that had led her to him, starting with her quest to retrieve her family's sword. Aidan nodded, piecing together this new information with what he already knew from Maggie's discovery of the sword in the first place and then Dar and Celeste's encounters with it, after that. He took a sharp intake of breath when he realized that it had been Brianna's grandfather who'd set the sword's entire course in motion. He wondered about the letter Brianna said he'd left for her, one that seemed to intimate knowledge about his granddaughter's destiny, and what it might mean, but said nothing, wanting to let her speak fully. He listened intently as Brianna spoke of her odd journey to Dunhill *Manor*, and her grief when she discovered that the heirloom letterboxes no longer graced the mantle there. Hearing her speak of these things, to realize they had deep and personal meaning to both of them, yet existed nearly a thousand years apart stunned him. When she told him what led to her hasty departure from her ancestral home, sharing in detail what she remembered of that last voyage with her parents —and the new information about the tragedy that she'd only just discovered from her aunt and uncle— he nearly wept for her tale and what she'd already endured.

"Och, Breea," he said, his heart breaking. "And I brought you aboard a ship."

"No." She shook her head. "Well, yes, but Aidan, you gave me back my sea legs, too, and happy memories I was never able to revisit before then, and so much more."

She told him then of her stop in Carlisle, how she'd been gifted the leather satchel and dress he'd first seen her in at a town fair. The woman in the booth, who he was sure was none other than Esmeralda herself, meddler and peddler extraordinaire. Then she told him of Abersoch and even though he should have known this was of course ultimately leading there, it never occurred to him that... that—

"You saw Lachlan, and Dar and Celeste? You *supped* with them," he said, barely breathing, so overcome with emotion that he closed his eyes and let his head fall.

"I stayed with them," she told him and began stroking his hair. "And their little boy, Griffin."

She gave him a few moments to gather himself before continuing her story, right up to the moment she spied his medallion as if it suddenly appeared out of thin air.

"Can we just take a moment," he said, standing and taking her with him.

She nodded readily and had just leaned into him when the door flew open. Both of their heads turned as Gwen hurried in, followed by Lady Madelyn and Anna as well as a parade of staff noisily preparing two tubs, all the while making no bones about their current displeasure with him. It was clear Gwen had failed to mention that he was back in her good graces, and so he threw a hand in the air still holding tight to Brianna.

Gwen pulled a face as she realized that it was her blunder that was the cause of his current distress, and quickly rectified the situation, alerting everyone of his restored favor. She shot him a look of apology and started to herd everyone out again. Aidan nodded his thanks as the staff bestowed him with smiles as they passed. He caught Brianna staring, her eyes widening in surprise, obviously impressed by the power Gwen wielded.

"You, too," Gwen said, turning to him, "Out."

"*What?*" he said, confused, and Gwen just nodded, her finger pointed to the door. He narrowed his eyes, none too pleased to have to put his conversation with Brianna on hold, but when he looked down at her, she gave him a small but reassuring smile. "I would have taken care of you myself," he said, relieved that they were on solid footing again.

"And I would have let you," she returned with a boldness that he'd not seen in her before—a boldness that was well-earned. Her smile broadened at the approval in his eyes. "We've become a good team, you and I," she said, her hand moving from his chest up to the nape of his neck, where her fingers tangled in his hair.

Aye, indeed they had, and his heart swelled with his love for her. "Breea. We will figure this out, and prevail together as we've done thus far." He leaned down, pressing his forehead to hers. "I love you. I…" he faltered as he realized how much he wanted, *needed* to hear the same words back. He knew to his bones that mere words mattered naught, not in the face of action. Yet after everything they'd endured, he was nearly ashamed to admit it was *this* that had him undone. "I—"

"I love you, too," she said, ending his misery, grasping his neck as if to strengthen her point.

He kissed her, then. The effect of her admission was so powerful, that it washed over and through him setting him to rights, and before letting go, said pointedly, "I'll be back shortly," turning to Gwen, Lady Madelyn, and Anna each in turn. When Gwen shook her head, he sighed but corrected himself. "Not so shortly, but not long either," he stressed.

"We'll see you at dinner," Gwen called, her firm tone leaving no room for further interpretation.

He raised a brow as he leaned closer to Brianna. "I find her *highly* offensive at times," he said, nudging his lips against hers, smiling at the chuckle he got from her.

"Aidan, out!"

And that was the end of that.

CHAPTER 27

For the next few hours, Brianna was treated to a fifteenth-century spa package worthy of her Medieval Black Card. From the glorious shampoo (which smelled every bit as good as her fancy salon brand, minus the thick lather) and the accompanying scalp massage, to a special body scrub concocted by Gwen and Lady Madelyn (apparently all the rage), and finally, and most unexpected, a mani-pedi—phenomenal, even without polish. Brianna didn't even mind the pruning and plucking here and there...or there either. It felt amazing to be sparkly clean and smooth all over, her hair perfect in a glamorous knot, and skin aglow. Gwen had even managed to furnish a sort of toothbrush and had given it to her with a toothpaste she'd whipped up, for which Brianna was eternally grateful.

Still reeling from her conversation with Aidan and truly unused to so much caring attention, it had taken Brianna a moment to let it all happen. But after today, which had been an emotional rollercoaster even Brianna 2.0 was ill-equipped for, she'd just gone along with it. Other than Aidan, no one—no one—had taken care of her like this since she was a child. Gwen, Anna, and Lady Madelyn carried out everything deftly, but with compassionate smiles. She had to say, their timing was perfect, especially after her harrowing morning.

By the time she was dressed again in a soft and lovely gown from Gwen's collection, most likely the ones she'd had made for her early pregnancy since she appeared to be very petite, Brianna almost felt as if the first part of the day had never even happened. Already, it all felt somewhat removed with everything that had happened in between...or maybe she was just compartmentalizing. But even when Alan and Richard arrived to deliver her bags to her (only to have them swiftly taken so her clothing could be laundered), she'd remained on an even keel—no memories of the morning overtook her, nor did she begin to spiral again. Her concern was only for their welfare, and theirs for hers.

Heading back downstairs, Brianna was so taken with her surroundings, that she wasn't sure where to look first, and marveled at how different she felt from when she'd first arrived at Seagrave. When she stopped atop the landing to look outside, she had to catch her breath, the view was so arresting. Gwen patted her hand and smiled knowingly, like it was something everyone did.

Still looking everywhere she could, when they

stepped into the great hall, her focus zeroed in on Callum and Grey. Their heads were bent in deep conversation, and Aidan was pacing in front of the fireplace. Seeing them all together like this, it was a startling scene to take in, with the men all so simply but sharply dressed in long-sleeved shirts, dark trousers, and tall polished boots. Striking yes, and even ahead of the times, a detail that confused Brianna until she considered the wealth and worldliness of this crowd—not to mention Gwen's obvious influence. Whatever the provenance, it suited them perfectly.

When Aidan looked up to see her, he threw his hands in the air and strode toward her. "Finally!" he grumbled, reaching her side and pulling her in for a hug.

Brianna's heart swelled at his reaction and she smiled, sinking into his embrace, hoping against hope her fears were misplaced. The thought of them parting was unimaginable. Aidan's earlier explanation had mostly soothed her nerves, but there was still something that she couldn't get past. Clearly, the whole Judith incident was resolved—which it *was*, at least what she'd been insecure about—but that was only part of it. What was lurking in the back of her mind now, however, was even more frightening. It was making her question her whole family history, specifically *her* history. Yes, fate had taken her where she was meant to go, and she did feel like she was *meant* to be here, but was it because she and Aidan were meant to be together and live happily ever after together, or …or was there more just around the corner?

"Breea."

Brianna startled at the sound of Aidan speaking her name. She'd been so lost in thought, that when she looked up at him, it took her a moment to recognize the worry and concern on his face. She smiled softly, hoping to assuage him but wasn't sure that this was the time to broach the subject again.

Saving her from having to explain, Tristan entered the room, and everyone turned to look at him. He had a little girl in his arms who looked like she'd just awoken from a nap. Brianna guessed it was his sister, but was confused when the little girl reached out as they neared Callum. Without even looking, Callum opened up his arms and took her into them. As she snuggled up against him, Brianna turned to Gwen who smiled softly and explained that Callum had stayed at Seagrave after his first wife, Fiona, had died and developed a bond with all her children, but especially this one.

Brianna nodded and turned back to watch—she hadn't, but should have expected that these men would be so tender and caring with infants and children, too. On the heels of her thought, Greylen and Gwen's youngest boy toddled into the room, and was scooped up by his father as he let out a happy shriek. Brianna smiled. It really was remarkable.

Tristan stayed close to Aidan after offloading his sister, and with hardly a moment for small talk, they all gathered around the table and took their seats.

When Brianna reached for Aidan's hand, he explained that the start of mealtimes was a bit more urgent. By the chuckles and smiles around the table, it appeared everyone agreed. As the children got settled, Brianna was struck again by the warmth of what felt like a true family table. Drinks were poured, platters and bowls filled with delicious food served, and it was all a bit overwhelming. She chose to observe instead of participate for a little while, just to let it all sink in. She had to suppress a laugh watching Callum pretend to serve Gwen's little girl the butter dish instead of her meal—the girl gave a wide-eyed look, staring in dismay between him and the small, covered crock on the table. After a moment, Callum laughed, and corrected his mistake quickly, adding a dollop to her bread, and they shared the sweetest smile.

After the initial chatter around the table died down in favor of eating, Aidan leaned in, and asked to share her earlier thoughts—fears, really—with those around the table. Knowing it would be better to talk about it and get a few opinions from people who had experience in this kind of thing, Brianna nodded, though she was nervous.

She leaned closer to speak into his ear, hoping no one else would hear, and was struck for a moment by how good, how right, it felt to be so near to him. "I want to be here with you. You know that, right? Forget about everything else," she whispered. It felt important that she stressed this to him, that whatever her doubts about Fate's intentions, she'd take every second with him that she could get.

"I know," he said, stroking the side of her face, then said loud enough to garner everyone's attention, "I...*we* have a subject to broach."

Brianna's heart leapt when she realized what he was about to say, but she swallowed and nodded when he glanced back and raised a brow giving her a chance to change her mind. She squeezed his hand for extra assurance and glanced around the table as Aidan continued, "Brianna...Brianna thinks..." he stumbled on his words, and she quickly looked back, surprised at his faltering. They shared a bittersweet look and she gave him a small nod, which Aidan returned. He cleared his throat and continued, "She's giving serious weight to the idea that *somehow*, in our case, fate's course may not apply as it has to the rest of you. I'm trying to convince her otherwise."

Suddenly all eyes were on her, and Brianna shifted in her seat under their scrutiny. "Well, I don't *want* it to be true," she said. "But what if it is?"

"How so?" Greylen asked, taking his wife's hand when she blindly reached for his beside her.

Brianna felt like a huge weight had been lifted just from this ready concern, and she turned to Aidan with a grateful smile—he'd been right to bring this up here. Glad to have somewhere to crowdsource her fears, Brianna told them about the bible at home, and how some of the pages were missing.

She turned to Callum who had made a move to speak. "Well, I wonder if the page on which your union would have been—*will be*—recorded is one of the missing ones," he said slowly. "The last entry I inscribed was for Dar and Celeste. Did you see their names?" he asked.

Feeling hopeful, Brianna thought about it and realized she hadn't seen their names. She shook her head. "I don't think so," she said. "I definitely would have remembered, too, especially at some point during my visit...with them...*Oh.*" At the sudden shock registering on the faces around the table, Brianna turned to Aidan. She grabbed his arm, tearing up herself. "You didn't say anything?" she asked.

He shook his head, looking just as surprised that he'd somehow forgotten. "With so much going on, it hadn't occurred to me."

"Them," Greylen said. "You mean..."

Brianna slowly nodded, as she recalled Aidan's reaction earlier. "Dar, Celeste, and Lachlan."

"He's okay?" Gwen asked, eyes wide. "Lachlan, I mean?"

Brianna nodded again, she'd forgotten that he had a heart condition that obviously would have had a different end here in the fifteenth century. "Oh, yes. He's unbelievably fit," she said. Poor Gwen, her head fell into her hands and she cried while Greylen did his best to soothe her, even Tristan moved to his mother's side then to offer his support.

"And Celeste, she's well too?" Callum asked.

Brianna grinned at the thought of her. "Oh yes, she's so sweet. Quiet, and at first, she was quite shy. But she's lovely. When she saw my satchel, you'd have thought she'd found a missing treasure. I didn't even know it was an original O'Roarke creation, but she knew it from clear across the room."

Callum was the one overcome then, and it took Brianna a moment to remember their connection. Celeste was the sister of Derek—who, according to the MacTavishes and lore—a twenty-first-century Callum incarnate.

"Their little boy, his name is Griffin, is two, maybe." At everyone's nodding heads, she assumed they concurred with the timeline. "And she's probably a little farther along than you right now, Gwen."

Realizing just how important these people were to them, Brianna went through the whole story again. Everyone had more than a few questions about her latest visit to Dunhill Manor—she'd barely made it through the telling of her arrival when the friendly peppering started. Brianna was relieved that no one seemed to be interested in dwelling on her childhood trauma, and everything she'd learned from her aunt and uncle on her last night there, but they *did* spend a considerable amount of time talking about the wee bit of magic that she'd been so resistant to once upon a time. So engrossed in their conversation, surrounded by these people who somehow felt as close, or maybe even closer than her family ever had, Brianna forgot herself for a moment and referenced the O'Roarke family lore. And, since she was learning that nothing *ever* went unnoticed with these people (even if you thought it did), at her mention of O'Roarkes marrying only in the case of true love, everyone jumped on it. Brianna glanced at Callum, somehow knowing that despite the centuries between them, he would not only understand but also realize their legacy, good and bad.

"The truth of the matter is, O'Roarke marriages come at a steep price," she said slowly. "They don't happen unless the love that binds it is true and enduring, which is great of course, but the *length* of these marriages is sometimes frightfully short."

Everyone nodded soberly, and Brianna had the sense that they all knew in their own way the truth of it, especially Callum.

Eager to move on, Brianna recounted her overnight stay at the inn and the fair, and when pressed again, described in detail the woman who'd given her the bag and clothing. When she got to the part of Dar opening the door when she arrived at Abersoch, she carefully recounted every single detail and every single word just as she had earlier with Aidan.

As dinner was cleared, Brianna realized she never had a chance to say how wonderful everything had been. She opened her mouth to do so, but was quickly drawn into another round of questions—everyone had returned to the subject of her worries that fate had not brought her here for an everlasting union, but for a different reason.

Everyone jumped in, trying to help her see another side—except Callum. Callum was quick to speak up, and it was clear he understood her point.

"You believe it to be more contrived," Callum said,

and Brianna saw Aidan's face set determinedly at his words.

She gave a small nod, conscious of Aidan's eyes on her.

"I have no desire to find truth in it," Callum continued. "I don't even care to entertain the thought, but Brianna's correct—we must. We cannot put our heads in the sand and ignore this very real possibility," he stressed to the others, then turned back to her. "I know I can speak for everyone when I tell you that we all believe wholeheartedly that *you* believe these things to be true, or at the least that they could be, aye?"

Brianna nodded, both grateful and terrified at his willingness to explore this. He looked pointedly at everyone before continuing, "Unfortunately, Brianna has a point, distasteful as we all may find it, *however*, if we consider, for example, mine and Margret's circumstances—how we each lost our first loves…" he shook his head. "The point is our losses occurred and two years later we were united, or reunited as," he paused, "*lore* will one day state. I suppose any sort of mechanization could have occurred." Callum said this pointedly while looking at Brianna, before continuing. "In which case, our tragedies might have happened differently, yet still would have occurred."

"Right. I hope you've finished." Aidan glared at Callum. "Thank you for your input."

Looking reluctant, Callum went on. "And…" he started, pausing for a moment as he glanced at Aidan.

If the daggers in his stare were any indication,

Aidan was none too pleased about what Callum was about to say.

"If not for the bargain my mother made," Callum continued, turning his focus back to Brianna, "I, too, would have suffered the fate of an impassioned, but frightfully short union."

He told Brianna the story then, one that she'd never come across in any of her family research, of his mother Isabeau offering a stone to an enchantress as payment to ensure Callum's happiness—the very stone which would eventually take its rightful place in the Wolf Sword centuries later.

It was such a beautiful, romantic story, Brianna almost forgot how they'd gotten on the subject, but quickly came back to reality when she looked over at Aidan, who was now glowering at Callum. Hoping to avert any possibility of Aidan leaping across the table to pummel him, Brianna squeezed his leg, and was grateful when Gwen jumped in.

"And what is it that *you* believe?" she asked her.

"I'm starting to wonder if everything I've learned, everything I was taught—of weaponry, my professional expertise in..." she glanced around the room, unsure of how much she should say aloud, but then continued, "in, well, objects of your world. I've been wondering if it was all leading up to today. If I was meant to be here with Aidan," she said, looking at him, "primarily to take that shot, and save him."

Between the gawking stares from Greylen and Callum and Aidan's loud sigh, Brianna figured out that he'd failed to mention this part of the story, too.

After Aidan filled them in (somewhat begrudgingly, Brianna noted, though he gave her a contrite smile after), she told Callum the only reason she'd been able to do it was because of Maggie—that starting with her, all the O'Roarke girls throughout the centuries were proficient in weaponry. He shook his head, clearly overcome, but quickly gathered himself and smiled wistfully at her.

"I nearly choked on my breakfast the morning she asked me to teach her to wield the sword."

Everyone chuckled, as he told the story of his precious Maggie, and there was no other way to describe her—the love Callum had for her was so obvious.

Brianna gasped with a sudden realization. "She learned with the Wolf sword?"

Callum lit up at that, and the effect was electric. "A fitting name indeed," he said with a gleam in his eye. "Aye, 'twas the very one, and I considered the sword hers until the night Dar left with it. Later, the sword was kept upon the wall in the Great Room and 'twas there that it rested while he and Celeste lived here with us. I was…" he got emotional then, and looking around, Brianna saw that they all did. "I was the one who put it into her hands, the day she was thrust back to her time—her rightful time."

Brianna gave everyone a moment to gather themselves before she spoke again. Aidan began absently brushing his thumbs across her palm and it was such a lovely sensation, simple and pure—in contrast to everything that had just come to light, the day itself for that matter. Still, it reminded her how grateful she was to be sitting there, and when Gwen caught her eye and smiled, something about her look struck her again. Here was a woman so truly happy and satisfied with her life, centuries away from what she was used to, and yet she clearly thrived.

Brianna was about to speak up, but it was Grey who broke the silence. "So, I still don't understand exactly what you're worried about," he said. "'Tis obvious you and Aidan are rightly matched."

Yes, they were, that was the hard part. Brianna had absolutely no doubt about their pairing—just whether it was really meant to be. She swallowed hard, unable to say her thoughts out loud. Across the table, Gwen's face fell.

"*Oh.* Oh, Brianna," she said. "You think that's why you're here—that it's the *only* reason."

Brianna felt tears build up behind her eyes as she nodded.

"You and Aidan are so obviously meant to be together, but now that you've settled the score, so to speak…"

Brianna nodded again, wiping away tears that had begun to spill.

"You could also be wrong," Grey said so firmly, but with such care, that her tears stopped, and she was able to get ahold of herself.

Brianna smiled weakly wondering if he'd done that on purpose. "I hope I am, but when I realized that we technically aren't married—"

She didn't get the chance to finish her sentence as

everyone—even Callum, she noted—leapt in with a deluge of justifications for why Aidan had done what he'd done. It was clear that *this* was the part of the story Aidan had filled Greylen and Callum in on while she'd been upstairs with Gwen and the consensus it seemed—if one defined consensus as everyone speaking over one another to tell her repeatedly—that although Aidan had given his consent the moment he realized they were meant to be together, he hadn't expected Brianna to give hers until sometime after their journey, knowing she was finding herself in a new place entirely, and surely would need the time to adjust, not just to that, but to Aidan himself. He hadn't accounted for the fire or their subsequent stay in Ayr, and he especially hadn't expected Brianna's reaction to the fire. When they got to relaying this point of his storytelling, she blushed, thinking back to that night when everything had changed for her. She was grateful for the way Aidan had told it, sparing her much embarrassment and stating simply that she'd "seized what fate had given to them." They figured it out anyway.

After a cacophonous few minutes, Brianna put her hand out, hoping to quiet the debate.

"I understand why he did it," she said loudly. Aidan was watching her closely, but his expression was unreadable.

"I haven't one regret," he said

She squeezed his hand. "And neither do I," she said, hoping no matter what, he knew she really meant that. And, despite her fears, she was so grateful for the little bit of knowledge they'd had of how fate had intervened, and how it had allowed them to throw caution to the wind, and just dive in completely with one another—however it might turn out, she couldn't imagine not having these past weeks with him. "But...but what if the fact of our marriage not being in accordance with O'Roarke standards is some kind of omen?"

"A technicality," Aidan stressed again, sitting up straighter as if his mere bulk would aid his cause. "Easily and quickly rectified."

That sparked another round of discussion, though this one much more civilized—mostly, an inquiry was made of the whereabouts of Father Michaels, whose name Brianna recognized from her family bible, so vows might even be exchanged tonight. Despite the positive feedback and the eagerness to make a plan to move forward, Brianna still felt uneasy.

Maybe she was overthinking things or simply being irrational, but still—she couldn't help but feel like she was waiting for the other shoe to drop.

Brianna looked at Greylen, and the others and suddenly felt so very tired. She wanted nothing more than to sit in comfortable companionship with these people, eat a good meal, and most of all—crawl into that soft bed, and into the security of Aidan's strong arms, and put this day behind her. So, she offered what was probably a pretty unconvincing nod and a shrug and picked up her fork. She realized that she'd been so caught up in the conversation, and answering their questions, that she'd barely paid attention to dinner and now they were well into dessert. She took a bite and almost groaned at how good it was—a cake made with fresh berries and vanilla, doused in a luscious, whipped cream—and at that, everyone took the hint and busied themselves with their plates and small talk.

After a little while, Callum stood and poured brandies, eyeing the table for takers. Although at first Brianna declined, she changed her mind and held up her hand, indicating just a little. Callum nodded and placed a small dram beside her, before serving Aidan and Greylen. When Callum took his seat again, the conversation turned toward Brianna visiting Dunhill once she'd had a chance to fully heal.

After a little while, Brianna noticed that Gwen had gone quiet, and started shaking her head, grinning from ear to ear. Greylen noticed, too, and returned her smile, then covered her hand with his own, giving it a small squeeze. Still smiling, Gwen spoke. "Look at our growing family. It's amazing," she said wistfully.

Callum and Aidan both nodded and raised their drinks to her sentiments. It wasn't the first time Brianna was struck by the warmth around this table, and how deeply entwined these people were. Looking around at the faces that were fast becoming familiar to her, it suddenly dawned on Brianna that she hadn't seen Greylen's mother since well before dinner.

"Speaking of family, where's Lady Madelyn?" she asked, the first words she'd spoken since her confession of doubt.

"Oh!" Gwen lit up all over again. "She's putting

some things together for Isabelle and the children so Aidan can take," Gwen started shaking her head as she looked at him, barely continuing, "them …with—" before stopping mid-sentence.

Brianna turned to Aidan, and saw him wide-eyed, shaking his head—exactly what Gwen had been mimicking, but Gwen had caught onto his signal a beat too late. Suddenly, it all made sense.

"You're leaving," she said, looking at Aidan, who nodded.

"I'm leaving at first light."

And there went the other shoe.

CHAPTER 28

Aidan had never intended to keep the information of his upcoming journey from Brianna—in fact, had he not been so swiftly banished from their chamber earlier, he would have told her then.

Now, however, he remained seated, engaged in a silent battle of wills with the worthiest opponent he'd ever encountered. Truthfully, he wasn't certain he had the desire to stay his ground—he hated that Brianna had yet again been thrown into a swirl of doubt and confusion—and so he was grateful when everyone around the dinner table abruptly excused themselves, muttering excuses about children who needed to be tended to and the like. While Brianna said her goodnights, Grey confirmed with Callum the ship's readiness for an early departure and motioned to the staff to return later.

Once the room was empty, Aidan turned his chair to face Brianna's, hoping she would follow suit. She did not, however, and instead, sat up straighter, then leveled him with her most intense gaze yet.

"You're returning the bodies, and the prisoners, aren't you?" she said. "And you'll need to check on Judith, I'm sure. I can imagine that you would feel some sense of responsibility toward her, especially now." She put her hand up to stop him when he made to speak. "I'm only saying that I know you well enough to know, regardless of the circumstances, you feel beholden to make sure your actions don't impact her negatively."

She was right, of course, but he feared she was placing more import on the venture than was really there. His greater concern, however, was her flat tone and expressionless eyes. He was learning his wife was a force of her own, especially when pressed, but considering her earlier worries, he feared she might distance herself from him because of it. After a moment, he used his boot to slide her chair around so she faced him too.

"Breea…. *Brianna.*"

"We're not married," she said, again, clearly fixated on the detail that was driving her. "I've been living in a magical bubble of false security."

"Och, when spoken like that I can almost under-stand your worry." He pressed his fingers to his eyes, and sighed, taking a moment before leveling her with a fervent gaze of his own. "However, no matter how we've come to be here, we *are* married. Mutual consent and consummation *are* binding."

"Not to an O'Roarke, not in the long run."

"It *was* before," he said, surprised by his heated reaction. "Save you, I'd strike down *any* who suggested otherwise."

"Aidan." She pressed her hand to her chest and shook her head, her tone at once contrite. "I wasn't diminishing what we have, you have my entire heart. If Father Michael could marry us right now, I'd be the one dragging *you* along to see him, just to satisfy my fear...but..." Her words trailed off. Seeming to settle on something in her mind, she leaned forward and grasped his hands, then spoke again. "...*But* I think there's a chance in the end—that it may not happen."

Aidan let out a small sigh, grateful that his fears of her pulling away from him had been unfounded. Her touch, too, was a blessing, though with her hands so delicate in his, he could feel her struggle, her worry, even. If he were being honest with himself, he must acknowledge its very real effect on him, and that of her words, so wholly unacceptable. But, he was Sinclair of the House of Pembrooke and that meant he couldn't be so quick to give in. He carried with him the full weight of his name and title, and even just the thought of this shored him up. He tried to at least find a spot of ground they could meet on. Leaning closer, his eyes locked onto hers, he said, "Dar and Celeste were separated, they're together and happy now."

It did not have the effect he'd hoped.

"You're speaking of your brethren. They're not O'Roarkes," she said with a sad shrug. "And besides, that still means that their union was lasting—there was simply a pause, during which neither moved on from the other."

He was surprised by the degree to which her words set him back. "A pause," he repeated. "A *pause*? I think not." He struggled to keep the offense from his tone. "I would say 'twas more of a transcendent gulf, to which I am sure you would agree now that you've had your own experience with such. Our unions are not some fair-weather affairs to flit to the wind, Brianna. When one of us finds his match, there *is* no other, nor moving on."

"What about Callum and Maggie?"

"I would not say their example applies to your *hy-poth-e-sis*," he enunciated, "but instead proves mine."

"How so?"

"They are one and the same. Maggie is another Fiona, and Callum, another Derek, identical souls born centuries apart." He gave her a moment to consider that, then asked, "Have you ever seen or come across past evidence or *known* an O'Roarke, other than Callum, to find love again after the loss of their one true love?"

Brianna shook her head immediately—she hadn't needed to even consider it, as he'd rightly surmised.

"Because they don't," Aidan said. "That's it, Breea," he said, casting his hands out, and feeling his fervor mount as he continued. "*This* is what we have, and what has proved true for all my brethren, those who don't bear the O'Roarke name included. Even Lachlan never entertained another after Ella. And Dar would not have moved on had Celeste never been returned to him. Celeste, too, would have mourned the loss of Dar for the rest of her years, for he could only have turned up in her time in another incarnation if he had passed in ours—at least that is how I understand fate's workings."

Brianna's brows drew together in confusion. "What do you mean?"

Aidan sighed. It was difficult to explain if you did not already know it. "I cannot prove it, but I believe that eternally matched souls will always have the possibility to find one another again should one-half die, even across time and space—not that it *will* happen, only that it remains possible. By whatever magic or fate that has brought us all together, I do not believe any of us *move on* from our destined love in the case of anything but death to either one of our partners or both."

Aidan had been so caught up in his hypothesizing that he hadn't noticed the shift in Brianna's expression. Something urgent crossed her face, and she said, "We need to get this all down on paper, *parchment*... now," she said, already rummaging around the room.

"Breea?"

She put down the etched bronze orb she'd been admiring, having been distracted in her search. "I was thinking about that letter my grandfather left for me. It's just..." When she trailed off, lost in thought again, Aidan raised a brow, hoping to prompt her when she next regarded him. "Right," she said, pointing his way with a knowing smile, and a clear nod to his manner, "You're probably not going to believe this, but I was somewhat of a handful when I went to live with him. I never misbehaved of course, but I was just…intense I guess."

You don't say. Aidan suppressed a smile. He could only imagine his Breea—so curious, so resourceful, so desperate to understand the world—as a young lass entering a whole new life after hers had been turned upside down. Rather than make any assumptions about her character, however, he simply said, "I'm sure he had no expectations other than providing a safe haven for you."

She smiled softly. "He did, but I mean to say that *more than anyone,* my grandfather would know I would need proof. He would have accounted for all this, so it's suddenly striking me as odd…"

She bent down to inspect the walnut games table, intricately inlaid with venetian glass, and trailed off again as she was apparently becoming wont to do. "What was odd?" Aidan pressed, eager for her to continue.

"Well, he mentioned ensuring our legacy, and that a part of me knew all along, but that doesn't necessarily mean that being *here* is my legacy. Maybe he just meant because of my fascination with Pembrooke and my training I would be *validating* our legacy for the future… or something."

Aidan thirsted for more. "Do you have it?" he asked, leaning forward. "This letter?" He had a desperate need now to see these words for himself.

She shook her head, sighing as she gave up on her quest for parchment, and came back to her chair, a carved chess piece in hand. She gave him an impish grin before setting the marble knight on the table and turning the small horse so that it faced her. "No, I left it on my nightstand before I went for a walk in the tunnels."

"But you said you didn't take your bag with you either."

Her eyes widened. "No, I didn't," she said. "It just sort of showed up next to me after …well, *after*. Packed with all my things, of course, at least the things I'd gotten from the fair."

"Did you check it thoroughly?" he asked, an idea forming in his head. "Being a true original, 'tis possible Dar or Lachlan would have slipped your letter into the bag's concealed inner pocket." Aidan tried to keep his excitement in check, but it was difficult.

"No," she said slowly. "There was nothing in there until I hid the medallion inside."

Aidan bit back his disappointment. Part of him had believed there would be a letter from the one person Brianna trusted above all else that told her what she needed to hear. But, she had checked the bag's hidden stores, so clearly their way of communicating with each other had been passed down, and she had known where to look. No matter. *He* would be her proof. *He* could convince her, and give her the stability she needed and so deserved. Aidan leaned forward and cupped his hands around her face.

"Breea, we will prevail. I have sworn allegiance to

very few in my lifetime and vowed but once to honor, love, and protect until my last breath—*you.*"

She smiled softly. "You've given me so much, I could never have imagined what this would feel like. I can't imagine living with...out—without...you."

Och, those eyes, so big, so haunting cut right through him. "You believe this, still?" he said. "That we may not be meant to be together any longer than is necessary?"

"So much it's killing me. I don't want to, I just can't help it."

For the first time, Aidan felt fear creep in, and he found himself wondering if she might be right.

"Well," he began slowly, "While I cannot foresee the future, I have every intention of returning to you whole and devoted after this journey is complete."

"I know. And I can't wait," she breathed clutching his hands.

Good God, she had put the scare in him. "I have every intention of returning to you," he repeated. "And you will be here, whole as well." And if she wasn't, he would move heaven and earth to find her.

She nodded, and there was a flicker in her eye that jolted him, and he leaned closer, somehow knowing what she was about to ask.

"I know we've had such a day," she began, "but maybe it's *because* of that... and this uncertainty of what our future holds that I need...I really need you to take me upstairs and make love to me. I need to be as close to you as I can possibly get."

He nodded, and with that same primal need

surging through him, he could not get her upstairs fast enough. Once he had her within their chamber, he could barely recall how they got there, so focused was he on his aching need to have her—*now*. He barred the door and immediately, they were on each other, all over each other, grappling their way to the bed while proceeding with the swift (yet careful of her wrist) removal of their clothing. He would not call what happened next lovemaking; it was certainly borne out of love, but in truth, from the moment they'd left the great hall until he'd buried himself deep inside of her and drew his first full breath, it was an act of desperation. He knew she felt it, too, this instinctive need, both raw and primitive at its core. Still, in the aftermath, he and Brianna both felt the tension of the day fade enough that they were able to share some welcome and carefree moments, smiling as they picked up their clothing scattered from the door to the bed and, as they washed, enjoying the unhurried familiar affection that had grown between them these last weeks.

After helping her into a delicate shift that he'd found freshly laundered and hanging in the wardrobe, he added another log to the fire, quickened his steps, and joined her in their bed, lest she make more of a mess than he could fix or worse, hurt herself. "Let me," he said, coming up behind her as she struggled to knot her hair with only one completely functional hand.

She turned and smiled as his fingers brushed through her hair before tying it just so, then hummed when he leaned forward and pressed his lips to her neck, which caused her to shiver. He liked that, and did it again, grinning when she made a sound of pure contentment.

"I did have a thought…" she said, rather optimistically, before her words trailed off and she scooted herself back between his legs.

"And?" he said, trying to quell the hope that was leaping in his heart.

He let his fingers trace the slope of her neck as he waited for her reply, watching as goosebumps raised in response to his touch. After a moment, she shifted herself again to look at him, though remained in the circle of his arms. Her eyes sparkled as she brushed her fingers across his forehead before tangling them in his hair. She glanced slyly at his cut and nodded in approval, obviously pleased with how it was healing.

Then, she finally spoke. "If I had a tally of the signs, the things that could corroborate that staying here, married to you is my legacy—"

"Do you?" he wondered, unable to help the interruption.

She smiled. "No, but the second I can get my hands on some ink and parchment, you can bet your dragons that I will."

He chuckled and pulled her closer, nudging his face to hers. "So, this tally of yours?"

"Right," she said, grinning. "I love everything about it here—most especially you," she whispered, brushing his lips. "There's Pembrooke and your proverbial dragons, of course. And, I'm also adding the matter of my clothing to the stay column."

"Your clothing?" he asked, puzzled.

She nodded, pulling back. "The outfit I wore that day I found your medallion," she said, her zeal growing with each word. "I realized it's gone, lost in the fire or sea, maybe that's a sign."

Aidan smiled without hesitation, but inside, his fear returned, taking a vise-like hold. "Well, there you have it," he said with false cheer. "Something positive after all."

"Yeah, I think I can see a bright rosy future with a keep full of our children, and the House of Pembrooke carrying on in fated glory."

She seemed completely satisfied now with this rationale, and fell asleep a short time later, in the circle of his arms. He held her for hours, banishing the thought prickling the back of his mind. He had that bundle of clothes in his possession, plucked from the pile he'd given to be laundered in Ayr, just before it had been whisked away. He stroked her hair and brushed his lips to her forehead as the sky grew to its darkest, and slipped from their bed only once, stoking the fire with a couple hours yet to spare. Brianna was still sound asleep when he stepped into the latrine, but only a moment or two later when he walked back into their chamber, she was up and quite obviously unnerved. Before he could alert her to his presence, she cried out, and in her sleepy state, fell with a thud from the bed. Aidan raced to her side, lifting her from the floor.

"I would never leave without saying goodbye to you," he told her, holding her tight.

She didn't say anything, but he felt her tears as she clutched him back.

"I don't want to go, Brianna. But I must."

"I know," she whispered, clearly trying to keep the emotion from her voice, downplaying her reaction. "I just panicked."

Aye. It was hard to forget all that she'd lost, those instincts ingrained from such an early age. "It's still very early, and I would love to lay down with you and hold you while we have the time."

She nodded but motioned to the latrine where he had just come from. He looked at her arm, "Do you need help?" he asked.

She shook her head, but he was waiting beside the bed when she returned anyway, and helped her up before crawling in beside her, careful not to jostle her injured wrist. Immediately, she pressed herself against him, wedging her leg between his. He was glad for it, in truth, he couldn't hold her close enough. She was quiet for so long he thought she might have fallen back asleep, but then she whispered, "It's going to be okay, right?"

"Without a doubt."

CHAPTER 29

Brianna was roused by a light tap on their door some hours later. Aidan tightened his arms around her with an affectionate hum just as her eyes opened, and brushed his lips across her forehead.

"Your breakfast is here," he said softly in her ear. "Don't move."

That she could do. While the night had all been a bit of a blur, between her panicked awakening and holding onto him for dear life afterward, Aidan had made love to her again. This time, however, it was unhurried and deliberate, and unforgettably profound in slow motion. She hugged the pillow they'd been lying on, breathing in his scent while admiring his broad shoulders and back as he walked across the room. He put on a soft pair of trews (in this case, long, drawstring shorts), that she was seriously considering confiscating for herself. They would be perfect for lounging or sleeping in.

Once decent, he opened the door, and stood aside,

allowing Gwen to lead a parade of staff quietly into the room. Brianna smiled softly, waving her fingers at Gwen to return her greeting. It was still so early, she guessed that Gwen had made it a special point to be up to ensure that Aidan was seen off adequately. Brianna watched as a large tray was placed on the table by the window, buckets of hot water were set on the hearth, and the fire brought back to a healthy roar. Then the staff left as quickly and quietly as they'd arrived. Gwen, however, remained, and that's when Brianna realized she was here to check on their wounds, particularly Aidan's since he was leaving so soon. After she gave him a quick once over, he sat down without being asked, so Gwen could get a better look at the cuts on his face, tilting his chin to catch the firelight.

Once she gave him a clean bill of health, Gwen nodded and smiled as she said, "Careful, she wants your pants," nudging her head toward Brianna.

Brianna couldn't see Aidan's expression, but whatever it was, prompted an eye roll from Gwen.

"No," Gwen said, "She's literally eyeing your pants."

Brianna stifled a laugh as he turned around and raised a brow in her direction, and when he faced her, Brianna just shrugged, and scooched herself back, against the headboard.

"Am I right, or am I right?" Gwen said as she came over, and now Brianna's laugh spilled out.

"Totally," she said. "They look too comfy not to take."

"I knew it! And how are you feeling?" Gwen asked, reaching for her wrist.

"Sore, but honestly not as bad as I thought it would be."

"Hmmm." Gwen took a long moment to inspect the abrasions and bruising and smiled. "Well, I'm very happy with how it looks," she said, wrapping it again. "Even the swelling is down."

Brianna nodded, watching as Aidan carried a steaming mug of ... her nose wriggled as she caught an aroma of— "Is that *coffee?*" she asked, grateful and horrified both.

"It is," Gwen said, then raised her hand, obviously clocking Brianna's flabbergasted expression. "But before you freak out, it's important that you know, we keep things under wraps."

At this, Aidan pulled a face and muttered something unintelligible.

Gwen sighed. "We *do*, despite what Aidan thinks. It's not like Captain John travels the world with my whims in mind."

At this, Aidan raised a brow and Brianna covered her mouth and giggled. It was clear this was an old argument.

"Okay fine! Well, at least he doesn't *anymore*. I can't help it Grey still surprises me with an occasional treat!"

Brianna reached out and patted her arm. "Guess what, I don't care right now. What I would love, is some of that."

Gwen smiled and handed her a steaming mug.

Brianna inhaled first, enjoying the familiar sensation, then took a deep sip and said, "Oh, this is good."

Gwen winked, then stood and started for the door before turning again. "Oh, I heard you're partial to Aidan's favorite tea blend, too. There's plenty more where that came from."

Aidan smiled sheepishly, and Brianna thought it was so sweet that he'd never said anything about it being *his* tea, he just enjoyed that it made her happy. She exchanged a wave with Gwen before she turned to leave, Aidan followed her to the door, where he motioned for her to wait. Brianna watched absent-mindedly, focused mostly on her coffee, as he turned to the wardrobe, then dug around in it before he pulled something out and pressed a bundle of some sort into Gwen's hands—maybe laundry? Brianna was too busy sipping coffee and admiring Aidan's trews, well, mostly just admiring Aidan *in* his trews to pay it much attention.

Then he was next to her again. "Just a quick moment," he said gathering her close, eliciting a sigh of content from her. He rubbed his chin on her head and whispered, "One day soon, we'll have the pleasure of waking together leisurely, with no cares, Brianna, only our lives before us."

She smiled, brushing her hand across his chest. "I can't wait."

He nudged her face with his and kissed her, then they spent a few minutes cuddling and finishing their coffees before washing up and getting dressed. At first, he'd urged her to stay in bed and relax, citing the early hour. She'd told him in no uncertain terms she would not miss out on seeing him off from the shore and watching until he had disappeared over the horizon.

This made him laugh, which made her nearly forget what they were talking about, that he would be going off on a ship, over the sea toward an uncertain encounter. She held Kitty as Aidan gathered the rest of his things, and when they heard a soft rap on the door, Aidan raised a brow and then looked at her.

"That would be Tristan," he said.

"It's okay," she said quickly and nodded before calling out, "Tristan, come in."

The boy opened the door, looking in cautiously, but she could tell he was relieved to be invited in. His eyes lit up as he hurried over to them, sticking like glue to Aidan's leg while saying good morning and giving Kitty a quick pat.

While Aidan grabbed their cloaks, he asked Tristan to keep an eye on her and Kitty in his absence, then draped the garment over her shoulders, fastening it with the clasp. When his hands moved up to brush her hair back, he looked into her eyes. His were filled with so much love, so much promise, that she nearly lost it, gone was her bravado.

"I will be back. And you will be here." He pressed his forehead to hers then and told her in a raspy whisper, "You are everything to me, aye?"

Brianna nodded, hoping she looked more confident than she felt as she followed Aidan through the door and into the corridor that led to the stairs, where Callum and Grey were already waiting.

"Hold on," she said, facing them. She knew that Aidan had sent word to his friend Ronan, and his brother Rhys and he was set to meet them in Ayr. But she hadn't considered that Callum and Greylen would accompany him as well. "You're both going, too?"

"They sought to kill you, an O'Roarke. One of my own," Callum said, straightening to his full impressive height as he did so. "It cannot stand unanswered, and for that, although Aidan doesn't need me, I will accompany him."

"Well, I for one, think he *does* need me," Greylen said, cuffing the back of Aidan's neck affectionately as the men chuckled. Brianna laughed, too, struck yet again at how much these men meant to each other. "As well, I'll take it as an opportunity to see the ship, or what remains of her, for myself."

At the sound of footsteps, she turned and saw Gwen coming down the hallway. "I'm so sorry," Brianna started, "I feel like—"

They all shut her down with a look as Gwen brushed passed her.

"Don't worry," Gwen said, waving her hand, "going by ship, they'll be back before we know it, and I'm sure with gifts and treasures abound."

At this, Brianna had to smile. If Gwen could be this casual about the whole thing, she would try to rest easy, too. She listened as they spoke of their plans, grateful she didn't have to participate. She was so engrossed in their conversation, that other than the feeling of Aidan's tight hold on her hand, she hadn't noticed anything as they made their way outside and into the courtyard, until they came to the readied horses, attended by a group of stable hands. Waiting there too, was a small group of men, including Alan and Richard. As they approached, the men started to say their goodbyes and Brianna felt her heart sink. She'd hoped she could accompany Aidan further, all the way up to the ship if she could.

Aidan grasped her shoulders. "'Tis still dark, love," he said brushing her hair back, sensing her thoughts. "And your wrist," he added quietly, glancing down.

She knew he was right, between the early hour and her injury, not to mention Gwen's pregnancy, it made sense to stay back. Still, it was a sooner parting than she'd expected.

"Give no breadth to unbidden fears, aye," he said, gently tapping her temple with his finger.

She smiled despite her sadness and shook her head. "I won't."

He smiled too, grasping her head in his hands and looking deeply into her eyes. "And know this, above all else—I love you."

She covered one of his hands, now resting on her cheek, and overcome with emotion, she mouthed the words back. Aidan broke his gaze from hers only when Gwen came up beside her to gently pull her back as the men mounted their horses.

Then, all too soon, Brianna found herself standing on the bluff, watching as the ship set sail, barely visible in the purply dawn. Just as the sun crested the horizon, Brianna was struck by the thought that this image of him was nearly identical to her first. Only this time, his formidable stature, flanked by Callum and Greylen in a clear show of might, was intimately familiar to her.

Tristan, who was standing to watch beside her, reached for her hand as Aidan's voice echoed across the water: "Brianna O'Roarke of the House of Pembrooke—never forget who you are." The boy looked up at her and grinned almost knowingly, then ran along the butte before leaping onto a cluster of rocks. Brianna watched as he lifted his hood and threw his hands in the air at the same time that Aidan and his men drew their swords in unison, raising them to the sky.

"And never forget who you belong to—Sinclair of the House of Pembrooke!" Aidan thundered, and his brethren (along with Tristan) echoed with a resounding rallying cry.

It was a fitting salute, and as she wiped away her tears, Henry pressed a linen into her hand. If she ever questioned her worth, that Aidan had left Henry behind with her spoke volumes. When she returned to her chamber, she found Kitty sleeping on the bed, and it was clear that while she was seeing Aidan off, the linens had been changed. She probably made a sound because Tristan looked at her funny. She didn't want to cry, but she would have at least kept his pillowcase. Hugging herself to mitigate the loss, silly as it might seem, she startled when Gwen came up beside her.

THE PROMISE

"Sorry, Tristan ran into the hall and said you were upset," she said.

Brianna hadn't even noticed he'd left the room.

"There's no way you would know this of course," Gwen continued, walking to the wardrobe, "but at one time, Greylen and I were separated for months, and while he was away, his shirt was like my security blanket. Anything of his really." She bent and opened the bottom drawer. "Poor Anna learned the hard way not to mess with certain things." Gwen pulled something out of the drawer, and when she turned back to Brianna, she was holding the pillowcases that had been on the bed. "See?"

She felt so foolish standing there blubbering over a pillowcase, but Gwen didn't seem bothered by it at all.

"His shirt and trews are in there too," she said. "Why don't you get some rest? I'm sure you could use a full day or even two of sleep."

Gwen—naturally—had been right. Brianna spent that entire day and part of the next doing just that. When she finally emerged from her chamber around noon the following day, she ran smack into Tristan, who had been hurrying down the hallway to check on her. As she bent to speak with him, a warm smile on her face, she saw his eyes flick worriedly toward Henry. Brianna looked over at Henry questioningly, but Henry just sighed and shook his head. She quickly put two and two together, figuring that Henry had insisted that she rest undisturbed and Tristan had insisted otherwise, clearly taking to heart Aidan's directive to look after her wellbeing, too. Amused at the tug of wills between the two, she did what she could to rectify the situation.

"You know, I heard how diligent you were in seeing after me," Brianna said to Tristan, winking at Henry. "I can't wait to tell Aidan when he returns. Maybe we could even write him a letter," she suggested. After all, she *had* been trying to get her hands on some parchment.

The boy beamed at once and puffed his chest out proudly, and Brianna caught Henry suppressing a smile.

The situation righted, she grabbed his hand. "Now I'm starving, do you think we can sneak into the kitchens and poke around?"

Tristan scrunched his nose as he grinned and Henry chuckled, both signs to Brianna that things were going to be just fine.

CHAPTER 30

Beset with strong headwinds, the ship's arrival in Ayr was slightly delayed. Not enough to make a difference, really, but enough for Aidan to enjoy the time he wouldn't have otherwise had with Grey and Callum. While all grown men now, in the confines of the cabin they shared, their reversion to boyhood rank prevailed. Their laughter caused a ruckus too, resulting in more than one crew member pounding upon the door or even a wall, so they'd cease their antics. They took it all in stride, however, and as they disembarked the ship, everyone acted as if it had never happened at all.

After mooring the ship, they disembarked to shore where Rhys and Ronan were waiting, and a cheerful round of greetings was exchanged. After checking with Captain John and what remained of Grey's ship, now hoisted from the water, the group headed to Glenn's to gather horses and be on their way. The Fitzgerald property was only a day's ride from Ayr, one that was completed with ease. By the time they'd dealt with the men who'd been involved in the ambush—also an easy feat, it turned out—the only matter remaining was that of Judith herself.

The five of them—Aidan, Callum, Grey, Ronan, and Rhys—stood now in the keep, facing Judith and two of her remaining family members, an aunt and uncle who both appeared relieved to be rid of Gil and Nigel. Although the Judith matter—or the betrothal that never was—was truly not his affair to sort out, Aidan did so anyway, hoping in return someone would have the character to do the same for him one day. However, while Judith appeared grateful to not be cast into the same lot as her brothers, it was clear that marriage had not been on her mind. Still, after some discussion, she admitted that she realized its importance, especially now with her father gone. And, in light of her brothers' heinous actions, she acquiesced that she might have trouble finding a suitable match—although she still did so somewhat reluctantly.

As the group discussed how to best go about a quiet inquiry into prospects, Aidan noticed Rhys paying particular attention to Judith, his eyes looking almost nowhere *but* at her. Judith either didn't notice (though Aidan thought that was unlikely), or she was ambivalent about his attention. A plan began to form in his mind—one that proved unnecessary when Rhys abruptly spoke up.

"I'll marry her," he said, with all the seriousness of one who'd come to the conclusion he was in the presence of his would-be bride. That Rhys made this all-important declaration so firmly while at the same time gazing warmly upon Judith said it all.

They all turned to Rhys, and by the looks on everyone's faces, no one had predicted that outcome, and yet no one seemed to be particularly surprised either. Judith, for her part, had blushed a deep crimson but did not seem in any way opposed to the union. Rhys gave nothing away, though Aidan knew this was his style—he'd lost many a game to Rhys when they were boys due to his brother's ability to keep a solemn face. Callum broke the moment with an unnecessary, but wholly expected, "Be sure it's sanctified."

While Judith and her aunt and uncle spoke between them on the merits of such an alliance, Aidan knew they would agree, especially given how Judith was regarding Rhys with bemused curiosity.

Now it was Aidan who had to suppress a smile when Rhys spoke again.

"Have you a priest among you?" his brother asked.

When the Fitzgerald family made it clear that they did not, Rhys expressed his wish to be wed by Father Michael, unless there were any objections. Frankly, Aidan had one, but only because he wished to return to Brianna posthaste, and Father Michael at the ready, *his* ready, and a wedding, no matter how quickly thrown together, including the summoning of said priest would add time.

In the end, Aidan and his brethren made the most of their delay, helping the Fitzgeralds sort through some affairs and put things in order once again. It was the least they could do, for after all, they had benefitted from their original alliance, which had allowed them to cross their land to build Abersoch. As well, Lachlan and their fathers would have wished them to roll up their sleeves, so to speak, and help in any case.

NEARLY A FULL WEEK LATER, Aidan was grateful to be back in Ayr. He hadn't wanted to say goodbye to Rhys or to Ronan, who both had matters to attend to, but he was eager to return to Brianna. They had just returned their horses to Glenn and were ready to board their ship to return home. Well not home exactly, but Seagrave—or was it Dunhill? He chuckled because it truly mattered naught. Brianna could be on the moon and he'd fetch her, no matter the price—at that thought, Aidan stumbled. He caught himself, then peered around to see if anyone had noticed, and saw his brethren casting odd looks his way. *No matter*, Aidan thought—surely if they knew what had just crossed his mind, they would understand. He continued his inventory of the area and caught sight of a woman just out of view several yards away. Heart thumping, he strode in her direction, picking up the pace the closer he got. If not for the quick thinking and strong-arming of his brethren, he would have succeeded in charging her, and mayhap taking her to the ground.

"Not a smooth one!" Aidan shouted at Esmerelda when he finally stood before her, Callum and Greylen each pulling him back. *"The path ahead is not a smooth one,* say you!"

She remained still, save a flicker in her eyes.

"I nearly lost her—to the hands of death!" Aidan's voice cracked as he said the words aloud. "And now...*still,* I fear she will be lost to me and beyond my reach!" he went on, surprised the words spilled forth.

"And you think this is your fate, Aidan Sinclair?"

Her words were a blow, feeding into his worst fear.

"*Is it?*" He balled his hands into fists at her vague reply. "My time with Brianna, *this*...was for naught?"

His vision started to blur as emotion swelled in his eyes, and if not for the tone in Esmerelda's voice when she answered, he would have thought her words were nothing more than another of her frustratingly veiled messages.

"True love, *true,* always requires a price," she said, looking at each of them in turn.

Aidan was not satisfied with her cryptic answer. "If you knew what this...what it felt like, you'd not meddle so."

She stepped closer, and Aidan flinched but did not retreat. Let her, or whomever she served strike him down if it be so. But when she reached out and took his face in her hands, it was not wrath he found in her eyes, but empathy and compassion, bottomless in its depth.

"I'm so very sorry," she said with such sincerity that his anger dissipated in an instant, leaving him wholly raw and exposed. "If I could take this from you, I would."

He knew she meant it because he now saw that she carried her own pain, too.

"I love her—with my *entire heart and all that I am.*" The emotion spilled to his cheeks with the weight of the words that he spoke, holding the depth of his fear.

She nodded, "Aye. And she you. You are each other's match after all."

Slightly bolstered by this, Aidan found the strength to ask the thing he most feared: "Will I lose her?"

"True love is never lost, Aidan. You'll always know each other, and recognize each other, whether you wake up beside one another each day until your last, or if you meet again in another form or another time. And if these past weeks are all you'll ever share, one day you'll know: True love is always victorious, and always worth the price. You gave her wings to fly, and do what she must. You love her for who she is, without conditions, none, which is quite a feat for a man of your ... temperament. You empowered her, and in that moment set her free—"

Aidan could hear no more. "I don't want her free," he said, rather ashamed to admit it. He thought of Lachlan and what it must have taken to walk away from Ella. He was not so strong. But then...it pained him to realize it, but he supposed never knowing Brianna would have been worse than having her even for the short time they'd been together. Still, he ached at the thought that it was even a possibility.

"Why...why do you do this, meddle so?"

She shook her head. "I understand why you and your brethren might think so, but please trust that I know your pain and that I try to be as helpful as the Fates will allow."

Aidan clutched her hands, and her eyes widened in surprise. "I beg you," he said, watching her eyes brim with tears now. "Could you be of aid *now*?"

She nodded and grasped his hands. "What you seek has been here—with her—all along."

CHAPTER 31

"Brianna! Brianna!"

Brianna turned, affection filling her heart at the sight of Tristan leaning against the window ledge, looking outside. She could see why Aidan and the boy had such an attachment to one another. They were both so serious, yet so warm and open. She'd spent nearly every day of the last week with him either trailing along behind her or directly at her side as she did whatever she could to keep busy and pitch in to help Gwen. While there weren't as many mouths to feed or children to tend to with Isabelle and Gavin no longer in residence, the whole household was still adjusting to their absence. It was obvious that they'd had a well-run routine while they were here, and everyone was missing them.

"Look!" Tristan said as Brianna made her way to the window. "Maggie's here! And I think Aunt Cateline has come, too, with Isla and the baby, look!"

Brianna's heart ticked up, and she rushed over to

look for herself. Sure enough, a small army stretched along the path that led to the gates of the courtyard with her family right at the center. Immediately, Brianna felt tears pricking at the corners of her eyes. She swiped a few away as Gwen burst into her chamber.

"Brianna, they're here," she said, clearly emotional too.

It was a big day. Brianna was meeting her family, the rest of her family, her true family for the first time. Gwen had received a letter from Maggie just the other day alerting them that she was going to be visiting, eager to meet "the famous Brianna," as she'd worded it. Apparently, Callum had written to her the day that he'd, well, that day he'd wanted to show Aidan who was boss, at least where his family was concerned. By the time Maggie's letter had arrived, their caravan was clearly on its way, albeit at a leisurely pace, since Aunt Cateline and Maggie's two young children, Isla and her baby Dougal were coming, too.

All three of them—Brianna, Gwen, and Tristan—hurried out of the room toward the stairs, Brianna fighting a losing battle of trying to stay in front of Gwen, who was always moving at a faster pace than seemed possible given her pregnancy. Brianna was worried Gwen would trip on the stairs, but Gwen only rolled her eyes when she saw what she was doing.

"We'll only both get hurt," Gwen muttered under her breath.

"True, but I've gained the favor of your guards, see," Brianna said, pointing to the sentries at the bottom of the stairs, who were looking at her and nodding.

By the time they made it outside, everyone had descended from the carriage, with the baby nestled in Aunt Cateline's arms. Brianna, of course, had never met Maggie before, but she was immediately recognizable. The moment Brianna appeared in the doorway, Maggie ran to her like she was a cherished and much-missed member of the family, calling her name as she got closer. Her voice caught and filled with such emotion that Brianna faltered, then began to cry herself as she started down the steps, chin quivering and tears soaking her cheeks. When Maggie reached her, she wrapped her arms around her, making the biggest spectacle ever, though Brianna found she didn't mind it one bit, sinking into the welcoming and nurturing embrace. When they finally broke apart, Maggie quickly smiled at Tristan and then at Gwen's little girl, before reaching for Aunt Cateline and wrapping them all in one big circle. Gwen and Lady Madelyn joined them, too, and it was another few minutes before they'd gathered themselves enough to pull away.

"Oh, look at you," Maggie said, grasping Brianna's shoulders and shaking her head. "So pretty." Her fingers tangled in one of Brianna's soft wavy curls, which had returned just the other day when the last of her Keratin treatment lost its hold. (Brianna had known the transformation was complete when she ran into Gwen who'd let out a squeal of shock and delight and could do nothing but point at her and mouth "Your *hair*!")

"Look at our family," Maggie said, taking them all in before stepping aside to let Aunt Cateline move closer, too.

Brianna allowed herself to be scrutinized yet again. The older woman stared into her eyes, then reached out to cup her cheeks. Brianna marveled at how her face rested in the (surprisingly soft) hands of her favorite ancestor Cateline De la Cour.

"You know those eyes came from my sister, Isabeau," Cateline said approvingly.

Brianna shook her head as tears filled her eyes again. She'd never felt so connected to another person since her grandfather died and hadn't felt so full since she'd lost her parents. She couldn't even speak, she was so choked up. She just leaned into another hug from Cateline and stayed there, listening to the baby babble until she was able to gather herself a bit. When she pulled away she noticed a few of the men, the older ones especially, were pinching the bridges of their noses to keep their emotions at bay.

"Come on," Gwen said after a moment. "Let's go inside and get everyone settled."

Brianna was about to follow everyone up the steps when she saw Gwen motioning at Maggie, pointing to the baby. Maggie gave her a smile, her eyes filled with a different kind of emotion as she took him from Aunt Cateline's arms and turned him around so Gwen could see him.

Gwen smiled, her expression contorting for just a second as she nodded and gently stroked the boy's face and crown. Maggie turned away for a moment and Brianna realized then that they had probably been pregnant at the same time, but Gwen had lost that baby. Hit with another, altogether different wave of feeling, Brianna fanned her eyes to stave off tears. After a long hug, with the baby in the middle again, the two women pulled apart and turned to Brianna, each latching an arm around her.

Brianna, who never really had close friends, surely not a sisterhood, suddenly found herself right in the middle of one. The three of them walked arm in arm up the steps and inside, still shedding an occasional tear, but laughing, too. After it was decided who was staying with whom (especially the little ones), Brianna made a few trips between Gwen's room and the others, distributing bottles of the new lotions, soaps, and scrubs Gwen and Lady Madelyn had made. On her last trip, something caught her eye from inside one of Gwen's open wardrobes and she nearly dropped the tray she was carrying.

"Wait," Brianna said, feeling her heart wither. "Why do you have these?" She asked, horrified as she bent down to grab the pile of clothing bunched up next to Gwen's shoes. It was the outfit she'd been wearing on the day she arrived in this time, clutching Aidan's medallion. Suddenly, something clicked into place. "This is what he gave you the morning he left, isn't it?"

"Oh, Brianna I'm so sorry," Gwen said, shaking her

head. "He did, but not to upset you. He just wanted to—"

She stopped herself as Brianna broke down again, all her old fears suddenly rushing back.

"Brianna, what's wrong?" Maggie had just appeared in the doorway and immediately rushed to her side. Brianna let herself be guided to a little sitting area, as Maggie looked at her with concern.

Knowing she could trust her newfound sisterhood, Brianna let all her feelings out, explaining to Maggie what she'd missed, with Gwen filling in the gaps, and translating for her when she was crying too hard to speak clearly.

"What if it means I'm supposed to go back?" Brianna said. She felt truly desperate about the possibility, and that realization was a surprise—suddenly her home, which she'd always loved and where she'd felt safest for the better part of her life, seemed stark and empty now. It would be cruel to have all she'd found here ripped away. "I just don't want to lose this, what I have here with *all* of you, not just Aidan."

"I don't understand why you think that," Gwen said, shaking her head. "I still have my clothing from —well, you know. In fact, much to my husband's displeasure," she tilted her head to the side, "and sometimes pleasure. Anna makes me all sorts of garments, some period-appropriate, others…not so much."

Brianna smiled a little at this. She knew Gwen was only trying to help, but she still wasn't convinced. She told them about Aidan's theory on fate, and its course when it came to all of them, curious to see how Gwen and Maggie would react.

"Well," Maggie said, "I suppose he's right. By the time I came to Dunhill, Derek had been gone for almost two years. Fiona, too. And trust me, Callum and I did *not* look at each other and instantly fall in love—we really didn't. But we had a lot of common ground, and it easily outweighed the uncommon ground. Who knows what would have happened if we never left the safety of our bubble." Maggie paused then, most likely at Brianna's wide-eyed expression.

"Bubbles are nice, but we can't stay in them forever," Gwen said, not missing a beat, apparently the bubble metaphor was already in use. "And once the tide has risen," Gwen pulled a face. "Bad choice of words. And now I'm mixing metaphors. What I meant was, once that love takes hold, there's nothing that will stop it, no matter how hard you pretend otherwise, or try to outsmart it." Gwen laughed, then said, "Ask Maggie, she tried."

Maggie made a face. "I just thought so long as I didn't admit to anything out loud, I'd be okay."

Brianna nodded, a small flicker of hope glimmering in her chest as she listened to Maggie's story. For all their ups and downs, and every struggle they had each overcome, in the end, they *were* still together, all of them.

"The crazy things we do while trying to outsmart a fate that's already been chosen for us."

"Well, you at least had a prophecy to give you some kind of clue—*and* let's not forget, you're head of the class too…" Maggie said, tipping an imaginary hat to Gwen.

"Not a detective," Gwen quipped.

Maggie made a sound. "Well, this detective was an epic failure. My greatest accomplishment came down to beating rugs at the abbey. Go Maggie," she cheered in a sad, faint whisper, twirling her fingers like pompoms, while making a disparaging face.

"Wait," Brianna shook her head, "Is that how you really feel?" She was shocked that this woman she had idolized her whole life saw herself in such a diminished light.

"I was a federal agent who fell apart and became a curtseying, scaredy-cat, people pleaser," Maggie said.

Gwen disagreed with Maggie's harsh self-assessment, too, and Brianna decided it was her turn to dole out some encouragement and set Maggie straight.

"Maggie," she said, "It's because of you and the legacy *you* began that I've survived here—and Aidan, too. Without you, I wouldn't have learned self-defense *or* weaponry—or at least not like I had. If not for your feelings after losing Derek and almost losing Callum, you wouldn't have ensured that *every* female O'Roarke for nearly a millennium—*a millennium*—never felt that way again. *THAT* is an incredible and powerful legacy. In fact, it goes way beyond."

Maggie nodded, clearly fighting back tears at Brianna's declaration.

"It's true," Brianna said softly. "You've always been a hero of mine." She gave that a moment to sink in, then added, "And what's wrong with curtseying, anyway?"

After an appreciative smile from Maggie, and another group hug, everyone was emotionally spent, and so instead of doubling down, or trying to further a point, any point, they all decided to give it a much-needed rest and focus their energy on *another* (they'd stressed) positive outcome. Brianna understood where they were coming from, but they either didn't realize or had already forgotten how the added disadvantage of her O'Roarke heritage—when it came to marriage, at least—could tip the scales. Brianna's fear that something would happen to pull the rug out from under her, or pull *her* from this reality had only slightly abated, but there was nothing Gwen or Maggie could tell her that would change that, and so she was happy to leave it for now.

That night, well after the castle had quieted down, there was a knock on Brianna's door, and Gwen came in. "Today was another win, Brianna," she said, and grasped her hands as if to shore her up and say, *'See you're still here'*. Gwen closed her eyes and quietly said, 'Thank you' like an amen. As Brianna looked up at her, she realized that this was what family and friends did for each other. Gwen's gesture was so sweet and so heartfelt, and so natural in its simplicity. The small act of kindness lifted Brianna's spirits enough to give her the courage to believe that the impossible could be within reach.

And just like that, the days began to pass, and the week that followed turned into a fun girl's stay-cay (well, girls plus the guards from both Seagrave and Dunhill, Henry, and of course, Tristan, his little brother, and baby Dougal). But still, it was the girls—from ages two to sixty-two if Brianna was calculating Aunt Cateline's age correctly—who were rocking down the house. And Gwen's thankful 'prayer' quickly became a nightly routine, and she, Maggie, Aunt Cateline, Lady Madelyn, and Anna all came to Brianna's chamber each evening after putting the little ones down for the night to remind her that she was still there. Sometimes Brianna would swear she could hear another chorus of voices whispering it, too, and she imagined the staff and guards just outside the door, doing what they could to ensure that she remained, too.

After nearly ten days at Seagrave, Gwen declared Brianna fully healed and they immediately made plans to travel to Dunhill Proper so Brianna could finally see it as it was then...or was it, as it was now...then, now...she threw her hands in the air. Whichever was technically correct, it *was* Dunhill Proper *now,* so there.

While Brianna had a difficult time containing her excitement about going to her ancestral home, she still couldn't shake the nagging worry that something was going to happen to extinguish the wee bit of magic she carried with her. So far, though, she'd staved off the demons, even when she overheard talk that Father Michael was needed to marry "the Sinclair" to Judith Fitzgerald. She forgave herself for that one—could anyone really be surprised that she'd thought the worst, especially when the remark included such phrasing as 'not making the same mistake again' and 'ensuring it was sanctified'. It was a stretch even for Brianna 2.0 with all of her growth.

Luckily, the news was overheard just before they'd sat to have dinner, meaning Brianna was in the company of many a wise woman. As they passed bread and butter around the table, they'd set her straight at once. It was a good thing, too, that she'd become used to their sharp wit and keenly shrewd ways, because timid and indirect they were not.

"You're right," Brianna said with a decisive (well, ninety-nine percent sure) nod. "It's going to be okay."

Gwen reached for her hand. "You sure have come into yourself, haven't you?" she said, smiling affectionally.

Brianna realized then that Gwen was right, she had never once felt so comfortable in her own skin.

Gwen seemed to intuitively understand because she reached out to give her hand a gentle squeeze. "That's what happens when you find your people," she said. "Your true people."

Brianna squeezed her hand back, "Well, genius *does* like company," she said with a soft smile, making her new sisterhood grin and erupt into muffled laughter.

The conversation around the table turned to Brianna's wedding then, the one that everyone insisted was imminent. When Maggie suggested that Brianna wear her gown, her jaw dropped. She didn't even know what the dress looked like, but it didn't matter. The offer was so meaningful, that Brianna was overwhelmed for a moment. Once she'd collected herself, she reached for Maggie's hand. "Oh, Maggie, I would love to wear your gown," she said. "But do you think it's bad luck since Aidan's already seen it?"

Gwen and Maggie both shot her peculiar looks, and it was so quiet for a moment, that Brianna worried she'd said something wrong. Then, Gwen finally broke and said, "Brianna, work with me here— you're technically married already." She paused, ostensibly to let that sink in, then with a small grin added, "Besides, Aidan didn't make it to that wedding. He didn't arrive until the day *after* the nuptials. So… he's never seen the dress."

It was too perfect to deny (*fated?* she let herself wonder for a moment) and Brianna felt immediately lighter.

"Oh. Well in that case, then, yes!" she said. "I would love to wear your dress, Maggie."

Brianna felt like she was floating. She was so happy, what with the revelation about the dress, coupled with the sighs of delight she heard as everyone started paying closer attention to the main course, which Brianna had prepared herself as a thank you for everyone's support and hospitality. She even managed to keep a straight face when Gwen whipped her head around to look at her, giving her a pointed stare before waving her fork in the air.

"Is this Coq au vin?" Gwen asked, jabbing the fork toward her.

Brianna shrugged. "Maybe," she said and held up her thumb and finger. "Just a little bit."

"And *I'm* the one who catches hell for making meals that mess with the time continuum?"

They sat around the table, laughing throughout the rest of the meal. After dessert, a fruit flambé of sorts served with a crisp pastry, that earned Gwen's eternal adulation, they headed upstairs to put the little ones to bed. It had become another evening routine, baths, bedtime stories followed by a parade of hugs and goodnights. Once Lady Madelyn and Aunt Cateline retired, Brianna soaked in a hot bath, too, eager to meet up afterward with Gwen and Maggie in the Great Hall for some tea, another part of their routine that Brianna absolutely loved. She'd never really liked being away from her grandfather or their home as a child, and as a result, had never attended any of the slumber parties she'd been invited to, but she felt like she was getting to experience a little bit of that here with Gwen and Maggie.

She still arranged her hair the same way she had been, since she arrived, but instead of the sleek glamour of smooth locks, now, her natural soft wavy curls gave her messy knot new meaning. Looking in the mirror at the few unruly strands that always escaped their confinement and fell about her face, Brianna had to admit it suited her much better. When she put on her favorite chemise, the one trimmed with lace that Aidan had gotten for her in Ayr, she realized she did feel better about her future here. Banishing her fears to the back of her mind, Brianna decided that she would stop waffling—the past was her present now and she was going to own it. After grabbing the robe that Gwen had given her just for these occasions, she caught another fleeting glimpse of herself in the mirror, and paused, marveling at her reflection. Brianna knew that the biggest changes were on the inside, but she liked who she saw there.

With a smile, she belted her robe and headed downstairs to join the girls, grasping the ledge on the landing when she saw the courtyard bursting with activity. She wasn't sure how she'd missed all the commotion, but she could see Henry speaking with Alan and Richard. *That must mean the men are back.* Heart racing, she rushed downstairs, excited to find Aidan, but when she came into the Great Hall, he wasn't there. She saw Gwen and Maggie already wrapped in their husbands' arms by the fireplace, but there was no Aidan. For a moment, she panicked, struck anew with the terror that something had happened after all, that her family lore had reared its head and was taking him from her, that she'd jinxed it all by deciding moments earlier that everything would be okay.

Brianna shook her head trying not to think the worst, and had nearly given in when she heard a faraway sound. She froze. Her eyes shot to the foyer, and she held her breath hoping her mind wasn't playing tricks on her, but then she heard it again, the familiar sound of Aidan's heavy steps as he came inside. She turned toward the door, and there he was, Tristan in his arms and deep in conversation with

Henry. She saw how his eyes swept through the hall, searching until they locked with hers. Her own eyes filled with tears as he shook his head taking her in from head to toe and back again as he put the boy gently down. Then he was striding forward, his pace quickening as she ran, throwing herself against him, surrendering to his strength as his arms wrapped around her, lifting her from the ground.

He breathed her name, rocking back and forth as they embraced, then set her down, and grasped her head, pressing his lips to hers. When they finally broke apart, he stroked the side of her face, touching her hair and shaking his head.

"How…What happened?"

Suddenly self-conscious, she reached up, but he covered her hand.

"Nay," he said, eyes misty. "'Tis beautiful, and suits you. I…I just don't understand."

Brianna almost laughed then, wondering how on earth she was going to explain it to him, but he didn't seem to expect an answer at least not now, because he pulled her back into his arms, covering her lips with his again.

When they next pulled apart, it was abruptly, and Aidan was looking at her urgently, like he had suddenly recalled something.

"Breea, love?" he said, gripping her shoulders. "Where is your satchel?"

"My satchel?" she repeated, altogether confused. "What do you need that for?"

"Breea, please love, where is it? Know that this is

important, or I would not be asking you now, of all nights."

"It's upstairs," Brianna said, still confused as to what he would want with her bag. "We had started to pack for Dunhill, so it's on the bench next to the wardrobe."

Aidan turned, nodding curtly to Henry who she realized had been waiting in the foyer for this very direction, and moved now quickly for the stairs. A few minutes later Henry was back, her satchel in his arms. Aidan gave a sharp intake of breath, then grabbed Brianna by the hand, pulling her over to the sitting area, motioning for the others (since everyone was now paying attention to him) to follow. Brianna looked at Gwen and Maggie, who both just shrugged, clearly in the dark also. Aidan sat down, bringing her down to his side, and grasping both of her hands in his.

"Do you remember when I asked if you knew of the hiding place within the bags?" he said, his green eyes intently focused on hers.

"Of course, I remember," she said, and rolled her eyes, feeling a bit unnerved. "It was only a couple weeks ago."

"*Bri*anna."

Usually, when Aidan enunciated her name in that way while giving her a good stare, it meant he was frustrated, but this time there was a bit of amusement in his eyes. Something was up, and Brianna was so curious what it was—and what it had to do with her bag.

He stroked the side of her face, smiling as he stared deeply into her eyes. "Would you please show us the compartment you told me about?" he said, calmer this time.

Brianna nodded and knelt in front of her bag, opening it and taking out the things she'd packed so she could show them the pocket hidden underneath one of the folds on the side of the bag.

"Is there anything inside?" Aidan asked when she showed it to him.

"Well, yeah, the medallion's still there," she said. At the mention of the medallion, Tristan lit up and started skipping around the room.

"Could you retrieve it?" Aidan asked, his voice even, measured.

"Retrieve it?" She recoiled at the thought. Brianna hadn't touched the medallion since they'd left Ayr. Once her fears about truly belonging in this century had started to grow, she hadn't wanted to tempt fate. The medallion was what had brought her here, and she worried it would sweep her away, the same way the sword took Celeste back to her time, catching all of them unaware.

"You're not going anywhere," Aidan said, his voice softening, reading her mind.

Brianna squirmed. "Maybe Tristan should take it," she said, figuring that would be a good compromise.

The boy went ballistic at this, clearly overjoyed at the prospect of the medallion being his.

"Right," Aidan said, "well let's save giving away any more of my possessions for later." There was a hint of a smile, which was a relief in the intensity of the last few minutes, and she blushed at his (correct) accusation that she'd forgotten the medallion belonged to him. "You're very cheeky, which I happen to adore," he said, "*however,* let's get back to your satchel, shall we? When I asked the other week if you had checked the compartment and you seemed to know what I was referring to, I assumed you were aware of how my brethren and I use them to communicate with one another."

She shook her head, still not understanding what he was getting at. Why did it matter whether she knew what the pocket had been used for in the past or not?

Aidan explained how they all used a recognizable marking to indicate a hidden store, be it something built into the masonry of a wall or even a walkway or entrance—or most often, a travel bag.

"Really?" Brianna asked, her historian's mind fascinated. "That's so clever."

The men seemed very pleased by her praise, but Maggie was looking at Callum with an expression of shock, like something had finally dawned on her. Callum was returning her stare, nodding slowly. Brianna didn't get much time to wonder what that was about, because Aidan knelt and pulled the bag from her arms gently. She watched first with curiosity, then with bated breath as he opened the bag wide and showed her a tiny etching deep within the recesses of the satchel, hardly noticeable if you didn't know what you were looking for—it could even be mistaken as a flaw, she realized, marveling again at the brilliance of it all. This must be the marking he'd mentioned. Then, he pulled a flap of leather back and Brianna gasped. She'd never noticed that extra piece there at all.

"*This* is what I was speaking about when I asked you," he said, and Brianna noted a slight quaver in his voice. "I thought you knew, based on what you had said. Should I, or would you like to?"

For some reason, Brianna was suddenly scared, but she wanted to be the one to do it. Slowly, she reached inside the bag, running her fingers along the seam Aidan had revealed, and slipped them inside the opening there. She gasped again when she felt something hidden inside. With her eyes locked on Aidan's, she pulled out not one, but three envelopes, all sealed in a waterproof sleeve. She recognized one of them, but not the others.

Aidan shook his head, his eyes filled with awe and emotion. "I cannot tell you what they are," he said. "I can only pass along what I've been told—that what you need, is there."

Brianna slid out the envelope on top and caught her breath. "This is addressed to you," she said, hardly believing it possible. "To all of you."

She showed the men the script which read, *To My Brethren,* then pressed the envelope into Aidan's hands. She nodded, imploring him to open it. It took him a moment to crack the seal without ripping it, but once he did, he read it aloud, passing around another paper that had been folded within. Everyone was now on the floor and their circle tightened, sitting so close together they were all touching.

To my brethren, if only we'd had more time,

We were all so moved by Brianna's unexpected presence, how interested she was in hearing our stories and of her family, that after she went off to explore for the morning, we thought nothing of the time, so very foolish in hindsight.

An envelope arrived soon after by courier from Dunhill Manor. It was from Brianna's aunt and uncle who reside there at this time and contained a note with their express wishes that the included letter be given to Brianna posthaste. We realized time was of the essence —and that it might already be too late.

Regrettably, I must make this short, as we need to go after her, however, I'm including a portrait I sketched only yesterday. Please know, we are all well and miss each of you so very much.

God be with you,
Our love,
Dar and Celeste

There were a few smudges where tears had marred the page, and when Brianna looked up, she could see there wasn't a dry eye in the room. They all passed the sketch around, which was of Dar and Celeste and Lachlan and their little boy, Griffin. It was so beautiful, heartbreaking, joyful, and bitter-sweet all at the same time.

The two remaining letters were addressed to Brianna, and written in her grandfather's familiar looping script. The first she'd already seen—it was the one she'd read sitting in the kitchen with Dar, Celeste, and Lachlan. The second was new. She fingered the envelope as she gave everyone a few more minutes to gather themselves. When they all realized what she was doing, they waved toward her urgently, and Aidan said, "Open it."

She took a deep breath, then cracked the seal carefully. Hands shaking, she pulled out the letter and ran her fingers over her grandfather's favorite stationery and his flowing script. A smaller page fell out when she unfolded it. Curious, she turned her attention to it and saw that it was a very old piece of parchment, kept preserved in another clear sleeve. It took her a moment to recognize it—

"Oh!" she gasped. "It's one of the pages.... from the...from our family bible."

She held it up and looked closer, her heart beating wildly as she read the tight script: *Brianna O'Roarke, daughter of Arthur and Meredith*—

She froze, staring at her parents' names. Not only was Brianna's name there, but her parents' names were there as well, when none of the other entries had ever included parentage. That's how her grandfather knew. It was *meant* to be distinctive, to stand out.

"Aidan," she breathed, her voice catching and held out the page to him. "Our names are on it!"

His eyes misty, he took the paper and looked at it

for himself, then gently cupped the back of her head and kissed her.

"Read the letter, love, please," he said.

My dearest Brianna,

I pray this letter finds you in the happiest of times. I'm enclosing the page from the O'Roarke family bible, the one inscribed with your name and that of your future husband. It is my hope that by the time you receive this, you have found one another. I also wish to recount a tale to you, one that I feel is going to be quite important to you and yours. It is an accounting of sorts, of the summer a few years past (the exact number, of course, depends on when you receive this).

While you were deep in your studies, I ran into a young man while doing my research at the university. As we began to speak, he seemed oddly familiar to me, and I believe he shared my feelings. Though as I pen this letter, I cannot in good conscience say our meeting was happenstance, given everything that has happened since.

We struck up a fast friendship, this young man and I, and he grew fascinated with our family lore, asking all sorts of thoughtful questions that I was all too happy to answer. I shared with him stories of our crest and our creed, and he told me of his family, the woman he loved, and the life that they shared. After some time, he asked if he could visit our ancestral home one day to see some of our family artifacts. Had anyone else asked, I'd have been suspicious, but he was a good man, and I could tell the journey would mean something to him. And, as I already had a sabbatical to Scotland planned, I extended an invitation at once.

His trip was brief, no more than a weekend, but it changed everything. If I had not witnessed what occurred with my own eyes, I would not have thought so much of our sudden alliance months past, but that all changed when I showed him the sword. I opened the case, and at the sight of our family treasure, Derek— that was his name—was struck with such emotion that his knees nearly buckled. When he looked at me, his eyes imploring and his hand shaking as it hovered over the sword, I, of course, acquiesced. The beauty of a man grasping the hilt of a weapon that is surely his by Providence is as indescribable as it is indisputable. That sword belonged to him, at least it did in that moment, and I could not in good conscience do anything other than see it rightfully returned to him, as odd as that might seem.

I heard of his tragic death weeks later, and though we had only known one another for a brief period of time, it felt as if I had lost a beloved family member— and, Brianna, in a way, I believe nothing could be more true. I can still recall, quite vividly, asking him to wait as I quickly penned a letter to you, one that would accompany the sword he was taking with him, knowing one day you would be shocked at my actions and want to trace it. Then, I dug around my study until I found the Wolf medallion—somehow, I knew that it must go with him, too. As he made his way to the door, he paused and looked at me with a gleam in

*his blue eyes (a blue I only then recognized as similar
to my own) and pointed quite decisively to one of the
stones in the wall. "Whatever you're looking for, my
money's on that one," he said.*

*It confused me at the time—this stone, for all intent
and purposes, looked no different from the others—so,
imagine my surprise when later, I dug at the mortar
that surrounded it and found that it easily came loose.
Then I pulled it out and discovered, I believe, the very
reason Pembrooke drew me that day, and I suppose
you as well. I've enclosed it here.*

*Rest easy, my sweet, your days ahead will be the
happiest yet. I beg you, do not waste one moment of
your birthright. Just bask in that wee bit of O'Roarke
magic knowing the love you share is true.*

I will always be with you, my precious girl,
Your eternal grandsire,
Dougal O'Roarke

Brianna read the letter over a second time, silently,
with tears falling, then again aloud at the urging of
everyone in the room. Then, she passed it around, and
they all took a turn, letting each word sink in and the
meaning of what happened. Both Callum and Maggie
seemed particularly affected, Maggie sobbing and
Callum holding her close, his head bent to hers as
they whispered between them.

After Maggie had calmed down a bit, talk turned
to a woman the men called Esmerelda—but who
Maggie referred to as "the old bat" and "crone",

respectively. It took a few minutes, but with a start, Brianna realized they were speaking about the woman who had given her the satchel, and she recalled that first night with Aidan at Seagrave, when she'd told them about her. The only person who remained silent was Gwen. She seemed to be puzzled by something, and when Greylen reached for her hand and asked what was bothering her, she shook her head.

"I think...I think the woman you're all talking about—the one Callum and Maggie met at the fair, and maybe even Brianna's 'fairy godmother', this Esmerelda person might be...my Aunt Millicent."

"Aunt Millicent, who first took you to Abersoch?" Greylen asked, eyes wide in understanding. "And told you of the tidepools?"

Gwen nodded. "Yeah. Do you think that's possible? That Aunt Millicent and Esmerelda are one and the same?"

For the better part of an hour, they all tried to explain what she looked like to Gwen on each occasion that they'd seen her, but they soon realized that she somehow appeared slightly different to each of them, even when they were in her company at the same time.

"How odd," Gwen said.

"Is it? Or clever." Greylen remarked.

"Well, I have to tell you, Aunt Millicent was a gem." Gwen made a face, "No pun intended."

They all chuckled, but after a moment, Brianna sighed. "I wonder if I'll ever get to see it, the stone that is," she said wistfully, still lying on the floor, her head on Aidan's thigh.

"Hey," Gwen said, trying to sit up, but wobbling until Greylen gave her a hand. "Did you have a backup plan? I mean, how were you planning to 'woo' your wife if you hadn't run into whoever this Esmerelda person is?"

"You're speaking to Sinclair of the House of Pembrooke, Gwendolyn. I can assure you I had grand plans—*grand*," Aidan said with so much fanfare that as he stared into Brianna's eyes, she was completely taken aback. She'd forgotten how romantic he could be.

"You did?" she whispered. "Really?"

He tilted his head to the side, a gesture now that was almost an old throwback, as he regarded her curiously, but looked almost stunned, too. "Breea." He breathed her name, clutching the back of her head, "I look forward to 'wooing' you every day for the rest of our lives."

She melted, despite the grunts and snorts from the peanut gallery. Aidan pressed a kiss to her lips and still holding her, he stood, holding her hands. When they pulled apart, Aidan was looking deeply into her eyes.

"Breea," he whispered only loud enough for her to hear, "we prevailed."

She had a feeling this was *not* a part of his 'wooing', but something that resulted from the happy end of their plight. And when his hands swept through her hair just before he kissed her again, the room broke out in a chorus of hollers, followed by a rain of pillows, gently thrown their way.

"Hey! Come on you two. Save it for later. Aidan, get back to it."

Aidan finally broke away, looking somewhat contrite. His expression shifted then and got serious. "Brianna—you have two choices, lass," he said, and for a moment she was taken aback by his tone *and* that he'd said 'you' and not 'we'.

"*I* have two choices? What happened to we?" she said, taking a step back.

"I'm battling for legacy here," he said, clearly exasperated. "And as *I* never questioned the sanctity of our union, I hope to show you the error of your ways —the sooner, the better."

Brianna didn't know what to think. Sure, he had a point, but he was taking all of this very seriously all of a sudden.

"Okay, then…one??" she asked, but so hesitantly that Aidan sighed and his oh-so-serious expression faded for a moment.

"Breea, love. I'm merely acting," he said, then arranged his face back into a mask of intensity.

She smiled, loving how they'd fallen back into their easy rapport. After taking a deep and calming breath, she grinned and repeated with a bit more bravado. "One?"

"You will stay here with me and let me love you like I was meant to for the rest of our days."

Brianna rolled her eyes. Obviously, she would pick one, why on earth would she even need to go on?

"I'm aware of the flaws in all of this, now that you needn't be convinced any longer," he said, "but play along, aye?"

"Okay, but I really, *really* like option one," she said, then gave a dramatic sigh. "But, two?"

He looked at her so seriously then, staring deeply into her eyes, so silent, she started to regret asking. Until he mouthed the word 'acting' and she breathed again, startling when he bellowed, "Henry!" This caused both Gwen and Maggie to startle, and Brianna even sucked in a breath herself, squeezing his hands for support, because she suddenly felt so off-balance. It was hard to remember this was an act, because when Henry pivoted on his heels, it was with such fanfare, that it rivaled any changing of the guard she'd ever seen. His boots echoed loudly as he strode across the foyer, and all the while, Aidan just stared down at her, his mouth set in a straight line, his look deadly serious. She watched the doors swing open just as Henry grew near as if on cue, and clutched Aidan's hands tighter, seriously starting to freak out. *Acting, right?* But when she looked up at him, his expression was still unreadable.

She gasped when Henry stopped atop the steps and reached for his sword, slicing it through the air before raising it to the heavens. A cry escaped her lips and she covered her mouth...then Henry bellowed—

"*RELEASE THE DRAGONS!*"

Brianna was so stunned she stood there frozen for a moment, then let out a laugh as the tension whooshed from her body. It could have been straight out of a movie. She gave Aidan a quizzical look, wondering if he knew what he was doing.

He stepped closer to her. "Don't you know by now, I would do anything to prove that you're meant to be here, with me?" he said, grasping her head in his hands.

God, she loved when he did that.

"How very clever of you, Mr. Sinclair," she breathed. She'd intended it to be another one of their quips, but she nearly melted at the love she saw in his eyes. "Will you take me home then? So I can finally see Pembrooke as it was meant to be seen?"

He smiled from ear to ear, and nodded, but said, "Not a chance, love—"

"*Wait*—what?"

"We leave at first light for Dunhill, where Father Michael will marry us *officially*, and so your over-bearing guardian Callum can scribe our names in the family bible."

"Great, yes, but then—"

Then he kissed her.

EPILOGUE

From his perch high atop the hill, Aidan spotted Brianna down in the garden below. He nodded toward her and turned to his man with a smile, slipping the small pouch that he'd delivered into his pocket for safekeeping. When he looked to the sky, he realized mid-morning was nearly gone and made haste for the stables. After allowing Merri to cool down after her exercise, he gave her a few extra pats, then scanned the property for his wife, catching sight of her, basket in hand as she left the garden.

He smiled again, taking note of the trail of wee ones that followed in her wake. Not any of theirs *yet*, though their valiant efforts had borne fruit, and she was indeed expecting. In addition to the children who tagged along behind her, Brianna was followed by a few 'pets' as well, even a...Aidan tilted his head to the side to confirm, aye, a goose he was sure he hadn't seen before. Shaking his head affectionately, he watched as she made her way to the keep, smiling and nodding to all she passed, spreading good cheer. She still hadn't seen him yet, and Aidan watched as Brianna stopped before the doors, and pressed her hand to the symbol. Their symbol. Then, she disappeared inside, and he stood there like a fool, beholding naught but the keep doors, just completely enamored. Whether he was simply caught in her allure, or if this was another marking of her surely more than a wee bit of O'Roarke magic, he cared naught.

By the time he'd washed up and entered the keep himself, Aidan found only warm smiles and an air of happiness that permeated their entire home, and truthfully the entirety of the Pembrooke estate. The past months, it had felt as if Pembrooke had been sprinkled with fairy dust as a result of their union, the sanctified one.

Aye, they'd indeed visited Dunhill Proper and had done so the very morning after he and his brethren had returned to Seagrave to the revelation that was hidden in Brianna's satchel.

Their ridiculously large riding party might have resembled an army, but it was a journey filled with laughter and joy. Brianna's delight when they'd arrived at the halfway-point cottage was infectious, and while they'd planned to have the women stay within the small dwelling for the night while he and his brethren slept beneath the stars, their wives had other ideas. After the children drifted off to sleep inside, the women slipped out to join them, to everyone's pleasure. Aidan was thrilled to be able to pull Brianna close and hold her throughout the night, sleeping on a makeshift bed as they'd done back in the early days of coming to know one another.

They crossed onto O'Roarke land the next morning, and though the border was invisible, it was as if some part of Brianna recognized it. Right away, her expression changed, she sat up straighter, more alert, and when she'd turned to look at him, her entire being appeared alight and overwhelmed at the same time.

"Breea?" he'd asked, momentarily filled with concern, but she shook her head, sending her soft curls dancing, and smiled.

"I feel them," she said, "all of them, Aidan—I'm home."

He understood, but still, she reached out for his hand and looked at him softly.

"I don't mean that you and Pembrooke aren't my home..." she trailed off and he took the opportunity to stave her need to excuse it.

"I know precisely what you mean, and that you feel this, sense this, is a gift."

"May I?" She'd asked, motioning with her hand, indicating her wish to ride ahead, to be with the land. When he nodded, she added, "You should come with me."

Aye, that he did, and what began as a steady and joyous canter in celebration of her homecoming, became something else entirely. He could hardly explain it with words, but he swore he felt her essence twine with the land and take root, and as Merri opened her gait, his stallion followed suit, racing across the meadow behind her in a full-on gallop. Aidan stayed a few paces behind, watching as Brianna's hair twisted beautifully in the wind behind her.

At Dunhill Proper, Brianna quickly turned down Maggie and Callum's offer to stay in the apartment that had once belonged to Fergus and Isabeau and later Dar and Celeste, and instead expressed her wish to stay in the chamber beside Aunt Cateline, to be close to her while they were here. Aidan hadn't a care where they stayed, as long as he was able to gather her in his arms at night and wake with her in the morn. Even better were the afternoons when they took advantage of the children's naptimes and absconded to the room alone, though, in those hours sleep was not involved in the least.

In the days that followed, Brianna gave him a tour of her home as she knew it. Though of course, he knew Dunhill well, to see it from her eyes was indeed an experience all its own. He would never forget her joy when Callum and Maggie, and even Aunt Cateline showed his wife treasures she'd never seen with her own eyes but had only read about. Her face, when she entered the 'informal' dining hall for the first time, running her hands along the drapery and admiring the spray of roses that dotted the tableware, a favorite of Maggie's was truly a gift.

If he were pressed, however, Aidan would have to say that her discovery of the letterboxes sitting atop the mantel where they would remain for centuries was the most precious of them all. Her eyes wide, head shaking, she'd walked over to look more closely, and when she gasped and turned to him, she said, "I can create a finish, to help preserve them." She ran back to him, grasping his tunic, "Aidan! What if *I* am the one who preserved them in the first place, so they'd still be there in the future for Celeste?" He hoped she didn't require an answer, for it seemed self-explanatory. He merely raised a brow and gave her an encouraging look, and she chuckled. "Right."

Aye, right.

Father Michael married them that first evening, and when Aidan stood upon the chapel steps dressed in his wedding finery, Brianna making her way across the courtyard in a gown that was already being touted as a family heirloom, the rightness that swept through him was beyond compare. They exchanged vows and rings, and though their marriage was now sanctified, in truth, their connection had been solidified weeks ago. Each of his brethren was there save Ronan, who they had not heard from since parting in Ayr, which was unlike him, and of course, Dar.

Back at the keep, they'd all made their way into Callum's study, waiting impatiently for the ink to dry as if they were in a race against time to ensure that their history would repeat itself. Aidan wouldn't have been surprised if they'd all held their breath as Callum removed the stone from the wall. It was an act he and his brethren had performed many times in the past, but it felt more significant this time. Once the compartment inside was revealed, Aidan and Brianna together placed the page torn from the family bible within. After the stone was set in place again, a round of sighs sounded throughout the room, and chuckles too, when Gwen suggested that if ever there was a time for a brandy, this was it and that she only wished she could partake.

Now, settled into Pembrooke and their lives together, Aidan could hardly believe all that it had taken to get them there. Shaken from his reverie, he stepped from the entryway into the parlor where Brianna was setting fresh flowers in a vase on the table. When she turned and saw him there, he wasn't sure who was happier to see the other, and neither did he care, his arms opened a scant second before she threw herself against him with a thud, and he chuckled, wrapping her tightly in his embrace, her growing belly between them.

His hands whisked through her hair and he tilted her head to kiss her, smiling as she hummed. When he pulled back, she leaned forward again. "More please," she whispered, coming up on tiptoes to nudge his lips. He obliged of course, and although he'd made slow, sweet love to her only hours ago, he sensed he might be doing so again. Posthaste. Then, he remembered.

"Wait, love." He chuckled at her pout. "I have something for you." He reached into his pocket and handed her the small silk pouch from within.

"What is it?" she asked. When he failed to answer immediately, she began to probe. "Is it fragile? Glass?" She gently shook it, "A baby rattle?"

He laughed and pulled her into his arms, then laughed all the more as she hugged him with one arm while peering at the gift with the other.

She looked up at him contritely and said, "Sorry," then made to toss the package aside.

"Nay!" he said, reaching out.

"Oooh, I knew it!" she shrieked gleefully, rubbing his chest with her free hand. "Is it porcelain? Crystal? A—"

"Why don't you open it and see for yourself."

She made a face, but saw to the ribbon and then carefully shook the contents of the small pouch into her hand.

"Oh, Aidan." Her intake of breath was so slight as she looked at the figurine, one to add to her growing collection, and then she cast her eyes at him.

Aye. The look he strived for each and every day, and there it was.

"It's beautiful," she said, the crystal bear with a wolf cub cradled in its arms sitting atop her palm.

"So are you."

"It's sapphire," she said of the little wolf and the one color she'd yet to acquire.

"Like your eyes."

She placed it carefully on the shelf with the rest of her collection of crystal baubles, then looked back. "It's magical."

"Like your love," he said, meaning it deeply.

She gave him a dreamy look, then startled, her eyes widening as she reached for his hands, firmly pressing them to her belly. Locking her eyes with his, they waited together, sharing his smile when their babe kicked, as they'd known would happen.

Then he pressed his forehead to hers and breathed the words he could never say enough: "You are everything to me."

THE PROPHECY

**EXCERPT FROM BOOK I OF THE LAIRDS OF
THE CREST SERIES**

The dream was always the same.

Gwen pressed deeper into the warm embrace, sighing as strong arms tightened around her. She rubbed her face in the crook of his neck, running her hand over the solid mass of back and shoulders until her fingers tangled in thick, soft hair. Large powerful hands followed her movements, pressing her closer as he cupped the back of her head and gently tilted her face.

She never felt his hesitation before. Tonight she did. She tugged on his hair, a silent demand to be kissed. Then he covered her lips, completely sealing them within his own. A deep sound rumbled through his chest.

This dream was different. She felt the warmth of his lips and the pressure of his hands, the texture of

417

his hair and the heat of skin. She heard sounds given and returned. It seemed so real.

His thumb coaxed her chin, and her lips parted as he moved between them. He spent an eternity simply joining their mouths...in every possible way. His tongue, reverent at first, was slow to explore, then became wholly demanding.

She gave in to him completely. In truth, she kissed him back with everything she had. They shared an urgency—taking satisfaction as they'd never been able to before.

She traced her fingers over his face—his broad forehead, straight nose, high cheekbones, his smooth, strong chin—and she pulled him even closer. My God, it had never felt so good.

She made a sound as he pulled back, a whimper he hushed with slow, passionate kisses over her forehead and cheeks. Then he covered her lips again before tucking her within the crook of his neck. "Sleep, love," he urged in a murmur. "The morn's but an hour away."

Gwen burrowed against him, silent tears wetting her cheeks—oppressive longing crushing her from the inside out. She'd never heard the sound of his voice. It would haunt her forever.

NEVER SAY GOODBYE

**EXCERPT FROM BOOK 1 OF THE BROTHERS
MONTGOMERY SERIES**

1774 Abersoch Britain

Amanda stood and walked through the expanse of the
ballroom, ignoring every compliment called her way.
She looked only at Alexander, holding his eyes until
she stood before him.

"My performance is over," she said firmly, quietly,
and with a deadly seriousness. "Good night,
Alexander." Then she left the room.

Glancing back, she saw him shake himself out of
his stupor. As he turned and made a move to follow,
Amanda hurried forward. She heard him behind her,
but he didn't reach her until she'd entered her room.
Grabbing her arm, he twirled her to face him. He
studied her closely, shaking his head as his hands
gripped her arms.

"Who are you?" he whispered, both a question and an accusation.

Amanda, ready to wake up from this hallucination, decided now was the moment for honesty. It's not like any of this was real anyway, no matter how real it felt. All of her obsessive reading about the Montgomery estate had apparently manifested in her subconscious after hitting her head.

And then physically *being* on the estate must have been the reason she'd imagined Alexander saving her life, not once, but twice. Thank her penchant for authoritative, powerful men for conjuring this vision of a man. Exquisite, elegant, masculine. Maybe also why being kissed by him may have been the single most enjoyable event of her life.

And Callesandra. Amanda had always wanted children, but had never found the right person to have them with. Had Callesandra been hers, she would have cherished her. Such a sweet girl. It broke her heart that they had both been treated so poorly by Rebecca, that the stories she'd read had been true.

For a moment, Amanda felt a strong pull toward this life, wishing it were real, for Alexander to be her husband and Callesandra her beautiful daughter. Wanting to touch him one last time before this was over, Amanda fingered his lapels and then flattened her hands against his chest.

"Tonight, I am your wife, I suppose...and the mother of your daughter. But I have never seen any of you before in my life."

ALSO BY KIM SAKWA

Lairds of the Crest

The Prophecy

The Price

The Pledge

The Promise

The Brothers Montgomery Series

Never Say Goodbye

Never Too Late

Never Say Never

Visit Kim's website for a complete list of titles

authorkimsakwa.com.

ABOUT THE AUTHOR

Kim Sakwa is the author of multiple bestselling romances, including *The Prophecy, The Price, The Pledge, The Promise, Never Say Goodbye, Never Too Late, and Never Say Never.* When not writing, you can find her listening to the soundtracks she creates for her novels. She's a hopeless romantic, hooked on happily ever after.

ACKNOWLEDGMENTS

THE PROMISE

I am so thankful for my talented, amazing team at Taggart Press. They are the reasons why my books are beautiful on the inside and out, and work tirelessly to get my books discovered by readers.

Sarah Beaudin
Graphic Design · Interior Design · Production
C'est Beau Design

Marian Hussey
Audiobook Narrator · Voice Talent

George Long
Cover design · G-Force Design

Julie Olson · Katie Price
Website development and design
Graphic design
Priceless Design Studio

Liz Psaltis
Content creation· Advertising· Promotion
EHP Marketing

Judy Rosen
Copy-editing · Proofreading
Precise Editing Group

Mandie Stevens
Promotion· Conferences · Advertising management
Finding Your Indie

Rachel Stout
Developmental editing
Rachel Stout Editorial Services

Jane Ubell-Meyer
Luxury hotel amenity placement
Major media coverage and events
Bedside Reading

Made in United States
North Haven, CT
21 October 2024

59197443R00262